'But who are these planners?' Bramble inquired. 'Who are our untouchable despots?' Spittle gathered on his dentures. His gums flashed scarlet. His newt-eyes rolled behind their double dazzling glasses. 'Do we elect them?'

'No,' roared the audience hungry for tears.

'We don't choose nor can we ever dismiss the real power over our lives: the State Planners.' His audience emitted a rumble like cannibals round a pot. Bramble's voice bit: 'Planners go on for ever, unquestioned, inviolate. Doing what *they* alone decide is right for us!' He swung on the man from the Airports Authority. 'And when were you last in the lovely Vale of Hampden?'

By the same author

# IVOR HERBERT

# Revolting Behaviour

**GRAFTON BOOKS**

A Division of the Collins Publishing Group

LONDON GLASGOW
TORONTO SYDNEY AUCKLAND

Grafton Books
A Division of the Collins Publishing Group
8 Grafton Street, London W1X 3LA

Published by Grafton Books 1987

First published in Great Britain by
Cassell & Co Ltd 1972
under the title *Over Our Dead Bodies*

Copyright © Ivor Herbert 1972

ISBN 0-586-06962-3

Printed and bound in Great Britain by
Collins, Glasgow

Set in Times

'The Gentleman in Whitehall does not know best'

The late Iain Macleod
Shadow Chancellor of the Exchequer, May 1970

'. . . but it may be that in the 1970s Civil War, not war between nations, will be the main danger we will face'

The Rt Hon. Edward Heath, Prime Minister,
United Nations General Assembly, October 1970

'The victory of the third airport suggests that the values of civilization are beginning again, after nearly two centuries, to displace the arguments of the engineer'

Leader in *The Times*, 29 April 1971

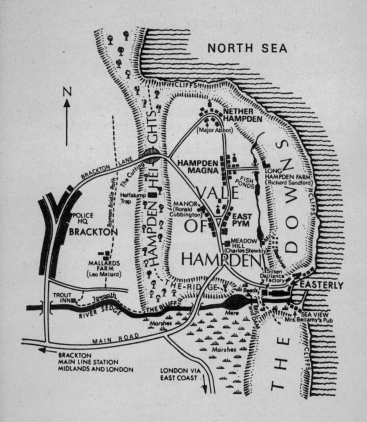

# Part One

# 1

'Two *hundred* and twenty shotguns,' Charles Stewkly repeated incredulously. 'In your area alone?'

Martin Stewkly, glooming out of the window, glanced round at his father's exclamation. The old man – he must be sixty-five now, he supposed – was half out of his tall chair at the head of the dining-table, gripping its arms and goggling at Mr Cubbington. The butcher raised a long white finger to his pale wide lips and nodded both at Martin and past him towards the drought-freckled lawn. Martin's mother, straw hat quivering on her grey bun, was showing the two visiting wives her beloved bantams.

Charles Stewkly slid back into his chair and asked in a lower voice, '*Sure*, Ronald?' But he knew Cubbington would be: his neighbour was too careful to get caught out in an overestimate. There were probably three hundred shotguns. 'And a few rifles, of course. ·22s, deer rifles?'

Cubbington said coolly, 'I've not yet asked. That would be a bit too obvious.'

Major Aston Abbot nodded briskly. He was equally astonished by Cubbington's report, but could not show it. As their accepted military leader he must trump Cubbington's calm. Charles Stewkly said, 'And Richard Sandford's area in the north – nothing like so many, I suppose? I've never thought of his bit as particularly *sporting*. So bare, those Downs.'

Every time his father leaned on the odd loose word as if he were off-driving it through the covers, the emphasis bundled Martin's childhood back, across the last two awful years in Africa. He turned from the window and sat down at the foot of the table.

Mr Stewkly hooped his eyebrows over his glasses and said, 'Martin, all this is absolutely confidential.'

Martin nodded. 'Of course.' But he looked at the others. Three pairs of eyes from a different generation regarded him over the jetsam of Sunday lunch. They were also, he realized with a shock, from an alien society: they none of them trust me an inch. Mr Cubbington had three butchers' shops in the area. His eyes were as grey as the North Sea which crunched against the cliffs to the east and the north of them. He looked too pallid for his trade, but he was fiercely ambitious.

Major Aston Abbot's eyes protruded, moist as a spaniel's. He had no ear for nuances, but those eyes caught every gesture. He was quick, but born just too late: in time for a major war he would have made a driving general.

Old Charles Stewkly smiled at his son. He hated Martin's habit of leaning on things – window-frames, backs of sofas – away from groups, annoying engrossed people not just by affecting languor, but by demonstrating how little he cared. He had done this even when he'd first met his cursed coloured woman. When she chattered of socialism, Martin had gazed out of windows. Perhaps he did it when he *was* intrigued.

Aston Abbot made a reluctant burble: 'Perhaps Charles, before we talk details, your son should withdraw.'

Martin was not offended. He hardly knew the Major. Aston Abbot had spent most of his military career abroad defending sandy British outposts until succeeding Governments had returned them, equipped with barracks and British graves, to their original owners. Major Abbot had accepted his own pointless privations. But had not forgiven the wasted deaths of men.

'Should be *asked* to withdraw,' amended Cubbington, resting his thin nose against his white finger like a flying buttress against a drainpipe.

Charles Stewkly, so happy to have his son home at last when he had believed him lost for ever, was genuinely surprised at his associates' suspicions. He exaggerated it, pouting his lips under his grizzled moustache, so that Martin for the first time since he'd landed, felt a giggle start to tickle the backs of his lungs.

He winked at his father, implying trust, but it made Mr Stewkly doubtful: Martin hadn't cared for English country life since he left school. In London he'd spoken out against it, attracted publicity and caused affront. He might still be laughing at us, thought Mr Stewkly regretfully.

Ronald Cubbington was saying disagreeably, '. . . only fair since our own families don't know any details.'

'And much better not,' said Abbot.

'Naturally,' said Martin rising. He stepped into the garden.

His mother bobbed up behind a brittle clump of dead lupins. She was comforting a bantam in her large hands. 'Martin, you haven't yet seen the horses. We were just going . . .'

Martin put his arm through his mother's. Her light fawn sleeve smelt faintly of exhausted rose petals, recapturing for him little silk sachets in her wardrobes, rustling as he reached up to touch. He gave her arm a squeeze as they went through the farm gate and out amongst the thistles and the dry cow-pats.

He asked softly, 'Is that the lot?' He jerked his head back at the dining-room. 'Of father's . . . gang?'

His mother pouted at the word. 'And Richard Sandford.'

11

'Ah yes,' said Martin, 'the Sandfords of Long Hampden. They would be in it.' He suddenly recalled riding on his pony with Sandford across his blowing downland oceans. Distant sheep grazed like drifts of snowdrops under black hedges below. Grey clouds bowled in from the sea cliffs, rain burst on to their backs and the sheep, coagulated into a bumbling carpet, dashed for shelter. He had suddenly cried for them.

'You *are* a melancholy little fellow,' Sandford had said, and from then on had always looked at Martin with some concern. Of all the Stewklys' friends Sandford was the least astonished when Martin ran off to Africa with Ruth.

He supposed that Mrs Sandford, frail as winter beech leaves when last he'd seen her, had long since fallen. 'What an odd foursome with father,' he said. His mother shushed him.

Davina Abbot, whose father had been a general in the days when red tabs counted, looked sharply around. Grace Cubbington, a good advertisement for both farmer's daughter and butcher's wife, peeped towards the cars in the drive. Their Jaguar waited with the Aston Abbots' BMW ('The Kraut can build a motor-car – you've got to give the bugger that') and the Stewklys' Land-Rover stuffy with dozing dogs.

The wives walked into the long, dipping field exclaiming at the horses who tweaked the grass, tails scouring flies from flanks.

'Isn't that Viceroy?'

'No, the bay one, there.'

Martin switched off. The plateau on which his father's small-holding stood commanded a great vale, counterpaned with hedgerows, sentinel elms, some knuckled oaks, clumps of osiers along the stream, and copses of beech. It was an unexciting piece of England but beautiful because it was old, composed yet fertile, purposeful yet calm. And flat. Nicely flat, nicely drained for the airport and the new town, which would link it with the still unmolested Anglian shore. The tower of Nether Hampden's Norman church, the spire of Hampden Magna's, the ridge-back of East Pym's splendid chantry all gleamed in the sun. They and their villages and their fields and woods around were all to be obliterated.

# 2

When his confederates left, Charles Stewkly said to his son, 'They can't prevent me showing you round, anyway. We demonstrate the horrors to come to every caller.'

They climbed into the Land-Rover. It was placarded: 'SAVE THE HAMPDEN VALE! HELP US TO FIGHT!' A little white flat with a red cross wobbled on the bonnet.

'We took St George for England,' said Mr Stewkly needlessly. A scud of rain blew down the valley on to the fly-flecked windscreen as they bumped down the farm drive and took the lane to East Pym. It seemed to Martin that the fields on either side were unusually full of Hereford bullocks and Friesian heifers. Mr Stewkly, perched high over the wheel like a coachman, glanced left and right at ripening wheat and great green encampments of potatoes.

Thinking of bare Africa, Martin began, 'It looks so particularly rich.'

'D'you want to talk about . . . ?' Charles Stewkly stumbled. He felt unable to pronounce the name, too self-conscious to say 'that woman', and unaware whether she was still his son's wife.

'No.'

Fields still ridged and furrowed from the medieval strips, pollard willows, and then a mill swept past grey, green and gold. Water glinted. 'No thank you, Father,' amended Martin ridiculously.

He saw miles of scrub, prickled with thorn trees, the glide of snakes, wakes of red dust floating where a crammed African bus burst along dirt roads. He heard the creaking of the dappled dead eucalyptus trees. He felt the hot, snoring million miles of bloody Africa beneath those purple, evanescent mountains menacing on the world's rim.

His father was inquiring . . . 'children?'

'Not mine,' said Martin, with a bright relief. But his father was not convinced. 'Probably M'Dinga's,' added Martin, too casually. 'She didn't go to him because he was African too.' He was anxious, even now, to be fair. His love for Ruth had not been as ludicrous as his father and his friends here had thought. What had destroyed it was the prime splitter of all relationships: divergent paths.

'But because he was on the climb – ' Martin's hand squeaked up the windscreen – 'a Government Minister, and I was the same as I'd been and she'd seemed in London – just helping people. I felt more helpful out there, in fact. But back in Lutanga she wanted more *power*.'

On that word he saw her arched on their rumpled clanging iron bed in the corrugated tin bungalow. Everything sweated. The night, stretched like an indigo drum, rattled with insects and hooted with birds. Jackals yapped beyond the bamboos.

Martin felt desire and hatred so sharply he had to twist in the Land-Rover's seat: bile spurted at the back of his mouth. 'Oh.' The palms of his hands tingled, damp with sweat.

His father touched his elbow. Slate roofs glistened with rain. A shut pub was passed. 'Look at the signs!'

On the golden-stoned outskirts of East Pym the Defenders' battle calls were painted on eaves, barn-roofs, cottage garden walls and across the old village school, now a Youth Hostel for the maligned young, many of whom walked hard and slept rough across the Vale of

15

Hampden to the sea. 'THESE MUST NOT GO,' declared the signs. 'DEFEND OUR HOMES!'

Little notices in cottage windows revealed the personal. In front of old Mrs Trimble's lace curtain was: *I'm 7th generation (Direct Descent) to live here and die. Why should they move me? E. Trimble, 79 in May.*

Behind the condemned privy, which she still preferred to the council's nasty, flushing thing, lay a long view over the proposed Airport to the site of the new industrial town. The summer drizzle had ebbed back across the Vale, shafted by silver sunlight.

Two farms appeared, byres and barns blazing with slogans, a new Dutch barn hung with tarpaulins shouting 'WHITEHALL! KEEP OFF!' and fluttering with the cross of St George.

There was a thatched booth where the village street widened. Here horses had been tethered, and pigs, sheep and cattle sold in a small monthly market which had left its legacy of drowsing pubs. The booth carried the legend 'HELP US TO FIGHT OR WE MUST DIE'.

Two large cars were parked outside, supporting chauffeurs. 'Americans,' said Charles Stewkly with relish. Inside a pretty girl was handing out pamphlets. Behind her back spread an illuminated painting of the Hampdens, East Pym, and the little port of Easterly. A shade revolved round a spotlight opposite, so that every ten seconds blackness obliterated the scene.

'Well, Pat, twisting their arms?'

'They've been *marvellous* today, Mr Stewkly. Of course it is Sunday and it was fine but even so – ' She lowered her voice and pointed at the Fighting Fund Collection Box. 'Over a hundred and ten pounds today.'

'But it's fantastic!' Martin blurted out, as his father introduced him to Patricia Fernden, the rector's daughter.

'You live here, sir?' asked the tallest American, stooping with concern. The Stewklys introduced themselves. The Americans buzzed forward in a rich chorus of protest. 'When we think what you fought for – !'

'Truly wicked!'

'We're with you on this.'

Sympathy illumined their anxious parchment faces. Dollar bills and pound notes crackled into the offertory.

'When we tell them back home – '

Patricia explained about the American Fund.

Mr Stewkly parked by the village Green, a triangle stockaded on one side with an avenue of chestnuts planted for Edward VII's Coronation. Under their dark-green skirts and pendulous branches smoothed by children's hands, a row of cottages peeped, prinking out damp gardens. There had been no large landlord at East Pym, since the Bestwode Estate had been broken up post-war to pay death duties. Till then, a paternal control of reasonable taste had governed two centuries of building. The land had been sold to tenants: five medium farms, twelve small-holdings and forty freehold cottages made up the village.

Charles Stewkly dismounted, landing with a little grunt, and struggled to extract his stick from the tangle of headcollars and stirrup-leathers in the Land-Rover's back.

Martin glowered. Why bring him to the prettiest village to squeeze out sympathy when he felt dry of care? Why agitate him when all he wanted was a cool green room with fluttering curtains? 'I'd like to sleep for six weeks,' he groused.

Mr Stewkly leaned against the Land-Rover and stared beyond the War Memorial at the church. The old windows bounced back the silvery sinking sun.

'"I will not cease from mental strife",' he hummed,

'"Nor shall my *sword* sleep in my hand"' (he struck the ground with his stick on 'sword' and raised his voice embarrassingly), '"Till we have *built* Jerusalem In England's green and pleasant land".'

Martin grunted peevishly. 'It's not so much "building" as "*not* building", isn't it?' He expected his father's face to turn to him wryly apologetic, but Mr Stewkly's eyes burned like a tiger's behind his glasses. He said fiercely, 'Get *out* and walk *about* and *feel* this poor bloody place!' He stumped off towards the Memorial. It was a slab of local stone, topped by a bronze body in the taste of 1920 proffering a laurel wreath.

Martin followed, turning up the collar of his nasty tropical suit. Cheaply bought in Lutanga, it felt not only wrong but clammy. Two old men, sighting the Land-Rover's flag, were distracted on their slow beat towards the pub. They went about and tacked towards the Stewklys. Hatted like pre-war gentry, they wore suits of thick lasting tweed. Steel watch-chains bounced on their bellies as they breasted forward.

Mr Stewkly waved his stick at them from the War Memorial. Two lists of names under crumpled poppies recounted the personal sacrifices of East Pym in the two blundering defences against Germany. There were twenty-two names under '1914–1918' listed by rank, and led in death by 'Major R. C. Abbot, MC', great-uncle of Aston. The bottom names were Troopers, for the Vale of Hampden had always been great horse country and a band of squires, farmers, and their labourers had fought together in the Yeomanry. Under '1939–1945' thirteen names were listed democratically alphabetically. But an Abbot (this time Lt-Col. R. G., OBE) still headed the innings of death. Aston's father had not got off at Dunkirk.

Mr Stewkly made a sudden scything sweep with his

stick, reaping in the entire village. 'They didn't die for much, after all, did they?' he said savagely, and wobbled.

Martin put out his hand to steady his father and made the usual excuses: 'They didn't know that. They stopped us being conquered and invaded.'

'Exactly!' exclaimed Mr Stewkly triumphantly. 'And now we shall stop Them invading us!'

The two old men hoved to and hailed him. Both were Potters, cousins of the village store Potter, of Bert Plumridge, who kept the pub, of Charlie Plumridge who farmed Church Hay, and of PC Plumridge, 'Old Plum', the village policeman. All descended from Silas Potter who built the smithy when he came back from Waterloo.

They shook hands briefly, the old men's eyes glancing off Martin and his suit and his excusing reference to Africa.

They don't trust me either, thought Martin, piqued. They think I don't belong any more. He began, 'I can't grasp what's happening here.' The Potter cousins and his father smiled. Martin went on exasperated, 'It's like preparations for some crazy manoeuvres!' He thought: It's impossible that they're serious.

He had been pike-fishing with the Potters on Sedge Mere just before he married Ruth. Slap of brown water at the punt's bottom; thicket of rushes like an army of lances . . . Blowing on scarlet hands, he had raved on about equal opportunity, the rights of the poor and our responsibilities in Africa. They had not listened to a word. But now they were attending to his father like two old Labradors expecting a day's shooting.

Mr Stewkly was saying patiently, '. . . But you're not *allowed* to appeal to the House of Lords in a case like this. The Minister was the final judge. And we've appealed to him and lost.'

'Ah, but when this Government do go out . . .' began Jack Potter.

Charles Stewkly sighed. Down among what their local MP still called 'the grass-roots', vision was obscured. Power and the Government were thought to be synonymous. The State's real power, gathering momentum regardless of change, was anonymous and, from this level, invisible. Here 'They' were the omnipotent Government which could seize, evict and lay waste slabs of England as the Saxons and Jutes had done here fifteen hundred years ago. So, the Potters reasoned, if one Government could seize, another Government might not.

Stewkly said crossly, 'There won't be a new Government, anyway. The Progressives' majority is 400 over the two wing parties combined. And they're all committed, for different reasons, to the extinction of these villages for the town and airport. Nor will the Minister wait. The contracts have been awarded. Costings depend on starting this autumn. They want to begin in September, before the frosts. We've got a verbal promise they'll wait till the harvest's in.'

As before a war, thought Martin.

'The last harvest,' said old Jack Potter. 'Funny the corn's turnin' so early this year.' Beyond the church a field of barley gleamed pale-gold, lime-green, as the wind wafted the whispery heads.

His cousin said, 'I can't abear that when I'm laid there' (nodding at the churchyard), 'they must dig me up agin or bury me under concrete for foreigners to walk upon.'

Jack Potter grinned like a skull. 'When they do pull that old tower down, you'll not feel a thing.' He cackled.

Mr Stewkly said, 'They intend to have the church down by Christmas.'

'But it's famous,' said Martin, appalled.

20

Jack Potter glared at Mr Stewkly. 'Then I hopes I'm ruddy dead.'

Charles Stewkly allowed for his son's excommunication in Lutanga by distance and disinterest. But he was pained that Martin knew nothing about the campaign that two thousand people of the Vale of Hampden and the Easterly sea-coast had been fighting for three years. It had become front-page news, a television topic, had attracted international concern and been called abroad 'The Little Englishman's Last Ditch'.

Driving home through the dusk Charles Stewkly said, 'We're still spending a thousand pounds a week to fight this thing.'

Martin was startled. 'How on earth – ?'

'Oh, Martin – think!' Stewkly exploded. 'Retaining solicitors, counsel, accountants, engineers and surveyors, hiring publicity, paying for posters, space in papers, on television – '

'I meant where from?'

'Through the Fighting Fund. People in the East End send us postal orders. We had a cheque from Monaco – they stayed here once with the Bestwodes, and the Princess loved the vale, she said. The Americans have raised their own fund for us. We've had gifts from a Russian poet, a Czech film-producer, that Greek singer. Some Persian Gulf oil sheik sent us ten thousand dollars because his son – studying the Civil War at Harrow – came across Hampden and Pym.

'We started from village fêtes, jumble-sales, Bingo by the sea, sponsored childrens' walks. Now probably a million people have contributed.'

'Honestly, Father,' said Martin. 'That's just not – '

'A *million*, in Europe and in America, have paid up, Martin. Because they know that this *is* the last ditch. If we can't stop Them we're all done for.'

'Done for?' repeated Martin. 'You mean overrun?'

'Oh, worse,' said his father. 'More ironic. Democracies haven't so much been *overrun* since the war. They've been eaten away from inside by the State's malignant power. Much harder to stop, Martin. And nobody has. Till us.'

thing. He felt unfit, middle-aged, stubborn and childish. His father could have killed himself six times when he was in Africa and he would never have known. He walked up quietly to Jupiter with hand held out. The horse, lured into expecting sugar, came to meet him, sticking his head out, nostrils wide, grey rubbery lips twitching.

'Leave him, Mr Martin!' called Wilkinson. 'I'll have 'im.'

No, I will, thought Martin, and don't you still mister me. His left hand crept out, pounced on the rein, gripped it. 'Stand still now!' he commanded, astonished by his authority. Jupiter plunged away like a tunny. The lunging rein scorched out across Martin's palms. Then he took a pull and hauled. Jupiter came in towards him, blowing and sweating, and stared. He looked no longer violent like a teenager, but bouncy like a schoolboy. A warm superiority flowed into Martin like new blood.

He looked back at his father, picked up the other rein as if he'd been driving horses all the last twelve years, clicked at Jupiter, and with an elation which lightened his feet, drove the horse back to his father.

Charles Stewkly, leaning on his stick and brushing off cow-pats and thistle-down, said drily, 'Well, you haven't forgotten. Better drive him home.'

The black tithe barn loomed over the house like a ship-of-the-line. It had graced a brewer's calendar and was the oldest building at Meadow Hill.

Its black doors, tall as the house, opened heavily, creaking. Beams with the glow of pale sherry flung arcs through the spotted gloom. Tiles had slipped on old pegs, so shafts of sunlight, thin as golden rain, seemed to lance upwards as the dust motes mounted in them. The place felt more treasured than any modern church. Four centuries of men had stacked their grain here like ants against bitter winters and long wars. Scores of martins' nests in neat clay cones hung like bats under the roof-beams. The earth floor in the barn's apse was crammed from dusky end to end with painted wooden vehicles. Martin gasped.

Where he remembered bales of warm hay and sharp wheat straw, there were now ranged more than thirty equipages. He saw a multiplicity of wooden spokes, glinting metal rims, bright coloured seats, boards and wooden shafts: dogcarts and station wagons, a Landau, two Victorias, four great farm wagons, a milk float, something like a barouche, a governess cart, a postchaise still being worked upon, a dashing gig, two tiny traps for ponies. Spare shafts and wheels, spokes and axles, harness, traces, bits, bridles, and blinkers were neatly stacked against the walls.

Charles Stewkly's eyes swung on to his son's face. Martin's mask had slipped. He leaned forward, eyes staring, as if at phantoms.

Then he breathed deeply in and sighed out, turned to his father and squeezed his shoulder. In that instant he knew simultaneously those two feelings which when combined can amount to love: admiration and sympathy. He both wished to follow his father's lead, and at the same time he wanted to care for him. The moment had been conceived by the danger in the Long Meadow. He loved his father. After those years in a wilderness, it seemed to him a revelation. He blinked. He wished to express the bond. But he could only say weakly, 'This *is* a surprise.'

But Charles Stewkly loved the squeeze of his son's hand on his shoulder.

'Not the only surprise,' he said a shade too briskly. 'Tell me, Martin, will you come in with us?'

Martin said truthfully, 'I've no real idea what "coming in" entails.'

'Well, first to stand up and be counted.'

'I wasn't planning to go away yet,' said Martin. 'I've nowhere actually to go.'

'I mean counted for the cause,' said his father. 'Next week our Petition goes to the Crown. We say that though we're loyal to the Monarch and to the Constitution we do not accept the Commission's findings nor the Minister's decision. And that we will defend our homes by every means we can.'

'She can't accept it, of course.'

'No, but it is our public declaration, not of independence, but of our refusal to be *erased*. It's not against the Monarch like the Barons against King John. She's as helpless as we are to change the monstrous State. It's not the struggle of Parliament against King Charles. Now its *us*, the little people of England, against the State.'

Martin said, 'Whoever signs will be regarded as rebels.'

'Justifiably.'

'If it comes to these.' Martin waved round at the waiting vehicles.

'Before that,' said Mr Stewkly.

Outside Wilkinson brought the young horses in across the cobbles. Their shoes rang sharply. One whinnied.

'We have got to resist, Martin. How long we can *endure*, I don't know.'

'You'd be a match for the local police I suppose.'

His father smiled. 'Just. There are only two of them left! And one is a sympathizer, wretched fellow.'

'Plumridge at East Pym, the cricket umpire?'

Stewkly nodded, 'Old Plum.'

'But what'll he do?' asked Martin. 'It's absurd to think of him against the whole village!'

'We assume they'll send a force from Brackton.'

'Plus the Army?'

'Perhaps. And then the big question: Will the Army

27

fire on us? We're not after all a rabble of youths in an Irish street. We're a hundred square miles of England.'

'Are you, by God?'

'I'll show you,' said Charles Stewkly, shutting the barn door on his conveyances and limping across the yard to his back door. 'Come and look at the map.'

Mrs Stewkly had a litter of puppies in a basket on the red-stone floor. A bantam cocked its beady eye at them.

'And you won't be *attacking* the police or Army either, I suppose,' said Martin following him in.

'We shan't attack anyone, darling,' said his mother firmly. She opened the oven door and a delicious waft of oniony, carroty stew blew into Martin's nostrils. He looked at the casserole.

'Perhaps you two men could wash your hands and lay the kitchen table,' said Mrs Stewkly, flicking the bantam aside with a slippered foot.

# 4

Aston Abbot hated Sandford's home, Long Hampden Farm House. As a child he had been frightened by its ghosts: a lame lady and her long-toed dog traipsing the oldest of its three squeaking staircases. Oak latches on oak doors clicked on still summer evenings. The house was never silent. At its quietest it tapped like a jug with trapped flies. Apart from the scratching dog and limping lady the long, dark complicated house felt inhabited by particles of people in agitated suspension. Occasionally you could hear a brittle anxious hum till casements loosed themselves. Honeysuckle, wisteria, and thorny Mermaid roses did not demurely caress the tiny Elizabethan bricks, but burst in at windows, rattling against leaded panes.

As Abbot went out into the dusky garden, fumbling with his fly, he struck his head on the lintel. 'You bloody beams!' he swore. The house, making him jumpy, provoked anger. 'Built for bloody Tudor dwarfs!' He sprayed a rosebed savagely, swinging the jet around. The courtyard, once an enclosure for wintering store cattle, was an ampthitheatre of rosebeds banked round the house. The roses turned their heads, floppy as old ladies' hats, towards the lattices. Drooping hundreds were on the petalled threshold of death: after the showers and the day's heat they exhaled last clouds of heavy scent.

A figure in white on the bench opposite the porch moved and coughed.

'My God! Belinda!' Major Abbot checked himself with a tweak of pain and buttoned up the offending object as soon as hygienically possible. 'I *am* sorry. Never saw – '

'Don't worry,' said Sandford's daughter. 'Kills the greenfly, Dad says.' She coughed again.

Sick like her mother had been, thought Abbot crossly. She'd be a responsibility later, blast it. It was the house's fault, lying under the Downs: its back was always cellar-damp. A hotch-potch of Tudor outhouses, a dovecote, Carolian hunting-kennels and Victorian pigsties, crouched in perpetual shadow. Sited by one Thos Sandyforde in 1588 for its sheltered water, its dank fish-ponds lay along the front. A slow stream connected these to the River Sedge, which debouched into Easterly's dying harbour.

Over his Downs Sandford's sheep mumbled. In his river meadows his big beef cattle grazed. He had a dairy herd, reared pigs, bred hunters and ran one of the country's last studs of heavy Shire horses. In any emergency Long Hampden had always been a vital part of the area's economy.

Two Tudor Sandyfordes and two later Sandfords had been knighted for valour, loans of silver (unrepaid), shelter for a Prince in transit, and the loan of a wife for a King's quick pleasure. But none had been ennobled or moved to Court. Younger sons in Army and Church had died in far-away places, red on the map, but the Sandfords farmed on at Long Hampden unnoticed by Governments; they were merely the last of England's squires.

There were trout in the stream and perch and pike in the ponds. Fields of barley creamed over the flanks of the Downs. Pheasants crashed vulgarly through beechwoods. Rarer partridges scurried through the damp green avenues of beet fields. Geese honked in the apple orchards, hissing at dogs.

It was known that in drought, pestilence, or war Long Hampden's 3,000 acres could feed all their own families. And all their neighbours. Such was the subject of Abbot's visit.

Seeing Belinda reminded him of Martin Stewkly. Before resuming their survey of the maps and list of names strewn across Sandford's desk, Abbot said, 'Martin's still odd, isn't he? Looks so bloody mournful.'

'I don't think conscience-struck Libs are ever merry,' said Sandford. 'And he had a bad time with that black wife.'

His colouring was that of one of his bay shires: red nutbrown face and black hair. But his eyes were blue and sharp. He still played village cricket and could easily, had he wanted to travel, have played for the county.

'She was a bitch any colour,' said Abbot. 'It could never have worked.'

'No, not here. But they never intended coming back from Lutanga. She never will presumably. She's done very well for herself now,' said Sandford mildly.

'She's of the right tribe,' said Abbot, who had commanded Askaris. 'That's how she came to run their Relief Campaign. And take up with His black Nibs. I was thinking in the rose-garden: Couldn't Belinda and Martin see a bit of each other again?'

'He's coming over,' said Sandford.

Abbot said quickly, 'Or they could meet in London. He could take her out from Sotheby's, say. They'd be better away from here before the balloon goes up.'

'His father thinks he may support us,' said Sandford.

Abbot said, 'I'm sure we ought to clear the decks of non-combatants and "doubtfuls" now.'

'If we can, without telling the world we intend to defend ourselves.'

'The Petition has *shown* who's with us,' said Abbot, impatiently. 'D'you realize – with an early harvest they could try to evict us in under three months.'

Sandford said, 'Let's go on grouping supporters into

31

Dozens. Their leaders will know who needs persuading out.'

Two glasses of whisky left damp rings on the maps and battle orders, as Abbot and Sandford sorted known supporters by villages or clumps of farms. They selected for each Dozen an acceptable leader with recommendations from Charles Stewkly – 'Keep Parish Councils as long as possible – ' and critical notes from Ronald Cubbington. Against the Reverend Frederick Fernden's name he had scrawled: 'Vacillating political with eye on Deanery. Omit.'

The selected names emerged with remarkable accord. Picking leaders from London streets or red-brick Midland roads would have taken months. Where people only sleep there are no obvious commanders.

But in the Vale of Hampden, the four men whose families had lived there for centuries knew the shepherds and the flocks. They picked the farm foremen, the head-keepers, the strong publicans, the village cricket captains . . .

'Three of the Parish chairmen are OK,' said Abbot. 'Staunchly with us. But what the devil do we do about Easterly? Browne's wife's the chairman there.'

Granby Browne, MP, a pink blancmange-faced politician, had his constituency weekend villa above Easterly harbour. Eyes agog for the chance of honours and awards, Browne was a little weathercock. When it seemed possible to thwart the Airport project, the MP had tried to muscle on to the Defenders' Committee. When his keen nose smelt defeat, he lunched the Minister of Aviation: the chairmanship of Hampden Vale Airport would be a political appointment.

The debilitated fishing port of Easterly was a problem in other ways: although most of its inhabitants had no wish to be removed to make way for the planned Sea-Link Base, a minority disagreed. The village had been ailing too long. The new base would offer jobs and expand trade.

On Easterly's outskirts on the River Sedge stood the only factory within siren-call of the threatened Vale. This, all swanking glass and vulgar concrete, was the home of 'Silken Dalliance', which manufactured the Feathered French Letter, last fling of the contraceptive sheath. Such had not been the Department of Productivity's intention when they gave Government grants. The place had been designed to make rubber covers for plug-leads. Too remote and casually managed, it proved uneconomic and its owners happily found a Pakistani entrepreneur from Brackton who wanted to take over their cemented elephant. His real name stuck on local tongues: they called him 'Cock Cover Jack'.

He had done well enough to be cordially disliked. Racial tolerance was all very well, if foreigners were poor and humble, or rich and brilliant. Jack was neither. But he was trebly happy: he was making money; he was keeping down the birth rate; he was giving pleasure in vital places. What European businessman could boast as much?

His enterprise afforded employment to fifty Easterly women who would otherwise have left for Brackton. It took on extra staff in the winter when the quayside cafés closed: Feathered French Letters stockpiled for the busy plunging spring. Waitresses and dishwashers between Michaelmas and Easter doubled the work strength under their militant leader, Aidan Stride, fervent Trades Unionist and the local Lothario.

Silken Dalliance had a hard organized core of resistance to the Defenders' plans. Most of its employees welcomed the Airport and Sea-Link. Uneasy, and already upheaved, they had grown accustomed to artificial daylight, taped music, conditioned air, cheap meals and free trade samples. Between gigantic Airport and Sea-Link Base they would be able to relish all a city's amenities without the expense of leaving home. The ladies dreamed of the arrival of rich but lusty executives, Steak Diane, discotheques, pink bidets and champagne in gigantic beds.

Aidan Stride's own sexual appetite was prodigious. A girl in the dinner-hour should have quietened him for the afternoon, but before the tea-trolley arrived he usually showed signs of firm desire as he paced down the aisles of bending bottoms. His palm patted and his fingers probed, and the girls' delighted cries ascended in an anthem.

For Stride the Airport would mean an increase in political influence and more girls.

'His women will do exactly as he says,' said Sandford.

'How can we get 'em out?'

Sandford shrugged. 'We can't. We *must* think of something for them to do here.'

Abbot snorted. 'The factory will stop instantly. Cock Cover Jack won't send in any more latex. I still think it'd be safer to cut out Easterly altogether. Our line of defence here – ' his chinograph pencil marked the map-talc where the valley of the Sedge cut between the constricting shoulders of the Downs. 'West of the freddy factory there's only the one road. We can flood it from the Mere. These woods here and yours this side give good cover . . .'

'I know we must plan for a fall-back line,' said Sandford. 'But if it's going to be a long siege, I agree with the others: we must have access to the sea and the saltbeds.'

'But it's a bugger to defend.'

'Not if the fishermen back us. And I'm seeing their leader Owen this week.'

Major Abbot had not so long left the Army that the

urge to 'get cracking' had died its customary civilian death. Now he fretted. For he had commanded sharply, earning respect if not affection from his superiors. 'No finesse,' Brigadiers decided, blocking his big leap up to a Lt Colonelcy, and the Army's golden bowler was a public boot. He kept trying now to bridle his impetuousness in this his last campaign, his only chance as Commander-in-Chief. But his three civilian confederates drifted on like rudderless democracies into war.

'Talk to Owen now,' the Major urged. 'The fishermen could lash the wartime harbour-boom across the jetty to the rocks. It's still there. Close the harbour entirely. Then from the cliffs . . .'

Sandford smiled and, to match the Major's zeal, telephoned Owen. He would come up right away.

Belinda looked in, pale, large-eyed, through the open window from the garden, illuminated by the desk lamp. She was framed in a tangle of honeysuckle.

Abbot jumped at the apparition. 'You look like – '

'Ophelia?' asked Belinda sardonically.

Sandford looked tenderly at the face so exactly like his dead wife's. It radiated the same inconsiderate calm which had so often irked him. He asked as gently as he could, 'What do you want, darling?'

'I saw Owen today selling his catch. He said, "Your father won't leave me out, will he?"'

'"Me" or "us"?' asked Abbot.

'He meant "*us*", actually,' said Belinda.

Abbot nodded. 'Good.'

'By the by,' said Sandford. 'Martin Stewkly's coming over.'

'You said,' Belinda glanced away.

'You don't want to see him again?'

'I don't mind seeing him. It's just that in his present state I'm likely to do him harm.'

'Don't do that, Linda,' said her father quickly.

Aston Abbot frowned like a spaniel.

'I'll walk down the farm-road to meet him,' Belinda said. 'I can't breathe in this house.'

# 5

'Like children.' Belinda pointed out of Martin's old car towards the lights of the house. 'Plotting and planning.'

Martin stopped in the courtyard. He had been pleased to see Belinda waving in the drive. But she had grown cynical since last they met. He wanted to ask about Sandford's position before he saw him too for the first time since Africa.

'Oh, come on,' said Belinda impatiently. 'They're all the same. Your father, mine, old Cod's-eyes Cubbington. The steaming Major's just roared off. Now Owen's brought an awful Hell's Angel yob. It's all a game for them.'

'Hardly.' Martin scowled. 'If they fail, they'll all be in God know's what trouble.'

'"They"?'

'We then.'

'Not me,' Belinda flashed out. 'And aren't you still the brave socialist idealist? "Greatest good for the greatest number" – all that rubbish?'

She thought Martin's face frowning was as Victorianly ugly as his home: battlemented, beaky with sharp bow windows, locked. His attraction still was the smile: like finding a friend at home in a hostile house.

'You're sure it'll come then?' he asked.

'Of course.' She leaned back, sucking slowly at her cigarette.

Martin was suddenly furious: 'Why so maddeningly complacent?'

'Because,' said Belinda, 'they say it must come – every

expert – except those briefed by our fathers. It's the best of all possible sites.'

'So you accept that?'

'Certainly. Otherwise, what's the point of experts and majorities?'

'And that we *need* another gigantic Airport at all?'

'Oh, come on, Martin. Time passes. We didn't need tarmac roads once. People fly nowadays. Hadn't you noticed?'

He glowered at her. She added smugly, 'England won't look the same. But it looked quite different fifty years ago.'

'The country was buggered about then by your sort of private enterprise. It *should* have been protected.'

'Are you a paternalist now?' asked Belinda.

'I'm *not* converted to seeing my home, yours, three villages, Easterly, the sea-coast and one hundred square miles of England blotted out. Are *you*?'

'Yes. I shall just live in London.'

Martin flushed. 'So Stuff You Jack, you mean? You'll be all right.'

'And you,' she said, 'have just found another cause – something you *need* to belong to. Like your silly black people.'

She started leisurely to climb out of the car. Martin shoved at her back. 'Oh, get out!' he swore. Then her father's voice called across the roses. 'Martin? Nice to have you home. Come on in.'

Martin got out, raging. An old Austin and an enormous gleaming motor bicycle with high handle-bars were parked by the wall.

'Don't think I will,' Martin shouted back, his voice rather too high. He saw Mr Sandford silhouetted against the light.

Belinda laughed out loud.

'Oh, yes please,' called Mr Sandford finally. 'Business.'
He went inside. Light from the open hall door carpeted
the steps up in alternate bars of gold. Peering past his
toes Martin blundered on, stubbing them. Belinda walked
quickly ahead of him into her father's study.

'Hello, Owen,' she said.

The fisherman was wearing a pinstriped-jacket over his
blue sweater. He was very tall with frizzy hair and huge
grey eyes with the stupid, friendly gawp of a calf. They
stared down fondly at Belinda's face. Then he saw Martin
and smiled widely. ''Lo,' he said again. Martin, hovering
uncomfortably, gave Owen the smallest possible nod.

Owen pointed proudly at the reedy youth in a black
leather sleeveless jacket punched with studs in bones and
swastikas. 'This is Slim.'

The youth reclined in an armchair. His tight faded blue
Levis stuck out in front of him. Ridiculous high-heeled
boots twitched. As Slim chewed gum his thin yellow
beard flickered. His eyes ran very slowly up Belinda's
thighs level with his head, but did not apparently like
them. He turned his head slowly to Martin. 'Young
Stewkly?'

Martin said stiffly, 'Yes.'

'Worked for y'r ol' man, once. Fired me for smokin'.
In the barn.' Fatigued by this exposition, Slim closed his
eyes again.

'Oh, yes,' said Martin. He felt his forehead and armpits
sweating.

Belinda was sitting in the armchair opposite to Owen's.
Her skirt slipped higher. Martin watched Owen's eyes
staring up. He turned angrily to Mr Sandford, 'I'll have
to be getting back.'

'Ah, wait a moment,' said Sandford, watching him
carefully. 'Owen and Slim are keen to co-operate with

us. Charles told me you were with us, so I thought we should all meet.'

Martin was nonplussed. What could be done with dreadful Slim and gormless Owen? His own enlistment seemed now an act of lunacy.

'Slim,' said Mr Sandford, 'is the leader of Easterly's Hell's Angels, as I'm sure you know.' His right eyelid flickered at Martin. 'Only they're called Slim's Bones!' He patted the arm of his chair. 'Sit down, Martin. He won't kill you.'

Owen let out a deep ho-ho-hoing laugh: 'No knives nor chains tonight, Slim.'

Slim gave a minute nod. There was indeed a very nasty chain around his waist.

Owen said, ''Bout two dozen o' our lot want to come along with you. We reckon if we're together, there'll *be* no Sea-Link. And the publicity like'll get folks here agin for the fishin'.'

Sandford nodded gravely. 'We're delighted, of course.'

Owen scratched his frizz of hair and pointing one huge carbuncled hand added proudly, 'Then Slim says his thirteen Bones with their great bikes don' mind helpin'.'

'Always thirteen,' said Slim expansively. 'Gotta 'Bonnie!'

'Triumph Bonneville 650,' explained Owen. 'With "apehangers". Others have Suzukis and Honda 350s.'

Sandford said, 'I've tried to persuade Slim that his team might be better off marauding *outside* the area.'

'Rather stay,' said Slim.

'Why?' asked Belinda, peeved at his disinterest in her.

'They'll bugger us about else,' said Slim.

'Nonsense,' said Belinda. 'It'll be better – more people, more shops, more jobs.'

'More Fuzz. More Yobs,' said Slim.

'He's cock now, Belinda,' explained Owen helpfully.

40

'He'd not be, if the Brackton Bootboys was in, see. Or the Brackton Skins.'

'If any of you resist,' said Belinda sharply, 'the police will simply knock you off. Pop you all inside. And bloody silly you'll look.' She got up and poured herself a brandy.

'They'll not get in,' said Slim. 'A few Fuzz!' He rolled up his eyes. Under the thick russet lashes they were astonishingly blue. He unhooked the gum from his mouth and flicked it into the fireplace. 'I said to Sandford we'll help.'

Owen added proudly, 'Sort of Shock Troops. Zoomin' in.'

Belinda laughed.

Slim did not look at her. He said with menace, 'We'll shock 'em,' and something flashed in a movement as magically fast as a gun in a Western, and a flick-knife struck towards Belinda. She froze. Everyone gaped. Nastiness polluted the air.

Belinda raised her eyebrows at her father: 'Well . . .' she breathed.

Sandford watched Slim's eyes. The knife disappeared into the tight white sleeve of the sweat shirt. No other part of him had even quivered. Owen said, grinning, 'Great with the ole knife, is Slim.' Belinda flushed, for her heart was still hammering, and looked across at Martin, who had resumed his sulking slump on the chair arm. He was aware he was expected to utter. He said reluctantly, 'Glad to have you with us,' sounding so like Noel Coward in a war-film, that everyone laughed, assuming a joke. He twisted a grin on to his own face.

Owen rashly gave Slim's black shiny shoulder a shove. 'C'm along then, Slim. What'll you tell the Bones?'

'Big Fuzz beat-up. 'Bout September.'

Belinda went out with them. The huge Triumph Bonneville 650 c.c. revved up, crackled, banged, roared, paused, roared up again. Gravel spurted back and clattered against the barns. The bellowing dropped as the bike shot under the gate-house, then came again drumming like thunder along the valley.

Martin had watched Belinda leave with loathing. He suddenly imagined her splayed bare-bottomed on the monstrous bike, bouncing, speeding away with Slim, gripping him tightly.

Martin said, 'That gang will be a liability.'

'Slim particularly dislikes Aidan Stride of the freddy factory,' said Sandford. 'Which could help us a lot.'

Martin said deliberately, 'You know that Belinda doesn't support us.' The word 'us', used for the first time in Sandford's house, sounded a final declaration of mad commitment.

Sandford nodded. 'We shan't see her again down here – till it's all over. One way or the other.' He saw doubt in Martin's eyes. 'She won't betray us, I assure you. She just won't be involved.'

Martin did not reply. Sandford added with emphasis, 'There's blood in her that started here in this room four centuries ago.' Martin finally nodded back.

He drove to Easterly and found Mrs Bellamy, the Sea-Tart, serving behind her bar. Her face glowed from the warmth: she was fat. Her arms swept across the wet bar-top like hams on an ice-rink. But her voice was oddly genteel. She murmured to her regulars, 'Mr George, *do* pardon me,' as she flicked back her mass of tangled hair, and 'Really, Henry, you *do* surprise me!'

Martin dreaded he might be too late. He bought her two double ports and asked if he could stay the night. She nodded cheerfully. 'Certainly, Martin dear.' Her breath smelt of chutney. 'Don't mind if you've Brewers' Droop either.' Martin looked round in fearful embarrassment but her customers by now were self-engrossed.

He slipped past the stuffed-fish cases into the black passage which smelt sour as wizened apples, and happily climbed the narrow stair into the Sea-Tart's bedroom. Its dormer window commanded, as from a private box, a spectacle of quay and moored boats, and curving sea-front houses either side. The faded chintz curtains fluttered in the night air. Mrs Bellamy slept with windows wide and never had a cold. The same great four-poster bed, hollow as a hammock, waited like a port. He had always liked the room: the mourning pulse of the sea all night, the scud of clouds under the moon on the steely horizon, and the gulls' cries at dawn.

He threw his clothes behind Mrs Bellamy's wobbly screen, and rolled over her bed's edge as if, exhausted after a long run, he was finally scoring a try. The bed was even softer and deeper than he remembered and the sheets lay perfectly between new cold and old fustiness. He found Mrs Bellamy's French farce nightie under the pillow, gripped it so that he would be aroused on her arrival and slid down the slope of sleep.

Mrs Bellamy looked affectionately at Martin and climbed cautiously into bed. Her bulk drew from the springs a twang of moans, like an orchestra tuning up. Martin opened his eyes, grinned at her, and again slept.

She sat down by his head, popped a pair of solicitors' glasses on to her nose and reached across him for her magazine.

'Don't mind, do you, dear?' she asked softly. 'I've not read me Uncle Kindly yet.'

She turned the pages greedily. 'Here he is, the nice old gentleman.' Mrs Bellamy had to follow some of Mr Kindly's phrases with her finger. Her big red lips moved in accompaniment.

Sex did not rear its pink head in Mrs Bellamy's bed till dawn, with English hesitation, finally filtered through the sky. Then Martin's bout was swift and remedial. Mrs Bellamy the Sea-Tart was hardly stirred from her slumber. When Martin collapsed she patted him on his warm shoulders and said in the voice of the Nanny she had been twenty years earlier, 'There, there, dear . . . we haven't had what we wanted for months, have we?'

It had been Mrs Bellamy's too generous concern for the father of one of her charges which had brought about her sudden change to a different branch of the nursing profession.

Martin thought how ugly Mrs Bellamy had grown but how beautifully kind. And with that he slept on till he heard the doomed gulls shrieking in the sun-shafts glittering on the sea. He started up thinking they were police-whistles. 'Old PC Plumridge!' he grunted. Mrs Bellamy said, '*He's* all right. It's the little one here, PC Benn, your Daddy ought to watch for with his naughty Petition, Martin dear.'

# 6

Percy Benn, recently married and appointed from Brackton, occupied Easterly's police house. His beat lay westwards along the Sedge Valley including the Downs and woodlands of Long Hampden. Its limit was the parish border with East Pym and the Hampdens which came under PC Plumridge, a grandfather within four years of retirement.

'Old Plum' had served with distinction with the Coldsteam Guards but the brutalities of combat had sucked his ambition dry. He had refused promotion to Sergeant since it meant leaving East Pym: his piqued headquarters at Brackton from then on largely ignored him. With the passing years he became an 'old-time copper', a term not used by his superiors as a compliment. But he had found the key to contentment for all unambitious men: he had tailored his job to his way of living.

PC Benn ridiculed his colleague. Thin, wiry, and small by police standards, with horny ears spread like a goblin's from his small skull, Percy Benn reckoned that a man without ambition was a man of wool. In Easterly he found lots of trouble: car-parking, traffic obstructions, licensing infringements, even some petty pilfering occupied his busy days. His grey van buzzed about his beat, making his mosquito presence felt.

Benn believed no man could be liked and respected. But he was not respected either, except by his wife who loved the way he treated her as a Victorian skivvy. She treasured the blows of his little fists as keep-sakes of his attention.

Off-duty, Benn ran. For long distances he ran across the Downs, but generally he pounded the road from Easterly, climbing past Silken Dalliance and then along the valley. He was happy panting behind the anal orifices of giant trucks up Easterly Hill, so long as he was getting in the mileage and racking his calf-muscles. Even on winter evenings PC Benn always wore his Brackton Harriers vest. He was directing his clenched teeth towards the County Championships. Brigadier Spratley, DSO, the Chief Constable, approved of athletes in his Force.

Plumridge, through all his rabbit-like friends and relations in the Vale, had known for a year that a real defence against the Airport was being talked about, but he had shut his mind's barn door. Now he stirred unhappily with the birds, staring up at his flower-papered ceiling, as all the week's whisperings rustled back to torment his brain. 'It's my Duty' had been his talisman for forty years, covering every unpleasant thing in the Army and the police. But which was his duty now?

He paced his vegetable-garden in vest and long pants wondering what to do. His heart and all his ties and relations backed any bid to stop the Airport and new town. He was against it from every angle except that of the uniform he must wear a little longer.

Because he believed that God was being specially pestered in the Vale of Hampden, he prayed briefly each Sunday Evensong, 'Please put off the trouble here, God, till I retire.'

PC Benn suspected that something was happening in Plumridge's beat. He had recently enjoyed a chat with Brackton's Duty Sergeant. The latter had overheard Inspector Wilson (known in the force as 'Shifty' from some imagined resemblance to a politician) saying, 'Plumridge is idle and has too many bloody relations.' Now if

46

Percy Benn unearthed something in Plumridge's beat . . .
The force was very keen on labour saving . . .

On the late afternoon of the Defenders' Petition Old
Plum did not answer his telephone, so Benn slipped
across to East Pym to find him marshalling petitioners
into the village school. He drew him indignantly to one
side: 'Not aiding an' abettin', are you?' he sneered.

'Preserving peace,' said Old Plum gravely.

Benn snapped: 'This Petition smells to me. More of a
Census, in'it?'

Certainly the cards carried not just names, but
addresses, qualifications, places of work, ages and telephone numbers.

'Why all these questions?'

Plumridge shrugged. 'It's legal.'

'It's bloody odd.'

PC Plumridge jerked his head. 'There's Mr Cubbington. He's one of 'em behind it.'

Cubbington hovered, pale face wary.

'Very full – this Petition,' said Benn, tapping the sheet.
'All these details. Not exactly normal, I'd say.'

Cubbington directed his pewter stare on to the little
policeman. 'D'you think Her Majesty wants to read a
mere string of names? She wants to know who her citizens
*are* And what they do. Adds life, Benn, don't yer see?'

Benn bit his lip and, muttering darkly, hopped into his
van and drove way past the thatched booth beset by
reporters. Peg-Leg Stewkly and the layabout son who ran
off with the nigger girl and the Rector's bleedin' daughter
were handing out drinks and cheeky pamphlets like they
owned the place. Bloody good thing when the Airport
swep' 'em all away. Benn whizzed past the placarded
cottages and called up Brackton on the radio.

'Looks as if there's more to it, sir,' he told Inspector

Wilson. 'Too well organized. Better come over to Cubbington's. They're addin' these things up at Manor Farm.'

The Cubbington's drawing-room was as brashly coloured as a paint advertisement. 'Tart's curtains,' whispered Davina Abbot glancing up from her pile of Petitions at the bobbled draperies. Her father, the General, had saved no money, but had inherited taste. Opposite the blue-marbled eighteenth-century fireplace was a vulgar bar with chromium stools, Mrs Grace Cubbington's proud delight.

Cubbington and Major Abbot patrolled a large baize table, round which four girls were sorting Petitions and tabulating details.

'Hello, Patricia,' said Stewkly. 'Your Reverend father not yet converted?'

'Consorting with revolutionaries?' said Patricia Fernden. 'He'd rather die!' She was collating the shop-keepers by areas and trades. The next girl was dividing 'farmworkers' into two groups by age. Stewkly cocked an eye at Abbot. The Major said quietly, 'Those over forty-five won't do in a fight.' He showed a list he held in his hand. 'These will. In their Dozens.'

Cubbington took the totals from the lists across to a map pinned on to screens. A band of pink encircled the four parishes joining the curve of the North Sea on the north and east. Below Easterly's steep southern Downs the pink frontier swept inland westwards along the River Sedge and the Mere to the bridge the road running out of the area to Brackton twenty miles away. The western frontier was the ridge of Hampden Heights, cut only by one lane towards the north end.

A few reporters still drifted on the buzz of talk, waiting for the grand total of petitioners. Their rivals had taken Cubbington's careful estimate of 'about 75 per cent of all adults support us', had already filed their copy and driven back to Brackton. An angled 'flood' left by the ITN crew hovered like a neglected stork.

A figure in sporting tweeds appeared in the doorway.

'Shifty Wilson,' murmured Cubbington, hopping off his bench towards the Inspector. PC Plumridge, rosy with embarrassment, rocked from one boot to the other in the hall.

'Come in, Inspector. And you Plum. Have a drink.' Cubbington waved at the bar. Grace Cubbington made pink welcoming motions like a sea-anemone, and pushed her hair back with a freckled forearm. 'Not on duty, are we?' added Cubbington, placing his finger against his huge nose and cocking his head at the Inspector.

'Not really,' said Wilson. He allowed himself to be persuaded. PC Plumridge declined. He asked the Inspector, 'If you're not needin' me, sir . . . ?' Wilson grandly nodded and waved Old Plum home, like a dog to its basket.

'Shifty' Wilson stood by the bar smiling a lot and moving his eyes carefully across the crowded room like a radar scanner.

Small talk – the harvest, weather, price of beef, abundance of pike – left his lips. He savoured the comic trivia of country life. But they were a dull lot these agriculturals, always *playing* at things: their shooting, cricket, village fêtes. Even their cattle markets and shops seemed, by town standards, old-fashioned and amateurish. And now this silly Petition. Grown men and women flapping round like chickens trying to put off a State decision which was as inevitable as death.

'Doing a good job on your Petition,' he said. 'Shame about the Airport. A wicked shame,' he amended, in a lower voice, lest his pearls be garnered by the porcine

Press. 'But there's progress. It'll come.' He let out a stage sigh.

'Over our dead bodies!' shouted a helper from Easterly, staggering in with a last box bulging with Petitions. Shocked silence doused the room. Inspector Wilson's eyes quartered the ground again.

The telephone rang loudly. Ronald Cubbington, eyes still on Wilson, listened carefully, then smiled. 'We'd be delighted . . . All four of us? . . . Fine.'

He turned to the others, ignoring the Inspector. 'BBC TV, Rupert Bramble, no less. Wants us on "Vision Now".'

# 7

The tweedy party padded onwards down the curving windowless corridors of the Televison Centre.

'Like Jonahs in the whale's guts,' grunted Major Abbot. He was wearing his regimental-tie under a stiff white collar. Davina claimed this gave him military authority, but it exaggerated his choleric cheeks and bulging eyes. His thick suit steamed and chafed. Sweating he urged his party on, lest laggards like the limping Stewkly might be picked off by hostile natives. Ladies wheeled tea trolleys superciliously past them. In Room 542 there was no sign of Mr Bramble.

'Rupe won't be in till later,' said a beautiful silver-blonde girl, bra-less beneath a slit sarong. Her voice was mildly accented. Was she a bleached Indian, wondered Sandford (Belinda had told him these were all the rage) or a dark-stained dolly from Birmingham?

Aston Abbot ogled her nipples pushing against the silk. She bent forward to offer cigarettes and Abbot saw there was suntan right up to their raspberry-coloured roses. He longed to grip them. His palms itched. He cleared his throat and the girl smiled at him. Apparently here in London you could pick girls up like jam-tarts. This one . . . His mind's eye stripped her and positioned her. 'What?' he asked.

Sylv went into the next office and said to the cropped-haired Research Supervisor: 'You can see that Major's thoughts pokin' through, Thelma!'

The men rose to greet Thelma's purple trousers and

Hapsburg whiskery chin. She said directly, with a voice like a truncheon: 'We thought you'd look rustic.'

The Defenders glanced quickly at one another, conscious of initial failure.

'I left my smock at home,' said Charles Stewkly drily.

Thelma's flat button eyes swivelled on to him. They must be kept down for Rupe. 'Waistcoats off, I think . . . Couple of you take yer ties off? No? Loosen 'em anyway.'

Abbot's moist spaniel gaze viewed Thelma with distaste. He could just glimpse Sylv in the next room arguing down the telephone.

Cubbington complained, 'We've been here nigh on an hour.'

Thelma noted his accent. Put him on the flank so that those broad aarhs would carry.

'We go out at 9,' said Thelma. 'In the studio at 8.30 with the others.'

'Who?' asked Stewkly.

'The other side. Your MP, Browne, who's in favour of the Airport. And two Civil Servants – Airport Authority and Land Board. Two dry-as-dusters. You should show well.'

Rupert Bramble appeared in a flurry of scent and apologies and like a properly primed minister, was knowledgeable over all.

He thought, peering at the four faces as they filed in under the lights, that real bumpkins would have been better. Viewers must regard them as homeless dogs, clawing at the railings within hours of the lethal jab. 'Battersea – that's the image,' he said and clacked his teeth and flashed his glasses. So they heard themselves introduced as retired-lawyer, farmer, shopkeeper and a soldier back from the wars. The audience, rehearsed by Thelma, loosed a blast of applause. The four bowed back, bemused that such enthusiasm for strangers could even sound sincere.

The two Civil Servants were already moist from their work-out with Bramble, and looked wary and sullen. The joy of Bramble's programmes derived from Victorian melodrama: the villains were instantly obvious. Then came the clown. Mr Browne, MP, transparent in his urge to please, was hailed by a youth planted by Thelma, who hollered, 'Which side you on tonight then, Greazy?'

Bramble demonstrated, scything down the Ministry men as if they were thistles, not just the doom of the Vale of Hampden. The audience, obliged to him for their free circuses of slaves, had all suffered Whitehall's claws. Helots themselves, they howled for revenge, as he inveighed against State Planners everywhere: motorways in London, Government offices, threat to St Paul's, new Buckinghamshire city, poison-gas plant on Berkshire downs, psychiatric prison in Stratford-on-Avon . . . Awful photographs flashed on the giant screen behind the panel.

A map of green England was stained blood-brown in patches like the Black Death under the fell hand of Whitehall.

'But who are these Planners?' Bramble inquired. 'Who are our untouchable despots?' Spittle gathered on his dentures. His gums flashed scarlet. His newt-eyes rolled behind their double dazzling glasses. 'Do we elect them?'

'No,' roared the audience hungry for tears.

'We don't choose nor can we ever dismiss the real Power over our lives: the State Planners.' His audience emitted a rumble like cannibals round a pot. Bramble's voice bit: 'Planners go on for ever, unquestioned, inviolate. Doing what *they* alone decide is right for us!' He swung on to the man from the Airports Authority. 'And when were you last in the lovely Vale of Hampden?'

The official mumbled that it had not been the task

of his department, which was rather to produce the statistics . . .

'Statistics?' hissed Bramble. '*We* talk of *people*. When were you last in Hampden Magna, Nether Hampden, Easterly or poor East Pym?' The doomed names tolled like a passing bell.

'Never been there,' muttered the Civil Servant.

The crowd started to rise and break, but Bramble stilled the billows.

'Or you?' He lunged at the man from the Land Board. The programme still had 30 seconds to run. Like an experienced lover he was withholding the climax.

'Been dealing till recently with Western England,' the Land Board Director blundered forward.

'Spending Englishmen's money,' snapped Bramble, 'to ruin Englishmen's homes down there?'

The audience's howl, by a quick boost of amplifiers, drowned the man's legitimate protest. Bramble, as with a baton, cut the tumult for two bars rest. 'These two gentlemen have not set foot in the Vale of Hampden. Yet they have decided on its destruction.'

Both civil servants burst into urgent tongue.

'Silence please,' hissed Bramble, glasses flashing dreadfully and great teeth clapping. 'You are not the masters here, thank God!'

'No! No! No!' cried the audience. 'Not the masters here.' One black man at the back squawked: 'And *we* are paying *you*, my goodness, what nonsense!'

'Meanwhile the people's elected representative,' said Bramble, raking the MP with a goggling fire, 'is powerless to intervene.'

Browne squirmed. 'I did my best,' he started. 'I strove . . .'

'To no effect, sir. You prove my point. Members of Parliament are impotent against the State.'

Thelma held up five fingers. She was grinning so much that her chin was wagging.

'Thank God, I say,' cried Rupert Bramble, gasping, 'for these four men, for *all* the brave men of Hampden. Who will *not* be slaves!' He sprang to his feet. His eyes rolled. He had reached his sort of orgasm.

The roar of the audience crammed the studio. They too rose, exhilarated by pride and sadism. In that instant the need to fight and to punish set their blood leaping. At Bramble's bidding they would have burned down ministries, lynched bureaucrats, gassed clerks.

Ecstasy galvanized thick Thelma, too. With lofted, beating palms she sustained the rumpus as the credits rolled up over four million television screens.

Charles Stewkly caught Major Abbot's roving eye. 'Aston,' he said quietly, 'Leave that blonde alone. Her name is Trouble.'

# 8

The Prime Minister caught the end of Bramble's programme as he walked into his second-floor flat in 10 Downing Street. He had been down in the White Drawing Room with his Foreign Secretary and his Minister for Europe who were at loggerheads on a number of questions which the Prime Minister intended casually to discuss without his Home Secretary: the tedious Channel Islands secession dispute, the United Ireland announcement, the Scottish Nationalists' Gorbals bloodshed, and the continued use in Europe of Britain's last remaining Army Division.

George Robinson, PC, OBE, MP, or 'Plain George' as his Press Secretary had persuaded the papers to dub him, had dominated the Progressive Party since he had created it from the overlapping wings and centres of the old Labour and Tory Parties. Fabian theorists of the Left, port-and-pheasant bores of the Right had been discarded. The great remainder reached their logical conclusion: unification under a new name and an acceptable leader.

Plain George, with cold eye and cold heart, was an expert balancer of men. His leadership possessed that knack which smoothly runs a marriage or a board-room: he could sow the seed of the solution he wanted in another's head, then praise it when it germinated. He had another asset too: he could smile on men he had condemned to liquidation.

He walked into the flat feeling sour, cruelly aware of what all Prime Ministers since 1918 have discovered on taking office: that they are playing world poker with a miserable hand. He decided he could gain a respite by removing his Minister for Europe: the Press had never liked the spry fellow.

Robinson's coat hung over his chair-back and the velvet slippers his wife had embroidered for him six years ago were ankle-crossed on a stool. He had his glasses on the end of his nose, moving them by wrinkling it in the way his wife had loathed but which his Personal Secretary Miss Ancilla Shergrove found amusing. Otherwise he was motionless as he watched the television, except to pluck his braces gently. He was only minutely riled by the show's wild applause.

He asked the switchboard upstairs to get him his PPS. The Prime Minister told him, 'John, get me a transcript of tonight's Bramble nonsense, would you, please? And tell the Chief Whip. And the Press Office better work on a counterblast now – for tomorrow.' He stretched behind him to Ancilla who was lying on the sofa with her long legs cocked over the end.

He said down the telephone, 'Wait. Dig up the background on these four Vale of Hampden fellows – tonight's mute, inglorious protesters.'

'*I* will, George,' said Ancilla, tapping his neck. 'Brisk task for the morrow.' He winked at her and put the telephone down, 'You can both unearth something.' He had a good deep voice under a flat Midlands accent which he toned up or down a class depending on the company.

Ancilla came round to his good ear and said softly into it, 'Poor love, it's a bad time for hounding,' and stroked the long white lock that overlaid his lobe. He always pulled out his hearing-aid when they were alone. He knew she wouldn't whisper dangerous things just out of earshot.

She said, 'I used to know Stewkly's son, Martin.'

'Hum?' He was recalling the switchboard.

'I'll do it,' she said. 'Who?'

'Home Secretary, at his home. Whom did you know?'

Ancilla told the switchboard to get Sir Frederick Chester. She said to the Prime Minister, 'Martin Stewkly, when I was at Cambridge. I loved him in fact.'

'Did you?' He never minded anything in the past.

The telephone buzzed and she picked it up.

But the switch-board had blundered: it was only Lady Chester. Ancilla mouthed 'playing bridge' across to George Robinson who made a clicking noise. Ancilla said, 'It's the Prime Minister, Lady Chester.'

And that's that damned Ancilla, thought Lady Chester, saying brightly, 'Hello, Miss Shergrove, it's *political* bridge, of course! Lord and Lady Delavine are here. I'll call Sir Frederick.'

'Loves putting me down,' said Ancilla cheerfully. 'Silly old cow.'

The Prime Minister gripped her wrist. He said, 'Tell the switch-board that when we ask for the Home Secretary that doesn't mean his blasted wife.' A slight to Ancilla insulted him. He had been politically associated with the Chesters all the way up. They still admired him, but they had been genuinely fond of his small wife Gladys. Too naïve for deep politics, she had always been frantically treading water. And George had been too engrossed to rescue her before her nerves finally collapsed and she had gone, five years ago, for that short rest in the nice Home in Surrey.

The Prime Minister envied the Delavines and their family merchant bank. They were needed by Governments in Europe, Africa and America. But they didn't have to answer for their deeds to the electorate. '*They* don't answer tomfool questions in the House.' He grinned at Ancilla. 'Not even any public shareholders to complain once a year!'

And old grandad had been poor Solly something from Hamburg till he lent money to princes, changed nationality and name, and bought his peerage.

'The PM,' said Lady Chester, clicking over the pine floor of her pretty drawing-room. There were flattering subdued movements round the bridge tables. Everyone enjoyed the *frisson* of power passing. She said, 'It's only that girl hanging on.'

Ancilla handed the telephone to George Robinson.

'Ah Freddy . . . Sorry to drag you away from your . . . er cribbage . . . This Hampden Airport thing . . . Yes, another thorn.'

Sir Frederick said he'd not watched Bramble tonight, but he'd see a report tomorrow. 'You don't envisage serious trouble there, surely, George? Agricultural backwoods . . .' He admired the Prime Minister's intuition, but he thought this time that his other domestic and European difficulties might have overstretched it.

Robinson wrinkled his nose, showing Ancilla his concentration. 'There's something odd, Freddy, about these four fellows. They're rooted, sensible, and yet . . . ?'

'Yet they come out publicly on this show.'

'Exactly. And show such a calm resolve there must be substance behind it. A firm *resistance*.' The Prime Minister had chosen exactly the right last word: it would set up in his Minister's mind the correct line of inquiry.

'I'll have a word with the Chief Constable, of course,' said the Home Secretary. 'He's said nothing so far.'

'Any good?' asked the Prime Minister.

'Getting on. About sixty. Spratley. Ex-Army Brigadier. A keen athlete.'

The Prime Minister laughed. 'At *his* age? Good for recruiting, I suppose!' He added, 'I thought you might see one of the four fellows. Casually. Let them feel the Party cares.'

'That the State isn't so brutish?'

'And that we can control it. And make their lot . . . easier – a suggestion . . .'

Ancilla watched his hand seemingly stroking an arch-backed cat: George's gesture when dangling lures. She thought proudly: he is marvellously clever with people. She walked through to her bedroom at the end of the flat and ran her bath.

Lying in it with the door open on to the passage she heard him talking to the Chief Whip . . . 'and ensure Browne never appears on TV again – ' Then to his wife in the Home, 'not too bad today, I hope, dear . . . ?' When he'd rung off, Ancilla came back into the sitting-room with only the face towel round her middle and leaned against the door post.

The Prime Minister shook his head. 'I'm pooped.' He gave her the wan smile which, snapped unawares by the Press, gave the impression, wrongly, that he was sneering. 'You look a bit whacked yourself. Why don't you take a few days off? Country air?'

'Bored of me?' Ancilla smiled.

'Don't be foolish. Who else could – ?'

Ancilla said, 'Well, I could invite myself to the Vale of Hampden again. I'd learn what really was happening.'

The Prime Minister's glistened.

'Martin Stewkly's married, George,' said Ancilla, quickly. 'To an African lady. *Very* Progressive, and I've not seen him for nearly six years. Before we were both married. And long before you and me.'

'We-ell,' said the Prime Minister sleepily, 'I dare say I'll manage. One of those Garden Girls down below seems pretty good. In the *office*,' he added, taking off his trousers. 'The other must wait. And it can.'

# 9

After Bramble's programme the four men talked behind the Albert Memorial (last rendezvous of London Nannies) out of earshot of all but a few al fresco lovers, coupling or recuperating on the warm, dog-sprayed grass. These sporting activities, common from Chaucer to the Regency and only suppressed under Cromwell and Victoria, caused the four countrymen no concern at all.

'These London ninnies,' said Cubbington, 'should walk up the sweet hedgerows of Hampden after haysel!'

'Go it, lad,' called Aston Abbot to a heaving back, just as Cubbington and Sandford urged on their bulls or Stewkly his stallion.

They were talking of their duties in the Vale. To Cubbington fell the organization of the trusted shopkeepers. After the Bramble programme he would recommend holding their maximum four weeks earlier. Stocks of paraffin and calor gas were to be quadrupled. The grocers were to accelerate stock-piling tins.

Doctor Quainton and the two small chemists were both enlisted and had begun the unobtrusive salting-away of drugs and medicines. The area possessed no hospital, and shortage of medical care did alarm the Defenders. There was only Easterly's old First Aid Post, used in the tourist season for jellyfish stings and sunburn, with Nurse Dinton, a thirsty supporter, in doddering charge.

The monetary position was sound. One Branch of the Anglian operated in Easterly. Its elderly manager, Mr Pennington, born in a Hampden cottage, had begged the job on which to free-wheel into retirement. He and Cubbington had overlapped at village school, and since returning to the area he had grown friendly with Richard Sandford. Discussing future developments hypothetically – 'If part of England was cut off, say, by war?' – it emerged that Mr Pennington would, by early October, have built up a large extra quantity of notes and coins from his Brackton Head Office. The bullion clerk there advanced branch requirements without query.

'As for credit,' said Mr Pennington, 'in the 1970 Irish bank-strike no cheques were cashed for six months and transactions were happily settled: cheque against cheque, the balance in cash or kind.'

Richard Sandford handled all the agricultural arrangements. The increase of stock which Martin Stewkly had first noticed on his return was one result of his two-year programme. He would now accelerate the rabbit and pig-breeding schemes on Cubbington's, Stewkly's and his own farms. Before D-day these would be dispersed – 'To each cottage two pigs and ten rabbits!' Bacon kept. Rabbits multiplied.

Sandford was also repairing the Vale's three water-mills and two windmills, on which all the grinding of wheat, oats and barley would depend for flour, bread, and animal feeding stuffs.

Major Abbot's task was simpler. His Dozens and their leaders were already organized. Zeal he had anticipated but not 'the proud obedience of the soldier,' which he had expected only from regimental tradition and group training. He said, 'I've found a fierce *local* tradition – good as any regiment. And picking the right leaders has brought discipline too.'

His three confederates in the mottled moonlight noticed a mounting restlessness in the Major. It sharpened every time a frog-sprawled couple emitted a particular cry of pleasure. Finally Abbot muttered, 'Said I'd meet this fellow from the Defence Ministry in the Cavalry Club,' and trotted away towards Piccadilly.

He had contrived to date the titillating Sylv, who had been stood up in the studio by her current 'steady', an exquisitely ugly one-eyed West Indian. He played drums with The Rancid Cheese and during their gig in Willesden Town Hall, reckoned he'd make a chubby fourteen-year-old, and buzzed Sylv to wriggle out. Sylv was not angry. None of The Rancid Cheese was much good after a session. Grotty little girls were always back-stage dropping their knickers at a tap of Joshua's drum. But her pride was piqued: 'Don't catch anything nasty,' she said sharply and rang off. 'Little runt.'

Sylv could not recall an evening spent alone. As she debated whom to ring to offer herself for dinner this extraordinary Major with the rather sexy wet eyes burst out of Rupe's programme and dated her.

Sylv burst out laughing. 'Delighted, I'm sure, sir. Where and when?'

This confused Abbot. Absence overseas followed by retirement in the Vale of Hampden had left him out of touch with London life. He had heard of its freedom. No one had explained its classlessness. He supposed there were places where one did not take girls like Sylv. He was accordingly astonished when she said, 'D'you mind Lindapil's?'

His eyes goggled moistly back. From gossip read in deserts and in the country, he imagined that that particular night-club was peopled by the aristocracy.

Sylv said helpfully, 'If you're not a member, I am.'

Aston Abbot collected her on the very wrong side of Notting Hill. The cars jamming the streets represented that bizarre assortment which so muddled the Major about modern London: huge collapsing Chevrolets bought by West Indians fifth-hand from USAF bases; clapped-out Austins of the English pensionaires clinging to declining standards like dormice to drainpipes; but also flash E-types, even Ferraris where the macabrely gilded heirs of Britain's rich kept their luxurious pads. Even in the sixties, thought Abbot, this jumble of people couldn't have lived in the same street.

Sylv was down the tatty path almost before Abbot's finger had left the bell, for she didn't want her house-mates to see 'the old goat who was gogglin' me tits all evening.' The Major, a gingery forty-five, was not the oldest man who had taken her out, but the others had been rich or famous. Obliging important guests was the best part of Sylv's job. Rich restaurants, night-clubs, and hotel-bedrooms no longer impressed her. She had risen a long way from the Nottingham slum. Her mother, hotel char, swung like a pendulum between rage and pride about Sylv's activities: 'Bloody cow don't you come home no more,' she wrote when Sylv told her about one-eyed Joshua of The Rancid Cheese. But next month Bramble's guest was an American Senator. 'My Sylvie slept with him. All night,' reported Mrs Bucket reverently to her hotel cronies.

Much of Sylv was displayed as she hopped into the taxi in a stimulating whirl of breasts and crotch. Abbot was overcome by a desire so violent that his hands and tongue were sucked out towards her. But he was engulfed by embarrassment: what would be thought or said or done about this nearly naked apparition in exclusive Lindapil's?

Nothing. In the first room glowing with beautiful women, Abbot's eyes rolled round like those of a poor Turk magically whisked into his Sultan's seraglio. Some elegant creatures in their forties had faces he vaguely remembered. But it was the ones like Sylv in their early twenties: bold but gentle, polished but loose in the '70s style, which kept his wet eyes brightly spinning. He need not have been ashamed of Sylv's accent. The same classless blend of adulterated cockney and broadened BBC prattled everywhere. One voice more stridently common than the others turned his head. A girl with bleached hair was talking to the Duchess of Hull. The Duchess recognized him and introduced her daughter. 'Gibraltar – the Governor's, wasn't it? No, I know – Zetland Hunt Ball. You're cavalry. We danced.'

They had indeed, the Major remembered, still astonished at the grinding of those graceful hips. The Duchess looked boldly at the little man. His eyes were so like lollipops one wanted to lick 'em.

Her daughter, peeved to be dragged out with her parents to celebrate Daddy finally getting the Garter, stared at Major Abbot. ''Lo,' said Lady Sarah, glib as a shop-girl with a cockney toss of her hair.

Sylv knew a dozen people on her slow way to him. ''Lo, Sal,' she said to Lady Sarah.

''Lo, Sylv.'

Weird place London, thought the Major, realizing with a cold pang that what he was about to do in Hampden must bar him from this sexy spun-sugar life, probably for ever.

The Duchess had spent twenty-five years of marriage with deep roots in Britain and friends around the world. Major Abbot had spent the same quarter-century whipped from Salisbury Plain to Malaya, Korea, to bloody Cyprus and to hideous Aden where his best friend's legs had been blown on to him. He had been trained like a gundog to wait for unreasonable summonses to defend people he disliked in positions of arbitrary, temporary importance. But twenty-five years of the dying antics of an imperial clown had not made Abbot a cynic.

His eyes quested through the delicious restaurant. The

Duchess's party was an exception to the clientèle. Middle-aged representatives of what his father had called Trade glowed everywhere, sucking phallic cigars, and stroking gorgeous things. The economies which had caused the continual withdrawals of Major Abbot's battalion from all those unpleasant outposts had not, it seemed, impinged here.

Another thought whistled through his mind like a cold ghost down a corridor: had he wasted his life, fighting for the like of these?

Sylv saw the shadow on his face and smiled. Feelin' his age, poor old boy. She leaned across and squeezed his hand. His eyes brightened electrically.

The Major's hand was burrowing up Sylv's thigh before the *consommé en gelée* had slipped down, and under her little bottom before her *tournedos* had disappeared. These attentions bothered her no more than those of a bumble bee at a picnic. When they danced Abbot's urgency was uncontrolled. He burned to fall on her. Would she let him? He was in a torment. It was not only sexual hunger after many lean years. He needed desperately, before it was too late, before he was excluded by their revolt, to plunge into this existence which simultaneously repelled and entranced him. He was literally bewitched.

But Sylv sucked her raspberries slowly, and sipped her coffee. The assiduous waiter (whose name she knew) offered brandy. She asked for Cointreau. Past two, they danced again. With room now on the dark floor, she gyrated in front of him as if he were a wretched teaser stallion. He watched her face dimly smiling, those breasts swinging just out of reach: thighs sliding, opening; belly moving; navel winking. The music beat in his ears. The dusky room swam, revolving out of focus behind her body.

And finally she was unlocking her front door, letting

him in. He had asked for nothing, only kissed and gripped her in the taxi.

Sylv had drifted into her customary acquiescence born of wine and dancing. Nor was the old fellow all that unattractive. And he had given her a super evening. She was undressed in five seconds, doing her teeth in ten, while Abbot still fumbled with his tie. 'C'mon, love,' said Sylv, flopping backwards on to the divan which served as bed and sofa in the dingy sitting-room. 'The bastards make me start at nine.' She supposed there'd be a touch of the mums-and-dads and then she could taxi him off before he fell asleep on her.

But Major Abbot's experience astonished her. The blind Chinese whores of Hong Kong, the athletic Kenyans, the famous Greta of Kyrenia had all contributed to an encyclopaedic knowledge. Sylv was ecstatic. 'Crumbs!' she gasped, relapsing into the tongue of ice-cream cornets, 'You certainly press the right buttons.' The Major seemed to have six hands and three tongues. 'Wow!' She moaned. 'Golly! ooh ooh ooh!' She shrieked. The Major, too, was in a whirl of heaven. Lying like a beached porpoise after the first long bout he groaned, 'My God, you're marvellous.'

'I love it,' she said simply. 'I specially liked you.'

Her fingers roused him again about seven. He produced two more tricks from his ragbag of Oriental erotica, and she yelped with such delight that laughter, banging, then abuse percolated the wall. It was while she was soaping herself in the bath that she saw him in the mirror fiddling about with his ridiculous old wallet. Still drying herself she caught him trying to wedge two five-pound notes behind the picture postcards.

'What's that then?' she demanded.

Abbot went very red and cleared his throat. He had no

notion of the fee for the likes of Sylv, but after Lindapil's he had no more money left.

'Well, what is it? What's it for?' She advanced towards him and he saw that she was not just pink from the bath: her face was livid, her eyes bulged.

'Why you . . .' she started, raising an arm. The towel became the wing of an avenging angel.

'I was . . .' began Abbot. He had intended to say 'grateful'. He meant he could not credit her passion. He added weakly, 'Happy.'

'And wasn't I?'

'I don't know,' said the Major blundering.

'You bloody knew I was!' shouted Sylv. 'And now you try to bloody pay me! I suppose you think I'm a common whore!' She dropped her towel, her right hand grabbed her Mason Pearson hair-brush, shot out and struck Abbot with such force across his ear that he was knocked sideways. He fell over the arm of her chair and crumbled into her pile of tights and pants. She hit him again as hard as she could. The soft body which he had so recently relished now reared over him all braced and blotchy. 'Pay me like a whore, would you? Get bloody out!' She screamed.

Knocking came through the wall again. 'Giv' over Sylv for Chrissake,' called a woman's voice.

'You've spoilt it all,' said Sylv and started to cry.

Abbot, clutching his ear, struggled out of the pile of her underwear. 'Honestly, I'd no idea . . .' he began, coming towards her like a crab, clutching a pair of her tights.

'Get out,' said Sylv very quietly from under her armpit. 'And drop me tights, will you? Get right out. Now!'

He walked to the door and turned. His face was quite pale and his eyes looked as wet and enormous as blackberry ices. Still sitting naked on the bed, she flung her head up. Her eyes flashed. 'Why! I don't even know your name,' she spat. 'You dirty old man.'

# 10

The Major bore Sylv no ill-will. He knew that during the guzzling complexities of the night she had found him neither dirty nor old but satisfactory. Major Abbot felt elated to have shaken off the sort of London life he'd sniffed last night. London already epitomized the enemy. At dusk he'd take his gun to Hanger Wood, as the fat pigeons came gliding in, ponderous against aquamarine gaps of sky. He patted the parcel by his side: a nice horsey Hermès scarf for Davina and her favourite Charbonnel Et Walker chocolates . . .

He urged the train homeward. The matter of the detonators, high explosives, the 2-in. mortars with smoke-shells and parachute flares, had gone off well. It had been surprisingly easy, via his old brother officer, now British Agent for an Arab State, to have two crates diverted.

'Under plain cover,' Jack Horsenden had said, 'like all our stuff. Although it's all above-board and exports. It's just that selling guns and ammo all round the world can lead to objections when you're arming both sides! Don't tell me who yours is for, Aston. Mercenaries, I know. Africa I'd guess, since otherwise I'd have had the nod. But don't tell me. It's going down here as quarry-explosives, and I've seen the necessary licences.'

The rolls of barbed-wire bought at Ministry of Defence disposal sales were already tactically stacked along the wooded Hampden Heights and in barns close to the south Downs. The marshlands by the Sedge and the lakes made their own defences, but the gap of open downland between the cliffs and the Sedge was their Achilles' heel. If he could only cover it with anti-tank guns from those old World War II gun-emplacements! But anti-tank guns were not things Horsenden's agency could provide off the peg.

Worried that Slim's Bones would prove useless in a rural campaign of partisans defending woods and hedges, he resolved on using them in a lightning blow, like Rupert's cavalry. With luck they too might gallop right through and get lost.

They had genuine cavalry of their own. The Vale of Hampden, once a famous foxhunting country, had so far yielded a hundred and twenty horses capable of galloping under armed men and a posse of sixty tough nimble ponies to form the courier service.

The Home Secretary said to Lord Delavine's son, 'The purpose of seeing this old lawyer is to assess mood. And to impress him.'

'Quite, sir.'

'In two ways. One, that we have hearts and understanding. Two, that we have complete authority.'

'Olympian,' Sebastian Delavine said neatly.

Charles Stewkly waited in the Home Secretary's outer office, a buzz of lowered voices, crackle of papers and snap of files all around him. Like boys doing prep, he thought amused. His wits felt sharp for the duel.

The door at the far end finally opened. Sebastian Delavine re-emerged and summoned him softly. Stewkly turned right through the opened door and found, to his surprise, the Home Secretary already coming to meet him, hand outstretched.

Stewkly had expected a large desk. There was none. At the room's far end stood a lovely long mahogany dining-table surrounded by a dozen chairs, some pulled back casually as if a handful of Georgians had just left.

'No, you needn't wait, Sebastian,' said Sir Frederick, waving his hand towards the fireplace on Stewkly's right. Two capacious armchairs and a very large sofa enclosed a low square table, bare except for ash-trays. The room was tall. From a dark-red carpet white walls soared upwards covered with portraits. The sunlit windows looked away from Whitehall. On the mantelpiece a heavy clock ticked strongly.

Both men watched each other with the sniffing wariness which foreigners often mistake for British duplicity. Politeness finally compelled Stewkly to utter: 'I understood you thought I might help in some way . . .' His stick tumbled against the table. 'It seemed thoroughly unlikely, but . . .'

'The Bramble Show is always so hysterical, I find,' said the Home Secretary. 'And even mild excitement tends to misrepresent.'

He examined the elderly lame gentleman sitting like a grey squirrel in the armchair, groping for his stick, and so apparently willing to please. It was these sensible retired people who gave such stability to English country life. The thought made him utter, 'I do so envy you living in the country.' He knew he had blundered. 'I mean – '

Stewkly raised his eyebrows but did not seize his advantage.

The Home Secretary said, 'We do feel sincerely sympathetic. But the whole process was – I hope you'll agree – painstaking?'

'And painful.'

'Ultimately, alas. But we moved with such care. The Committee took nine months to hear the evidence; another three to conclude.'

Stewkly bowed his head.

The Home Secretary continued, 'And even when the Report came out convincingly for Hampden it was fully debated in the House. Finally, we in the Cabinet weighed it again most carefully.'

The Home Secretary changed his public political tone for a touch of the pub personal. Leaning across the table, he gazed frankly at Stewkly. 'I've experienced a little of these difficulties myself. My own weekend cottage near Newbury. Peace for recharging the old batteries, you know. And then the M4' – He shrugged like Fagin. 'Bang past the door.'

'You still live there, sir?'

'Oh, no. Impossible. Neither was *I* offered any compensation. The road lay on my neighbour's land, so for me – nothing. As that learned Judge said, laying down the principle, "No man has a right to a view." Unlike you, *we* couldn't claim "adverse affects".'

'You'd had it long?'

'Four happy years,' said the Home Secretary, satisfied with a correct conversational move.

'Some of us have lived in the Vale of Hampden for four centuries,' said Stewkly fervently. 'And make our living there.'

Sir Frederick was surprised, but stepped forward boldly. 'But wasn't fair compensation by valuation offered?'

That had been the first battle by the 'Defenders of the Vale of Hampden'. To treat with the District Valuer appointed by the Airport Authority the Defenders had persuaded all landowners and tenants in the area to fight through only one firm of Estate Agents.

Stewkly saw the Home Secretary frowning, and he smiled. Schedules listing cottages, fields, woods, lanes, and streams had been delivered to everyone in the area with a copy of the draft Compulsory Purchase Order.

The Schedule's final column asked owners for their own valuation. All had calculated a reasonable price between willing buyer and seller and then multiplied it by 900, appending a note on every schedule: 'for the 900 years or more we have been free in the Vale of Hampden.'

'You all put in absurd valuations,' said the Home Secretary, peeved even now at these howls of Press laughter.

'We simply did not agree, sir, with the Government that a man may not value happiness, history and his home. Contrary to the opinions of the State, we *did* try to put a price on a summer day.'

Sir Frederick hopped back from emotion and abrasively cleared his throat. 'You meant your valuations to be impossible.'

Stewkly shrugged. 'The Acquisition of Land (Authorization Procedure) Act, 1946, permits us to suggest our own valuations.'

The Home Secretary retorted, 'That Act continues, "The Minister may, if he thinks fit, make the Compulsory Purchase Order with or without modifications."'

'Which is what he did,' said Stewkly.

'But he also set up a Public Local Inquiry,' said Sir Frederick angrily, 'Under his Inspector at which you all had your say – a great deal of say, Mr Stewkly. The inquiry lasted the record length of seventeen days.'

'But after all,' said Stewkly, 'this is a record attempt at seizure.'

The Home Secretary grimaced.

Stewkly continued, 'And the abominable "Notices to Treat" were then promptly issued to us all.'

'Which you all then ignored.'

'Yes.'

'Voluntarily? It was rather surprising that no one from the entire threatened area returned a Notice to Treat.'

'We were all equally threatened,' said Stewkly flatly, 'by the State.'

The Home Secretary did not pursue the point. 'So the Compulsory Purchase Order for the area was made final.'

'And next follow,' said Stewkly, 'the even more iniquitous "Notices of Entry".'

'Ah, wait,' said the Home Secretary, putting Stewkly in mind of an executioner playing with his axe. 'Surely the Ministry's Solicitors must first apply for a Court Order?'

'That is the procedure, sir, between mere citizens. Here the State acts with its special powers. The Authority has statutory powers now to serve its "Notices of Entry".'

The Home Secretary bowed. 'Unless, of course, some way could be found further to soften the blow.' He looked steadily at Stewkly, expecting the brightening of interest usually fanned by generosity. 'The offers from the District Valuer – values, compensations for disturbance, loss of profit and so forth – were considered quite inadequate by you all?'

'Quite inadequate,' said Stewkly.

'Well,' continued the Home Secretary, with the concentration of a bowler walking back for his final crisp wicket-taking delivery, 'I've no doubt, even at this late hour and without a precedent that all those matters can be – er – comfortably adjusted upwards.' His finger-tips met again. 'Although that is not properly in my department' – the tented hands moved gently – 'The maintenance of order is.'

'We meant,' said Stewkly with considerable emphasis, 'that no compensation can buy us off our land.'

'That – er – ridiculous Petition was meant seriously?'

'In every way, sir.'

'A sort of resistance, Mr Stewkly?'

Stewkly bowed.

74

'Not,' asked the Home Secretary gently, 'to overthrow Her Majesty's Government, I imagine?'

'Oh, I doubt that,' said Stewkly, smiling. 'We're not contemplating treason.'

'But passively, you might,' the tented hands flipped, 'resist the legal demands of the State.'

'We are in defence of our homes.'

'Like Mr Gandhi's Passive Disobedience in India?'

As he uttered the name Sir Frederick knew he had blundered.

Stewkly smiled. 'If you find the analogy apt, Home Secretary, we would be pleased to accept it.' Confidence tingled in his finger-tips. If Gandhi's campaign could free a sub-continent from the British Raj . . .

'We do not, of course, Mr Stewkly, want to use the big stick.'

'No.' Stewkly peered carefully into Sir Frederick's eyes but could not fathom how great a threat lurked.

'Government decisions are the expression of *vox populi*,' said Sir Frederick, unconvincingly.

'But our people do not intend to be dispossessed.'

The Home Secretary knew he had rendered this little man obdurate: he would return unpersuaded to his accomplices. Sir Frederick supposed there might be unpleasantness: old people lying down in roads, bailiffs, evictions even, the wretched police standing by.

'What can we do, Mr Stewkly? You know the arguments . . .' He shrugged and smiled. 'As inevitable as death,' he said with sudden chill, and glanced at the clock. He also pressed his hidden bell, for Sebastian Delavine materialized. 'Your next appointment, sir,' he murmured.

Sir Frederick nodded firmly, extended a hand to help Stewkly, and had him moving towards the door. 'Reasonable of you to come . . .' Stewkly limped through the buzzing outer-office. One of the young men called out brightly, 'Lifts are on the left,' as if nothing of importance had occurred. Yet oppression bore heavily on Stewkly down the dark corridor. He had expected to feel joyous. He did not. 'I feel condemned,' he muttered and caught sight of himself in the lift mirror: he was gritting his teeth. 'Doomed almost,' he murmured.

The Home Secretary shrugged aside the discussion. A lengthy memo from the MP, Browne, discounted any trouble in his constituency. The Chief Constable reported the quiet collection of the Petition and the responsibility of its organizers, all well-known, respected people of good character. 'The crime rate in the designated area is overall particularly low.' Brigadier Spratley ended, 'In my opinion rural Englishmen today may still bark about local grievances, but they have all long since lost their bite.'

The Home Secretary said to Sebastian, 'I shan't even ring the PM about this. We'll draft a short memorandum . . .' He recommended that the Airport Authority's Valuer should add a bonus to all its compulsory purchases *affecting tenants*: a special Dispossession and Removal Grant. 'If the little men (who have less to lose) can be persuaded, the landowners (who are men of some business acumen) must either concur or enrage their tenants.' He recommended some police surveillance over the area: 'A few Special Branch personnel might watch for secret assemblies or build-up of arms.'

He said to Sebastian Delavine, 'Apprise the Ministry of Defence, just in case. Have a word with your opposite number there, Sebastian. We could meet the Secretary of State. He could anyway alert his Home Security Committee.' He was flapping his hands.

Sebastian thought: he's a little uncertain.

The Home Secretary continued his memorandum: 'The

service of "Notice of Entry" should be delayed no longer. Simultaneously with the extra carrot, let us now raise the stick.'

He concluded, 'Stewkly is an amiable, crippled country dweller from the professional classes. He is hardly the stuff of which revolutionaries are made.'

# 11

Roger Sturgeon, Military Assistant to the Chief of the Defence Staff, read the brief notes on the Hampden situation already made by the Home Security Committee. It would develop into a Defence Staff Scenario: 'Run up to Crisis Situation.' 'Twilight Period.' 'Aftermath'. He told the Committee's Chairman that he knew Abbot well from the Army. The Brigadier suggested, 'Sniff the breeze.' Sturgeon knew that affairs of State in Britain generally begin and sometimes end as casually. 'The top of the nation,' as Sebastian Delavine had remarked that lunch-time to him in the Guards Club, 'sticks together on a spider's-web of friends.'

Before setting a staff to work upon a scenario the breeze should be sniffed. 'We don't want to waste a moment working out landing logistics for that piddling little port of Easterly,' said the Brigadier waving Sturgeon off. 'We're not dealing with *Uhuru* for the Vale of Hampden, I don't suppose!'

Sturgeon said from the door, "Specially not, sir, as the nearest battalion is at Nottingham. Or would be if it wasn't meant to be resting after Arabia.' At which both laughed. It then transpired that the Anglian reserve of Sappers and Ordnance Corps units were in Ulster and Scotland filling gaps left by the NATO manoeuvres across Europe.

Sturgeon's office colleagues were busy brooding over a nasty clutch of reports about Chinese troop movements in Tibet. The Vale of Hampden situation and Aston Abbot's part in it receded from Sturgeon's mind. It would not do to bother the Chief of the Defence Staff. 'When my Master is busy stalking tigers,' remarked Sturgeon, 'it's the profferer of flea-bites who gets his head snapped off.'

For a few days after the 'Vision Now' programme the Vale of Hampden buzzed in a swarm of public interest. Reporters teemed like rain on the yellow August country-side. The Defenders anxiously watched their crops.

The training of the cavalry was combined with examinations of the corn. Martin Stewkly's Dozen, shotguns slung across their shoulders, were trotting up a tangled hedgerow when PC Plumridge appeared in the gateway. Old Plum's eyes moved to the shotguns. The men stood, their horses swinging their heads, bits clinking, hoofs pawing the soft earth.

'Best possible way of potting pigeons, Plum,' said Martin.

'Ah,' said Plum, 'I heard you shootin'. They'll stand for it, will they, the horses?'

'They will,' said Wilkinson proudly. 'Look here,' and he whipped his gun off his back, into his right shoulder in a sweep of black-steel. Pigeons were feeding on the lodged barley.

Wilkinson fired. 'Got him!' A scatter of slate-grey pigeons slashed with white shot up, wings clattering.

'Sir?' called young Pete. 'May we?'

'Go on,' shouted Martin. 'Quick then!'

Four guns fired twice. Five pigeons crashed breast-heavy into the barley. Spumes of tiny white feathers drifted downwards. The horses, bar a toss of head and flick of ears and quick stamp of hoof, had not budged.

'Better nor any Pest Control Officers,' said Plum grinning. 'D'you want 'em – the pigeons?'

'I'll take a brace,' said Wilkinson, stepping off his horse. 'And the rest are yours, Plum, eh?'

No harvest had meant so much to the Vale of Hampden's farmers. Even in war corn had still come in from the Canadian prairies, and deficiency payments from the Ministry of Agriculture had aided local farmers when crops failed. But elms dripped. Nettles and giant cow-parsley flourished in puddled ditches. And the farmers were about to be completely on their own.

The Home Secretary's recommendations had been acted upon. Revised Letters to Treat offering all tenants the new Grants had gone out within a week from the Airport Authority's Valuer. The carrot offered was the equivalent of eighteen months rental. Space had been taken in the *Anglian Observer* and *Brackton Mercury* to parade the new terms.

Thousands more copies of the Compulsory Purchase Order were nailed to gates, trees, deserted barns, and stiles, where Ministry inquiries had not revealed the occupier. 'White signs of Whitehall plague!' the Defenders cried and rushed through the Vale like a spray of disinfectant whipping them down. But new copies menaced like the pox on dripping tree-trunks. Ministry vans delivered further loads and minor officials, long goaded by public gibes, hammered them home with a will.

'Bloody people have got to learn who's boss, Harry,' said one Assistant Supervisor, peering at progress from the wheel of his Ministry Austin.

The people of the Vale were now threatened every-where by the stick. The old Notices to Treat which, at the behest of the Committee of Defence, had been ignored in the spring had not all been destroyed: in cottages and seaside flats they were removed from hiding-places and re-examined.

'Most of you and yer old men,' shouted Aidan Stride

to his workers in the Silken Dalliance canteen, 'will be a hundred quid better off by taking the grants. Get those forms back to the Valuer, sharp.'

'Yeah! Stuff the Defence Committee!' shrieked one lady. 'We want our rights.'

'Rather stuff you, Mabel, right or not,' said Stride, sharp as a razor. ''Tis Mabel, i'nit?' He pretended to peer. 'See you later then, eh?' He made brisk gestures with a forefinger. 'Dead serious. We *want* the bleedin' Airport. We *want* the money. Bang them forms back.'

Stride was in his usual posture when addressing his women: lying elbow-propped on the ping-pong table on the rostrum. He modelled himself on a picture he had once seen of 'The Great God Pan'. The ladies looked up with beady hunger at his skin-tight jeans. He was really beautiful, they knew. He smiled back at a sea of loving faces. Who would Aidan take this dinner-hour? they wondered, as his great brown eyes roamed over them. 'Sorta stroke yer bosoms through yer overall, those eyes,' Mabel remarked to her fat friend. 'And if Aidan wants us to send those forms back, so we will,' declared the fat lady to Mabel.

And even among the Potter and Plumridge relations round East Pym youngsters banged the new Grants down on kitchen-tables and said to their parents, 'Christ, Pa! Christ, Ma! 'S money for rope. You gotta grab it.'

Mothers protested, 'But I don't *want* to go.' And fathers repeated, 'Why *should* we be shifted?' But the rootless young bayed like hounds, 'They'll shift yer, they will. They allus do.'

Fathers smote at sons, 'Call yersels rebels. Yer load of pissy crap!'

'We can't win, Dad!' Sons moaned back.

Daughters put on sensible voices, 'No one's ever beat 'em, Ma!'

'Think of the money!' cried the young.

'Think about our bloody rights!' the fathers swore.

Dissension crackled. The Defence Committee at Meadow Hill argued on into the damp night. Anxiety and fatigue shredded tempers. Like nineteenth-century generals perched on hills, they saw the tide of battle turning against them in the Vale. The depth of the enemy's strength came horribly into view.

Abbot said, 'A show of force now. To rally the doubters.'

'No. Why disclose our strength?' asked Richard Sandford.

Cubbington, who had risen from labourer to rich butcher by taking care, backed Sandford. 'Don't show our cards, I say.'

Abbot snapped, 'Our supporters are melting.'

Charles Stewkly asked, 'Could we fight now?'

Abbot said bitterly, 'You can't tell if troops are ready till you train 'em. If I can't show 'em, how can I train 'em?'

'Ammunition?' asked Cubbington.

'Ample,' said Abbot. 'It's been here since June. *And* the explosives have come. And mortars, flares, smoke-shells. As for rifles . . .' It was another bone of contention.

Stewkly was rigidly opposed to rifles. 'They'd make us look like Mexican gunmen or the IRA. Our whole conception of this – a defence of England by Englishmen – would be ruined.'

'Why wait?' asked Abbot.

'Till they come to evict us, Aston,' said Stewkly wearily. 'We must let them make the aggression. The evictions are their attack. We agreed that years ago. We are the *Defenders*.'

Sandford said, 'And if late September turns out fair

82

we'll get the harvest in. And that'll free more men for you, Aston.'

'Sit and wait then,' said Aston.

'For twenty-two days,' said Charles Stewkly, glancing at the calendar.

'Unless they rush us,' said Cubbington.

Martin thought the time ripe to mention his letter from Ancilla Shergrove. 'She works in Downing Street.'

His father looked surprised and pleased. 'Ancilla! Your great friend until – '

'The same,' said Martin quickly. 'The one who so admired you.' So she had, that marvellous girl looking – he'd taunted her – for a father. Political hostess of a mother like a parakeet, something to do with a Press Peer. It had been extraordinary seeing the envelope's back with '10 Downing Street, Whitehall' engraved in black gothic letters, and on the front that flowing hand he had once thought he truly loved.

'For "Plain George"?' asked Cubbington incredulously.

'Only as one of his staff,' said Martin modestly.

Something did not ring quite true to Charles Stewkly. He pressed his son: 'Staff? She was very intelligent. Wasn't she at Girton? Spoke several languages?'

'Yes, Father, yes,' said Martin impatiently. 'I suppose she's one of that pool of confidential secretaries.'

Abbot asked, 'But why's she written, Martin?'

'She just said she'd heard I was back and unmarried again and wouldn't it be fun to meet again? It would. It couldn't hurt.'

'It could,' said Cubbington bluntly. 'She's probably been told to see you.'

Groans drowned him. Abbot said, 'Oh, spy trash, Ronnie.'

Sandford said, 'I hardly think the Prime Minister would send a secretary to spy on us.'

# 12

Martin asked down the telephone, 'Which restaurant? I've been away for years, eating mealies and bean soup in iron shacks.'

Ancilla never dithered. She asked, 'You still OK with knives and forks? Some Cypriots I know have opened a new place in Chelsea called "Seventy Seven".'

'More formal than 69?' asked Martin weakly, but she laughed. The thought summoned up sight, scent and touch of her, but he felt neither of the two things usually cast up drowned in the wake of his affairs: despair or disgust. He visualized every part of her precisely, every fold, but felt only a gentle regret.

'7's are straight up-and-down people,' said Ancilla. 'And so's the food. Also it's quiet, and it really will be very nice to see you again, my old revolutionary.'

Martin, waiting in the cool, glassy bar, lost among a sea of polished, affluent Londoners, suddenly felt fear. The last insurrection against the State had been the '45: the Young Chevalier at Derby with 6,000 men, the London road open, and the panicking German king packing his bags to flee.

He looked around the chattering faces, gripped by the realization that almost certain failure awaited them, meaning imprisonment, exile, or death.

He attempted the confident mien of a rebel, but glimpsed his face ludicrously haughty in the mirror. He had to smile. At his reflection a beautiful strange girl smiled widely back. It was as if he had inhaled oxygen. He grinned at her.

At that moment, Ancilla Shergrove's voice murmured from behind him, 'You old Narcissus.' Martin protested. Ancilla gave his shoulders a little shove. 'Well, then, you're picking up strangers.'

Martin swung the bar stool round. There she stood with that same diagonal grin as if life was really funny, so long as you didn't let it catch you laughing at it. Marvellous great eyes, wide-open, lustrous, direct.

'Your hair's even longer,' he said, kissing her and touching the back of it. It smelt deliciously washed. 'Compliment . . .'

'Yes, that's why I'm late,' said Ancilla. 'I supposed you'd remember about the washing.'

'When you went off me, you never bothered.'

'Well, I have now,' said Ancilla, sliding on to a stool. 'And it wasn't a question of "going off". The relationship petered out, didn't it?'

Martin had no wish to argue. His eyes followed the outer rims of her pupils. 'You look marvellous.'

Ancilla laughed. 'And you look attractively fit. Why aren't you wasted away, gaunt with giant orbs, sick with beriberi? Or,' she added, 'with love?'

Martin said, 'I've been home two months.'

Ancilla waited.

Martin added reluctantly, 'And that's over.'

Ancilla had her head slightly tilted. The barman, without looking at Martin, had pushed a pale Cutty Sark poured over ice-cubes across to her. She continued to look at Martin.

'All right,' he said, 'I miss her.'

'Well said.'

Martin grunted.

Ancilla said, 'But it interests me.'

'Honestly?' He was astonished.

She nodded. 'Why shouldn't it? We were lovers and friends.'

'Yes.' He smiled. She was splendid to say things like that.

'You've still a soulish look,' she said.

'Soulful,' said Martin pedantically.

'Not the same thing,' Ancilla said firmly. Two overlapping thoughts bowled through her mind like high clouds merging: she had been right in thinking him not ready; and he very much needed looking after.

'It was the sex, really,' said Martin, harking back.

'Yes,' said Ancilla. 'You said. At the time I didn't think all that of you and her.' She swirled the ice-blocks round and sluiced the whisky back. 'She did rather use you, too.' Ancilla had two gold inlays at the back of her lower jaw. An accident? Or had some man hit her? She could provoke.

'Are you well?' asked Martin, 'Happy?'

'Yes, both.'

'But you got married too. Why are you still called Shergrove?'

'It's still my favourite name.'

'But what happened to whoever it was?'

'He was a homosexual MP.'

'What!' Martin stared at her to see if it was a joke. 'Didn't you know?'

'I put the doubts away. You know, like bills on summer mornings.'

'Not like you.'

'Perhaps not, but otherwise he was a tremendous man. A barrister. Brilliantly funny. Marvellous about pictures. A junior minister. I suited him, he thought. We met at one of my mother's political receptions. He immediately took me to France: Versailles, Barbizon, then along the

Loire. I wasn't *bouleversée*, but I was *enchantée*. It was such *fun*, Martin, I can't tell you.'

Even now her eyes danced. Martin grimaced. 'But why couldn't you *tell*, Ancilla?'

He sounded like a testy schoolmistress, she thought, correctly correcting. She said lamely, 'He looked normal. He was endowed, as you might say – '

'I wouldn't say,' he flashed out, feeling a stupid pang. 'I don't at all want to hear those things.'

'You asked me, love.'

Martin nodded and put his hand out and held her upper arm and gave it a squeeze. It was soft but not pudgy, firm but not hard. Feeling him, she fluttered her hand, making the muscles in her arm move inside his palm.

He asked, 'But didn't he *do* anything?'

'Not really. He'd be tired, after all that driving, he'd say.' She smiled at Martin. 'He did look tired, I must say.'

'For how long, for goodness' sake?'

'We were away most of September . . . He took a lot of baths – he was always on the bidet or making me. I thought he just had a cleanliness fetish. Law people are tremendously clean I've noticed: washing away crime's contagion. He'd turn me over always and start – '

'Don't,' said Martin, scowling down. 'I honestly don't want to know.' Then he looked up at her. Her eyes were swimming wet.

'Oh, Ancilla, I *am* sorry.' He leaned across to her, put his arm round her shoulders and his cheek against hers and said into her ear, 'I am so sorry, love.'

He heard her breath come sweeping in till it made a click in her throat. Then it sighed out again. She continued in her crisp voice. 'He *assumed* us to be already engaged. We were staying near Amboise. I heard him ringing his secretary – who was a man, yes – to put the announcement in *The Times*. He started shouting down the telephone, "Then go! Bloody go! You are dispensable." He put in the announcement himself. The whole machinery had begun. He rang my mother. She sounded thrilled.'

'But, darling, you were *never* carried away.'

'I was, by his personality. He had charm and power and intellect – a very magical combination to a girl. When we got back the Press took photographs. Everyone was congratulating us. The Prime Minister expected –'

'You to do your duty,' said Martin bitterly. 'What a *mess*!'

Ancilla looked quizzical.

'All right,' said Martin, 'like mine.'

'So we had this grand wedding you didn't read about.'

'No. In Lutanga they don't report St Margaret's.'

Ancilla laughed, so he did. She went quickly on, 'We lived together in his house for three weeks. He tried to do things to me which hurt terribly. My mother said, "You'll cure him, darling. You stick it. He'll be Prime Minister. Truly they can be cured." She was having her toenails done at home in Smith Square at the time. I tried three more nights. He was like a surgeon, a torturer even. Then it was Friday and he said he was going sailing. I thought, marvellous. He went with his secretary. They didn't find the boat for three days. Half-sunk. The two of them were in it, drowned. And clutching each other together.'

'Oh God,' said Martin. He thought of the salty bodies slapping about entwined. 'Anyway thank God for you.'

On the menu the word *Poissons* appeared, glided away. He saw Ancilla in that hotel bedroom in Cambridge. Plain box of a room. Awful print of King's Chapel. Boxes for furniture.

The piped radio had suddenly blared out at tea-time, stirring them. 'Like Donne's busy old fool, unruly sun,' he had said. She had said, wide-eyed, as if the shock had jerked her into truth, 'Darling, you know you're not ready for settling. So we'll stop now for a little and I'll go away.'

Ancilla said now, 'I've always wondered if my mother could have been right: that I could have cured him.' She shrugged. 'Could one?'

'I don't know,' said Martin crossly. 'They say not, don't they?' He stared at her, brooding. She thought: Sometimes he's very attractive. Anger suits him like many a clever face.

He asked, 'Why *you* though?' as if blaming her. 'You're not butch.'

'He wasn't that sort. That boy-friend of his was the woman.'

Martin asked angrily, 'But why after us did you go to Greece without another word?'

'Being unready. Waiting and thinking.' She grinned and Martin wanted to, but he pulled a sulky face. 'That left me on my bloody tod. London, night after heaving night.' Twenty different girls after Term ended, till hot, dusty September and everyone away and Ancilla gone from Greece to Crete which he had never seen and could not imagine. It had been a loathsome autumn.

'You never wrote anything,' he said. In an unknown place with people he'd never heard of, she was lost. Worse than dead, because she would reappear the same or different, both capable of disturbing, disappointing or cruelly hurting him. 'You amputated me.'

'No.'

'You didn't *know*, Ancilla.'

'I'm sorry,' she said and chose the wine. The instant he sniffed it, he saw the garden at Meadow Hill earlier that

Cambridge summer: a warm weekend; wisteria dangling pale-blue, frail as old ladies. His father and mother sitting at a trestle table at the top of the garden, eating chicken drumsticks. Outside the blue pool of shade the lawn glowing, the border dazzling. Pigeons above their head in a complexity of green-lit branches purred like grey cats. A wagtail strutted, flew a few paces. His mother smiled under her straw hat, talking of bird-boxes. Bees too heavy for their engines cruised very low over the lavender that lovely summer.

'You remembered the hock,' Martin said, delighted. He made a business of inhaling it. It smelt of early summer gardens before the air thickens with fallen petals.

'Your father brought a bottle out in a stable bucket. The label floated off, I nicked it.'

Martin smiled warmly at her. She was clever. 'It's lovely being with you again. You're good with people.'

Ancilla said, 'Twice not.'

'Twice?'

'I wasn't so good with you.'

'You were terrific,' he said indignantly.

'Ah, together. But not perhaps when I lurched you.'

'No.'

When he was paying the bill he asked flippantly, 'And have you now, Miss Shergrove, a steady lover?'

He was shocked when she instantly answered, 'Yes.'

She saw his crest fall. Men are conceited idiots, she thought, expecting one to sit around unchanged in waiting-rooms. She said deliberately, 'I said I was happy. That's why, I suppose.'

Martin winced. 'Do I take you home to him?'

'No, I've my own widow's nest.'

'Will he be there?'

'No, but that doesn't mean you can – '

'Ancilla, I'm not asking that. Do I know him?'

'Well, of him.'

'Another pompous politician.'

'I don't think so.'

Martin angrily shoved his money and the bill away. He got up, muttering, 'Better take you home then.'

Ancilla hadn't stirred. 'To the Vale of Hampden?'

'Home to your widow's nest to wait for Mr Whatsit.'

His voice was raised enough for people to notice, so she got up and slid her arm in a conciliatory sweep through his and murmured, 'I would really like to stay at Meadow Hill again. I did love it, you know. And Charles, your father. And your mother. I have some leave due.'

Martin's anger ebbed. He was flattered. Then caution braked him. He said casually, 'I'll ask my parents.'

She said to the taxi-driver 'Lancaster Terrace', and it moved off. She asked Martin, 'Where do you stay?'

'With my crippled aunt in Kensington.'

She laughed. He said crossly, 'She is my aunt. She is arthritic. And she lives behind Queen's Gate.'

'Oh, don't be such a porcupine, Martin. You made it sound pathetic.'

He said, 'But I wanted to see more of you.' She squeezed his thigh in a friendly way and said, 'Me, too.' But her hand felt so different from its touch of six years ago that Martin was disheartened by the loss. Relationships never recover, he thought. But it was ridiculous that one live hand could now feel dead.

The taxi stopped. She said, 'Look, I'll make you coffee. But I mean the black stuff we drink. Not the old euphemism. OK?'

Martin said ungratefully, 'What else with your lover creaking in the wings?' He watched her slim legs climbing the steps. It was a neo-Georgian house, not at all a nest, and must have cost a fortune. Martin ran his finger over a William and Mary walnut table in the hall. Ancilla called back, 'Oh, it's "right" as dealers say. It was in his family.' The kettle started to hiss. 'It came over with William's party in 1688.'

But Martin was looking at the letters on it: 'Miss Shergrove; Mrs Shergrove; Ancilla Shergrove.' She couldn't live here regularly. On the other hand they weren't just brown-enveloped bulb circulars, or vouchers for costly erotica. People must believe she lived here.

He prowled around. It had an unlived-in disinfected air like a suit back from the cleaners. She was tinkering in the kitchen: pans clanged. Someone kept food in, then. He looked for elderly male impedimenta: hat, *Financial Times*, cigar box, Regimental invitation. Nothing. But the rooms reeked of a personality.

Martin pried into the study; red hessian walls, leather books, Alken prints, a fine Partner's Desk. On it a photograph of Ancilla in shirt and trousers standing precariously on a boat on a wide river – the Loire, Martin guessed – and laughing wildly. She did indeed look ecstatic. And also like a boy.

The telephone bleeped. The gilt carriage-clock beneath the Ferneley was striking midnight too noisily for him to overhear. It stopped. From the kitchen Ancilla was saying . . . 'Yes, he's fine . . .' He watched her long legs swinging. Even sitting on the table her thighs looked deliciously slim. 'Yes, I will . . .'bye.' She called, 'Whisky's on the cabinet. Help yourself. That was mama just checking. She sent her love.'

'Thank you,' said Martin, feeling as cool as a successful spy. The voice on the telephone had been that of a man. Carrying the cut-crystal decanter, he walked into the kitchen and watched Ancilla carefully. 'How is she?'

'My mama? Still busy. And liking it. Your coffee. D'you want to sit here?'

'I'd rather.' The kitchen could have been anyone's. He grinned at her.

He's better like that, she thought. I don't go for his hang-dog line.

He drank his whisky quickly, gulped his coffee, leaned sideways to kiss her cheek, said brightly, 'Thanks a lot, love. I must fly,' and was into the hall before she could utter. She was very surprised, but she called out, 'Shall I ring for a taxi?'

'Nonsense. I'll walk.'

He bounced across the Bayswater Road and into the dark, murmuring Park. He was elated at having caught her lying. The evening's succession of raked-up uncertainties – what he felt, or she, what either wanted – dissolved instantly. She had declared war, and shiftily, and thought she'd foxed him. He felt thoroughly on top. When he reached his aunt's flat there was a note by his bed in her upsettingly shaky hand: 'Please ring your father when in, nothing wrong.'

The telephone only rang twice. His father coughed down it. 'Hello.' He sounded older and frailer. 'Oh yes.' It was his mock-vague voice. 'Would you ask Miss Shergrove to stay the weekend after next?'

'But I thought you said – '

'Friday week.' Charles Stewkly's voice turned crisp as a water-biscuit. 'We would like her to stay, Martin.'

# 13

'Aston discovered about her first.' Charles Stewkly was leaning against the black flank of his barn. 'There were some more reporters up here after the Bramble show and Ancilla's name cropped up.'

'But how, Father?'

The men were backing the horses into one of the big farm-wagons. 'A reporter lobbed her name into the conversation. To see if it disturbed a fish.' He called across to Wilkinson, 'All right with those traces?'

Wilkinson was perched up behind two pairs of fairly balanced horses. The two wheelers were massive and calm.

'Go on then,' called Stewkly. 'Spring 'em.'

Young Peter at the lead-horse's head dropped his hold of the nearside rein. Wilkinson clicked his tongue and flapped his reins on the four poised rumps. The horses started forward, then steadied as they took up the considerable weight.

'Jump up, too, Pete,' shouted Stewkly. The wagon, built to cart half a field's cut corn, was laden with rolls of barbed wire. Its blue body had red wheels and underframing. The tailboards were splendidly inscribed in black and blue with Charles Stewkly's father's name and 'Meadow Hill 1886'.

The wagon creaked forward dipping like a galleon crossing the harbour bar. Wilkinson, as proud as a peacock, clutched two fistfuls of reins. The lad swung up behind. 'Nimble as a cabin-boy. Or as a farm-lad before my childhood,' said Charles Stewkly with a flush of excited achievement. The thing was working.

Mrs Stewkly, hearing the squeak of axles, clop of iron horse-shoes, rumble of wood and ring of iron rims on the cobbles, dashed from her kitchen as the great dray lurched through the farmyard gate and rolled down the lane, the brilliant tailboard glinting in the sun.

'Oh lovely!' she called. Five tiny Jack Russell puppies rolled down the stone steps behind her like little white sausages, and the bitch who had chased the dray came arrowing back to the sound of their whimpers.

'He's going into East Pym, round the Green and back,' said Stewkly, limping as far as the gate to catch a glimpse of the great equipage banging along the road.

'But about Ancilla?' repeated Martin. He was still in his London suit.

'The fellow simply said she was the Prime Minister's mistress. He said it was common knowledge in Fleet Street and the House. Aston rang up a few of his Army friends: even they had heard the story.'

'But do they know?' Martin demanded.

'Where there's smoke in public places . . .' began his father.

Martin interrupted, 'I meant, don't Ancilla and that Robinson *know* that they're "Common knowledge"?'

Charles Stewkly said, 'My clients used to believe their affairs were secret months after strangers knew. Love is certainly blind in that sense.'

'The grander you are the more you believe you're immune.'

'Hubris,' said his father. 'Power blinding the gentleman. Apparently she appears on all those guest-lists for his official parties.'

Martin said, 'It was him ringing at midnight.'

'Did you mind knowing?'

Martin paused. 'Yes. Not that it was the Prime Minister. I minded her having a permanent lover. I'd enjoyed seeing her.'

The team's four heads swung into view nodding along the lane to East Pym.

'Good, aren't they?' asked Charles Stewkly. 'We can put over sixty horse-drawn vehicles on the road,' he said proudly, and jollied his son's elbow. They walked back into the kitchen.

Mrs Stewkly, staggering with a side of beef, came out of the deep-freeze room, now lined with regimented fruit-bottles and jam-pots.

Martin grabbed the pink slippery white-ribbed monster from her. 'That's far too heavy. Where to?'

'For salting,' said Mrs Stewkly, bumbling on down the stone passage to the long-disused laundry. There, in huge zinc troughs, in wooden wine-barrels stamped Bordeaux, and in galvanized rainwater tanks, slab after slab of meat lay rosily submerged in brine like picture-postcard Britons at the seaside.

'You'll feed an army!' Martin exclaimed.

'We don't suppose they'll let us have our electricity very long,' said his mother reasonably. 'In that one, dear.' There was still room in a long Victorian bath, brass handled with a tall brass plunger. 'That's the latest beef,' said Mrs Stewkly, noting the date on its label.

'Do you mind about Ancilla?' she asked, pattering towards the kitchen. 'Look here!' she flung open another out-house. It was piled high with cans of paraffin, thousands of pyramids of pale nightlights and ten thousand white candles faggoted together. 'We've been saving up for over two years,' said Mrs Stewkly, proud as a child of its piggy-bank.

Martin stared. 'Mind about Ancilla what?' he repeated.

'Being held here, of course.'

Martin shrugged. 'I don't know. It seems absurdly melodramatic. I don't see how she can be forced . . .'

'Well, your father and his Committee have got all that arranged,' remarked Mrs Stewkly, re-emerging from the deep-freeze room with two large hams. 'I gather it won't be easy for anyone to get away after it starts.'

'I thought everyone except Aston was against taking a hostage?' He took the two heavy ice-cold hams. 'Same bath?'

'No, the Vicky bath's for beef. The big white one near the boiler's for the hams.' Mrs Stewkly took out a pile of bacon three foot deep and followed Martin down the stone passage. 'In my father-in-law's time the labourers lived on bacon. Cold for their weekday dinners in the fields. Hot on Sundays. But it's different holding the Prime Minister's mistress, isn't it? The public can't say we've seized an important Minister. We're not upsetting the country.'

'She's important to him, though.'

'That's the point, dear. But poor George Robinson wouldn't dare to make a fuss. What's more,' said Mrs Stewkly triumphantly over her wobbling bacon slabs, 'He wouldn't like to bomb us or to gas us with her here.'

Martin's hams slid into the bath with a double splash. 'But father doesn't think they'll bomb us?'

'They've been doing nasty things in Ulster and Glasgow. And the resisters weren't all in a group there.' The pile of bacon trussed with twine sank into the brine. Mrs Stewkly dried her hands on her apron. 'Look how quick the salt forms.' She pointed between her fingers. 'Anyway,' she said comfortably, 'they won't touch us with Ancilla as hostage.'

She trotted ahead to the kitchen. 'So stupid of married public men to take mistresses – always ends in tears.' She bent over her stove. 'It's next Friday she arrives, isn't it? I'll get her room nicely aired.'

Martin burst out laughing. His father stuck his head through the kitchen window. 'You wouldn't take a load of rabbits up to Hanger Wood? In the dogcart to practise the pony? Sandy Potts is putting hutches in the pheasant-pens.'

Martin asked: 'By the dew-pond?'

His father nodded. 'Potty's got a lot of box trees there. For his beer.'

'I'd forgotten about beer.'

'We made it here last century. Hops wouldn't thrive – too chalky – so they used box leaves and twigs, and marsh-trefoil as they did on the continent. One ounce of trefoil leaves was worth half a pound of hops, they used to boast.'

'He'll like my mead,' said Mrs Stewkly. 'Look Martin, I'll show you.'

But her son, grinning, said, 'Later.'

'Different flavours depending where the bees were browsing.'

Martin loaded twelve cages of young rabbits into the yellow-wheeled dog-cart, some under the side-seats, some on top. 'Leave a perch for yourself,' called his father from the barn door. They were putting another pair of horses to a harrow. 'Where you going, Father?'

'Just to practice these in the Back Paddock. Dung needs spreading anyway.'

'Take care then.' The grey pony looked very smart in black bridle and blinkers between the yellow shafts. Martin climbed gingerly up through the little door at the back, and locked its brass handle. He clicked at the pony and, with a roll like a dinghy in harbour, the trap set off. The pony took very little hold, but she spanked steadily along, her steel shoes clopping along the lane, her quarters swinging, her firm neck stuck out.

Martin whistled. He recaptured the joy of a journey: high enough up to see over the hedges which hid the country from modern cars; quiet enough to hear the cries of birds and animals, trees creaking, even the wind through the wheatears. He was going slowly enough to digest the views. He gazed across tangled pink-and-white streamers of dog-roses, dusty beads of blackberries and dark-purple clumps of elderberries under their bitter leaves. Rose-hip syrup, blackberry jelly, elderberry wine were to be his mother's specialities. 'We'll be terribly healthy, darling. That's what's so nice about it all. So few good deeds are physically good for you.'

Martin slowed the pony up the flint track into the woods. She dropped her bit gratefully. The rabbits were getting jolted. Their eyes bulged and their ears were pressed nervously back and outwards like furry razor-shells. The pony's breath panted as she climbed steeply between the hazel-bushes bright with green-sheathed nuts, and the elephant trunks of the beech trees. The cart squeaked. Otherwise it was wonderfully quiet. The trees jerked backwards slowly.

Martin heard the sound of chopping. 'Sandy!' he called. The axe stopped. The keeper whistled. Sandy Potts was on the edge of his pheasant-cages in old khaki trousers and boots. Like most countrymen he seldom stripped so his body was white except for a scarlet vee below his neck and scarlet forearms. Drops of sweat stuck in his fair hair.

'Phew!' The keeper swotted a horsefly which fell off his neck in a spot of blood. 'You're smart, Martin.'

Martin nodded at the pony, but it was his suit Sandy meant. 'I only got back from London at lunchtime. I'd forgotten.' His clothes were smeared with brine, green scum from the pony's mouth and sawdust and cabbage-leaves from the rabbits' cages.

'Well,' said Potts, 'we'll none of us want London suits again week after next.' He grinned. 'I'm really lookin' forward to't, Martin. Look there!' He pointed. A cut-out figure of Britain's unassailable Premier stood 200 yards down the glade. It had scared the hawks away that summer above the flocks of cheeping pheasants.

'Watch me knock his bloody crown off.' Potts picked up his ·22 rifle with muzzle silencer and telescopic sights. He knelt, elbow on knee like a front-rank infantryman in the squares at Waterloo. He fired: phut. The tin crown flew spinning off. The pheasants squawked as it spun. 'That's for Plain George if he durst come here,' said the keeper.

'Bloody good,' said Martin. 'Could I?' He took the rifle and leaned across the high side of the pony-cart resting the back of his left hand on it, as if on a barricade. Sandy Potts said, 'You look like one of them partisans.' Martin cocked his head. The keeper corrected himself. 'Or do I mean gorilla?' Both laughed. 'That's what we'll all be,' said Martin with real pleasure. He looked through the telescope. The Prime Minister's grinning face loomed in the sights. Lecherous sod, thought Martin, thinking of Ancilla. He held the T of the sight under Plain George's leering mouth and squeezed the trigger. The target rang out and started spinning like a whirligig. 'Sod you!' said Martin aloud.

They began to unload the rabbits.

# 14

West of the Vale the thick beechwoods of Hampden Heights rang with the scream of power-saws. Cubbington and Sandford, owners of the trees, rode through the stippled glades dabbing arrows on the trunks to show the direction of fall. North and south of the cutting through which the lane from Brackton ran, beech trunks five foot thick crashed sideways, branches unlopped. These splintered underneath, and stuck wildly outwards and upwards for twenty feet. The foresters had not felled the trees low to the ground as good woodland management demanded. The stumps, like wartime 'dragons'-teeth', stuck up six foot high, almost tank-proof.

Richard Sandford hated seeing his trees tortured. They had been planted in their thousands by his grandfather as his last act of faith in his country and his heritage. They went in soon after his younger son (who would have been Richard's uncle) had died in terror in South Africa as a Zulu assegai turned slowly in his bowels. Sandford's father had tended the trees well, culling them with foresight, so that they grew straight and tall.

'They'll not pay my father's Death Duty now, Ronnie,' he said, 'but perhaps we'll never have to!' They trotted through a spruce plantation. The air, cooled by the conifers, smelt delicious but Cubbington's white face looked pinched. He had bought 300 acres of woodland fifteen years ago. As the saws screamed through the pale golden wood in a white dust flurry, he could feel their steel teeth devouring his investment. He rode badly, pumping up and down on his square-gaited cob, and sweating. The horse-flies hung about him like grey sharks for blood. 'Hope it's all ruddy worth it,' he puffed, 'in the end.'

'It must be.' Sandford cantered ahead with the maddening ease of a man who had ridden from childhood. Cubbington admired him. This thing had brought the people here tightly together. 'Like in a lifeboat, Ronnie,' Grace had said. That showed the way she looked at it: escape. 'No,' he had said, 'Like in the castle of Nether Hampden Hill that never was taken by the Royalists. Not after a ninety-eight-day siege.' They'd last longer this time. Cubbington kicked his heels into his cob's flanks as if booting despair behind.

Sandford was peering over the edge of an old quarry tangled with briers, stunted yews, sycamores, and spears of rosebay willowherb. He was stirring his paint-brush in the tin slung on his saddle bag. He looked poised and bright.

'Old flint quarry,' said Sandford. 'Then after the flints, they dug out the chalk. Must be thirty foot deep.' He swung off his hunter, took up a large flint, and lobbed it in. It took a long time falling, crashing through the undergrowth. Three rabbits scuttled up, white tails bobbing, and portly cock-pheasant gaudy as a toastmaster burst out cackling.

'Heffalump trap,' said Sandford grinning.

Cubbington did not take the allusion. 'Ambush?'

Sandford nodded. 'Let's get Aston.' He pulled out the little straight copper hunting-horn and blew it: *Too-aroo-aroo-aroo*.

Below the escarpment in what would be enemy territory, Abbot's own horn toot-tooted back. He was riding along the hem of the woods with one of his mounted Dozens watching for traces of police reconnaissance. Soon they heard his troop crashing up and Sandford rode forward swiftly to stop them. 'Look,' he pointed behind him to where Cubbington slumped on his cob. 'Natural tank trap. Hop off and walk back, so we don't make tracks on the ground.'

'All we've had down there,' said Major Abbot, 'is a little man from the Forestry Commission who'd heard some talk about clear-felling. Soon put him right. You can't see your barricade from down there, y'know.'

Sandford took Abbot to the edge of the quarry. 'You're the military man. Suppose we stop the felling either side so there *appears* to be a gap . . . ?'

Abbot squinted professionally at the quarry's lip. 'We'd have to camouflage it carefully, bring the ends of the beeches across it . . .'

'Will you then?' asked Sandford. 'I said I'd see Owen in Easterly this afternoon. The boom's ready. PC Benn caught three fishermen working on its cables. They said it was for the Festival of St Peter, Lord-Lieutenant coming and all. Little Benn was delighted! Owen's trying to fix the explosives to it.'

'Don't let him,' said Major Abbot. 'Far too tricky. I'll see to it.'

# 15

Martin watched Ancilla staring all round out of his beflagged Land-Rover: what an obvious spy!

The southern end of Hampden Heights tumbled down on the left, plunging in layers of chalk into the River Sedge. The road back from Brackton Station followed the marshy valley. The way they'll attack us, thought Martin, looking with invaders' eyes. Ahead the Downs began again; the last hump before the sea. But here the road swung left and the old packhorse-bridge appeared. It had been the way out of the Vale for the wool off the sheeps' backs, and the way back for the gold the wool bought to build three lovely churches.

'It's so pretty!' exclaimed Ancilla. They had shot up the wooded ridge and the Vale, lively with dancing banners, lay below them. 'This,' declared a gigantic notice, 'is the start of Doom Valley. Give Generously Now.'

They drove on without speaking. On the edge of East Pym, a dozen women and children and a few men were standing in the road, in the manner of English crowds observing accidents. Out of the group burst the Rector's daughter wearing her St George's arm-band. She flagged Martin down. 'The Brackton bailiff's here!'

'Today?' asked Martin, looking at his watch. 'Now? He's not meant till Monday – ' He was aware that his agitation had alerted Ancilla. He affected a more casual tone. 'Really? What's the fellow up to?'

'A final warning. Apparently they do this unofficially.'

Patricia caught sight of Ancilla. 'Oh, hello, I didn't see. Another supporter?'

Ancilla mumbled and Martin saw with glee that she was blushing. He introduced them, parked on the verge and eased his way through the little crowd. Ancilla, peering out, saw him warmly greeted. A small man at the crowd's back shouted, 'What say we chuck the bugger in the pond, Mart?' Three women started to roll up their sleeves as Ancilla had only seen people do in films. She was surprised how quickly Martin had been re-accepted. Annoyed too; it hadn't occurred to her that he could be involved with this ludicrous resistance. Illogically she then felt pleased for him, but also: That's the second damn silly cause he's got mixed up in . . .

She was surprised at his authority. He was striding up the garden path, looking tall, stooping under the pergola. She had recalled him only as he had been in that summer years ago, and, when he differed, had thought the difference wrong. We don't expect – nor like – people to develop when they're away.

The pergola was covered with old-fashioned climbing roses. Heavy-headed, deep-purple dahlias made columns either side. Chrysanthemums were coming on. Behind, filling the last corner of the tiny plot, were potato-rows, three apple trees and a giant marrow. A beehive and a tepee of beansticks waited for next summer.

Ancilla thought furiously: What a cottage to pick for the first eviction! Wasn't there some uncared-for hideous heap to take? She wanted to ring George.

As Martin, the dog-collared Rector and a man in a dark suit came out and stood under the orange honey-suckle berries, a growl and yelp went up from the crowd.

The Reverend Fernden raised both his hands and proclaimed in the high voice he used for psalms, 'Please, Mr Macdonald is only doing his job.'

'Traitor,' shouted a big man, and two women yowled: 'Call yourself *our* Rector, Creepy?'

A quick obscenity greeted this; guffaws drowned his reply. Patricia, scarlet-faced, was making her way up the cottage path. 'Can't be *your* daughter, Rector,' shouted a very small farm-worker, 'She's too much guts.'

Martin, to support Patricia, took both bailiff and Rector by their elbows and propelled them under the pergola to the cottage gate. The crowd, swollen by another twenty villagers, glowered across the clipped hedge.

Martin called out, 'Mr Macdonald doesn't have to do his job till Monday.'

'Aye – rot his guts!' shrieked Mrs Potter from the village store.

He started again, 'He's come off his own bat, to warn – '

'Fat good – ' shouted Mrs Potter.

'Save 'is breath!' It was ancient Mrs Trimble with the notice in her window.

''E can eff off for a start!' bellowed the fat man.

'*And* on bloody Monday!' Plumridge from the pub shook his fist.

The Rector made a final appeal as his daughter, rosily bedraggled, wriggled out through the wicket-gate. 'Good people,' he intoned. 'I beseech you all to obey the law of the land, and to disperse.' He remarked fretfully, 'Can't *think* where PC Plumridge is, Martin. Surely he should be here?'

'My cousin's more sense!' shouted the publican.

The Rector resumed his lofty note. 'I am sure it would better serve your neighbours – '

The fat man mimicked the Rector's voice. 'As thou thyself hast thy long snout,' he chanted, 'verily right up the Bishop's majestic-sit-upon.'

A hub-bub of laughter burst out. Cries of 'Brown Nose!

106

Snouty Nose!' were lobbed up. In a little pause, old Mrs Trimble called out clearly and with bayoneting truth, 'With the likes of you, how can the churches be aught but empty?'

Two youths on motor-bikes from the Easterly garage studied the crowd's fringe while their engines throbbed. The pair in ordinary overalls were not Slim's Bones. One shouted: 'Garn! Git! You're bein' bloody well compensated!'

The crowd swung round like a patterned carpet being shaken out. The menace in their eyes made the youths let in their clutches and roar off, bottoms raised, making the customary gestures with their fingers.

It was the only support for the Airport Ancilla had seen. What allies! she thought and began to giggle. Charles Stewkly's face darkened the Land-Rover's window. 'Good-day, my dear.' He took her hand courteously but with some difficulty and gave it a mole-like squeeze. 'It's so nice to have you *descend* on us again.'

Ronald Cubbington standing like a sea-captain on the bonnet of another bedecked Land-Rover lurched into view from the village Green. He hailed the crowd through a tannoy: 'This is *not* the eviction . . . *not* the eviction . . . please wait till Monday.'

Major Abbot clattered up the road at a canter with a rattle of horsemen behind him. His big eyes roved over the crowd like a shepherd. Spotting several of his Leaders he beckoned them sharply out. The women began to disperse, muttering.

PC Plumridge, upright as a ceremonial trooper on his small motor-bike, phutted into earshot. 'C'm along now, Mrs Potter, please. Hey, Harry, what's the racket? You're not meant to be standin' in the road, Peter, are you? And old Mrs Trimble, surely it's time for your tea!'

Ancilla felt considerable relief at his arrival.

The Rector approached Cubbington who turned his back. The Rector called out, 'Good *Eeevning,* Major!' to Aston Abbot, who grunted. Escorted by his daughter he drove away.

'Poor man,' said Ancilla.

'A Trollope toady,' said Charles Stewkly, suddenly mimicking the Toady Mince; head sideways slanted, hands clasped over bottom, little neat steps and smile. Ancilla let out a hoot of laughter and Charles Stewkly tottered.

'You are an idiot, Father, showing off,' said Martin arriving with the bailiff. Close to, Mr Macdonald's appearance was far from pugilistic. Certainly he was tall, and had large hands. But they were not those of a bruiser, and had, even in summer, a shiny petunia chilblained look. Ancilla stared into his grey, mournful eyes, seeing him somewhere behind white slabs. An undertaker's assistant?

'Mr Macdonald,' Martin introduced him. 'Former fishmonger.'

'Still partially so employed,' corrected Mr Macdonald. 'But now, sadly, a County Court bailiff, whose unpleasant task it must be on Monday morning – '

'When?' Mr Stewkly asked sharply.

'Between 9 A.M. and 10 A.M., let us say, sir. We usually do it then. The male inmates – as we tend to call the unfortunates – are by then out at work. The lady neighbours adjacent have commenced the wash – Monday, for that purpose, being our favoured choice.'

Charles Stewkly nodded understandingly. 'How many evictions have you got listed, Mr Macdonald?'

'Ah, sir, it won't come to that, believe you me. The actual throwing out of persons! Surely not in this day and age.' He lowered his voice confidentially, 'But I have instructions for the whole row, sir. Regrettable though it

108

may seem, for the gardens are particularly well-tended, I would say. Though,' added Mr Macdonald lighting on some good cheer like a crow on a run-over rabbit, 'the insides of the dwellings do require modernization. Or, that is to say, would have.'

'Why these in particular?' asked Ancilla.

'Privies in the garden,' declared Mr Macdonald in hushed tones. 'By no means sanitary. I did note that "Now Wash Your Hands" was imprinted on the toilet-paper – if you'll permit me, madam – but where would they wash? I asked myself.' He shrugged exaggeratedly, then shook his head, adding hoarsely, 'At least they were in possession of toilet-paper. Too often the grimy daily paper, the shiny magazine – '

'Many of you coming?' asked Charles Stewkly offhandedly.

The bailiff smiled, 'Only my colleague Mr Wilberforce and myself, sir. We never require more. The constabulary will attend as per. In an observatory capacity only, of course. That'll be PC Plumridge, I recall. Sometimes a colleague from a neighbouring beat attends. And in this case, I dare say, another police officer from Brackton Headquarters may accompany.' He paused, 'In view of the publicity.' He turned to Ancilla, 'You're not the lady from the Welfare, I take it, madam? No. There'll be one of those, WVS, Meals-on-Wheels, Child Care Officer, and the furniture removal vans. Brackton Council acting as agent for the New Town and Airport Authority have the removals all nicely in hand.'

'Where to?' asked Ancilla, in a small voice.

'Council Isolation Hospital near Brackton,' said Mr Macdonald. 'That's where we currently direct all evictees, as I term them.' He turned to Martin. 'Prisoner-of-War Camp it was, but some of the evictees – not itinerant gipsies – have made parts of it quite pleasing.'

The bailiff removed his soft grey hat with a finny flourish. He caught Ancilla looking at it. 'I will, of course, be wearing the official bowler hat on Monday morning, madam. But this being an unofficial visit . . .' Martin steered Mr Macdonald to his car.

Charles Stewkly said to Ancilla, 'I suspect they picked on these houses first, because the road is narrow here.' He gestured at the cottages crowding in. 'The bulldozers which will eradicate our village and church prefer, apparently, to move three abreast. For economic reasons, they say, but I fancy it gives the drivers some mutual support, as used to be the case with mass hangmen.'

He spoke without bitterness, but regarded Ancilla so steadily through the Land-Rover window that she had to look down. Her London shoes – she had come straight from Downing Street – looked secure and rich among the straw-covered pedals, binder-twine, oats, packets of seed-barley and spent 12-bore cartridges.

Stewkly continued, 'Not that these cottages will be wasted.' He waited for her to look up. 'Their rubble will make the foundations for the minor service roads.' He added, 'Sad how soon the sum of generations makes dust for next year's wheels.'

'Is that from a poem?' asked Ancilla savagely. 'It certainly ought to be.' Her eyes were quite moist. But her cheeks were flushed. She was very much confused. Expecting opposition she found everyone conciliatory. She had been angry in London, and would have become furious in the country at any direct challenge to poor George's complex, thankless rule. But after all those rumours and reports there seemed to be no resistance at all. They're like Jews to the gas-chambers, she thought, helping each other to death.

She regretted coming. She felt as if, being at some-body's deathbed, she too needed to confess. She wanted to tell Martin that she had come to spy.

110

Ancilla could not comprehend the unreal air of acceptance, almost of content. But those villagers who could recall the difference between the Munich crisis of 1938 and war's outbreak the next September recognized the same relief: the great issue, after debateable delays, was now to be resolved.

After dinner Charles Stewkly went out, and Ancilla asked whether she might telephone London. 'My mother.' She saw Martin's head flick. If he'd ears, he'd cock 'em, she thought.

'Of course,' Mary Stewkly said politely, pointing to the telephone at the back of the sitting-room. Ancilla could not resist squeezing Martin's shoulder as she crossed the television. He was staring rigidly at a Brillo soap pad ad. He heard her start, 'Hello, Mummy . . .' and later go on . . . 'and everything's fine . . . quite calm . . . Martin sends his love . . . the easiest journey possible . . .' She offered to pay the cost of her petty treachery.

'It goes on Charles's farm account anyway, my dear,' said Mrs Stewkly, who had a bantam between her slippers in front of the old electric-fire. 'And counts for tax. Or against it, whichever is the sensible way round. Though I suppose I shouldn't say that, seeing who you work for.' She lowered her voice with such reverence that Martin thought she must be teasing. But her face was quite solemn. Martin couldn't cork his laughter. Ancilla stared across at him, surprised and suspicious. Martin said, 'I don't suppose Prime Ministers are frantically worried by retired solicitors' tax-fiddles, mother.'

Mrs Stewkly, disturbing her bantam, and followed by the three remaining Jack Russell puppies, slippered away over the floor to make cocoa. Ancilla relaxed. She shook off her shoes, stretched out her beautiful legs towards the sharp heat of the fire, and let her soles toast. She was aware of Martin watching her. She said softly without

111

turning, 'Do you remember my feet that day in Cambridge?'

'Barefoot on some professor's lawn,' said Martin immediately, 'Just cut without a box: there were white daisy-heads – wrinkled as buttons – on the soles of your feet.'

'We'd been playing tennis,' she said, 'soon after we met.'

'No time to waste,' said Martin grinning.

The game had continued out of sight: *flip-flap – flip – 'ooh!' – flap!* 'Good shot, Jack!' A heavy spring scent of apple-blossom. Her dark hair falling out of her scarf. They had dived under dark, glittering leaves: rhododendron? laurel? 'Do they prickle your back, the leaves?' he had asked her, solicitous as a hostess about an armchair. The taste of her ears, tongue, feet, thighs and all the time his ears listening for the pattering continuance of tennis. She had yelped with delight and tickle, in a marvellous mixture of girl and child. Each time he stopped, head cocked, propped on a painful elbow, she had pulled him back under those dark acrid leaves. Her carefree pleasure had astonished and delighted him. It was the first time he had given something in making love; not just received satisfaction. It was absurd, no, it was awful – to think she lived with that near-dictator, that paunchy white-haired executive of over sixty.

Ancilla continued to curl her toes like a baby's before the fire. She recalled the strange man staring with the cruel urgent look that April Sunday in Professor Prince's garden. And yet he had been so tender . . . She smiled at Martin now with such vivid warmth, that he had half-risen to come to her, before he collected himself.

Lady Shergrove, always happy to participate in affairs of State, had promised to relay Ancilla's message. She was glad, returning to her sparkling dinner-party in Smith

Square, that things had worked out so well for her daughter. Of course, her marriage had been tragic, but darlings, so blessedly brief! Think if she'd married that wretched Stewkly boy! She'd have been cooped in some miserable cottage in Anglia, miles from anyone, anywhere or anything important.

As she sat down in her Louis XVI fauteuil with a rustle of lace and satin, she whispered to Sir Frederick Chester, 'Ancilla. All *very* quiet.'

The Home Secretary slightly inclined his head. He was relieved, but not surprised. He glanced down the table towards Sebastian Delavine, seized his attention, and lifted an eyebrow. Sebastian nodded.

After dinner, with only two tables of bridge, some of the richer guests including Major Roger Sturgeon and his heiress wife arranged to go on to gamble at the Claremont. As Sturgeon walked behind him, Sebastian murmured across the sofa's silken back: 'All's quiet on the Hampden front.'

Sturgeon's mind sprang back to work like good elastic. 'Hampden?' he queried softly. 'Tibet, you mean?'

Sebastian frowned, rose, took Sturgeon by the elbow and explained about Ancilla's visit.

Sturgeon looked astonished.

'Not our idea, of course,' said Sebastian. 'PM's own.'

'Miss A's, you mean,' said Sturgeon, 'Meddling bitch —'

Lady Shergrove called imperiously, 'What are you whispering about? Roger! Sebastian!' She stamped on anything which excluded her. 'If you're not going to play bridge, please do not distract us.'

The two men, looked abashed, apologized. Lady Shergrove nodded brightly like a Dresden doll. 'Really, darlings, shop on Friday night! One ought not to be in London at all.' She swung back to her table.

113

Sturgeon said quickly to Sebastian, 'We never thought much would come of that Hampden thing.'

Sebastian nodded. 'Old men,' he said scornfully, then added because he coveted the beautiful Ancilla, 'Plain George will be without his warming-pan tonight.'

Hetty Sturgeon, whose Marriage Settlement provided their life's jam, champed by the door. The party for the Claremont, disturbing the bridge-players again by their ill-timed thanks, at last departed. Even when they were on the stairs, Sir Frederick called over, 'Sturgeon! Your master. Where is he this weekend?'

'Fishing in Sutherland, sir,' said Sturgeon. 'A remote, contented General.'

# Part Two

# 16

Sunday, the last day of September, was so warm in the Vale of Hampden that Martin had difficulty in persuading Ancilla out of the house. It was too hot for walking, she declared. Martin, equally determined to keep her away from the stables and the barn, finally took a picnic and his mother's Mini – 'Don't touch the Land-Rover on pain of death!' his father whispered – and drove Ancilla up into Hanger Wood from where she could see nothing of the last day's preparations.

In the late afternoon, PC Plumridge finally fell off his damson-tree with sufficient force to break his leg. The sharp crack of his snapping thigh-bone hurt less at first than the four attempts which had painfully bruised his old back and shoulders. Mrs Plumridge, who had observed her husband's antics from her scullery, had suffered dreadfully, convinced that Ernest would kill himself in the process.

At his great cry: 'Tibby! I've broken me leg!' she was down the back path like an elderly whippet and had him cradled in her fusty lap. 'You old fool,' she crooned, 'you've not done it *too* bad now after all that, have you?'

He looked suspiciously up at his wife and was about to protest his innocence when pain sprang on him like a red-hot vice. Her pink face, the brown apple-tree, his russet cottage roof, some puff-ball clouds, the green-and-golden beechwoods on Hampden Heights all became suffused with dark-red blood. He mumbled, 'Don' ring Brackton till later,' and passed out.

She telephoned Doctor Quainton and was surprised to

hear that he was round at the Stewklys. 'Nothing wrong, I hope,' said Mrs Plumridge, who knew why Ernest had chosen that Sunday afternoon to fling himself repeatedly out of the damson-tree.

Representatives from all three Parish Councils were meeting at Meadow Hill. Chaired by Charles Stewkly, they were discussing the final wording of their joint Proclamation.

'Ridiculous nonsense!' muttered Ronald Cubbington, fretful lest the Easterly garage was selling too much petrol to visiting trippers. His impatience with Stewkly's constitutional pedantry was boiling over when Mary Stewkly popped in with the message for the Doctor.

There was a ripple of sympathetic approval. The Resistance had its first hero. 'Trust Old Plum,' said Cubbington generously.

'First of the wounded,' said Major Abbot smartly. The doctor had risen. 'Shall I come back to sign?' he asked Stewkly.

'Sign now,' said Cubbington at Stewkly's side in the bow-window. 'Time's runnin' out fast.'

Urgency gripped the meeting. Charles Stewkly read out the final Proclamation.

'*We, duly elected Counsellors representing the Parishes of Hampden Magna and Nether Hampden, of East Pym and of Easterly, in the County of Brackton . . .*' The quiet voice gently paced forward . . . '*decided that the proposed Government plans and counter-offers are not in the best interests of our parishioners . . . enjoining the ancient rights bestowed on the Vale of Hampden since Saxon times and never rescinded . . . declare our allegiance to the Crown . . . but are now resolved reluctantly*' (the word to which Abbot and Cubbington objected) '*to defend our rightful homes.*'

Shoulders crowded over the table. All signed.

The meeting had dispersed before Martin and Ancilla returned. A bottle of the same fragrant hock had failed to ease Martin's obvious anxiety. The woods had looked very beautiful, but he had been twitchy, watching everything that moved along the roads. Ancilla, too, watched. She remarked on the number of cars. Martin snapped, 'Sunny Sunday. Bloody trippers,' and that was that.

At precisely 4.30 P.M. PC Percy Benn, as was his habit on alternate Sundays, slipped on his Brackton Harrier's vest, his little blue-striped shorts and socks, and the running-shoes Nel had polished. He drove his grey police van to the foot of the hill leading out of Easterly and carefully locked it. Then he set out on the longest run of his training schedule. The Chief Constable had dropped him a few crumbs after his last 5,000-metre effort, but had sown doubts, too: 'Have you the *stamina*, er – Benn? That's what I wonder.' This Sunday Benn would run 10,000 metres across the Downs timing himself with his flagellant stop-watch.

A good run was important, for he'd be tied up with the Evictions next day, helping Old Plum in East Pym even though they were sending down a bod from Brackton.

He set off up the hill out of Easterly. Considerable day-tripper traffic overtook him. Easterly's last visitors had spent nice afternoons snug in their cars on the quayside, windows tight-closed against the nasty sea smell. Now, burping from synthetic ice-cream, they drove fractiously home, squeezing the little figure in the running vest into the gutter to show who owned the road.

PC Benn, head forward and teeth gritted, endured with a martyr's satisfaction the grimaces of children through rear windows. 'Nut Case!' one plump girl shrieked as he passed Silken Dalliance and turned down the lane.

The traffic noise should by now have disappeared, but

PC Benn still heard the throb of motor-bicycle engines. Turning his head spoilt rhythm and concentration, so he padded on downhill to the little bridge across the Sedge. It seemed to him someone had been expanding the salt marshes behind the town, but he needed his energy for the long climb on to the Downs. He did notice on his left a small breach in the sea-dyke through which a trickle of sea-water was flowing. Naturalists' Trust probably messing things up for its bleeding geese and waders. He spat out a gob of phlegm and trotted up the hill.

Sheltered from the sea-breeze by the shoulder of Downs a dozen engines sounded close behind him. But this lane went nowhere. Petered out on grass. Was only used by picnickers and now at five o'clock . . . He shot a glance behind him. Slim's Bones, kitted out in full regalia, black and menacing, were riding behind him. He ran on another twenty strides. Then looked back again. Slim led, then came four files each three abreast. They were all out then, thirteen of the bastards. Benn felt peeved. Wondering what offences they might be about to commit agitated his correct breathing as his brain rehearsed possible charges. His balance suffered. They would, he supposed, stop at the lane's end. He would lose them on the grass. His feet were already burning and the thought of the quiet turf ahead and the silence in which he could suffer alone lured him on like the sound of pipes.

But the engines were still behind him as he left the track and felt the wind blowing in across the darkening sea. Indeed, as he struggled on to the uplands the motor-bicycles fanned out behind him like the teeth of a creeping trap. They pressed him closer. Slim in the centre was only a dozen feet behind him. He sat at ease, hands right up on his 'ape-hanger' handle-bars. He was wearing a German helmet. Steel bones glinted on his sleeveless

120

jacket and a steel bicycle chain jiggled and flashed round his waist. He was smiling slightly.

The two wings either side of Benn now pressed forward so that he was running in the centre of a crescent scythe. A strange fear touched him. Still running, he glanced at his watch. In 3½ minutes he could turn and run back. He had come far further than he had reckoned. He might come too soon on the last cliff over the sea.

The other Bones in their white sweat-shirts under their chopped-off leather jackets looked across at one another and grinned when they saw Benn look at his watch. Slim in the centre held his finger to his lips for silence and motioned them closer. The drumming of thirteen engines, the Bonneville, the Suzukis and the Hondas, beat all round PC Benn. He jinked quick as a hare and so nearly crashed into the flanking Honda that he felt the heat of its exhaust pipe. He jinked again across the moving scythe and was nearly run down by a Suzuki. Straining on, knees still shooting forward, ball of foot striking ground, torso cast forward, his spiked shoes tore at the turf, but his head was swinging left and right, left and right, and his eyes were rolling. The Downs, ochreous in the dusk, rolled emptily ahead to the rim of the cliff. He slackened pace. The wheel of Slim's 'Bonnie' crushed his running-shoe, sending him stumbling, almost falling. He darted ahead, then spun round and tried to cut through between two of the black onrushing bicycles. Panic twisted in his little face. But he was through them. He was headed home for safety.

Then, in a moment the engines were behind him again. They were inland of him, so far as he could judge against the indigo sky and the blur behind his eyes and the regular shooting jabs of pain. They were nudging him on. They were turning him round. I've lost my direction, he realized in a wild fright. He jinked left. He jinked right.

He could hardly see. But his brain seemed to split from his head as the engines roared closer. His lungs' bottoms shrieked with pain. He started to moan. He would stop and face them. But even as he started to pause, whirring wheels nudged him on. He was staggering now. His steps wandered. The light had failed. They pressed him still. The Downs spun. Night seemed to have fallen like a sack. Another hot nudge: a burn of flaming pain. In a desperate leap he flung himself forward like a little monkey. His hands were outstretched to grasp the turf, to lie, to be at rest, to be cool, to be silent. But there was no turf. His fingers, gripping at cold air, closed on to his palms. His nails in terror gouged into his palms. There was silence except for somebody screaming. The air rushed through his Brackton Harrier's vest as he fell and so, when they pierced him, did the sharp black rocks at the foot of the cliff.

# 17

It was quite dark outside the police-house before poor Nel Benn became uneasy and dithered round the telephone. She was afraid of its inanimate voices, which in a police-house bore either ill-tidings, mad inquiries, or sharp commands. She was particularly frightened of it at night. Percy, to stop her calling her family, told her of people electrocuted by it in summer storms.

Bravely she tried to ring PC Plumridge again: the number was perpetually engaged. During Dr Quainton's visit to his cottage, the receiver had somehow fallen from its rest hidden behind a chair.

Shortly before 11 P.M. Sergeant Jenkins rang. He had been unable to raise Benn on his van's radio. Where was he? Mrs Benn was in a quandary. Perhaps he wasn't meant to run so late. She hummed and hedged.

The Duty Sergeant, sensing her anxiety, said, 'Percy's probably got cramp on this crazy running lark of his. Mind he turns out tomorrow, though, for old Plumridge is off sick. Just heard he's broken his thigh in his garden, the old nit.'

Nel Benn made herself cocoa and then astonished herself by falling instantly asleep in a quiet bed. It was an inadmissible joy, to crawl alone and no longer nervously between those loved and dreaded punishment sheets.

Six miles to the east Ancilla Shergrove was staring from her bedroom into a night full of minute, suspicious noises. The air, soft as velvet, was scented from the stocks massed below her window. She had heard Martin leave in the Land-Rover. 'After some ruddy poachers,' he'd said, kissing her cheek with averted eyes. His parents had already seemingly retired.

Martin and six men, four cross-beams, a pile of red-and-white 'Road Closed' poles, six large notices and red lanterns were beyond the Sedge bridge on the main Brackton road. Their three Land-Rovers were parked in the woods north of the river. From beneath the bridge rose wading, scraping and drilling noises. Aston Abbot's demolition squad in frogmen's suits was at work in the black water fixing the charges below the two main arches.

The torches on their heads occasionally shone downwards on to the water. Martin, thirty yards away, saw their reflections spinning in yellow discs. When he could notice his own breathing and the pale tobacco-cough of Cubbington's cowman, the noise from under the bridge sounded colossal.

Two field-telephone lines ran back along the road for half a mile to the point where it forked for Easterly and East Pym. Beyond the bridge the wires ran half a mile south towards Brackton. Each telephone outpost was manned by two members of the Major's force wearing knitted caps above blackened faces. On one was Sandy Potts the game-keeper, whose eyes and ears were sharper than most. On the other one, chosen for the same abilities, was his customary enemy, 'Flighty' Wing, the keenest poacher in the Vale. United against Whitehall, they still competed to be first with their early warnings. On the passing of any car or cyclist they twirled the field-telephone handle. The bell rang by Major Abbot's ear beneath the bridge. He whistled for doused lights and total stillness. Past the men hidden in the woods with the barricades, over the heads of the squad under the bridge, the citizens drove home, snatches of chat and cigarette packets drifting out of opened windows.

After eleven, few cars passed: work was hardly

impeded. Just before midnight, Abbot came up the bank rubbing his hands and called all his men out. He gave three sharp twirls on his field-telephone to check on the scouts. There was no ring back. Road clear then. He rang three times again to recall them. Then he climbed on to the centre of the road, and looked both ways up and down it, peering for the two crews with the poles and wire. He gave one long shrill whistle.

At the same time came the roar of a motor-bicycle along the road from Easterly. Its headlights lanced at the sky as it topped the rise where Sandy Potts and his mate had been on guard. But they, lugging their telephones and coiling the wire as they ran, were scrambling back through the woods towards the Land-Rovers. The bike roared down the slope towards the bridge. Suddenly its brakes squealed as its rider saw the lights, the board, the barricade. The men in the Land-Rovers peered out. They were unarmed and apprehensive. The Major was out of sight. They were without orders. Then the rider looked around, saw them and called across, 'Abbot's lot?' It was Slim's brother.

From the south the sound of a car was growing closer. Flighty Wing and his mate padded back down the road, crossed the bridge and reached their vehicles.

Aston Abbot stood in the centre of the bridge, gripping the wires which ran over the parapets to the detonators beneath. He judged the distances, put down the wire reels and plunger and raced back towards the interior road-block. He imagined Slim's apes had made a balls-up of putting Benn away. 'What the hell's the matter?' he asked over the spluttering of the Honda. The lights of the car appeared beyond the farther barricade: it was slowing down. 'Turn your light and engine off,' he ordered, and slid off the road and crouched down. 'Get down here.'

The youth surprisingly obeyed. He said, 'Fuzz Benn went over the cliff.'

'What?' Abbot was shocked. 'You were only meant to lock him up.'

'We didn't chuck him orf. Bleeder jumped. 'E's barmy. Or was.'

'Dead?'

'Reckon so.'

'Murder,' said the Major with distaste.

'Nope, no one touched him. 'E coulda stopped. But no. Bleeder kep' lookin' at 'is watch and run-run-runnin'.'

Beyond the bridge the car had stopped at the barricade. Its clanking engine told its age. Not the police anyway, thought Martin, sitting up straighter to look.

The old Consul's doors opened uncertainly and five figures, pink in the lanterns' glow, lurched out. They wandered up to the barrier, peering at the notices. 'Sez Road Up Dangeshish Brish,' a voice protested. 'S'orl right earlier worn't it, Joe?'

The drunken voices wafted clearly across the bridge.

'Carn't git 'ome, anyhow,' answered Joe and gurgled happily.

'Back t'strip club then.'

'Aye. Back to t'nudies. See that coon agin. Cor!' Lips smacked.

'Squeeze of titties.'

Belly-laughter rumbled.

'Wives won't credit it.'

'Late back. "Dangeshresh Brish!" Ethel say, "Thash new, y'sod."'

They piled back, giggling, into the car and started to turn with much engine-revving and squeaking of brakes.

Slim's brother whispered, 'Bleedin' Yorkshire trippers. Blow the fuse on 'em, Major.' There was some soft laughter from the Land-Rovers. Abbot held up his hand. Silence.

The Consul was finally lumbering away. Abbot ran back to the bridge, recovered the plunger and reels of wire and brought them into the ditch by the barricades. 'Right,' he said. 'You in the Land-Rovers there, and you, Martin, away with your lot to Hampden Heights. Potty!' he called.

'Major!' answered a voice.

'Get my BMW on to the road, engine running, ready to go.'

'Can't we wait, Aston?' asked Martin. There was a chorus of approval.

'Well, back on the ridge, then. But remember in a few seconds, there'll be no more petrol coming in.'

'We've lots o' corn for the nags tho', Major,' said Flighty Wing cheekily.

The Land-Rovers pulled away to the ridge and everyone got out, a black huddle of bodies and heads against the lemon flush in the sky from the lights of Easterly. Potts turned the BMW and stopped. 'Further on!' shouted the Major. 'I don't want stones smashing it, do I? I'll never get another.'

'Gor!' said the Bone. 'Blow 'ere, would they?'

'Yes, some,' said Abbot. 'Shouldn't you be back with Slim?'

'Wire's up across the Downs.'

'Right across the open piece?'

'Yep. All the way. And electrocuted, them coils are.'

'You got the generator?'

'S'easy. Lying by me Dad's garage. Towed it up there.'

'Well done,' said Abbot, delighted. 'Working?'

'Chucked a rag on it – Fizz! It's all over straw and petrol, y'know.'

127

'Smashing,' said Abbot, carried away. 'Want to watch this?'

'Well, you are, aren't yer?'

'OK. Stand by.' He pressed the plungers. The explosion ripped out in red and yellow rays sideways under the bridge, upwards through it. Then another explosion. The double noise in the dark night was immense. One split in the masonry shrieked as the stones ruptured and crashed. A shower of stone fragments rose in the blaze of light like charred papers above a bonfire.

'Bloody hell!' squealed Slim's brother. 'Well *done*, Major!'

The night was full of thundering stones and the crash and splatter of rocks on to water.

Abbot glanced at the youth. He was about sixteen, had pimples, sideboards, some beard-fuzz on his chin, and his eyes sparkled. At that instant on Abbot's orders, he would have leapt on to the crumbling bridge. Lighter pieces of disintegrated stone hurled higher up were still pattering into the tree-tops. Several hit the road near them in a clatter. The boy ducked. Abbot said, 'No danger now.' The boy grinned. Abbot thought, They only need a war, these lads, a war they're winning, with lots of blowing-up. It's all they *think* they want, anyway. As I did.

'Come on,' he said. 'Make sure we've done the job.'

He walked briskly towards the bridge, but the lad had run ahead, clumping in his boots. 'Smashin',' he shouted back. 'Orl gorn.'

Abbot was delighted. Not only had the two arches blown, but so had the central support on which he had feared the police could easily balance a temporary bridge.

He looked down into the river. It had swallowed the stones like pills and flowed on smoothly and darkly towards the lakes, the marshes, Easterly and the sea.

From the bulwarks on either side came the continued pattering of flaking stone. Aston Abbot sighed wth satisfaction.

'Tell Slim it's blown.'

'Sure, Major.'

'You know what you're on tomorrow?'

'Yep. Patrollin' the wire and the refuges.'

'Refuges? Oh, refugees.'

'Yep. Seein' them refuges out.' He vaulted on to his Honda, roared up the hill past the waiting Land-Rovers back to Easterly. As the throb of his engine faded the clock in East Pym's beautiful church tower was ending its twelve strokes of midnight.

'Good timing,' said Major Abbot sliding into his BMW. His protuberant eyes glittered. 'That'll show the buggers we mean business.' He could not have defined whom he meant, and would have denied he intended the khaki-shades of those red-tabbed Major-Generals who at the critical points of his career had turned him down. But it was they he imagined cowering from the blast of his explosion.

'Well, Potty, war's begun.' He blew a long sustained Victory Vee on his horn, which was answered by the Land-Rovers. The party drove rapidly north-eastwards through the Hampdens and up to the Heights on the only other road penetrating the Vale. We're fighting not only against Them, decided the Major pursing his lips. He thought of his father dying at Dunkirk, and his great-uncle wasted amongst the rats and blood-stained mud of Flanders. We fight for our own people. Against more waste.

# 18

The normal traffic flow on a Monday early morning was always out of Easterly and the Vale towards Brackton. Nobody came into the area to work. Few of its inhabitants worked outside. The economic causes which made the area close-knit and remarkably self-sufficient postponed the discovery of the revolt.

The Yorkshire trippers' wives, furious about their husbands' absence, mocked them when they telephoned Sea View to report that the bridge had disappeared.

'Get orf it, Joe,' snapped Mrs Ethel Birtwistle. 'Pissed as a fart you were last night and no mistake . . . Quiet, Joe. You get back here sharp, the lot of you. To do some bloody good explaining.'

Joe was appointed spokesman for the guilty five who had drifted from the Strip Club to a black brothel in a back street: crowded, probably poxy, and wickedly expensive.

'Disgraceful, the police,' Joe agreed with his wife. 'No diversion signs. And we all had pockets picked in the Club.'

'Club?' screeched his wife, for the other wives in a bristling phalanx of dressing-gowns, tight girdles and loose curlers pressed behind her in Sea View's lounge.

'Local Rotary like,' said Joe.

'Wallets nicked in a *Rotary*?' Ethel demanded, turning to her four associates with stagy astonishment. 'You've told police?'

'Just goin' down there, love.'

'Mind you get it back, Joe Birtwistle.'

The husbands shuffled reluctantly into Brackton Police Station where Sergeant Jenkins was listening on the telephone to the local manager of Anglia Traction, one of whose drivers, he was explaining incredulously, had just rung in from a farm near the Sedge.

'Bridge *disappeared*?' repeated Sergeant Jenkins. 'That *is* Mr Barnett, the manager?'

Joe and his penniless and dishevelled friends squeezed along the counter, aware of every itch on their bodies, scratching themselves furtively and sweating on the consequences. 'If it's t'bridge on t'Easterly road like, that's right. T'weren't there last night.' They were so delighted that the vanished bridge had been not an alcoholic hallucination that they began to chuckle, and punch each other's shoulders and jab each other in the ribs: 'That'll fix t'Missus proper. Knew she thought I was lyin'.'

Sergeant Jenkins, having assured Mr Barnett that he would look into this extraordinary business, told the eavesdropping clerk to check immediately with Brackton RDC about any roadworks on the Easterly road. The Duty Sergeant then bent a dark, dubious Welsh eye upon the still grinning Yorkshiremen. He drew a pad towards him and poised a pencil over it with such menace that the trippers' new gaiety popped like soap bubbles.

He had just asked Joseph Woodrow Birtwistle his home address, when one of the telephonists dashed up to him. 'PC Stansgate with the bailiffs reports the Sedge bridge has been dynamited!'

The Yorkshiremen gazed bemused at one another. 'That ruddy bang we heard.'

'Weren't the ole flivver, after all.'

'Gor – might've been us, a little later.'

Sergeant Jenkins walked with steady but extended strides to the radio room.

PC Stansgate driving to East Pym for the evictions in

his blue-and-white Panda had suddenly come upon the red Anglia bus, two private vehicles, five furniture-removal vans, two wholesalers' delivery trucks and three anxious ladies in runabouts from the WVS, Meals-on-Wheels and Child Welfare. The road was jammed this side of a barricade. A score of people were peering into the gloom of the river and arguing in agitated knots. One of the private vehicles contained the two bailiffs: Mr Macdonald (in a state of shock), and Mr Wilberforce recriminating (the police were certainly responsible). PC Stansgate had found the bridge totally vanished.

'Don't be bloody stupid, Stansgate,' said Sergeant Jenkins sharply.

'Sarn't . . . You can just see some little bits at the bottom of the river this side.'

'Where's Benn then?' asked Sergeant Jenkins. 'Didn't you see him the other side?'

'There's no one the other side, Sarn't. No one at all. And what shall I do about the bailiffs?'

'Keep them there. Send the rest away. Put some of your accident-beacons back at the junction to close the road. The Inspector will be along immediately.'

Certainly no one could be seen beyond the river and it could not occur to PC Stansgate that forty armed men were established in slit-trenches in the woods and closely observing him.

Under the cover of the trees the Defenders looked at each other, bright-eyed and bursting with mirth like schoolboys, and stuffed fists and grubby handkerchiefs into their mouths.

There was no one on the road beyond the river because Slim's Bones were on point duty at the Easterly fork. The patient English quietly queued to inquire what had happened, clicked sympathetically when they heard a bridge had fallen down and made the long detour to

Brackton through East Pym and the cutting over the Heights.

Cubbington was loudhailing in East Pym, Sandford in Easterly and Charles Stewkly in the Hampdens. Copies of the Parish Councils' Proclamation were displayed on notice-boards, telegraph-poles, barn doors and in supporters' windows. The Defenders exhorted anyone who wished to leave the area to do so immediately by the cutting to the Brackton Lane. 'After 10 A.M., we're closing our frontiers against Whitehall.'

The five Yorkshire wives craning over the laurel hedge in Sea View's arid garden thought at first it was a Students' Rag Week. The little port bubbled like a saucepan. The police-house was vainly rung: poor Nel Benn now left the telephone shrilling.

She had answered it several times in the early morning, but it was always that cruel Sergeant Jenkins shouting from Brackton, 'Tell us what is *happening*, Mrs Benn, for goodness' sake! Look out of your window, Mrs Benn! What do you *see*?' Finally she left the receiver swinging under the desk on its cord with Jenkins's voice shouting to and fro as it swung. She tottered upstairs and sat down on the cool lavatory-seat with her spinning head between her knees. She had hated the way Sergeant Jenkins's shouts, as if squeezed into the wire at Brackton by electric force, had spurted out of that black mouthpiece as it swung like a serpent under poor Percy's desk.

Mrs Ethel Birtwistle spotted Sandford's flagged Land-Rover coming up the road towards Sea View. There were two young thugs on motor-cycles in front of the thing, and a couple of young fishermen perched on its bonnet. Standing up behind with a grey loudspeaker was a dapper-looking gent with a sunburnt face and very sharp eyes. 'This is an Emergency . . .' he was shouting.

Ethel Birtwistle burst open the rickety garden-gate and,

sidestepping the first Bone, pushed her way in front of the Land-Rover. Her friends huddled like cows in the gateway, mooing distressfully, 'She'll be killed for sure.' But the Land-Rover stopped and Richard Sandford bent down and asked: 'Madam, can we help in any way?'

Mrs Birtwistle was momentarily stunned by his courtesy. Then she recovered. 'Well, if you're anything to do with this *rubbish*, you can! We don't live in this dump. Our men are in Brackton with the Consul, and we – '

'Consul?' Sandford interrupted, his chain of thought suggesting a diplomatic mission.

'Aye,' said Mrs Birtwistle, surprised that he should inquire about the car. 'Have yer seen it then?'

'No, I don't think so,' said Sandford gravely.

'Well, then,' said Mrs Birtwistle. 'There's no bus come in, nor ever will, for t'bridge is exploded. So how the bloody heck do we get out?'

Sandford frowned. The lady's hair was in curlers, and she was on the large side, but she was not unattractive. Frustration made her glow. She had character and, he thought, sex. The excitement of revolt had gone to his head. He began, 'Madam, could you use your charms to get a lift to Brackton by the back road – '

'Lift!' screamed Mrs Birtwistle, 'We've been lookin' for nowt else the past hour. No one bloody wants to go to Brackton. They all live here.'

'In that case,' said Sandford, bowing extravagantly, 'I'm delighted you choose to stay here, madam. You are a lively asset to us, a lovely one, may I say? And your equally desirable lady-friends there.' He was revelling, like an actor too long rested, in his moment on centre-stage. He brought the other four into his audience with a grandiloquent gesture. 'Ladies, we beg you, stay and enchant us!' It was the rashest invitation he had ever issued.

134

The two Bones, the fishermen, and the small crowd compressing the procession, examined the five deserted wives with lively interest. The wives were flattered. They nudged one another, flushed, looked into each other's eyes, and giggled. Richard Sandford added, tapping Owen's shoulder below him, 'And we've a lot of jolly sailors here to keep you happy.'

Mrs Birtwistle and her friends had been half-charmed already by this extraordinary and handsome gentleman. But this insinuation – 'That's a bit much. If you think – ' she started.

Sandford, savouring each exchange, raised his hands. 'I only supposed, madam, that your husbands, deprived of your delicious company, must have been relieving themselves in Brackton's squalid Strip Club, and so – '

'They were, the buggers,' shouted the thin-beaked wife from the gate, who looked short on satisfaction.

'Relievin's right,' snapped Ethel Birtwistle. 'Knowin' Joe.'

'Rotary Club,' said the Junoesque wife with fat red lips, comforting herself. 'That's all it were.'

'No,' said Sandford firmly. 'There's no Rotary Club in Brackton. But in the Strip Club they make a nasty practice of stripping trippers.'

'Pickin' pockets?' inquired the thin wife.

Sandford nodded. 'I'm a magistrate.' Then he corrected himself. 'That's to say, I was, before the Emergency started.'

'That's it!' shouted Mrs Birtwistle, impressed by his authority. 'He's right, girls. They've done us. We'll bloody do 'em.' Giving the nearest fisherman first a shove to make room, and then a tug to get up, she landed next to him on the Land-Rover's bonnet. She gave Owen's waist a squeeze, ruffled his frizzy hair, and let out a hoot of

135

laughter. 'Girls! We'll have *our* holiday now. We'll give 'em bloody Strip Club!'

The procession, refreshed by its first outside allies, moved on, but Richard Sandford was laughing so much he could no longer speak into his microphone. Handing it to his comrade he collapsed shaking on the seat behind Mrs Birtwistle's vermillion back. He had imagined rebellion would be grim and terrible. He had been mad to think so. He spluttered, 'Everything Britain's done post-war has been a bloody farce! Trust trippers' wives to get involved!'

For the rest of Britain the first news that anything was amiss in the Vale of Hampden was tucked casually away in a road report on Radio One. Mixed in a pot-pourri of Heavy Loads, High Winds and Autumnal Pageants, an adenoidal disc-jockey advised motorists to avoid the Brackton to Easterly road where a bridge had been damaged. 'Police diversions are in operation.'

County Police HQ was more than diverted. The silence of PC Benn was now causing alarm. Inspector Wilson had finally been able to talk to Mrs Plumridge: her husband was 'very poorly, in shockin' pain. No, sir. I've not heard a word about a bridge. What were wrong with which bridge, sir?'

Shifty Wilson's suspicions were temporarily allayed by a surprise telephone-call from Doctor Quainton. 'My patient, Ernest Plumridge, one of your police officers, is in a state of trauma following his accident. But he keeps begging me to tell you how much he regrets not being on duty.'

Inspector Wilson thanked him and then asked, 'You've heard nothing of PC Benn, by any chance?'

Dr Quainton regretted. Was he ill?

'Actually, Doctor,' said the Inspector, 'he's disappeared.'

136

'Absconded with the petty cash?' asked Dr Quainton, naughtily.

'No, no,' said Inspector Wilson irritably. 'He carries no cash anyway. Possibly case of nervous strain. Very keen long-distance runner. Might have collapsed. Which reminds me,' added the Inspector as casually as he could. 'What's happening about the bridge?'

'Bridge?' asked Bill Quainton. He could not resist inquiring, 'Police Bridge Tournament?' He heard the Inspector gulping under the strain of self-control.

'No,' said the Inspector at last. 'The Sedge bridge has been deliberately exploded. By criminals,' snapped the Inspector. 'I'm on my way out there. And, Doctor, if you've anything to report on this extraordinary business, you will ring me, won't you?'

The Chief Constable, returning from the Scottish Police Athletic Finals, had not arrived in Brackton before Inspector Wilson left. The sports, as he called them, had been weakly competed and sparsely watched. There had been prior calls on police time in Glasgow, where weekend fighting had been particularly brisk. When the force should have been out in their singlets running and leaping round a track, they were crash-helmeted in the Gorbals hurling and snatching. It had been a wretched blow to the current recruiting campaign. 'Get Fit in Blue,' muttered the Chief Constable peevishly, 'with photographs of 'em limping off Clydeside with broken elbows!' Brigadier Spratley was therefore in ill-humour when he quick-marched into his office, and found his assistant quivering over Inspector Wilson's report.

The Chief Constable read it grimly.

His assistant said nervously, 'I've alerted Special Branch and Regional Crime Squad, sir.'

The Brigadier grunted. 'Airport Resistance, of course.

137

Get me Wilson on the radio. And have you heard from the Home Office at all?'

Shifty Wilson had four policemen sniffing like hounds round the bridge-buttress and fanning out along the marshlands which bordered the deep river. They had brought no boots: their shoes and socks and trouser-bottoms were already soaking. They muttered crossly to one another, keeping the belt of woodland on the opposite bank of the river under observation, as they stumbled over the boggy grass. Movements under the beech-trees seemed to confirm their uneasy feeling of being watched, but they could identify nothing. PC Stansgate was snapped at by Shifty for saying, 'I think there's a man there, sir.'

'Police officers don't think. They bloody know. And they don't move until they do.'

The Defenders, at ease in their trenches, amused themselves by drawing beads on the blue uniforms plodding below. They swung their gun barrels on them and pretended to squeeze their triggers. A gaudy cock pheasant strutted past Flighty Wing, dragging his tail within a hand's pounce. Wing hurled a sharp flint in a sun-shaft. It struck the pheasant's burnished back. Firing off squawks of protest it rocketed away *kok-kok-kok-koking* over the river. The sudden noise arrested the police below. They all stared upwards. The Defenders froze.

Police voice wafted up: 'Did a good job on the bridge.' Inspector Wilson detected admiration in their tone. He called down haughtily, 'They did a dam' bad job for themselves. They'll face charges under Highways Act, 1855, Explosive Substances Act, 1883, and Public Order Act, 1936.'

PC Stansgate also knew his Moriarty. He piped up, 'And Highways Act, 1959, too, sir. Section 141: "Damage to Highways".'

Wilson scowled down at him. 'You've forgotten the Malicious Damage Act, 1861, Stansgate, Section 61. Easy one to remember.'

His driver summoned him from the Jaguar. 'The Chief Constable on the radio, sir.'

'And where,' inquired Brigadier Spratley, 'are the bailiffs?'

Shifty Wilson was not sure. He did not know them. He looked around anxiously, but did not see them. He asked into his microphone, 'Why, sir?'

'Because we must get them into East Pym and occupy the houses and arrest those responsible for this nonsense *immediately*, Wilson. They're laughing at us in there now. And in an hour the Nation will be splitting its sides.'

'I was just collecting the bailiffs,' said Shifty Wilson, 'prior to moving them in through the Hampden Heights cutting.' He had a map on the white roof of the Jaguar and was desperately working out the route with his finger. 'We'll come back via Brackton.'

'Can't you cross the river?'

'We've been reconnoitring carefully, sir. It's not fordable here.'

'Swimmable?'

'Surely not with the bailiffs, sir?'

The Chief Constable, thwarted, supposed he was right. He looked at the map on his office wall. 'You can't get round over the Downs into Easterly?'

Shifty Wilson had no idea. He knew Easterly hardly at all. PC Benn should have been at hand with all this information. He peered at the map. There was no other road into Easterly from the south. He said, 'My knowledge of the terrain, sir, suggests we must go by road via Hampden Heights.'

'Very well. And men?'

'I've four here, sir.'

'Of course you have. But you've got to watch that road, haven't you? You'll need as many as we can muster, Wilson, to take you in. Men blowing up bridges aren't just a shower of yobs.'

'No, sir. Clearly dangerous and determined. I was going to suggest twenty men, five cars, and the van. With the bailiff's car and the furniture-vans we'll make an impressive convoy.'

'Good,' said the Chief Constable. 'And I'll come with you.'

Shifty Wilson dropped his microphone and groaned.

# 19

The convoy was only assembling when the first newsmen reached Brackton Police HQ. The kind WVS ladies, the removal-van drivers, the Welfare women, the bus-driver and the five Yorkshire trippers vied with one another to describe the vanished bridge. The BBC News reported, 'It is now thought possible that objectors to the Vale of Hampden Airport may have been responsible for the explosion which wrecked the bridge near East Pym where seven families were due to be evicted by bailiffs this morning.'

The rest of the communications hounds in full cry on a strong scent were struggling to glimpse the quarry. ITN and BBC News teams were hiring helicopters. News Editors in London and Manchester were screaming for anyone in the office who'd ever been to bloody Hampden, who had a contact there. The telephone-lines via Brackton to the villages in the Vale were jammed with inquiries. Best placed were the reporters on the *Brackton Mercury* and *Anglian Observer* who knew a few of the locals, and were selling themselves expensively on the telephone to the big London dailies. But information leaving the Vale was scant. Those in the know disclosed nothing. The rank and file could only, like bystanders after an accident, report confusion.

Aidan Stride was no exception. Dreading assault from the Bones who were patrolling the gates of Silken Dalliance, he babbled down the telephone to Brackton.

His Pakistani employer tried vainly to soothe him.

'Goodness me, Mr Stride, calm yourself, I beg you,'

jabbered Cock Cover Jack. 'Just because a bridge has been exploded by noiseless agitators does not mean an essential factory should cease production . . . It does not matter that the manager has not yet arrived. You must for the time being take his place. I will myself be over most shortly. In the meantime, you have supplies of laticiferous materials and of feathers. Please persuade your ladies to return damn quick to their work-benches, Mr Stride. As only you know how, by golly!'

It was an ill-timed jest, for Aidan Stride's agitation had another cause. The previous day four of his lady workers had wagered that he could not satisfy them thrice in the night. He was in fine trim and happily bet his week's pay against all theirs. Thirty-five quid to a hundred: he couldn't lose.

The ladies repaired to his flat eager for either treble gratification or financial victory. For once allied, they were shy of showing wild desire before accomplices. Others, they implied, might pant for Stridey: we take him or leave him, really. They grinned over his shoulder with winks and yawns.

Stride struggled on through the night under the increasingly scornful, yet greedy gaze of his three ladies perpetually in waiting. 'Why don't you help, rotten cows?' he squealed at 2 A.M. 'You're as bad as upper-class sacks!' At 4 A.M. he was only on the second lap. He lay exhausted, heart hammering, aching horribly, panting for respite. Then a fresh substitute leapt on to the field of play, turning him over with harsh bullying hands. 'Leave me alone!' begged Stride.

'You quit?' asked Mabel.

Stride nodded with eyes shut.

'Pay.'

They dressed, chattering among themselves like a winning netball team.

142

Stride gloomily counted out his losses.

As he had dreaded, his failure grotesquely exaggerated, had raced round Silken Dalliance. Outside, two of Slim's Bones, letting their bicycle-chains swing menacingly in their hands, bestrode their bikes. And there was no answer from the police-house.

Stride rang his Union's Branch Secretary in Brackton but was brushed aside. 'Blown-up bridges is no union matter, Aidan. Hours and conditions of work unchanged, eh? . . . That's their Protest, lad, not ours. We're up to the eye-balls here with the new Rubber Goods Supervisory Testers' claim for Related Bonuses plus Free Holiday Contraceptive Devices (Female). It's a sod, Aidan, 'tis really.'

'The police,' protested Stride. 'Can't you tell the police?'

'What? You bein' attacked or somepin'? . . . Wot yer mean "not really"? Pull yoursel' together.'

But Stride was still physically exhausted and mentally distraught when *The Star's* Industrial Correspondent finally got through to him. *The Star's* man pressed him for the nature of his work and his boastful wit had yielded some good quotes in the past. 'You're saying there's no revolt up there? Working normally? Slim's whose? . . . Bones? Yobs on motor-bikes! Aidan, old boy, Britain's bulging with yobs on bloody bikes.'

Without his lost tournament of the night, his exhausted cringe to work, and the menacing patrol outside his factory, Stride would have heard the Proclamations and all the news. But now, pale, yawning, he tottered into his office, put his arms on his desk and his head on his arms and slept. The ladies looked through his glass door, sniggering. They had not after all wholly relished those days of sexual subjugation from which they were now unbound. 'We've cut ole Stridey down to size,' boasted Mabel, and everyone laughed.

Ancilla Shergrove reading restlessly in bed heard the explosion at midnight, knew that some kind of armed resistance had begun, ran to her window, but saw nothing. No fires burned in the darkness. There was no noise in the house. From the stable-yard there floated up straw-rustlings, hay-munchings and snuffles of nostrils. Must be hundreds of horses, thought Ancilla. She felt slightly alarmed, as if something bigger than she'd guessed loomed ahead of her in fog.

Should she ring London now? She started down the corridor and paused at the stair-head. But I've nothing definite to tell him yet. A light-shaft from the sitting-room crossed the hall.

'Ancilla? Are you all right?' Mrs Stewkly called, pottering into the hall, and looking up the staircase's twist. She could see Ancilla's long legs vanishing softly upwards into a tiny nightie which from that angle covered nothing. She is beautiful, thought Mrs Stewkly. How Martin could ever have liked Ruth! Horrid, really, thinking of this poor girl with old George Robinson . . . She recollected her position. 'Ancilla, can't you sleep?'

'No,' said Ancilla, coming deliberately downstairs. 'I was just thirsty.' The rays of the light by which Mary Stewkly had been doing her tapestry shone right through Ancilla's nightdress. She saw Mrs Stewkly looking at her, and said cheerfully, 'They're the new thing.'

'Lovely,' said Mrs Stewkly appreciatively.

She approved that Ancilla dispensed with social modesty. Or modesty at all, she supposed, as the image of the Prime Minister, deaf-aided, white-locked, pipe-smoking on the nation's telly screens, came whistling up. She had noticed Ancilla looking at the telephone. She asked, 'Some aspirins, my dear? A sleeping pill?'

'They're still out?' asked Ancilla.

Mary Stewkly nodded.

Ancilla withdrew. Mrs Stewkly heard her bare feet creak up the staircase, pad along the corridor and return to her room.

Later in the night Ancilla thought she heard Martin tiptoeing down the corridor past her room. She called 'Martin', softly. The creaking ceased but there was no reply. She opened her mouth to call again. I can't. He'll think I want him in bed. She turned on to her face, and pulled the pillow down behind her head like ear-pads. Finally she slept.

When she came down to breakfast, both men were out again.

'Poachers must be a real menace round here,' remarked Ancilla sardonically.

Mrs Stewkly was evasive. 'Oh, they are, they are.' She shook her head.

'Could I call my mother?'

'Oh dear,' Mr Stewkly looked upset. 'Charles has got such an important call coming in for him he told me strictly to leave the telephone quite free.' She cocked her head at Ancilla like one of her bantams. 'To keep it unengaged, you see.'

'In the village, perhaps?'

'Yes.' Mrs Stewkly thought she could telephone from Potters' village store. But she was so sorry all the cars were out.

Ancilla walked down the drive from Meadow Hill. More than a dozen cars overtook her going towards East Pym. Youths on motor-bikes were patrolling them. Handfuls of people like toys on a model farm were standing fixedly on the Green, watching the traffic pass.

145

The buildings were covered with rousing slogans and the red cross of St George burst defiantly from windows and branches. Ancilla's arrival on foot was greeted with suspicion. Heads turned balefully.

The two elderly Potter cousins detached themselves from a group and stumped slowly towards her with inquisitive, unfriendly looks. Ancilla explained she was staying with the Stewklys. The two villagers stared. Ancilla asked, 'What's happening?' Neither answered.

Flinging an arm out and looking, she knew, too dramatic, Ancilla expanded, 'All these cars . . . an explosion . . . these people waiting . . . I mean,' she ended firmly, 'what's going on here?'

'What do Mr Stewkly say?' asked old Jack Potter, cunningly.

'He's out,' said Ancilla.

'And young Martin?'

'Out, too.'

'Ah,' said his cousin, comfortably, 'they'll be up to no good, that I *do* wager.' Jack Potter nodded. The two old men regarded Ancilla steadfastly. She found herself blushing.

'The village store?' she asked. 'To telephone.'

Mr Potter pointed. 'My family's,' he said. 'And there be a maze of people millin' in an' out.' Ancilla could not conceive of telephoning her mother, let alone No. 10 from the store. She thought crossly how ill-arranged everything had been: if one was to report things, plans should have been made for radios, contacts, all that sort of thing. She knew she ought to wander through the crowd, marking and inwardly digesting, but she felt dispirited. She turned away and faced the sad dead names on the village War Memorial.

# 20

A light mist with the sheen of oysters hung about Hampden Heights, as the stream of cold air from the North Sea mixed in the warmer tangle of the beechwoods. The Defenders were pleased. They deployed along the ridge and poised themselves each side of the cutting. Below and between them the last straggling strangers were leaving the Vale. Martin and his father squatted on one ridge of the steep bank and looked down on caravans and dormobiles whining up the rise, bobbing over the crest, and then speeding away downhill and across the flat cultivated land to Brackton. The ground between the Heights and Brackton was free from the mist: the wooded escarpment retained it like a dam.

This suited Major Abbot, for he had his forward mounted scouts posted ten miles into enemy territory. They were hidden ahead in farm-house windows covering the Brackton lane. At the foot of the escarpment he had four mounted Dozens screening the fields north and south of the lane against any police move to scale the Heights. His own group of horsemen clustered in the narrow lane itself at the foot of the steep hill. Manned field-telephones ran forwards to the farthest scout and backwards up the hill to Ronald Cubbington's observation-post: a rope-laddered platform high in a tall beech-tree.

The few vehicles approaching from Brackton found the lane blocked by a dozen mounted men, dressed in corduroys and worn twill trousers, polo-necked sweaters and old tweed coats, but carrying shotguns strapped across their backs, so that the blue-black barrel-ends gleamed over their shoulders. Each wore a St George's brassard. There was no other uniform. But there was a firm authority. Vehicles belonging to the Vale were urged homewards. 'Get a move on now. The thing's started.' So were a wholesale grocer's delivery van for Potter's store and a petrol-tanker for Slim's father's garage. Their drivers looked perplexed rather than frightened by Major Abbot's peremptory: 'National Emergency – Home Guard manoeuvres'. The combination of shotguns with a host of horses wild-eyed, white-toothed, sweating, stamping and with nasty swinging quarters induced obedience.

To the few strangers seeking to enter the Vale, Abbot's men were equally firm. 'No way in. Area's bein' sealed off. Defence Manoeuvres.' Some drivers proved querulous, but they were turned around in gateways and sent packing back to Brackton. There were several late holidaymakers hopefully towing wide wobbling caravans. Abbot eyed their retreat with delight: they would impede the onrush of the police.

The field-telephone by the roadside whirred frantically. 'They're coming, Major. Coming.' Sandy Potts in the farthest outpost rang back to Abbot's checkpoint. 'How many?' asked the Major calmly. Sandy said breathlessly: 'Four police cars – two white Jags in front – a Black Maria, some trucks at the back moving sharply.'

'OK. Fine. Gallop back in, Sandy.'

Abbot blew his whistle shrilly for the Dozens on his flanks to hear, and his signaller rang Cubbington's observation-post on the Heights. At the same time Slim's brother Red, acting as Abbot's link, roared back over the crest on his Honda, and down into the Vale to tell the Bones to block the road.

Sandy Potts and the other outlying scouts sprang into their saddles and galloped helter-skelter across the pastures and ploughland to the foot of the escarpment. They had started behind the police convoy but their horses were making thirty miles an hour in a direct line jumping the fences, and the police cars were squeezed to a crawl in the winding lane by the rejected caravans.

The four mounted Dozens screening the base of the Heights withdrew into the woods' fringe and watched across the flat land towards Brackton. Behind and above them the mist was starting to blow off the ridge and they could hear other Defenders clambering about. Then they saw Sandy and two other scouts land over the far hedge and come galloping across the fields towards them. Sandy's face shone and his eyes sparkled. His horse was sweating and heaving. 'Get up in there!' shouted young Doctor Quainton. The doctor squeezed his horse forward from the edge of the wood and every quarter of a mile to north and south another leader did the same. They peered across country. They listened for an assault across the fields. Rooks cawed and some distant heifers lowed peacefully. A covey of pink-brown partridges flew whirring back towards Brackton. Nothing could be coming from there then. The Leaders along the line whistled a long low note. Then there were three long shrill whistles from the ridge: Abbot's signal to withdraw to the defence line.

Overlooking the cutting Charles Stewkly and Martin waited for the signal to roll. Below them they could see the blue winking lights and the white roofs of the police Jaguars leading a snake of vehicles towards them. Four dozen men were poised on the cutting's two rims behind piles of huge trees. These were held back like fifty-foot grey torpedoes by ropes lashed round their bellies, then anchored to the standing beeches. Abbot's next signal blew: Victory Vee.

'Right. Roll 'em.'

Woodmen's axes hacked fiercely through the taut

ropes. The ends spun up like snakes, frayed and yellow-ended. Then the great trunks, levered by the men, began to roll slowly over the lips of the cutting. Their weight groaned. The tearing of their grey bark whined. The sounds accelerated slowly.

'Quick! Quick!' urged Martin, jerking a crowbar under a sluggish tail. He was sweating already.

The trunks at last gathered momentum, banging together first like sentinel drums, then resounding like thunder. Some went askew, rolling at an angle away down the slope towards Brackton. The cutting was filled with the rumble of trunks, the crash of branches on one another and with fragmented sticks, chips and dust as trees bounced and reared and dived into the lane. In two minutes the thirty-feet-deep cutting was filled to its brim with a tangle of three hundred tree-trunks. One trunk caught on the angle like a roller-coaster was still rumbling downhill as the Chief Constable's Jaguar raced past the point where Abbot had checked the traffic. Its driver suddenly saw the tree cavorting towards him in elephantine bounds. He slammed on his brakes as the car was still turning and it skidded into the right-hand ditch with its body across the road.

'Get out!' screamed the Brigadier. The tree-trunk was thundering towards them. He pushed his driver out and squeezed across, and the three policemen in the back were doing the same when Inspector Wilson's Jaguar, making up for lost time, shot round the bend and struck the boot of the Chief Constable's car a squealing blow. The Chief Constable and his men were pitched into the ditch. Their own car teetered ominously above them. The Inspector's Jaguar's right wing impaled itself in the other's boot, and the impact whipped its own tail viciously outwards. Its rear-wheels ripped into the left-hand ditch.

Shifty Wilson cut the side of his head, and the smaller

150

of the three policemen with him was breathlessly crushed by his two larger colleagues sliding on to him. They emerged bruised and shaken as the tree-trunk, with a final crazed leap, struck both Jaguars a mammoth blow, splintering their windows and driving them like white nails deeply into opposite ditches.

It took some time for Brigadier Spratley and his men to crawl out under their car along the soft-bottomed ditch, full of dank stinking leaves. When he emerged he was plastered in mud and in a gibbering rage. His feet left the ground in grotesque hops, and his black and bleeding hands flailed the air as if he was beating off mosquitoes.

Inspector Wilson eyed the Chief Constable warily, as he held the side of his head. Blood started to ooze between the webbing of his fingers. He felt faint. He leaned against the side of his half-sunk car. The sight produced a further furious bellow from the Brigadier. 'What the devil are you *doing*, Wilson? Sun-bathing?'

On to this scene the dozen men from the Black Maria were suddenly decanted. They saw two white police Jaguars practically destroyed and locked together. Farther up the hill it seemed as if the forest had crashed into the cutting. Unsure who needed rescue or attention in the presence of their superiors, they waited anxiously for commands.

When Mr Macdonald the bailiff saw the sight he howled like a banshee and fell back in his seat. His colleague, Mr Wilberforce, made clicking noises over him and loosened his collar. The lady from the WVS, who had brought a little brandy for the evicted families, tripped forward and began to spoon it between Mr Macdonald's pouting, quivering lips. She was aware of bellowing in the background, but could not believe it concerned her until a man, caked in reeking mud and leaves from bald head to brogue shoes, gripped her elbow and yanked her backwards. 'Madam!' shouted the Chief Constable, 'Have the kindness to leave that useless civilian alone, and come and treat my men.'

Behind the hub-bub the Child Welfare Officer and the drivers of the furniture removal-vans conferred together. Heads were generally wagged. Crashes, blocked roads . . . heads were nodded. They returned to their vehicles, started them and began to reverse them away.

The Chief Constable bellowed to a policeman: 'Stop them!' Four of the hovering group, delighted to be instructed, surrounded the irate driver of the last furniture-van. 'Where are you going, blast you?' shouted the Brigadier, running up as athletically as he could.

'Home. We're all goin' home.'

'You were detailed to remove the furniture – ' began the Chief Constable.

'For gawd's sake,' said the driver, 'can't you see the road's blocked? We're goin' home, I tell yer.' The Brigadier looked apoplectic, so the driver added pertly, 'And our orders was from the Council. Nothin' to do with p'lice.'

Brigadier Spratley ground his molars. He could order them to wait, but what was the point? He turned sharply and his shoe, softened by the mud on his slippery sock, shot off across the road. One of the policemen bounded after it like a retriever. Behind him the hopping Brigadier could still see Inspector Wilson slumped against his Jaguar's upturned wheel. 'Wilson!' he shouted, 'Inspector Wilson! Muster two parties of men. At the double! We're going to assault the ridge. I shall go left-flanking with the smaller party.' He hopped closer to Wilson, the policeman following him with his shoe like a pageboy. 'I want you to cross the escarpment to the south. What have you done about these wretched cars?'

'Radioed for a recovery vehicle, sir,' said Shifty Wilson pulling himself together. 'The drivers say they're not repairable here.'

'Obviously,' said Brigadier Spratley, grimly.

'Sir,' said PC Stansgate running up and saluting. 'The bailiffs are leaving. The big one's collapsed. The other's taking him to hospital. And the WVS lady is going with them, sir. She said to tell you she didn't like the situation, sir.'

She had in fact said she wouldn't tolerate that vulgar madman's noise a moment longer, but PC Stansgate intended a career in the Force.

Shifty Wilson asked the Brigadier, 'Shouldn't we keep the bailiffs here, sir? After all – '

'What good is a collapsed bailiff, Wilson, for God's sake? What we must do is to arrest the ringleaders and charge them under the Public Order and Criminal Law Acts. Then the rest of this impudent affair will collapse like a pack of cards before the world gets to hear about it.'

But he was too late. The first reporters and photographers, blocked by the Black Maria on the road, were already outflanking the dark-blue cluster of police across the fields and trotting happily towards the Chief Constable and Inspector Wilson like hunt-terriers after bedraggled rats.

'Keep the Press off!' shouted Wilson, but even as Stansgate and his colleagues started to form a line, the cameras were flashing. The reporters' eyes sparkled at the sight of mud, blood and wreckage. They had already questioned the discomforted bailiffs, surly van-drivers and the livid WVS lady in retreat down the lane. Now their own eyes filled the slender gaps in their imaginations. The crashed cars beneath the prodigious pile of tree-trunks were superb. Several photographers staggered up the road for closer shots.

The Defenders, crouched above them on the ridge, watched them carefully. 'The police assault's taking a dam' long time to get mounted, Ronnie.' Aston Abbot grinned at Cubbington. 'First basic principle gone wrong for 'em.'

'Ah,' said Cubbington, peeping through the stockade of trunks at the agitated group on the road, 'in war you'd charge 'em now, I reckon.'

'With just a quarter of our horsemen here we'd cut 'em to pieces.'

With rather too much shouting and whistling and instructions to the Press to get behind, the two parties of police climbed over the fences to the left and right of the road. The Chief Constable's party struck northwards making an angle up the slope towards the ridge. They were in a tight group.

'One four-inch mortar would obliterate them,' said Aston Abbot.

Shifty Wilson had deployed his men carefully like beaters. Armed with long staves they entered the lower fringe of the wood and disappeared from the Defenders' view. Martin Stewkly heard them crashing through the low tangle of brambles. One shouted, 'Lot of horses bin through here, sir.'

Inspector Wilson struggled through the undergrowth to have a look. The ground was churned up with hoof-marks. 'Heading uphill,' said Shifty Wilson after a careful scrutiny which afforded his men several minutes respite. 'You can tell by the shape, you know. Come on now. They'll be our men.' He sent PC Stansgate off to tell the Chief Constable.

Stansgate slithered down one bank of the cutting, sitting on his backside like a boy on a slide. He shot past some photographers, who snapped him, and went up the other side like a blue squirrel. He heard the Brigadier's party clumping towards him higher up. He shouted up, 'Sir, it's PC Stansgate. Inspector Wilson said to tell you we've found a lot of hoof-marks.'

He could see the silhouettes of the police against the shining mist which swirled through the trees above him. They looked disconsolate. They had found the impenetrable barrier of tangled tree-trunks on the ridge. Brigadier Spratley had urged two men to climb it, but one had fallen back and twisted his ankle between two slippery branches and the other had got impaled through his tunic on the barbed-wire.

The Brigadier had decided against outflanking northwards. He was coming south to join forces with Wilson. As he plodded along the great wall of beech trees on his left, he feared that this situation might be too large for his own force to deal with. But he could not be sure until he had reconnoitred the ridge all the way till it met the River Sedge and the blown bridge ten miles to the south.

The Defenders crouched in their trenches behind the stockade could hear the police party clumping along and caught snatches of muttered conversation. The morale of the attackers sounded encouragingly low.

As the Chief Constable and his party came out into the sunlight at the foot of the cutting, he was intercepted by six reporters who pestered him for details like sea-lions for fish.

'Some line of fortifications along the ridge,' snapped the Brigadier.

'Fortifications?'

The reporters dived after the unintended herring.

'What *sort* of fortifications?' asked one.

'Pretty stiff opposition then?'

'Concrete pill-boxes, you mean?'

155

The Brigadier, striding on, shrugged them off.

'Did you say gun emplacements?' panted one portly reporter.

'But you couldn't get through,' persisted another.

The Chief Constable did not reply and started indecorously to climb the farther bank. The photographers took some lively pictures of backsides and bootsoles clambering up the slippery slope. One of the reporters waddled down the road to find a telephone. The rest, like anxious schoolboys keen for teacher's scoop, padded after him in a herd.

Brigadier Spratley met Inspector Wilson only twenty-five yards from where Martin lay hidden. The police, wearied by their long climb through thorns and brambles, were clambering laboriously over the outstretched branches of the felled trees.

Martin looked left and right: some of his men waited in slit-trenches, some were lying among brambles and bracken. They lay still and the browns and fawns of their country clothes blended into their backgrounds. Beyond the stockade the uniformed police stuck out like sore thumbs. Like Boer farmers and British redcoats in South Africa, thought Martin watching the countrymen, cheeks against the walnut stocks of their shotguns. All had their ears cocked, listening to the police. Would they ever fire at them? Martin himself could not possibly, at that moment, have pulled the trigger. The police looked the reverse of authority's fist: frail, bewildered, exhausted. Of course, if they, when they attacked . . .

'Might be a bit big for us, sir?' Shifty Wilson suggested, gesturing at the huge stockade.

'Certainly not,' snapped the Brigadier, 'merely a matter of finding a gap.'

'Frankly what I thought too, sir,' said Shifty Wilson. A

whipping branch had started his forehead and face bleeding again, and his head ached horribly. His men struggling behind knew that, without the Chief Constable, old Shifty would have led them back and blown for reinforcements: he could probably lay his hands on a couple of hundred extra men given a day or two's warning.

The men were young and had been involved only in a few backstreet affrays: the Brackton Boot Boys fighting the Brackton Skins, and both indulging in the working-classes' bloodsport: Paki-bashing. The yobs on Brackton United's ground hurled things during matches and burnt seats after them. But that was the sum of local violence. This long, high, unclimbable fortification stretching silently on and on and on along the top of this bloody ridge was weird. 'Real sinister. That's what it is,' one agreed with another.

'How many in there, you reckon?'

'Take hundreds to build this lot, wouldn't it?'

'Would that.'

'Armed?'

'Probably.'

'Revolution then. Organized.'

'What? In the country? Lot of farmers and such!'

PC Stansgate had made his way keenly to the head of the group. He was questing along like a dark-blue labrador puppy when he came to the gap in the stockade.

Martin on one flank of the pit, and Aston Abbot on the other saw him check, peer, then run back towards Inspector Wilson. They heard him call out excitedly, 'Sir! We've come to the end!' It looked as if he was wagging his tail and giving a dog's pink, panting grin.

The tired party of police started to jog forward, stumbling over the briers, two men pitching flat. They came to the end of the stockade and looked into the wood opposite. The mist's tail-feathers still dragged between the trees. Shafts of noon sunlight pierced down through the branches. Snippets of sky overhead were rinsed blue. The men caught distant glimpses of the Vale dappled in sunshine, patch-worked in green pastures, brown plough, and fields of yellow stubble. Pillars of blue-grey smoke stood up from the umber tiles of cottage roofs.

Inspector Wilson said reluctantly, 'Might be a trap, sir.'

The men looked at the Brigadier. Instinct had suggested the same idea to him, but he could not now admit it. The morale of his tired men was in the balance. So he said firmly, 'Nonsense. Need some trap to catch twenty fit, trained and efficient police officers, wouldn't it?' And he laughed as scornfully as he could. 'Right then,' he ordered. 'Spread out either side of me – in case of snipers – and crouch down. And when I shout "Forward" I want you to charge with me across the ridge. We'll consolidate there.' He pointed beyond the gap towards the next thick lump of trees which concealed a delighted Dozen. 'Then we'll get down in the Vale and put an end to this nonsense.'

The police spread out and crouched down like runners on their marks. They looked warily ahead seeking to penetrate the bushes beyond the gap. There was a menacing sense of enemies waiting. The Chief Constable knelt down in the middle of the line with Inspector Wilson at his side. He wished to give his men enough time for a breathing space but not enough for them to reflect on what manner of gun-fire they might meet head-on beyond the ridge.

Suddenly the Chief Constable screamed, 'Forward! Charge!', leapt to his feet and launched himself like a Rugby wing. His men to right and left hurtled forward too, heads down, eager for his praise and aware of how wide their bodies were for snipers' shots. Thus it was that all twenty in line abreast charged over the camouflaged lip of the quarry and with an outbreak of imprecations, a scream, shouts and desperate grunting, started to crash tumbling down through the undergrowth. The longest lasted a few lurching, pitching strides before their feet too trod air and they sank through the sharp and stinging boughs. The heaviest, like the Chief Constable, sank the deepest. His roaring muffled oaths boomed from beneath twelve feet of tangled wood, like the bellowing of a sea-monster.

Sound crackled fiercely as bodies snapped through lighter branches and thudded horribly against the heavier ones. The boughs themselves reared and keeled over, pitching the police like little blue canoes down into the darkness below. There was no purchase for their wildly scrabbling hands. Their bodies were wedged deep down, but the thinner branches above their heads snapped off as their hands hauled at them.

Inspector Wilson, following the Brigadier, had pitched straight forward and struck his head on a lurking tree-trunk. Something flashed behind his eyes and he lost consciousness again for a minute. He came round, head downwards, body jammed, and nothing but bending branches to grip at. He screamed 'Out! Out! It's a trap! Back everyone!' The panic in his voice transmitted itself to his men who, from bravely trying to struggle onwards and upwards, gratefully accepted the official cry and began to burrow their way out backwards. The branches in the quarry rattled crazily overhead as the police scrabbled for home like a pack of moles.

Some aided their friends, pulling on painfully out-stretched hands, straining to part two boughs where an ankle, knee or elbow was fast gripped. One by one, bleeding from tears on their faces, with great rents (some blood-stained) in their uniforms, the police crawled back over the lip of the quarry and sprawled exhausted on the ground.

The Brigadier, curiously silent, crawled out last. He had lost his dentures. His tweed suit was torn down to his muddy underclothes. There was a sharp gash across his bald head. He signalled Inspector Wilson to limp nearer. 'Lishen,' he whispered. 'Form up men, ashemble all walkin' wounded. Fit men carry oshers.'

Inspector Wilson issued his orders. Only a few of the party were still sound. Hopping, limping, slithering, sliding and grunting with pain, the police attack fell back down the steep escarpment and disappeared from the Defenders' sight.

Martin gazed entranced. He had been working all night, but he felt now as elated as if he had put away a bottle of Bollinger. Victory had been accomplished without a shot. The fates must be with us. We must be meant to win.

Aston Abbot could control himself no longer. Leaping from his slit-trench he dashed to the stockade and raised the banner of St George on it. 'Hooray!' he bellowed. 'God save the Vale of Hampden!' And all along the ridge cheering from two hundred throats broke out in a rippling roar. The noise came crashing through the trees, and the police party halted, whipped round and stared up at the woods. A dazzle of flags had appeared along the ridge of the escarpment. The rumble of cheering rolled down towards them like the dread heralds of an avalanche. 'God save the Vale of Hampden,' shouted two hundred voices. 'Save the Vale . . . the Vale . . . Hampden!' the voices rose. 'Hampden! Hampden!'

Looking now with real fear over their shoulders the police party, dragging its wounded, hobbled urgently towards the remaining two Panda cars and the Black Maria. Bloody and muddy, they squeezed in, and the acrid smell of alarm joined the sweat from their bodies.

# 21

Evening papers across Britain led with THE BATTLE OF
HAMPDEN HEIGHTS and on the Continent space was found
on front pages for the latest British madness. TV News-
crews had filmed the retreat of the bedraggled police.
The tale had instant appeal. The police had not been
attacked. No one had even thrown anything at them,
with the exception of the beech-tree which had knocked
out two Jaguars. And that accident, as local farmer
Mallard put it, 'was more of an act of Providence, as you
might say.' Some English countrymen had defended the
outposts of their Vale against a police attack, to protect
their neighbours from that day's due evictions. A leader-
writer declared with pride: *'Even today Englishmen
cannot be pushed around for ever willy-nilly.'*

News editors strove to push reporters into the Vale.
Those who had covered the initial repulse were ordered
to penetrate the barricades immediately: 'Buy your way
in, old boy.' But the few who finally arrived gasping on the
ridge were intercepted by Abbot's patrolling horsemen to
whom, in the flush of victory, a city bribe was a bloody
insult. Adamantly they turned the newsmen away. Only
one keen young reporter remained to snoop and have his
brains picked by the others on his return. All papers
reported that regiments of armed cavalry were defending
Hampden Heights. Reference to 'Fierce horses' and
'grim-faced men with glinting rifle-barrels' and 'as I
struggled up alone on to the ridge', were telephoned by
thirteen reporters from pubs along the way to Brackton.

The stouter scouts of Fleet Street had not left the landlord's 'snug' at all. As one said sagely – 'Didn't dodge the sodding Arab snipers to get knocked off at home, thank you very much.' His climbing days were over. He exchanged a bottle of the publican's best malt whisky ('to making contacts') for an earful of the young reporter's copy.

An enterprising local man brought a rubber-dinghy to the broken bridge and set off paddling wildly. The Defenders carefully observed him. The current slung the boat swiftly downstream, spinning it in its eddies. After a struggle the young man, too trendily dressed for rowing, ran it aground on the inner bank. He was bending down to tie its painter to the bare roots of a willow when he heard a faint noise. Martin Stewkly and four men with shotguns stood around him. He let out a puff of breath, looked around the watching faces and said, raising a hand Indian fashion, 'Greetings, Great White Hunters. Please take me to your Leader.'

Two of the men growled angrily and edged closer. The reporter looked anxious.

'Who are you?' asked Martin.

'Terry Speen, *Brackton Mercury*. But I'm the stringer for two London dailies.'

'You can't land,' said Martin.

'Go on,' said Sandy Potts, padding up with his ·22 at the ready. 'Buzz off back or I'll hole yer rubber toy.'

Speen asked, 'Know which side your bread's buttered, do you? We're on yours.'

'Whose we?' asked Martin.

'The whole Press. Even the hang-'em and flog-'em old Tories. The TV people. Even the BBC religious broadcasts. Haven't you listened?'

'No,' said Martin, 'We've been busy.'

'Certainly have,' said Speen admiringly. 'They say

Hampden Heights was a Famous Victoree!' He grinned at Martin, who finally smiled back. 'So if I could briefly exchange words with your Chief . . . ?'

'No,' said Martin, 'I'm sorry. You must see we can't let anyone in. But I'll do this. We'll ring you tonight in your office with a sort of report, a bulletin. How's that?'

Speen handed out a batch of cards. 'Phones still working?'

'They were.'

'OK, then,' said Speen, stepping delicately into his little boat.

'Hey!' called Sandy Potts. 'Keep the old newspapers for us will you?'


The Chief Constable, cursing the loss of his dentures as he urged his Panda down the lanes to Brackton, was sharply aware of personal defeat. He made dispositions in his head as the car buzzed homewards. Sightseers were already joining press men and these, held up behind a few delivery vehicles still trying to get into the area, blocked the road.

'Mush keep lane open,' he mumbled to Inspector Wilson.

Shifty Wilson could not quite see why, since it was already blocked by a pile of tree-trunks 30 feet deep, but he readily agreed. 'Lines of communications, Sir.'

'O' corsh. Goin' back in dare sharp.'

Shifty Wilson looked nervously about him.

'Wish shupport,' the Brigadier spluttered sardonically. 'Shoon as back to office, shpeaking to neighbouring HQ.'

'To borrow reinforcements.'

'Yesh,' hissed the Brigadier grimly. 'Plush cranesh and bulldozers to pull treesh out.'

'Warrants, sir?' asked the Inspector.

The Brigadier's mind was jammed with military plans

for his new assault. He looked crossly at his Inspector. Wilson explained. 'Warrants for the arrest of the ringleaders.'

'Can you name 'em, Wilshon?'

'Of course, sir. All those who signed the last Proclamation.'

The Chief Constable nodded impatiently. 'But we can arresht without warrant – they're committing a treason.'

The car reached Brackton's grimy outskirts. Knots of people gawped. The Chief Constable glared at them. 'What?' he asked Wilson.

'I said, but we can't arrest the ringleaders, because we can't reach them, sir.'

'That's why I shaid "Isshue warrants",' spat the Brigadier. He said to the driver, 'Go in round back. Mob of goggling loafers.'

Wilson was saying . . . 'Sedition, anyway: "exciting discontent, disorder, tumult." But can we charge 'em under the Treason Felony Act of 1848?' The car drew up in the police yard. 'That's levying war against the sovereign. They've not done that.'

The Chief Constable, a fiercesome sight in his torn mudcaked clothes, followed by the filthy and bleeding Inspector strode through the corridors, leaving a wake of gaping faces.

Wilson panted on, 'Riot, anyway. "Three or more persons constitute a riot, an unlawful assembly." We can arrest the ringleaders on the spot, sir.'

The Chief Constable found his spare false teeth in a drawer and jammed them in.

'God all bloody Mighty!' he shouted, pounding his desk and champing his dentures. 'That's what we intend. When we get in. Meantime you issue warrants for 'em under the Public Order Act, 1936.'

'Sections 2 and 5, sir? Quasi-military Assemblies and offensive conduct?'

The Chief Constable glowered at Wilson, looked away and snapped at his assistant: 'Get me the two Regional HQ.'

'Sir,' said his assistant. 'The Home Secretary wished you to call him the moment you return.'

Brigadier Spratley hesitated. 'Get the other two Chief Constables first.'

But the telephone on his desk buzzed. His assistant snatched it up. He listened, 'It's the Home Secretary, sir.'

It was in fact Sebastian Delavine, who thought Spratley an anachronism. Nearer London retired Army officers did not run police forces. He said coldly, 'Brigadier Spratley? The Home Secretary would like a word with you.'

Sebastian, on a parallel line to his master, overheard the conversation. It was somewhat one-sided. The Prime Minister had spoken most harshly to Sir Frederick, calling his memorandum 'as feeble and misleading as a couple of kiddy's aspirins'. The Prime Minister referred to the general decay of law and order in the last two and half years; a period which coincided precisely with Sir Frederick's tenure of the Home Office.

The Home Secretary goaded by fear – for hadn't Plain George axed three Ministers for mishandling the Glasgow troubles? – now passed the can, red-hot, on to the Chief Constable.

Brigadier Spratley gasped. 'Sir, to be fair,' he protested, 'how could anyone guess that twenty men wouldn't suffice – '

'You're not there to guess, Brigadier,' said the Home Secretary icily, and Sebastian in his outer office smiled like Cleopatra's cat.

Spratley was now trying to outline his plans. Again the Home Secretary cut in: 'No more police action for the moment, please. Simply contain the area. The Cabinet is meeting tonight.'

The Chief Constable tried again. 'I had it in mind, sir, to fly over the area. In a police helicopter.' He went on quickly, forestalling another interruption, 'First, to reconnoitre. Secondly, to warn the inhabitants of the charges against their ringleaders.'

The Home Secretary paused only for an instant. 'Right,' he said. 'Do that. And report to me directly you return. And Spratley,' he added, 'don't for God's sake and the Government's, do another single thing which makes us look ridiculous. If you could *see* the evening papers!' He made a heaving gesture with his hands and his voice went faint.

'What, sir?' inquired the Chief Constable.

'No more blunders, Spratley.'

The Home Secretary summoned Sebastian. 'Call your opposite number at the Ministry of Defence and ask your master kindly to step across for a word with me.'

Sebastian bowed and started to withdraw. Sir Frederick said lightly, 'I'll call back the Prime Minister, *privately*, Sebastian.' Delavine nodded. The Home Secretary said, 'You'll ensure the Chief of the Defence Staff gets alerted, won't you? It will mean troops now, of course. So we'll want their people in readiness outside the Cabinet Room this evening.'

Sir Frederick's report to the Prime Minister was concise. George Robinson thought: he's got a good brain, pity if he has to go.

Sir Frederick concluded: 'Just one thing, Prime Minister. I believe you told me that your Private Secretary, Miss Shergrove, might be going into the – er – rebellious

166

area . . .' He paused. The Prime Minister said, 'That is so. She is there. Or was.'

'You mean you've heard nothing from her?'

'Nothing,' said the Prime Minister so savagely that Sir Frederick knew he was rattled.

'Is it possible, she's being held as a hostage?'

'Quite possible, Freddy, I'm afraid.'

'I'm so sorry, Prime Minister. That could be rather awkward.'

'The situation's a mess, Freddy, when authority becomes a laughing-stock. See you this evening.'

The Prime Minister summoned his Press Secretary for a résumé of all news media. He said, 'Do what you can – after the Cabinet's met – to get the balance right for the "mornings".'

'Short-handed police, sir, struggling against odds?'

'Yes. And play down this noble yeoman line. We want no village heroes in the Vale of Hampden. And one more thing. Did you know Miss Shergrove was in the rebellious area?'

'Yes, sir.'

The Prime Minister was nastily surprised. 'Did you, How?'

'Pinchman Chapter rang me from Fleet Street to check, sir. He'd heard it, of course. And as they're always anxious – '. He hesitated, wondering for the thousandth time if the Prime Minister realized how many people knew about his mistress.

'Yes, yes,' said George Robinson. 'But they'd nothing concrete?'

'A report from a local man seeing her at Brackton Station. Going off with – '

'That man Stewkly's son,' said the Prime Minister. 'As arranged.'

His Press Secretary nodded. The Prime Minister continued, 'It would be more than unfortunate if the Press imagined that anyone from the staff here could be held by these people.' He paused. A worse thought struck him. 'Or if a diseased imagination believed that Miss Shergrove might support them.'

The idea seemed so wild to the Press Secretary that he burst out, 'Oh surely, sir!'

The Prime Minister said, 'She did know Stewkly's son many years ago. Quite well. Before her marriage, you understand.'

'I didn't know that, sir.'

'No reason why you should. Private matter entirely. And really it was a private notion of hers to go up to Hampden.'

The Prime Minister's capable Press Secretary nodded. Plain George was shelving even that personal responsibility, in case things went wrong. 'I told the columnist that Miss Shergrove was fishing in Scotland, sir. And I telephoned her mother immediately so that she was forearmed.'

'Thank you,' said the Prime Minister, and suddenly smiled.

# 22

'Look here,' said Ancilla, jumping up so violently from the kitchen-table at Meadow Hill that all the teacups rattled, 'You've bloody well got to let me telephone.' She started to squeeze between Mrs Stewkly's warm Aga and the table end. Ronald Cubbington, still wearing his rubber boots and St George's brassard, got to the back door in front of her, slammed it and leaned against it. His long white face looked at her with loathing. He disliked Government supporters, the Upper Classes, immorality, Londoners and pretty women: he loathed Ancilla Shergrove. 'No, you don't,' he said.

Ancilla, flushed, turned back to the table. Richard Sandford, who might have supported her, was occupied in Easterly: there had been an attempted run on the Anglian Bank there till Mr Pennington, the manager, had come out boldly behind the Defenders. 'I am one,' he had said, displaying the Proclamation in the window of the Bank. 'I have ample funds to last the length of any Emergency, rest assured.' The effect was magical: the Bank could never support anything unsound or illegal.

Queues had formed, too, at Slapton's the bakers, till Richard Sandford had explained the mills were in full production. 'Home-grown, home-milled, home-baked bread from now on, m'dears,' said the baker, again and again. 'Good for virility, long life and make your hair grow glossy as a chestnut. No shortage either.' There was some expected whining: 'No sliced white then?' but no riot.

And Abbot's away, too, thought Ancilla, and he would

have comforted a pretty face. But then so too should Martin and his father, staring gloomily at her across the kitchen-table.

'Oh dear,' said Mary Stewkly. 'I *am* so sorry.' She addressed herself busily to the clutch of bantams in their cardboard box by the Aga.

'Where to?' repeated Martin toughly. He looked exhausted. 'Who d'you want to ring? Your mother?'

Ancilla nodded.

'Again?' asked Martin sarcastically.

His father motioned to restrain him.

Ancilla began, 'She'll be frantic – '

'Like poor Plain George,' said Martin.

Ancilla stared at him and went scarlet. But she didn't glance away. They looked steadily into each other's eyes across the table.

Mrs Stewkly scrabbled so keenly over the bantams that the uprooted hen squawked across the stone flags.

Charles Stewkly studied his nails.

Cubbington asked from the door, 'Did you think we didn't know?'

Ancilla looked round at him, then back at Martin. She asked, 'Is that why I was invited?'

Martin looked uncomfortable. He said, 'You asked yourself.'

She nodded. 'True.'

'To spy?' asked Martin.

'Of course, to bloody spy,' shouted Cubbington.

'Please, Ronnie,' said Mr Stewkly raising his head.

Ancilla asked, 'Well, may I go home now please?'

Cubbington stared: 'My God – !'

Charles Stewkly said quietly, 'Ancilla, I'm sorry. We can't let you.'

Ancilla asked Martin, 'You planned to hold me then?'

Martin nodded once, regretfully. He hated the way she

stared at him. He burst out: 'You planned to spy, didn't you? Yes, we are going to keep you here.' He nodded his head forcefully several times. 'You can't get out anyway. All our frontiers are guarded, you know.'

Cubbington called across, 'Martin! Watch it.' He asked Stewkly, 'Charles, shouldn't we lock her up?'

'I suppose so,' said Charles Stewkly.

'Where?' asked Ancilla.

'Only in your bedroom, dear,' said Mrs Stewkly, dusting her hands on her apron. 'If you'd like to come along now?'

Cubbington started bullyingly, 'And put a padlock on –' but his voice was drowned by a roaring engine in the sky. He opened the back door and the kitchen reverberated. A pale-blue helicopter with 'POLICE' along its fusilage was hovering just over the black barn, no higher than the first-floor windows of the house. Its rotor blades flogged the air with the flop-flop-flop of carpets being beaten, and its engine raged on.

'The horses,' shouted Charles Stewkly, hobbling across the kitchen. 'They'll be driven mad.' Martin followed him across the yard. Cubbington, white face tucked into pleats of hatred, was already pounding towards the barn. Ancilla looked for Mrs Stewkly. She was in the scullery craning out of the window.

The door of the helicopter slid back and a capped head and uniformed shoulders appeared, holding a megaphone. 'This is the Chief Constable,' he hailed them, his voice descending through the rotor whirr like that of Zeus through a Delphic storm. 'Come to East Pym *now!*'

Wilkinson, young Pete and the others were out in the yard staring up at him.

'Get to the *horses*, Wilkinson!' shouted Charles Stewkly.

The Chief Constable's voice twanged out again. 'You

can avoid serious trouble . . . sedition . . . treason . . . coming to East Pym *now*!' The helicopter was drifting away. Cubbington was running under with his shotgun. He paused, raised it. The helicopter suddenly lofted as if puffed up, and sped away.

The horses' heads stared at the departing speck. Stewkly said to Wilkinson, 'I'm going down to East Pym.' Martin joined him in the Land-Rover. They drove off.

The huge barn door was ajar. Ancilla slipped inside. The warm air smelt of paint and leather. She saw the wagons, carts and carriages waiting in rows. She was so astonished that she leaned against the old oak supports, pale as dry sherry. She thought in a rush: they plan for this to last for years; and they have been planning it for years. A mixture of fear and respect swirled in her head. Her heart was thumping. She picked her way between the vehicles, touching them, smelling them. They were beautiful, bold, foolhardy. The new paint glistened. The axles were freshly greased. The leather looked soft as snakes and dark as pickled walnuts. A scene leapt into her mind from a Polish film: their cavalry with lances and red-and-white pennants charging the German tanks in September 1939.

She put her head quietly through the far barn door and looked into the stable yard. Wilkinson and Pete were filling water buckets. Pete saw her. 'Hello,' he said cheerfully.

Wilkinson looked up. 'Arternoon, miss,' he said, 'Shockin' noise them things make.'

Ancilla nodded. Perhaps he had not been told to watch her. She walked on into the stable yard.

Wilkinson paused with a heavy bucket in each hand. He put them down on the neat raked gravel. Ancilla thought: he's going to grab me.

Wilkinson flexed his biceps. 'We've a lot of horses in,

miss,' he said proudly. 'Why haven't you been riding, yet? You were good as a kid.'

Ancilla said quickly: 'I'd love to. I'd really love to, Wilkinson.'

He looked dubious.

She asked cunningly, 'Would you be allowed to let me?'

'My horses, my yard. As you'll remember. The Guv'nor puts me in total charge.'

Ancilla smiled at him. Wilkinson asked, 'Now?'

'Why not? No time like the present. And everyone's busy.'

'Pete,' said Wilkinson sharply, 'Saddle the grey mare for Miss . . .' He looked inquiringly.

'I'm still called Shergrove,' said Ancilla. 'Look, I'll help.' She followed Pete into the tack-room. He picked up a saddle from a rack of twenty. He said proudly, 'We've forty horses out on Hampden Heights right now. Seein' those buggers don' get in.'

Wilkinson bustled across to give her a leg up on to the grey. 'Don't be long, Miss, will you? They're fed at six.' He was anxious now, peering up at her under his cap, his face partly gritty like old sandpaper. She couldn't answer him honestly. 'I hope I don't get lost,' she said, and as she rode out keeping the barn between her and Mrs Stewkly in the house, she thought cynically: Lost? Hoping not to be? That's a Freudian slip.

The police helicopter, a pale-blue chattering dragon-fly, was circling the cottages of East Pym as the Stewklys' Land-Rover followed by Cubbington roared up to the Green. A mounted Dozen coming off their day's duty on Hampden Heights were jogging slowly into the village from the far end. Someone gave an order: the shotguns came glinting off their backs in a whirl and they stopped under the trees by the churchyard. Groups of two or three armed men came running out of the cottages, coatless, in braces. They had been at their teas.

'Major Abbot?' Someone shouted urgently.

'He's on the Heights still,' Martin called back.

Cubbington began to run across the Green towards the War Memorial. He had taken the flag from his car. It unfurled behind him. 'Any Leaders,' he shouted as he ran. 'Follow me here.'

The police helicopter came into sight again behind East Pym church, as twenty men came running across to join Cubbington by the Memorial. He saw Martin. 'Quick, tell the horsemen to wait under the trees till the police get out. Then charge 'em down.'

'Firing?' asked Martin.

'If the police do.'

The voice of the Chief Constable, a little hoarser, wafted towards them . . . 'This is an unlawful assembly . . . Return to your homes immediately . . .' The helicopter moved in towards the War Memorial. The clump of armed men round it raised their shotguns.

The helicopter hovered. The Chief Constable still showing himself bravely, shouted again. 'I have warrants for the arrest of the ringleaders. These men must come forward and the rest of you must return to your homes . . . Under the Public Order Act this is a riot . . . police authorized by statute to call on others of Her Majesty's subjects to assist us . . . misdemeanour to refuse . . .'

Martin was running back out of the trees. The horsemen were longing to fire. He ran past Potter's Store. There was a van outside. Potter had been unloading boxes crammed with lavatory paper. Martin stopped and grinned at him. 'Look,' he said, 'With those and a dozen men!' Potter laughed. They roped in the nearest bystanders.

The helicopter was still hovering near the War Memorial, but Cubbington and some of the Defenders were hurling abuse up at the Chief Constable. Feeling threatened from above and impotent, they snapped back fiercely like terriers beneath an eagle, 'Go on. Git!'

''S our village!'

'No bloody Airport!'

'Up the Vale of Hampden!'

'Up! . . . Up! . . .'

'Hampden! Long live East Pym.'

'Eff off, effing Fuzz!'

The Chief Constable's voice was reciting again . . . 'Edward Aston Abbot, retired army officer . . . Ronald Sidney Cubbington, farmer of – '

Cubbington pointed his shotgun at the Chief Constable, and shouted, 'Belt up you, you bugger! Or I'll fire!' And they they all heard the sound of another helicopter thumping in the south. It was moving in low and swiftly. Cubbington and the Defenders looked round. The Chief Constable, catching their movement, paused, and swung round staring.

Martin's group were running in like crouching monkeys towards the Memorial. They raced under the tail of the police helicopter. Cubbington, Charles Stewkly and the Defenders round the monument, aware of the darting movement, swung away from the other helicopter.

'Now!' shouted Martin, and opened his coat. The centres of the rolls of coloured lavatory paper had been wedged with stones, and their gummed ends torn free. There were some decent East Pym cricketers with Martin. The rolls flew up, trailing, were whirled out by the blades, and sank in a confusion of rubbish over the helicopter's slim tail. A long burst of laughter rose from the group round the War Memorial and spread to the villagers on the outskirts of the Green. They started running in towards the police helicopter, laughing and pointing and jeering.

The Chief Constable looked out of the door and peered back. The tail was festooned with pink, green, blue, white and yellow trails of lavatory paper. As some were dislodged, the Defenders rushed forward, stooped and lobbed them back.

At that instant the other helicopter, a hired Westland, arrived. Both its doors were wide open and crammed with press photographers. Cameras clicked and lights flashed. They took the Chief Constable's furious face, the word POLICE partly obliterated by strands of paper and beneath, the laughing, mocking, crowd.

Foolishly, the Chief Constable waited for silence. He waved his hands vainly. A group of village boys raced towards his helicopter, pelting its sides with old apples and squidgy pears. It hovered uncertainly, and sank a few feet lower. The Press Westland slowly circled it, overflowing with black camera snouts and white grinning faces. The Chief Constable, purple in the face, withdrew inside.

The horsemen under the trees, thinking the police intended to land, galloped forward on to the Green in line abreast, hallooing at the tops of their voices, right hands brandishing their shotguns, left hands on their reins up their horses' necks, heels drumming their flanks. The roll-throwing party gave a final salvo. Several apples smacked through the open door of the helicopter. It was slammed shut. The aircraft rose and rotated as if to make off towards the south, tilting nose down like a dragon-fly. The cavalry galloped beneath it across the Green, firing rather wildly upwards at it in full stride. A fusillade of shots crackled out from the steps of the War Memorial. Pellets rattled against the belly and thin tail of the helicopter. It lofted quickly and scurried off against the darkening sky, and the lights in its cabin were suddenly doused.

Prolonged cheering rose from the village Green. Horns blared Victory Vee. In the tumult the Press Westland landed. In the dusk flashlights popped. Reporters thrust forward microphones. Pads and pencils materialized in palms. Cubbington and Stewkly raised their voices above the din. Charles said to Martin, 'Get the horsemen back.' Martin ran off.

Cubbington stepped down from the steps of the monument and approached the Press. He was engulfed. Charles Stewkly heard him shouting, 'You can't land here.'

'We're with you,' called a reporter.

'Thank you,' said Charles Stewkly gravely.

'Bloody Whitehall!' shouted another reporter and a photographer coaxed: 'You two a little closer please . . . there . . . fine. Hold your guns up, so's we can see 'em. Guns higher please . . . there. Hold it. Again.'

'No!' snapped Cubbington. 'We don't want you here because you'll reveal our strength. Get back on board.'

'Please,' added Charles Stewkly.

'Which ones are you?' called a reporter. 'Abbot? Cubbington? Sandford?'

'Get on board!' bellowed Cubbington. He turned back over the heads ringing him to shout out, 'Are you loaded, men?'

Cartridges were slipped into breeches. Barrels snapped shut. Some photographers who had already shot their fill scrambled back hurriedly into the Westland. They took long shots now over the crowd's heads.

'Thirty seconds,' called Cubbington and began counting. '. . . five, six, seven . . . Raise your guns!' he shouted. The reporters began to scuttle back into the helicopter. Cubbington went on counting . . . 'fourteen, fifteen . . .'

Charles Stewkly limped after the laggard pressmen.

Charles Stewkly limped after the laggard pressmen. 'You do understand, I hope,' he called after them. 'We do value your support.'

'Twenty, twenty-one . . .' shouted Cubbington.

'Ring us at home tonight. The name's Stewkly.'

'Get the hell off!' roared Cubbington. He murmured to his men, 'Over their heads when I say fire.'

The last of the reporters were now back in the helicopter shouting, 'Have you enough food?' 'How long can you last?' 'Here! Some fags.' A packet, then two more were lobbed out. A half bottle of whisky thudded on the dark grass. A voice cried, 'Give Robinson a bloody nose, boys!'

Charles Stewkly stepped aside and waved courteously.

'Fire!' shouted Cubbington.

The reporters saw the barrels blaze in the dusk, and slammed the door. The Westland soared upwards. Pale faces mooned, pale hands waved from its windows.

Charles Stewkly said, 'Ronnie, you were very tough. They do support us.'

Cubbington grunted. 'But they can give us away, too.' He broke off. 'Gord,' he swore, banging his hand against his forehead. 'The girl!'

'Ancilla!' said Stewkly, aghast.

At Meadow Hill Wilkinson on a sweating cob was waiting uneasily in the yard. 'I've looked everywhere, sir, and shouted. Must have had an accident.'

Cubbington in huge heavy strides ran into the house and started ringing all the outlying farms, Richard Sandford, Mr Pennington at the Bank, Slim's father's garage, Patricia Fernden, Doctor Quainton, and old Nurse Dinton at the Easterly First Aid Post. 'Can't tell PC Benn, anyway, poor sod,' said Cubbington grimly. It was the first time in the long night and day they had thought about the policeman's death.

Martin was hovering agitatedly. His father asked, 'Ronnie, shouldn't Martin go round the outposts, warning them to watch for her?'

'Land-Rover, Father?' asked Martin eagerly.

'Of course, And when you find her, Martin, don't let her go, will you?' He put his hand on Martin's shoulder. 'I'm afraid it's no accident.'

'I know, Father, I know,' said Martin curtly, and roared away down the drive.

Cubbington glared up from the telephone. 'Bloody snotty bitch. I'll handcuff her. And Martin wasting precious petrol.'

Charles Stewkly gave a thin smile. 'At least the telephone's still working, Ronnie. And I suppose it's free: We'll get no bills from Brackton – or anywhere else outside – till it's over.'

Cubbington said enraged, 'But when they come they'll bloody murder us.'

# 23

Dusk drifted through the valley and stacked up against the trees. In the wood it was owl-dark. The noise of the distant helicopter was snuffed. Ancilla kicked the grey mare along the track, not frightened of pursuit, but anxious that she might not find the way. But when the wood ended she saw the Sedge and Mere below her and cars' lights moving in a lemon and pink necklace towards Easterly.

The high ground on her left, Sandford's downland, led only to the cliffs on the North Sea. Beyond the Downs on the far side of the Sedge lay the way southwards. She recalled a lane, picnics near a wartime gun-emplacement. That way she might escape.

She reached the road and was thankful that the mare's white coat showed up in the cars' headlights. By the side of a modern factory she did not recall, a lane dipped down. Ancilla thankfully trotted on. The grey mare was fit. Her ears were cocked against the factory lights and the faint glow of Easterly. The lane dropped steeply into darkness again. She smelt the brown river, then heard water gurgling against the little grey bridge. It was the right way. She crossed over. The great shoulder of the Downs loomed ahead. Stars drifted in the sweep of the sky. The mare's feet touched turf and Ancilla let her canter on silently up a winding track.

Then the mare started to stop, head up, ears cocked enormously, staring left and right. The old gun-emplacement lay ahead. The mare's body went rigid between Ancilla's thighs. 'Oh, go on,' said Ancilla crossly, slapping the mare's quarters. But the grey stopped so suddenly that Ancilla pitched on to her neck.

The darkness swam with people. Hands gripped her calf, knee, then her waist on one side. Fingers the other side tugged her. Something was hauling savagely on the mare's bridle. The mare was struggling to back away. Ancilla was being torn both ways. Pain flashed electrically through her thigh muscles. She was splitting. She screamed, 'Help!'

Hands wrenching her left arm and leg dragged her from the saddle head first on to the ground. She saw the horse's belly on top of her, still going backwards. Then the mare whipped round, loose, and thundered away down the track. Ancilla thought: she'll be killed on the road. The ligament hinging her legs at the top of her thighs was torn: the pain gnawed. She tried to free a hand, but her arm was jerked back fiercely. 'Leave yourself alone, bitch.'

Another voice said something. There was some sniggering. 'Yeah . . .'s right. Slim'll do it.'

A voice very close to her ear on the ground said in a la-di-dah tone, 'Miss Shergrove, we presume.' Another voice said, 'Plain George's bloody scrubber.' There were half a dozen youths in oily jeans and sweaty T-shirts. The youth kneeling on her arm got off it, and lugged her to her feet. Hands on her other side grabbed her wrist again and pushed her forward towards the gun-emplacement.

'What are you doing?' Ancilla asked hoarsely, tugging again at her hands. 'Can't you let me go?' Fists thrust her forward. 'Oh, good God, I can't get away now, can I?'

The lah-di-dah voice mocked, 'Takin' of you to our Leader, ma*dam*.'

The old gun-emplacement reeked of stale beer, urine, tobacco, sweeter 'pot', armpits and dirty socks. She felt

181

her gorge rise. 'Here she is, Slim.' She was jerked forwards.

Slim was sitting on a crate, like a caricature of a tribal chief on a throne, for two of his henchmen were crouched on either side of him. One was rolling a fag like a witch-doctor and humming to himself. Beer-bottles and coke-cans left damp trickles in the dust. There were two oil-lamps and a small calor gas cooker on which three tins of baked beans were boiling in a blackened pan.

Slim looked steadily at Ancilla. She stared back.

Slim said softly, 'Light her up.'

A boy of about fifteen picked up an oil-lamp and held it in front of Ancilla. She felt its heat through her sweater, and as the paraffin sloshed about the lamp smoked with a sickly smell.

The youths watched Slim as eagerly as hounds for a biscuit. He moved his eyes under their pink lashes very slowly up Ancilla's thin-trousered legs till they came to her crotch. Here they paused. He stuck his head forward, eyes agog. The gang sniggered. Ancilla tugged at her wrists. 'Stop that!' A youth's furry chin was against her ear: his breath was a puff from a septic tank. Slim's eyes crawled slowly over her belly and up to her breasts. They stared at one and circled, and stared at the other and circled that. The gang sniggered again.

'You like her, Slim?' asked the youth behind her. He put his elbow into the small of her back to make her belly jerk forward and her breasts quiver.

'That's better Slim, i'nit?' asked the youth anxiously.

Slim stared silently.

A knee was pressed sharply against Ancilla's buttocks, jerking them forward. Hands pulled her arms backwards so that she was bowed out towards Slim. 'Look Slim,' said the stinking voice in her ear. 'That's better, i'nit?' The youths at each side crouched forward, examining the shape of her exactly through her jeans tight-stretched between her legs.

Slim did not reply. A murmuration of excitement broke out of the boys. They all stared at Ancilla, hands deep in pockets.

'Got to frighten her, he said,' Slim said, moving his eyes downwards again. Ancilla wriggled. 'Who said?' she asked.

'One of the bosses,' said Slim.

'One of the *other* bosses,' said one of the gang, greasily.

Slim smiled briefly at him. The knife appeared flashing in his hand. He said, 'Bare her top.'

The youth behind tugged her sweater upwards. She kicked backwards and caught the side of his head. He grunted and rolled over, cursing.

Slim murmured, 'You and you: her feet.' Two youths tackled her ankles. 'Apart,' said Slim. 'Leave her sweater.' He got up and walked very slowly towards her and held his knife under her chin. She stood perfectly still, watching the blade.

'Don' move for Chrissake,' murmured the voice in her ear.

'Still,' said Slim, like a photographer. The point of his knife jabbed into her sweater at the bottom of her throat. She felt the prick of it like the sting of a wasp. Then he ripped it downwards to her belly. She had pulled herself in as far as she could go against the knee behind her. The knife touched her only just below her bra. It raced down to her stomach like the flick of a whip.

The sweater gaped. There was only a trace of blood, thin as a line on a map, from below her breasts to the start of the curve of her belly.

'Nice, Slim,' a youth grunted. 'Nice, nice,' murmured the other greedily. Some had their tongues stuck between their teeth. Their eyes bulged.

Slim, as if deboning a sole, flicked the flaps of her sweater back with his knife-blade, then slipped its tip under her bra between her breasts. 'Still,' he ordered.

Ancilla took a deep breath and closed her eyes. She felt the blade of the knife quite cold at first, then growing warmer from her skin. Slim flicked it upwards and her bra snapped. The two pieces fell away.

'Gutsy,' said Slim.

The gang craned round to get a good look. Hands reached forward, fingers twitching like monkeys' paws. There was a murmur of approval. A voice breathed, 'Smashin' . . .' Another started, 'Gor, I'd like to get me teeth – '

Slim frowned, 'Got to frighten her, haven't we? So she don' scoot agin.' He looked carefully into her eyes. 'You frightened?' She didn't answer. Slim said sharply, 'Well, turn her round. Can't slash her zip, can I?'

They turned her round away from him, and she felt the point of his knife prick the small of her back above the top of her jeans. The gang crouched still, eyes glowing.

'Still,' breathed Slim. 'Very still.'

His knife ripped through the canvas, she felt it prick her backbone, graze the bottom of it and then plunge on down the crack between her buttocks. Her split jeans fell away. The knife came on round till the youths in front could see it poised upwards. Then it stopped. She screamed. The gang looked carefully at her, breathing heavily.

Slim said, 'Scarcely nicked yer.'

Ancilla screamed again, tugging and wrenching at her wrists and ankles.

Slim said quietly into her ear, 'So you must be frightened.'

She nodded violently.

Slim said, 'Say "I'm frightened, Slim".'

One of the youths begged through wet lips, 'Her nicks, Slim. Slit her nicks.'

'Say "I'm frightened",' repeated Slim

Ancilla kept nodding, but she was shaking all over.

Slim said wearily, 'Turn her round again.' He put the blade of his knife beneath her navel and the band of her pants and pressed it. He pierced the elastic. She was quivering so much that her belly vibrated against the point. It smarted like salt in a wound. She looked down. There were little spots of blood.

'You'll have to be *very* still this time,' said Slim. 'Won't you?'

She felt a slight pressure on the knife point, as if he were preparing to strike.

'I'm frightened Slim I'm frightened Slim I'm frightened Slim,' babbled Ancilla and burst into floods of tears.

'Let her go,' said Slim, putting his knife away.

'Hey, Slim, you said we could all have her.'

'Like always when we get 'un.'

'Slim, you promised.'

'Nothin' of the sort,' said Slim. 'She's going back to Stewkly. Aren't you?' he said to Ancilla. She was finding it impossible to hold her jeans and sweater together. She nodded.

'Won't scoot agin?'

She shook her head.

'Kneel down here and say "I'm frightened of you, Slim", once more.'

She stopped holding her sweater and her jeans. They fell away and she knelt down in the dirt. 'I'm frightened of you, Slim.'

Slim smiled. He sat down on the beer crate and put a bottle in his mouth and sucked it. 'Run along then,' he said. She got up and, hobbled by the ripped jeans around her ankles, stumbled out on to the Downs.

She felt as cold as ice. Shock, she thought. Her teeth chattered. She tried to run. Her jeans kept slipping down. She took them off. She thought twice she heard the sound of Slim's motor-bikes roaring on the hill, and lurched forward over the bridge and up the lane. Headlights turned towards her from the road. She crouched down against the hedge, holding her sweater together over her breasts. The lights widened, brightened, loomed, dazzling her. An engine stopped and she heard Martin's voice. 'My God, Ancilla! What's happened?' The Land-Rover door was still banging as he put his arms round her. 'Darling, what happened? The mare? An accident?' Ancilla could say nothing. Tears sluiced down her face. She was howling.

# 24

When Ancilla woke up sweating, the slit between her bedroom's curtains was still glassy black. It reflected, like a wavering wheat-grain, a child's night-light on the dressing-table.

Ancilla looked for her watch. It had been taken from her wrist. She swung her feet out of bed and immediately felt dizzy. She looked down: she was wearing flannel pyjamas with very faded stripes and thick brown socks. Martin's? More likely old Mr Stewkly's. Brandy, hot milk, Mrs Stewkly's sleeping pills . . . Before that, a bath so hot on her cold body it had taken a minute for her to wince at its bite . . . Before that, the Land-Rover: weeping, shivering, wrapped in a pungent horse blanket, cuddled against Martin, asking about the mare, asking, '*Who* said I was to be frightened? Was it you? Was it you?'

Not at all nice, and I'm not safe yet. They're all in it. She opened her damp pyjama top: pink cut of the knife point between her breasts and rosy scratches doodled across her white belly. She felt sick and got up. The room tilted. She lurched across to the basin. Plug? Turn tap first. She retched. Vomit swirled down the plug. Bitter bile in the back of her mouth. Tears boiling behind her eyeballs. I'm pathetic: some stupid local louts . . . She ran the cold water over the nape of her neck. Delicious. She let it trickle on and breathed deeply in and out.

She found her watch on the dressing-table. It was just after midnight. She opened the door: an argument crackled fiercely up the stair like a bonfire. She listened:

187

Martin, his father . . . bloody Cubbington . . . another voice, military, the man Abbot then . . . and another. No sound from Mrs Stewkly. Ancilla began to creep down the twisting staircase.

Martin's voice sounded sharp as a terrier yapping. He was saying, '. . . poison the whole thing. If they're not out, I'll kill the bastard.'

His father said wearily, 'Don't be dramatic, Martin.'

'I bloody well will, father. With pleasure.'

Ancilla craned eagerly over the bannister. Her cheek touched her arm: it was glowing.

Cubbington growled, 'We've agreed all o'that, Martin.'

'We? We? It was your bloody idea.'

'Shut up, Martin.' It must be Richard Sandford. '*I* suggested bringing them in.'

Charles Stewkly said, 'Martin, we had to have everyone in who wanted to join us.'

Sandford's voice said defensively, 'They *have* been useful. They kept Stride and the factory under control. Slim stopped the rush on petrol at his father's garage.'

'Slim – ugh!' said Martin.

Sandford went on, 'They've produced discipline. Been our police force, if you like.'

'I don't bloody like,' Martin burst out. 'Nor would anyone who cares one fart what we're meant to be standing for. They're just bloody thugs.'

'We have *got* to be democratic,' Charles Stewkly intervened. 'I've taken such pains all through.' His voice was thin.

'Democratic? With these yobs?' asked Martin.

The military voice said, 'I'll tell you how we can be rid of 'em to good purpose.' Major Abbot's face popped round the dining-room door to see if the hall was empty. He glanced up. Ancilla saw his bulging eyes.

'Good God!' exploded Abbot. 'Are you the woman?'

188

There was a commotion of chairs in the dining-room. Martin yanked the door open and pushed past Abbot. He ran up the stairs towards Ancilla and gripped her, 'Are you all right?'

'Perfectly,' said Ancilla.

'What are you doing?' asked Major Abbot.

'Eavesdropping,' said Ancilla.

Charles Stewkly had reached the door. He stared up at her, head twisted like an agitated owl.

'Glad I did,' said Ancilla, giving Martin's shoulder quite a friendly squeeze. 'Otherwise I'd have thought you *all* wanted me murdered.'

A murmuration of protest from three men. Cubbington skulked in the dining-room. Ancilla waited for the apologies to peter out. Then she said coolly, 'I must say your young friends don't quite fit the image of honest countrymen defending hearth and home.'

There was some clearing of throats, but nobody answered. Ancilla added, 'I really would get shot of them. If you want to keep any public sympathy at all.'

Martin said, 'They're going, love. I swear it.'

'How?' she asked fiercely.

There was a movement of heads towards Aston Abbot. He said, 'It'll be done. But . . .' He shrugged uneasily. He was still in his muddy breeches and leather jacket. Must have come straight off Hampden Heights, thought Ancilla. She said drily, 'But you can't tell me, because I'm a spy.'

Charles Stewkly limped forward and held out his hand. She went down the last step and took it. 'Ancilla, my dear, we must suppose you are a spy. Because you do work directly for the Prime Minister. And he must be taking steps to subdue us.'

'Must be,' said Major Abbot, 'mustn't he?' He looked inquiringly at her.

'Well,' said Ancilla tartly, 'he has a duty to maintain law and order, I suppose.'

'Exactly,' said Abbot, 'As we have here.'

Ancilla thought: they're mad. They think of themselves already as a separate state. But she smiled and said to Mr Stewkly, 'I'd be very happy to be your *guest*. I can't say I won't try to get away. But I don't quite see how I can. I will try to behave like a good prisoner.'

'Oh, Ancilla,' began Mr Stewkly.

'Like a good prisoner,' repeated Ancilla firmly. 'But could you try to see I'm not physically ill-treated any more?' Saying the words squeezed out tears of self-pity. She gulped and turned and said tightly to Martin, 'I'm going back to bed.'

He supported her up the stairs. The others retired into the dining-room and shut the door. Martin paused at the door of Ancilla's bedroom. He said: 'They're getting out a new bulletin. To give our side of the picture. The BBC say the policeman from Easterly has been found dead and we're supposed to have . . .'

'What?' demanded Ancilla. 'Murdered him?'

Mrs Stewkly's voice called out, 'Martin? Is that Ancilla? Not in bed?'

'Just going.' He pulled Ancilla inside her bedroom. He said, 'We didn't kill him. He was in his running clothes. He'd fallen over the cliff.'

Ancilla sat down on her bed. She said savagely, 'Near Easterly, of course.'

Martin nodded. 'But that doesn't mean bloody Slim killed him. He might have just – ' Martin broke off as Ancilla looked up searchingly.

'What?' asked Ancilla. 'He might have done what? Threatened him with knives?'

'I don't know,' Martin said urgently. 'We don't *want* any violence. We've forsworn it. We're not hooligans like the Government are now saying. We only want to defend ourselves. To take a last stand.'

'Have you seen what they did?' asked Ancilla, opening her pyjama top and pushing down her trousers a little way. Martin stared. He made a revolted noise. He put out a finger towards the marks. She said, 'In fact, they don't hurt any more. But they do look bad, don't they? Rather satisfactory.' He bent down and kissed the marks on her belly feeling them with the tip of his tongue. She felt very hot. She put her hand on the nape of his neck. He said, 'You've been sweating.'

'Do I smell?'

He laid his cheek against her belly. 'Yes. Lovely.'

She squeezed his neck.

'Were you frightened?' he asked.

'Terrified.'

'I meant even back here?'

'Yes. Nightmares.'

He turned his head round. 'I'll stay with you here for the night.' He went on very quickly, 'Oh, just to – to reassure you.'

'For a cuddle,' said Ancilla. 'For moral support?' She was smiling.

'Yes.'

'These pyjamas and socks are terribly hot. You wouldn't mind if I . . . ?'

'Of course not,' said Martin politely.

Ancilla laughed for what seemed to her the first time for years. Martin grinned. 'I mean, of course, I'd like it!'

Ancilla smiled. 'It wouldn't tease you?'

'A man of iron,' said Martin. 'Though that's the wrong word.'

'Anyway, I *would* like you to stay.' She squeezed his arm. 'Get out of your smelly old clothes.' He pottered

191

about uncertainly. 'Go on,' said Ancilla, 'Use my toothbrush. We always used to share, didn't we?'

He lay very gently with his arm beneath her. She rested her hand against his cheek and leaned across and kissed his forehead. 'I think you're a nice man, Martin Stewkly.' She sighed, 'Thank goodness.' And fell asleep.

# 25

Ancilla was awoken by banging at the door and Mrs Stewkly calling, 'Your mother's on the telephone. Are you all right now?'

Martin had gone. Always was discreet: she hadn't felt him the whole night through. 'Coming,' she called. But probably less discretion than catching police in traps again.

It was just eight o'clock. Lady Shergrove had much more energy than people who sat around in factories and offices all day; she always put her feet up for two hours after luncheon. Though her dinner-parties never ended before midnight, she was woken at 7.30 daily with china-tea, lemon and the newspapers, and began to ring her friends 'While their little minds are bare and bright as slates!'

'Well, what's happened to you?' she asked Ancilla. 'We've been trying to reach you for two days. The line's always jammed or something. Our friend is desperate.'

'Is he? Honestly?'

'Of course he is. About you, I mean. Not the situation. He'll soon sort that out. Can you talk?'

Ancilla looked round the cold empty sitting-room and pulled her dressing-gown round her. 'Not really. Yes and no, you know.'

Lady Shergrove demanded, 'You a prisoner?'

'Yes.'

'Hostage?'

'I suppose so.'

'They haven't threatened you.'

'N-no.'

'You mean some people have?'

'Because I *tried* to escape.' She added in a louder voice, 'I don't think I can.'

'Locked in?'

'Not with keys.'

'Well, honestly, Ancilla . . .'

'Well, honestly,' said Ancilla fiercely. 'The whole bloody frontier's guarded.' There was a click on the line. Ancilla heard her mother shrieking, 'Hullo, Hullo! My God! These telephones. I'll have a word with the Minister!' Ancilla's mouthpiece was as dead as flannel.

Mrs Stewkly came in and said, 'Ancilla, I'm sorry, but Charles said you weren't to give things away, so I had to cut you off from the kitchen.'

Ancilla scowled. 'They must know the whole area's defended.'

Mrs Stewkly said solicitously, 'You'll catch your death of cold. Put on something warmer, dear, really. These October days . . .' She pottered out. Lady Shergrove's voice was still yelping from the telephone. Ancilla called, 'Mrs Stewkly, could I just tell my mother I'm all right?'

'Hasn't she asked?'

'Actually not,' said Ancilla. 'She always assumes one is.'

There was another click in the telephone and Ancilla said, 'Shut up squawking, I'm on again. But I can't talk.'

'Can't you help our friend at all?'

'How?'

'Say what's happening.'

Mrs Stewkly's voice came on the line. 'Oh, Lady Shergrove. It's Mary Stewkly. We did meet ages ago.'

The politeness flicked Lady Shergrove on the raw. 'What the hell are you doing to my daughter?' she demanded, furious as a lioness.

194

'Nothing,' said Mrs Stewkly, mildly. 'But there's so much coming and going and rough people around. You know what I mean, I'm sure. We are taking good care of Ancilla.'

Ancilla cut in, 'Protective custody.'

Lady Shergrove uttered a little shriek. 'The impertinence! The Prime Minister's Private Secretary! You tell those rebels, Mrs Stewkly, they can all hang!'

'Oh, surely not.' Mrs Stewkly was stirring away at some scotch broth while trying to listen.

'Surely, yes,' snapped Lady Shergrove. 'Treason. A capital offence.' She slammed down her telephone and flopped back in her beautiful bed beneath its damask curtains, gasping and wriggling in her silvery bed jacket like a fresh caught mackerel. 'Really!' she kept muttering. Then she rang No. 10. 'The Prime Minister, please . . .' Normally now Ancilla's voice would come on either in the second-floor flat if they were still up there, or in her own office on the left of the Cabinet Room at the back of the ground floor.

A woman's voice answered: either a Duty Clerk or one of the two 'Garden Girls' who always travelled with him. A pang gripped Lady Shergrove: George might find someone else.

When the Prime Minister came on, he sounded irritable. 'Well, have you got her?'

Lady Shergrove explained. She started, 'It seems quite ludicrous that a band of yokels – '

'They're more than that,' said the Prime Minister shortly. 'But we'll cope. Couldn't she tell you anything helpful? Their plans, numbers, food, fuel situation? No?' He was now angry. 'Nothing at all?'

Lady Shergrove said, 'Prime Minister, she is a *prisoner*.'

'Is she all right?'

'Well, she's very agitated. I think the sooner – '

'Of course,' Plain George sounded blunt. 'When you hear something, ring me again.'

The Home Security Defence Committee reported to the Minister of Defence that it had no Intelligence about the area. Air photo-reconnaissance confirmed the continuous defence-lines along Hampden Heights, some barbed-wire rolls across the Downs south of Easterly and an apparent boom across the harbour mouth. 'But what we want,' the Prime Minister had reiterated yesterday evening in the Cabinet Room, 'is what the ordinary people up there *feel* about the situation. We know they can't all be behind this gang. After all, there's this miserable parson keeps ringing up.'

The Reverend Frederick Fernden (with his eye on a Deanery) sneaked off to the Rectory telephone whenever his daughter was out, to talk melodramatically to Inspector Wilson. But references to 'masses of horses galloping everywhere' were not concrete military intelligence.

The Chief Constable found himself a laughing-stock. Photographs of his helicopter streaming with rolls of lavatory paper were on all front pages with '*Brigadier Spratley's Flying Loo*', and '*Police Chief caught with Pants down*'.

The Prime Minister rang the Home Secretary in bed and said, 'When this nonsense is over, Freddy, pray remove that buffoon Spratley.'

Sir Frederick, feeling the draught of a knife behind his back, readily agreed. But he added, 'By the by, Prime Minister, that press leak about "murdered PC" . . . a shade premature. Spratley tells me that the fellow's injuries were consistent solely with a fall.'

The Prime Minister's Press Secretary awaited his master in his office. Preposterous communiqués were being issued to the Press from what was called 'Committee of Defence Headquarters, Vale of Hampden'. These were calm reports and the morning papers gave them great prominence. George Robinson rode huffily down in the lift. The Press Secretary had the less mocking papers at the top. But the Prime Minister did not want to discuss them. Instead he asked, 'What do we say about Miss Shergrove? She is definitely a hostage.'

'We had decided to keep that very quiet, Prime Minister.'

'How can we? She's in the very house where these damned Defenders meet. They'll say something about her.'

'What, sir?'

'I'm asking you. What will the Press make of it?'

The Press Secretary knew that the revelation that the Prime Minister's mistress was in the enemy camp would produce a bellow of mirth in Fleet Street which he would hear along the Embankment and across Whitehall.

His silence maddened the Prime Minister who roared out, 'If you think they'd dare to print that Miss Shergrove is anything other than my Private Secretary . . . !' He glared at his Press Secretary who stared fixedly at the worn toe of his shoe.

When he had finally pinched the smile out of his face, he looked up diffidently. 'There's a line, I suppose, sir, that these brutes have seized a poor girl – ' He had been about to say 'Innocent', but could not have uttered the word without grinning.

The Prime Minister nodded, 'Get out something on those lines and let me see it.' That was dealt with. 'Now. When do I speak to the Nation?'

'Your next "Man-to-Man" is in three weeks, sir.'

'Too far off.'

The Press Secretary agreed. 'Perhaps then, sir, when you've made the military dispositions the Cabinet agreed last night?'

The Prime Minister nodded and dismissed him. The Press Secretary returned to his office by the front door and started to telephone a few Editors and Political Correspondents with what he called 'Minor Wise-ups'. But Fleet Street had got the bit between its teeth. The Vale of Hampden looked like the joke of the decade, and if it rocked the boat, so what? The Government should have steered the damn thing better.

# 26

The State's 'military dispositions' were made with such speed that Operation Snuffbox evolved from one rushed Ministry of Defence scenario. Its basic strategy, approved by the Chief of the Defence Staff, was passed to GOC Midlands Command for action. The CDS's Military Assistant, Major Roger Sturgeon, had attended the original briefing in the Ministry. He now accompanied his reluctant master to meet the Chief Constable, and the GOC Anglia. The Commander of the only active troops left in the area, Lt-Col. Jack Bradenham, 5th Armoured Regiment, was also present, though his battalion was officially resting after their Arabian operations.

During the meeting in Brackton Police HQ Sturgeon's thoughts drifted away to Hampden Heights, visible from the Chief Constable's office as a golden wall beyond the plain. Somewhere up there his old comrade Aston Abbot was presumably digging defences and making plans. It seemed absurd in England not to telephone him. In other circumstances he would have looked him up for lunch. Sturgeon mentioned this to the CDS, but Lt-General Sir Roderick Sloope said sharply, 'Don't be a fool, Roger. This isn't social weekends any more. Your friend over there is the enemy now.'

Sir Roderick had sulkily acceded to the Prime Minister's request to waste half a day in this miserable Anglian town. Commanded to No. 10, he had been left kicking his heels in the ante-room behind the screen at the end of the passage leading to the Cabinet Room. Then the Prime Minister with his nauseous matiness had said . . . 'So important – after the horrible muck-ups by the police – that the country should see the good old Army can take the job seriously. So if *you* could pop down . . .'

The next blow fell after lunch when the General was telephoned by the Minister of Defence. The Minister, on direct orders from Downing Street, had put under his command for Operation Snuffbox a company of African troops. These were Lutangans in Britain on a training and goodwill mission. 'I'm sorry, Roderick,' said his Minister. 'This is a political requirement. And the PM is adamant as a diamond.' The Minister of Defence could hear the CDS seething down the telephone. He added, 'A few men of whatever colour can only help. We're woefully thin on the ground, aren't we?'

Sir Roderick was sorely tempted to reply that it was the Government's mad political requirements all round Europe which spread his troops so thin, but he said, 'The PM still doesn't believe – and nor do you, Minister, I take it – that our troops will fire on these villagers?'

'One can't assume it,' said the Minister of Defence. 'You recollect the Army's reactions when intervention was contemplated in Rhodesia? . . . Exactly . . . We hope, of course, that force won't be necessary. But if so, these Lutangans . . .'

'Won't be so inhibited? Are they cannibals, by the way?' Sir Roderick asked caustically.

The Minister clicked his tongue. 'Lutanga is a member of the Commonwealth. Their help here demonstrates the solidarity we're trying to achieve in Africa.'

The Chief of the Defence Staff retorted, 'If one black foreign soldier kills one English civilian here in Anglia, the black areas of the Midlands will be burned to the ground. I intend to put my views in writing to you, Minister.'

The CDS flew back to London leaving Sturgeon behind

for liaison. The GOC Midlands promptly handed over to his Battalion Commander, and drove back to his depleted HQ.

Colonel Jack Bradenham said cheerfully, 'I've always found Africans excellent fighting men.'

'So did Aston Abbot,' said Roger Sturgeon, drily.

'Ah,' said the Colonel. 'You know the fellow, of course.'

'Knew him,' said Sturgeon. It already felt as if Aston was either dead or in prison.

'Now, how would he *think*?' asked the Colonel. 'Defensively? Cautious? Or a glory-seeker? An armoured thrust, perhaps?'

'He has only a few horses, Colonel, I gather,' said Sturgeon unhelpfully. He had no wish to be drawn personally into this business. But tactics and Abbot's reactions had to be discussed when the two tactical commanders arrived: Major Frank Radnage who commanded the only squadron of 5th Armoured which GOC Midlands had decreed could be spared; and Major Ngyoto, impeccable in the dark Brigade of Guards barathea which the Lutangan President had adopted for his bodyguard.

'Dam' glad to be here, Colonel,' exclaimed Major Ngyoto, his white teeth grinning in his handsome black face. 'My chaps are fully cheesed off at Aldershot, I can tell you.' He rubbed his pink palms together. 'Bit of a dog-fight – just the thing.' He let out a melodious chuckle.

Roger Sturgeon and Major Radnage exchanged nervous glances. The Colonel cleared his throat, and his Intelligence Officer laid maps upon the table.

It was decided to place Major Ngyoto's company of Lutangans on the right flank. 'Right of the line – pride of place,' he beamed. Based below the shoulder of the Downs south of Easterly they would make a two-pronged attack: one platoon seaborne in an LCI to land at Easterly harbour; the other two platoons to penetrate the wire defences on the Downs and to advance into Easterly down the lane behind the Silken Dalliance factory. 'You will thus grip Easterly – ' began Colonel Bradenham.

'Like the head of a hunter,' cried Major Ngyoto, 'in a jolly old crocodile's jaws!'

Major Radnage's squadron of the 5th Armoured – 'ample', GOC Midlands had remarked with a pitying glance at the Chief Constable, 'for this petty police action' – would assault the left and centre. Of the squadron's three Troops, No. 1 and No. 2 would be landed by helicopters to hold East Pym. Those Troops would be without their Ferret armoured scout-cars. HQ Troop, supporting a detachment of Royal Engineers, would threaten the blocked cutting on Hampden Heights. 'This,' said Colonel Bradenham, 'should draw off the rebels from the blown bridge.' There No. 3 Troop, covering an RE bridging party, would cross and join up with the other two Troops in East Pym. With the Lutangans in Easterly the two main centres of the rebellious area would thus be secured.

'Then,' said the Colonel to the Chief Constable, 'you can take over, arrest the ringleaders, restore civil control and all that sort of thing.' After the Chief Constable's earlier blunders, he wanted him kept well out of the way.

Brigadier Spratley distrusted the Colonel's blithe attitude. He said, 'There are far more men in there under arms than you allow for. When I tried to land at East Pym – '

'But, Brigadier,' said Colonel Bradenham cheerfully, 'you were alone with a few rozzers. This'll be the Army going in. Civilians haven't a chance in open country.' He added with a tinge of regret, 'I'd have liked more time for reconnaissance – of course I would. I'd like to *know*

202

what we'll find and *then* move. But political pressures don't allow time.' He shrugged. 'The Army's used to it.'

'Indeed it is, Colonel,' agreed Major Ngyoto. 'Nothing is simple for we pure fighting men.' He begged leave to return to his chaps. 'They may be pranging the local natives a bit!' He went off laughing his deep rumble.

Lutangan males had been reared over five centuries for only three activities at which they must prove expert or perish: hunting, fighting and sex. There was still plenty of hunting and fishing in Lutanga where recalcitrant tribes on the country's edge had to be hacked to pieces with good made-in-Birmingham bayonets. For the élite there was still plenty of sex in Lutanga, too, for the President not only allowed his bodyguards to sleep with whom they chose without fear of civil action, but he also granted annuities to mothers producing children by them. This practice known as 'Gongo' kept his guards content, improved the country's stock and ensured future recruits, for male offspring sired by bodyguards were taken free into the Lutangan Sandhurst.

Major Ngyoto's Company had found things very different in Aldershot. There was no hunting, no fighting and no Gongo. Indeed, the wives of Aldershot, so far from offering themselves instantly to the bodyguards, had been hustled by husbands behind the locked doors of their married quarters. The Lutangans were very dissatisfied with the British way of life.

Their cold, damp, tented camp below the Downs south of Easterly was even worse. In the deserted wastes of the autumnal countryside they could not even find Aldershot's helpful whore-ladies. 'Plenty of Gongo when we finish these rebels,' Major Ngyoto promised them hopefully. 'Meantime amuse yourselves with one another as our grandfathers did when they were long time away hunting beyond the purple mountains.'

203

The Government's 'military dispositions' were instantly reported to the Defenders by a deep belt of supporters who surrounded the area: farmers, delivery-men, corn-merchants and agricultural engineers, who kept their eyes and ears open.

The arrival of the Lutangan company caused dismay. 'These extra ninety fully-armed troops won't hesitate to fire,' said Major Abbot. News of the squadron of Ferret scout cars on the Brackton lane arrived the same day. Leo Mallard, the nearest farmer to the border, reported two large Army helicopters – 'and the milk-lorry ruddy nearly pushed in the ditch by a convoy of Engineers with bulldozers and cranes'. The Brackton corn-merchant said that another Engineer detachment was on the outskirts with what looked like pieces of bridge.

He was talking to Martin behind a haystack near the Brackton lane. 'They'll have you both ways, Martin, I reckon. Quite apart from those black fellows on t' other side. Hadn't you best pack it in?' His heart did not want them to, for he supported the Defenders and liked a fight. But his head did not want friends and clients killed.

The Defenders had not yet found out where the British and Lutangan assaults were aimed. 'Until I know, I can't dispose our horsemen,' said Abbot. Stewkly clung to the belief that British troops would not fire on a crowd of villagers and horses. But the crowd had to be thick enough to block the lanes otherwise the troops in their armoured cars would quickly outflank them. 'And there aren't enough of us to cover all the border.'

'We could fall back on the gap behind the freddy factory,' said Abbot. 'As we planned, Richard.'

'And give up Easterly and all our friends there?' asked Charles Stewkly. 'Without a fight?'

'Slim's Bones will fight,' said Sandford.

Abbot said coldly, 'Thirteen yobs on motor-bikes even

behind their electrocuted wire, won't hold up those Africans for five minutes.'

But they were not, as it transpired, to hold them up at all. Next morning Slim telephoned Richard Sandford: 'They've got Red. We're goin' to get 'im back.'

'Who have?'

'Brackton Bootboys.'

'But how?' asked Sandford.

'Went in to get some reefers,' said Slim impatiently. 'So the Bootboys got 'im. And they'll shop 'im to the Fuzz.'

'How d'you know?' asked Sandford, exasperated by this crazy tale.

'Met the Bootboy Boss,' said Slim. 'Near where them coons is. Showed me Red's jacket. So we've got to get 'im. 'Less you'd let the Bootboys have the girl for swaps.'

'Ancilla Shergrove?'

'Prime Minister's bit what I tickled with me flick.'

'To give her to those Skinheads?' asked Sandford incredulously.

Slim grunted. 'They'd all screw her, I dare say. Bootboys has no control.'

'No,' said Sandford fiercely.

'Thought you'd say that. Well, ta then.' Slim rang off.

Sandford telephoned the Stewklys. Martin said, 'Good riddance.'

'Leaves Easterly quite unprotected.'

'Listen,' said Martin, 'I'll ride over. Knowing Lutangan habits has given me an idea.' He added, 'And thank you for not sending Ancilla off. I wouldn't have liked that one bit.'

'No,' said Richard Sandford, 'I didn't think you would. Pity for all our sakes you didn't marry her really. Hers, too, maybe.'

* * *

Mrs Bellamy was delighted when Martin introduced her to Mr Sandford. 'Of course, I've never met your Belinda, sir, but I was Nanny to the Brunchams' little girl, the Honourable Emily as she was then, and she was a schoolfriend of Belinda's at Heathfield.' Richard Sandford looked bemusedly round Mrs Bellamy's parlour where she was entertaining them to morning coffee and chocolate digestive biscuits. Over the fireplace framed photographs of Mrs Bellamy's former charges jostled one another. 'There's Emily on her pony at the Lawn Meet at Bruncham.' There were stacks of old engraved invitations to society weddings. 'I believe your Belinda was bridesmaid to Lady Mary, wasn't she, at the Hull wedding? Such a pretty girl, Lady Mary, I always thought, even if she did have her mother's naughty moods.'

In such an atmosphere Sandford felt incapable of even mentioning Martin's suggestion. He said, acutely embarrassed, 'Martin had a little plan to mention to you, Mrs Bellamy.'

'Professionally?' asked Mrs Bellamy, pulling her diary towards her.

Martin nodded and expounded, but the plan did not slip as sweetly down as Californian Syrup of Figs in Mrs Bellamy's former nurseries.

'They would be coloured gentlemen, Martin, I take it?' inquired Mrs Bellamy.

'You've no particular objection?'

Mrs Bellamy pondered, sipping coffee with little finger extended. 'That charming Rajah sent his son to me when I lived in Town. For his Introduction, when he was twelve. A forward little lad, but with perfect manners! He picked it all up so quickly.'

Martin made encouraging noises.

'His Daddy was ever so grateful. A real gentleman, the Rajah. When he came to me himself, he always made me

dress up in polo clothes and he played the pony!' Mrs
Bellamy chuckled affectionately. 'But they were *Indian*
gentlemen, of course, and the Rajah had been at Harrow,
which is quite a nice school . . .'

'These are very nice Africans,' said Martin.

'But there would be so *many*,' said Mrs Bellamy, 'and
I'm not so young as I was.'

'Good gracious, Mrs Bellamy,' said Sandford, unable
to restrain laughter, 'we weren't suggesting that on your
*own* . . .'

But Mrs Bellamy drew herself up. 'I'm the only professional lady practising here,' she said stoutly. 'I am *the*
Sea-Tart, as naughty young Martin calls me.'

Martin made abashed sounds, as if caught not eating
his cabbage.

Mrs Bellamy continued, 'I don't count those women
from the factory. They're not professionals in any way.
More,' she added tartly, 'of an 'areem for that foreman
of theirs, by all accounts.'

Martin glanced across at Sandford, who nodded. Martin
said, 'Mrs Bellamy, we do think these African gentlemen
may do nasty things here, if they're not – pacified. They
do just terribly want to be loved by English ladies.' He
could see Mrs Bellamy weakening. He pressed on, 'They
are far from home, alone, cold . . .'

Mrs Bellamy said briskly, 'Very well, Martin, I will do
what I can. But I must have assistants.'

Martin beamed, 'Of course. And under your control.
Nursery maids, one might say.'

Mrs Bellamy nodded comfortably.

Sandford said, 'Owen the fisherman and I know of five
or six, we think.'

'Here?' asked Mrs Bellamy. 'Amateurs then.'

'Amateurs now,' Martin corrected her. 'For these special duties they will, of course, become professionals.'

Mrs Bellamy said keenly, 'I would charge an overall fee, then give portions to these assistants. That would be the correct way, I'm sure.'

Martin agreed. He saw Mrs Bellamy was awaiting a figure. 'There may be as many as ninety visiting gentlemen.'

'No, Martin. That is too much. Certainly with untrained girls working under me. Twenty would be quite sufficient.'

'But if we asked the girls from Silken Dalliance to help too – '

'Under my control?' snapped Mrs Bellamy.

'Absolutely.'

'We-ell,' Mrs Bellamy smiled. 'You always *could* charm birds off trees, Martin.' She dredged the brown sugar up from her coffee cup and delicately licked her lips. 'I will receive the gentlemen here at ten pounds per gentleman. I know it sounds a lot, Mr Sandford, but my assistants may not be cheap and I do like my own holiday in Gibraltar every November: cornflakes, *Woman* dear Mr Kindly, British bobbies and Cooper's Oxford marmalade. That's the old Rock, even now. And that's what Abroad should always be like, *I* think.'

Richard Sandford and Martin proffered their gratitude. Mrs Bellamy coaxed them to share the last digestive biscuit. 'Thousand a year or marry a marquis, as I always said over nursery-tea,' she beamed. Then she added astutely, 'Those rough girls from the factory will not undercut me?'

'Of course not, Mrs Bellamy.'

They walked happily out into the hock-coloured sunshine of an early October noon. Martin asked, 'You've definitely got those Yorkshire trippers' wives to help Mrs B?'

'Owen says they're rampant for it. Full of sea air and sea-food. They're on to Owen's home-brewed stout now, powerful stuff, and longing to teach their absent husbands a sharp lesson.'

'They know Africans are on the menu?'

'Their appetites are particularly whetted.'

So too were those of the lady workers of Silken Dalliance, who had been largely unsatisfied since the night of Aidan Stride's defeat. As Mabel said, 'When I called him Droopy I never dreamed it'd stay that way ten days!' The miserable Stride had consulted old Nurse Dinton at the First Aid Post who, misinterpreting his whispered 'I can't do it,' had treated him for constipation and purged him cruelly.

So Richard Sandford's conversation with him in his office was disjointed. 'Pardon,' Stride kept interrupting, 'ruddy toilet calls again.' Stride's mind was occupied with supplies to keep the factory running. 'Seein' the manager can't get in through yer bleedin' barriers, Cock Cover Jack's put me in sole charge,' he said proudly. As with many a businessman, sudden sexual failure produced a new commercial urge.

Sandford suggested, 'Couldn't you think of something else you could make here? We could help with lots of materials, but not rubber or latex, I'm afraid.'

'I have somethin' in mind,' began Stride, 'stemmin' from the predicament of a friend o'mine.'

'Good,' said Sandford. But he put his immediate proposition. 'We would naturally pay you a management fee on top of the ten pounds per girl used.'

'Form of productivity bonus, like? Linked to output? Good.'

Martin was finding keen enthusiasm from the ladies at the work-benches. 'Well,' said Mabel, 'I call that really fair, I do. We've never been paid, have we, girls, like that old Bellamy bitch? But this way we'll be savin' our homes and such from destruction – for these coons can

209

be violent, that I do know from *Jungle Busters*. And the tenner would be sorta expenses like, not *pay*.'

'Wear and tear,' shouted her fat friend, cheerfully.

So it was arranged. Final details were worked out with Doctor Quainton and Nurse Dinton, and Martin reported back to a delighted Committee. 'Bloody brainwave, Martin,' said Cubbington almost jovially, 'I do admit it.'

Charles Stewkly came quickly in from the stables looking excited. 'One of Wilkinson's scouts beyond the Heights this morning heard that Slim's Bones were seized by the police in Brackton in an ambush.'

'All caught?' asked Martin. 'Slim, too?'

'Twelve. Fighting with another gang. And apparently,' added Charles Stewkly, 'the tip-off came from old PC Plumridge, struggling from his sick bed.'

Martin, Cubbington and Abbot stared at him.

Charles Stewkly said slyly, 'Well, I thought it could only do Old Plum good in the eyes of his masters – ' he made his glasses pop up – 'Whatever happens here.'

# 27

In spite of their officer's exhortations Major Radnage's Squadron found it impossible to keep their mouths shut amongst friendly Englishmen. In hot Arabia they had been as mice, surrounded by darkly hostile (and uncomprehending) aliens.

But here the troopers, hardened by the hostility of foreigners, relaxed among compatriots, and were easily drawn over second pints.

The Squadron should have been confined to its cold tented camp. But their rest period had been interrupted, they were very low on recruits and Major Radnage was a kindly officer. Were his Colonel not constantly jollying him along, he might have taken a graver view of Operation Snuffbox. But Colonel Bradenham was carefree: this thing was merely an exercise.

Reports that East Pym was to be the objective for the helicopter raid were now so frequent that Major Abbot based his defence plan upon them. He would himself command there with 300 men, leaving only a light screen under Cubbington on Hampden Heights and three Dozens under Charles Stewkly facing the bridge. Richard Sandford, Martin and the fishermen would be in Easterly facing the Lutangans with fifty-four women.

Major Abbot asked Patricia Fernden to imprison her father in the cellars of his Rectory till the action was over. He then called together the Leaders of the East Pym Dozens in Cubbington's house, outlined his plan and conducted an exercise.

Then he waited. All the Vale waited. At 6 P.M. Sandy

Potts was perched near the Brackton lane on a straw stack. Suddenly he scurried like a fox along the hedges, jumped on his horse by the willows and galloped back towards the Heights. 'They're loading into the helicopters,' he shouted up to Ronald Cubbington in his observation-post on the ridge. Cubbington rang through to Abbot in East Pym.

Abbot said, 'Warn the whole escarpment to watch where they cross.'

The men crouched under the trees, ears cocked towards the enemy plain. But there was no sound of aircraft engines. Cubbington from his eyrie could faintly see the soldiers repeatedly emplaning and deplaning to the raucous barks of bossy sergeants. The Army were plainly regarding the exercise as a mere practice manoeuvre. 'By God, we'll show the buggers!' Cubbington swore, his long white face puckered in fury.

Night fell, overlaying a blanket of cloud with a black eiderdown. All along the ridge the Defenders listened. Then at 10.35 P.M., half-way south between the cutting and the end of the escarpment, the sound of helicopters whirred towards them. The watchers whistled shrilly. Cubbington rang back to Abbot whose tactical base was East Pym graveyard. 'Plenty of good cover,' old Potter cackled.

Abbot blew his whistle. Light after light in the village went out like doused candles. He heard the end of the evacuation as the last occupants left their houses through their back gardens and made for their rendezvous in the copses round the darkened village. Then he heard the helicopters approaching. He saw that they were impudently showing navigation lights. He heard them hovering over the Green. White landing-lights flooded out from under their bellies. They touched down. Their doors flew open. There were two pale glows from the interiors.

Against these Abbot could see a press of huddled, jumping figures. The rotors ceased. Orders swept hoarsely across the Green. Abbot heard running feet and orders coming closer. He guessed they were setting up defensive machine-gun groups at the three corners of the Green.

Flighty Wing's pricked ears picked up the squeak of bolts and chink of rifle-barrels from the far corners. 'You're right,' he whispered to Abbot behind their tombstone.

'Anything from the houses?'

Wing listened. Silence breathed. Wing sniggered. 'Someone's left their telly on t'other side.'

'Cut off the main supply, Flighty. They may have left cookers on, too.'

Flighty Wing glided away to the Electricity Board's junction box. The gate had already been forced and the door opened. He slipped in and lifted the main switch. The television set across the Green died. Abbot heard some of the soldiers' voices quite close – 'Not very welcomin', the natives.' Some low laughter. A young officer shushed them.

Wing was silently back at Abbot's side. Out on the Green the soldiers blundered into the bus shelter, and tripped over a bench. One struck the litter-bin a clang. The helicopters squatted near the Memorial like two roosting pheasants. Abbot saw the door of one open again. Someone climbed in, stooped, picked something up. In the silence the young officer's voice bellowed through a loudhailer. Abbot saw with scorn that he was clearly visible, a perfect target in the light of the helicopter. He was reading from a little notice: 'People of East Pym. This is an Army operation under the Emergency Powers Act, 1964. We are here to restore order. Please remain quietly in your homes. Thank you.'

He blew his whistle. A general movement stirred across

the Green. Aston Abbot and Wing heard the sound of army-boots crossing the surrounding roads. Garden gates clicked open, squeaked, clacked shut. Boots crunched up gravel paths, rang on stone doorsteps. The officer's whistle squealed again from the centre of the Green. Fists banged everywhere on doors back and front. The officer's voice twanged out through the loudhailer. 'People of East Pym. We are about to search your homes. Do not resist. Open the doors. We will do no damage. Open your doors *now,* please.'

Silence enshrouded the village. Flighty Wing had his fist stuffed into his mouth. He and Abbot could clearly hear from all around the village the uncertain scrabbling of boots and whispered discussions.

A Very light whizzed from the officer's helicopter, its crimson path slashing into the night's belly. On the signal, back doors and front doors were wrenched open with rattles and bangs which reverberated through every cottage. Army-boots, quickened now, rushed up wooden stairs. Bedroom doors banged open. Windows rattled and squeaked.

'People of East Pym!' The young officer's voice sounded anxious. 'Please put on your lights.'

Flighty Wing, unable to suppress himself, snorted with delight. 'Quiet,' whispered Abbot across the tombstone of some distant relation.

Uncertain shouting erupted from various cottages: 'Sir! No one here!'

'Who's that?'

'Sergeant Powell, sir. These cottages are empty.'

'Empty? No furniture, you mean?'

'No, sir. Fully furnished. No people.'

Another voice from the opposite side: 'Sergeant Evans here, sir. All empty here.'

The cries of other NCOs, more amused than anxious,

teased their young officer in yelps round the Green: 'Here, too, sir. No one!'

'Whole place empty, sir,' shouted Sgt Muldoon, grinning.

Second-Lt Downley shouted: 'Who's in the pub? It should be Sergeant Flint.' His voice had got higher.

Sergeant Flint came out of the pub door and shouted back, 'No one here, sir.'

'The church!' shouted the officer. Downley was just nineteen and had not yet commanded in action. He had carefully rehearsed every detail for an orderly organized search of cottages. Certain listed people were to be found and held for the police. He had not planned for desolation. He became agitated. 'Try the church! They've got to be somewhere. Haven't you any torches?'

Troop-Sergeant Muldoon shouted back, 'You have them there wid yer in the choppers, sor. Shall we come back?'

'No, stay there. Send back runners,' shouted the Lieutenant. 'And Sergeants Flint and Powell surround the church with your Troops.'

'Come on, Flighty,' whispered Abbot. 'Time we slipped away. But where's their Commander? On the Heights or at the bridge?'

'This orficer's sweatin' nicely anyroad,' murmured Flighty Wing. The two men slipped through the graves to the steps down the ha-ha wall and padded silently off across the farm called Church Hay.

They heard behind them a tremendous racket in the graveyard as the soldiers tumbled over the tombs and stones and barked their shins on granite curbs and rusty iron-railings. Glass pots of dead flowers crashed over.

'Clumsy sods!' whispered Flighty Wing in the shadow of Charlie Potter's Dutch barn.

'We'd be as bad in their villages,' said Abbot fairly.

'I'd be better, Major,' said Wing. 'I doubt there's any poachers with them sodgers.'

Abbot's plan depended on the troops not occupying the cottages. He could not believe they would. Unless Army training had altered since he left they would consolidate on the Green, machine-guns in each corner, with probably forward-positions on the roads to Easterly and the Hampdens.

Second-Lt Downley called up Major Radnage on his radio. 'Village occupied, sir.'

'Any resistance?'

'None at all, sir.'

'Somebody must have stood firm.'

'No one here at all, sir.'

'What d'you mean, Dick? Where are the people in the houses?'

'Gone, I suppose.'

'Heard you coming, you mean?'

'No, sir. Gone before we landed. The place was silent.'

'Not a sausage? Not hiding in the gardens, barns?'

'The village is quite empty, sir.'

'Bloody odd. Let's hope they're all up on Hampden Heights . . . OK. You consolidate as planned.'

Major Abbot on Church Hay listened to the soldiers pottering about below. His Leaders gathered quietly in the warm straw of the Dutch barn. They had posted scouts who normally harrowed, harvested and ploughed their fields to watch the lanes. The first reports came back: the soldiers were leaving the cottages. They were unrolling ground-sheets and bedding on the Green. They were noisily setting up outposts on the lanes leading out of the village. Aston Abbot gave a huge sigh. Those twenty-five years he had worn khaki may not have been utterly wasted after all. A great victory lay within a few hours of his reach. Oh Lord, he prayed, deliver the enemy into our hands . . . And another prayer, from Britain's last Civil War, spiralled into his brain as the clock tolled midnight. 'Oh God, Thou knowest how busy I must be this day. If I yet forget Thee, do not Thou forget me.'

He was not a dramatic man. Honour and glory had never been his grails. He was dutiful, had served, had hoped to succeed. But in all his post-war actions he had never fought when either the cause was clear, or the rightness of his side obvious. He felt both now so plainly he could almost grip them. Looking down on the ugly shapes of the helicopters squatting round his village's War Memorial, which listed his relatives and friends and neighbours, he felt at last dedicated and therefore fulfilled.

# 28

The Lutangan platoon picked to make the seaborne landing, Major Ngyoto's 'jolly old right hook', grumbled terribly as their old Landing Craft Infantry pitched and wallowed in the rolling swell. The Lutangans, an inland people, were in terror of the shifting, slapping, roaring mysteries of the sea. They were cold on the long journey. They huddled together, muttering. Sickness boiled scalding from their bellies. They lurched to the cold sides which leapt up, banging chins and elbows, and were sick.

Major Ngyoto, Sandhurst-trained, was keen to introduce his chaps to amphibious warfare. The army offered four black rubber Assault Boats. 'Crew?' asked Major Ngyoto, 'Sailor fellows?'

But the establishment did not allow for crews for Assault Boats. 'If you had a small LCI, Major, we could loan you an RN bos'n and his mate.'

So the antique LCI chugged up the East Coast, collected a platoon of African troops on the orders of two Majors, black and white, and set off northwards on Operation Snuffbox.

The naval bos'n and his mate scanned the black night for the lights of Easterly. They were strangers to the shore and were working off charts. Their ETA off Easterly's harbour-wall was midnight. It was five past now but their groaning cargo had kept down their speed. They were conscious of cliffs looming to port and heard the swell smashing itself on rocks. But where were the village lights? Their Admiralty Chart marked a light-tower at the end of the mole. No light burned.

'There!' shouted the mate from the bows. 'Off the port bow. Harbour-wall.' His voice blew back over the sagging heads of the seasick Africans. The bos'n reduced speed and stared to port through his night binoculars. He could just discern the darker arm of the wall. He called for'ard to the Lutangan platoon commander: 'Hey, Chico! Plenty soon Easterly, savvy?' He had served steaming years in Far Eastern waters. 'Ready quick, boy! Looky sharp-sharp!' he shouted.

Murmurations in a heathen tongue bubbled up from the depths of the LCI. The Lutangans seemed reluctant heroes. Then the bos'n heard the word '*Gongo*' often repeated. Interest was roused, voices deepened and quickened. The Platoon began to pull on its webbing equipment. They were heavily armed.

'Hey, Chico!' called the bos'n. 'Me turny thataway. Stop motor. Shush-shush.' He held his hand to his mouth. 'When big wall that-a-side' – he pointed to port – 'all boys jumpy up quick soon, savvy?'

The Lutangan platoon commander stumbled aft until he reached the bos'n. Then he remarked softly in a pleasant pre-war Oxford accent: 'Thanks awfully, old fellow. Our orders are pretty plain. And we know the form.' The bos'n goggled. The Lutangan could not resist adding as the LCI glided towards the harbour mouth, 'Plenty good sailing-boy bos'n, savvy?'

At that moment an astounding submarine explosion beneath the LCI's bottom flung its bows into the air. It was followed rapidly by the sound of a chain scraping. The boat canted wildly to starboard and three larger explosions rapidly succeeded. The Lutangan platoon poised in the bows of the LCI were catapulted into the water like black clay-pigeons. They began to thresh wildly towards the dinghies and small craft tied up beneath the slimy harbour-wall.

'Mined the bloody entrance, they have,' announced the bos'n surprised, plaintive for himself, but also rather proud of his countrymen's actions. He smartly put his LCI hard astern. 'I'm standing off. Those cheeky nignogs can fend for theirselves.' His mate agreed. Nothing had been said about mines or opposed landings, and the two sailors were firmly agreed that it went against the grain to loose foreigners on an English village.

'Fought all our wars for that, Shorty,' said the bos'n, 'I mean keepin' foreigners out. Then soon as we wins, we lets 'em all stream in.'

'Bloody mad,' said his mate.

The bos'n heard the voice of the platoon commander rousting his men along from the top of the harbour-wall. From the grunts and cries it sounded as if most of the Lutangans were scrambling up the wall from the boats. The bos'n stood off shore a little farther and put out sea-anchors. He had orders to wait till instructed. 'Just a bloody taxi,' he grumbled to his mate. They opened their Thermos of tea, set their backs resolutely against the coast and lit up fags.

The Lutangan Lieutenant collected his platoon on the sea-wall and they crouched down behind him in the approved fashion, section leaders heading each file. The fishing village was in darkness. It remained silent. The Lieutenant beckoned and started to creep forward silently in his rubber-soled US Army combat-boots. His platoon were snaking along behind him with uncomfortable squeakings and pinchings of wet uniforms when an illuminated sign suddenly leapt out on the wall of the public-house facing the harbour. Inscribed in colossal letters of fluorescent paint and dazzlingly lit by the pub's floodlights were the words: 'GONGO! GONGO HERE!' and underneath written in their own tongue the Africans read: 'WELCOME BRAVE LUTANGANS!'

A rumble as of jungle drums coursed through the platoon. They began to press their Lieutenant forward. His sergeant said: 'It is the other two platoons, sir. They must be here before us.' The Lieutenant nodded. Then the lights in the saloon and public bars flashed on. The Lutangans froze. They stared. Two barked. Several moaned. Through the windows five stark-naked white women were displayed standing on the bar, lying on it, swaying on tables, beckoning spreadeagled from chairs. A howl of delight burst from the platoon and the Lieutenant had to run his hardest to keep ahead of them. The door of the pub opened as they approached and Mrs Bellamy, gigantic in her black French nightie, filled the passage. She held out her hand to the Lieutenant. 'Good evening,' she said brightly, 'Do come in.'

The Lieutenant was forced past her into the bar by his panting troops. But Mrs Bellamy checked the tide. 'Their wet clothes, Lieutenant,' she said, 'they must remove them for drying. I must care for the health of my Gongo girls.' She turned to introduce them. The five Yorkshire wives, a little alarmed by the closeness of twenty dripping, goggling Africans, had snatched up beer-mats and were trying modestly to cover themselves with the little discs advertising potent brews. Mrs Ethel Birtwistle greeted the Lieutenant, who was even taller and stronger and finer looking than she had imagined.

'Hi!' said Mrs Ethel Birtwistle, and her fingers tapped her beer-mat.

'But you too will be awfully good for me, I trust,' said the Lieutenant. Mrs Birtwistle looked puzzled. The Lieutenant bent forward to touch her beer-mat. 'Guinness,' he said. 'Small joke.'

A titter quivered through the ladies.

'Great pleasure,' said the Lieutenant and issued a sharp order to his men. They instantly stripped off. Interest now overcame the ladies' caution. Like savages approaching explorers, they crept forward beady-eyed.

The Lutangans' equipment and uniforms were soon flung in a great pile over their discarded machine-guns and rifles. When the ladies first glimpsed their visitors naked they set up a chorus of unbelieving whimpers. The Lieutenant, puzzled by the sound, glanced along his platoon as if inspecting rifles. 'I apologize,' he said to Mrs Bellamy. 'Cold water, madam, has a shrinking effect. In a moment, rest assured – '

Mrs Ethel Birtwistle could not believe her ears. 'Apologize?' She shrieked, 'For those whoppers?' She could not contain herself either and darted forward.

'Gaw!' cried the thin-faced wife, pale eyes goggling, and the wives oozed towards the front rank of the soldiery, hands outstretched to touch and grip, and bodies not far behind. The Africans recognized flattery in their grasps, and also stepped forward boldly towards a multi-racial unity.

Mrs Bellamy tried vainly to interpose herself, for no proper introductions had yet been made. But she could more easily have restrained great engines from coupling with their trucks. '*Please*, ladies! The proprieties. In the *bedrooms*, like ladies, please,' she begged, but the handsome Lieutenant courteously peeled off her nightie and stifled her protests. She was borne over backwards on to her bar-room floor. She glanced frantically left and right: the floor leapt with vanilla and chocolate couples sandwiching, interlocking. Round them hovered a hot black circle of stiffly waiting ranks, some crouching, some standing, but all just as the Lieutenant had assured her.

Squeaks of pain arose, for the Africans, wasting no time on preliminaries, were cold and salty from the sea. 'Oooh . . . Ow!' shrieked Mrs Ethel Birtwistle. 'Wait half a mo, love . . . ooh . . . aaah . . .' But the Lutangans, too long without their Gongo, were like stallions: half a dozen grunting thrusts, a mighty final one, a gasp, a sigh and they were done. The Yorkshire wives looked up astonished, but they were disappointed for only a moment, for the next rank sprang grinning on to them. The ladies, thus briskly roused, were kept in panting suspension as their partners changed, till final ecstasies engulfed them. Mrs Bellamy in a moment's respite surveyed her floor like a general his battlefield. Some of the early-comers were again in action. Some sprawled on bar seats or leaned, huge and provocative above her head.

Gracious! thought Mrs Bellamy. The drink! She had been too carried away to recollect the purpose of the night. The glasses of beer stood ready as rockets behind the bar. Green and white tranquillizers had swiftly dissolved in the alcohol. She carried the glasses round, watching anxiously as the thirsty Lutangans took them to their lips. But down they went. And seconds. How many had Doctor Quainton said were safe? And thirds . . . Mrs Bellamy waddled to the window, opened it a crack and heard to her horror the rumble of more rubber boots and strange expectant cries. The 'GONGO' sign was flashing brilliantly over her outhouses. In its winks she saw the odious Adrian Stride marshalling his women like a Sergeant-Major. As his reinforcements trotted on to the quayside to take up their first defensive positions she saw that they were wearing only little Silken Dalliance aprons and Silken Dalliance hats.

A black host of new Lutangans headed by Major Ngyoto thundered on to the quay and checked in goggling astonishment. They had run three miles across the Downs lured onwards by Martin's signs: 'GONGO AHEAD'. 'I MILE TO YOUR GONGO'.

Mrs Bellamy hastily closed her window and drew the curtains. She looked nervously round at her Lutangans.

Outside she heard the first deep baying as the new troops chased the lady-workers into the yard. But in the bar her Lutangans had their minds only on their jobs. With throats' thirsts slaked, they demonstrated the recovery of other urges and tottered towards the sated Yorkshire ladies yet again.

Mrs Bellamy glanced at the Lieutenant, magnificently dark with sweat. But he was slowly savouring his fourth pint. Perhaps the drug had failed? Sharp cries arose from Mrs Bellamy's outhouses. But the Lieutenant turned heavily to Mrs Bellamy. 'Goodj beer, mad*am*,' he said drowsily. 'And mosh besht Gongo ever, by dam!'

Aidan Stride, believing that Africans only desired fat ladies, had been through his stock like a farmer before market. His heavyweights lined the walls of Mrs Bellamy's tea-room like contenders for a freakish beauty competition. All but Mabel were frightened: rubbery thighs and ballooning breasts quivered, as Major Ngyoto burst in with his revolver extended, backed up by a dozen soldiers.

'All against walls please, dam' quick,' he ordered. There was no movement. 'Ah,' he chuckled, 'you all *is* against the walls already! Good show.' His great eyes roved round the mammiferous range. 'Um,' he laughed, '*Dam*' good show indeed.' His eye fell on Aidan Stride. 'What you do here, fellow?' the Major asked. 'You play Gongo with us?'

'No, sir, thank you,' said Stride nervously.

'Skipper of this side then?'

'That's right, sir.'

'Bang on,' said Major Ngyoto. He examined the fat ladies closely, and made a little moue of distaste. He said to Stride, 'Actually, old boy, I prefer ladies model-type – dam' thin. Fallen into bad white tastes, what!' He guffawed with laughter. 'Any more younger chicks?'

'We have all sorts here,' said Stride, eager as a Mayor with visiting Royalty. 'If you'll follow me.'

The Major re-holstered his revolver, and used his smart leather-covered cane to prod, probe and flick aside the aprons. He said over his shoulder to Stride, 'Officers take first crack at Gongo. Open my innings with these, old boy.' He selected three slim young blondes.

'You virgin-girl?' he asked hopefully. They shook their heads. He complained, 'Where does a chap find virgin-girl in the UK now?'

Stride, with ears cocked for sounds from the bar, led the Major and his young ladies into Mrs Bellamy's parlour. He bowed Major Ngyoto in. The Major paused on the threshold. 'Good officer sees men fed first. Man-management at Sandhurst – part of a good show.'

He issued sharp orders and his men began to swarm towards the work-ladies like bees into honey-combs, tearing off their uniforms as they ran.

'Good show, skipper,' said Major Ngyoto, 'Gongo innings has begun. Let's hope no batsman retired hurt, eh?' He laughed uproariously. 'Bowled middle stump, skipper.' He drew his three young girls close together to explain their special duties. Stride could see they were surprised by the Major's requirements but they began willingly to undress him.

Major Ngyoto shouted out over their heads, 'Bring beer for my chaps at half-time, will you, skipper,' and lay back on Mrs Bellamy's sofa. The girls moved over him in an interesting tangle of heads and tails.

Stride beckoned to those ladies not engaged and raised his hand to his lips. Stepping carefully over the copulating couples, the girls carried round the doctored drinks.

Stride entered the parlour with a jug and glass for Major Ngyoto. 'Half-time already, skipper?' asked the Major, boisterously surfacing like a seal between two pairs of white legs. 'Change ends, eh?' His revolver and whistle lay on the table. 'Put the booze there, old boy,' said Major Ngyoto, starting to sink again beneath pink buttocks.

'A beer now, Major. To drink to your health and to good Gongo,' Stride suggested urgently, extending a foaming glass. He was in terror of the violence of these mighty Africans. But he had struck the right chord: Major Ngyoto was a polite man. His face reappeared again like a prune in a bowl of Turkish Delight. Then his arm and hand, darkly sinuous as a mamba, writhed out and took the glass. 'Quite right, skipper,' he said, 'bottoms up.'

# 29

At 0330 hours Major Abbot dispatched his Leaders. Files of armed men crept from the woods and down the dark hedgerows leading back into East Pym. Lt Downley had properly posted his sentries, and Abbot knew they would be on duty till 4 A.M. By now, after three and a half hours of night-watching in an empty English village, they would be bored, cold, weary and off-guard.

A breeze slapped at the doors and windows left open by the soldiery. The sentries, jumpy at first, had grown accustomed to these trivial rattles of the night. The Defenders stole into their cottage backgardens, into their graveyard, into the pub's small carpark, into the backs of their farmyards and their barns. In twenty minutes three hundred men who knew each crunching path and squeaking stone were emplaced in upper-windows and on roofs overlooking the Green. To the east over the sea the base of the indigo sky was lightening in palest lime. It was possible to pick out huddles of soldiers snugly sleeping on the Green.

Sandy Potts and Flighty Wing scurrying along with their 2-in. mortars reached their positions commanding the other two corners. Abbot crouched behind the battlements on the church tower. He heard the old clock wheeze beneath him. He checked his mortar and looked down at the pile of shells. The great clock gave a long sigh and began to strike. One, it tolled. Two . . . three . . . At the brink of the fourth note Abbot dropped the first shell into the mortar and a white magnesium parachute-flare soared up high over the Green. Wing's and Potts' mortars rocketed up almost simultaneously from the two far corners. The three dazzling flares, langourously suspended below their parachutes, cast down a vast brilliant radiance all over the Green. Soldiers, like startled ants panicked by the sun, scrabbled about bewilderedly. They gawped outwards peering into the dark. Abbot's hunting-horn rang out. From all sides of the Green three hundred shotguns fired instantaneously across the open space.

The soldiers were hooped in a ring of flashing fire. The noise had been deafening, and its extent terrifying. Blinking in the brightness they swung round and round trying to penetrate in the darkness the source of the barrage. As the shots whistled over their heads like driven hail, Abbot's voice bellowed through his loud-hailer: 'Three hundred guns are trained on you! The next barrel will *kill* you. Drop your weapons *now*!'

The soldiers paused, awaiting orders, but Lt Downley was silent. He had been dozing, saddened to have met no opposition against which to pit his skill and make his name. He had been woken by an encircling crash of gunfire, the scream of shot, and now it seemed the voice of God was booming His orders from His own church tower. Downley's mind did not race, as those of heroes are supposed to do in peril. It felt numb, heavy, full of cold glue.

Then Potts' voice roared from the opposite roof top. 'You are surrounded! Drop your weapons *now*!'

Across the Green Wing bawled through his loud-speaker: 'You can't escape. Drop all weapons *now*!'

The heads of the soldiers, like those of some naughty Old Testament tribe in trouble from Jehovah, twisted from one voice to another. Then Abbot's voice boomed out again: 'Officer in charge! You have ten seconds only to surrender.' He blew his horn.

As rehearsed, all the three hundred men opened and shut their shotguns' breeches with a rattle which ran round the village like a giant grinding its teeth. The horn twanged again. Then all three hundred voices yelled in tremendous chorus: 'Surrender!'

Lt Downley still hesitated. But the roaring voices all round were too much for the younger soldiers. 'It's a killing-ground!' one shrieked and, dropping his rifle, darted in snipish zig-zags towards the helicopters. 'It's a killing-ground!' screeched another twenty-year-old with only a few months more to serve and a pregnant wife in Nottingham. 'They'll kill us here!'

Sergeant Muldoon's voice bellowed, 'Stop! Hamilton! Stop! Scratchit! You lousy cowards!'

But it was too late. A dozen other troopers needed only one example of discretion. Flinging their arms aside in their corners of the Green they rushed back towards the helicopters, knocking their sergeants aside and bowling over the gawping Lt Downley.

'Officer in charge!' boomed Major Abbot. 'I am about to give the order to fire.'

'Surrender!' shouted Lt Downley breathlessly, for he was still prostrate and immobile and under the direct gaze of the man with the terrifying shout. 'All surrender!' He was unsure of the proper words of command: surrendering was not taught at Sandhurst. 'Put down your arms!' The rest of his soldiers, most eagerly, some with feigned reluctance, and a few with disgust, dropped their weapons.

'Stand where you are!' boomed Major Abbot's voice.

His horn now thrillingly blew the huntsman's 'Gone Away' and the hundred horsemen held in reserve on Church Hay, swept round the church, and galloped down on to the Green. They seemed at first to be carrying lances at the charge but as they thundered closer the magnesium flares showed that these were wicked pitch-forks. Twin tines hooked and brightly polished came rushing towards the soldiers' bellies and kidneys. 'Aar-raarharrh!' roared the cavalry, swooping down and round the soldiers as if they were rounding up heifers. The horses lined the edges. The pitchforks were levelled at the soldiers' bowels. The Defenders swarmed down from the cottages to seize their discarded weapons, and the outposts down the two lanes, left without orders and aware of panic, trotted back to join their comrades on the Green.

A few disarmed soldiers started to sneak towards the helicopters, but old Wilkinson's troop of horsemen galloped in and cut off their retreat.

Sgt Muldoon's voice cried, 'Mr Downley, sor. 'Tis a bloody shambles. Shan't I form the men up, sor?'

'Form up . . . ?' Probably that was right. 'Thank you, Sgt Muldoon. Carry on, please.'

Sgt Muldoon took over and the troopers, delighted to be instructed again, fell in smartly, right-dressed, eyes-fronted and stood to attention in front of the helicopters.

The horsemen trotted about in the background laugh-ing. Major Abbot came through the crowd and climbed on to the steps of the War Memorial. The white flares were drifting away down wind. Their dazzle faded and left long quivering shadows. But dawn suffused the village in watered gold. 'Three cheers for the Vale of Hampden,' bellowed Major Abbot, as if after a school match. 'Hip-hip – !'

'Hooray!' roared back the Defenders. 'Hooray! Hooray!'

'And now,' Major Abbot called out, 'would you take our guests back with you for a little nourishment. We have no quarrel with *them*, after all.' To set an example he shook young Lt Downley by the hand. 'Abbot,' he

230

said, 'Aston Abbot, formerly of the 7th/10th. I dare say you'd like a hot bath. My place is just down the road.'

It had after all, thought the soldiers with relief, just been a sort of exercise. There was Drippy Downley chatting with this ex-Army type. Only the sergeants stood around uneasily, muttering to one another. Major Abbot approached the group and peered at their faces in the light of his torch. 'Corporal Muldoon!' he exclaimed, 'Aden, wasn't it?'

'Thought it sounded like your voice, sor,' said Sgt Muldoon, coming to attention, 'Major Abbot, isn't it now?'

They shook hands. Abbot said, 'Ah, *Sergeant* now, I see. Well done.'

Sgt Muldoon said, 'You made right fools of us, sor, I must say.' He lowered his voice. 'But to tell you the truth, Major, the hearts of my boys weren't in it at all. They need a few bombs flung at 'em, you know, to get 'em fightin'.'

Major Abbot was magnanimous. He had won his battle. 'Ah, well, having something to fight for makes all the difference.'

'You're right there, Major. You wouldn't be shifted, and who's to blame you?'

Major Abbot grinned like a dog and vigorously shook the Sergeant's hand again. Victory lofted him up like a god. He said to Sgt Muldoon, 'I heard Sir John Betjeman, dear old man, talking on the television about preserving our country. And he said, "There's part of yourself that *needs* what's been there always." We know what he means.'

'And so do I, sor,' said Sergeant Muldoon.

# 30

As dawn flooded across the sea, Martin, Sandford and his Dozen and Owen and his fishermen peered into Mrs Bellamy's outhouses, Bar and parlour. The floors were covered with the comatose bodies of the Lutangan Company. Sometimes a leg twitched, sometimes a head lolled, but that was all. They lay, in knotted piles of splendid black gleaming bodies, fast asleep. Only Major Ngyoto had tried, as the sedative overcame him in Mrs Bellamy's parlour, to reach his equipment. He lay spread-eagled on the sofa, arm outstretched and finger pointing like Michelangelo's Adam on the Sistine Chapel's ceiling.

The Yorkshire wives had long since staggered back to Sea View, all, bar Mrs Ethel Birtwistle, twittering with consciences and shame. Some had endured moments of real terror, for the drug had struck suddenly: pulsing living bodies hammering into them had collapsed instantly in dead black weights. Two, thinking their mates had died on them and being unable to shift their huge frames had mewed piteously for help.

But Mrs Ethel Birtwistle was gay as a lark. 'Just think of Joe and your ruddy husbands in Brackton's Strip Club,' she said with scorn. 'I've never had a holiday like this in all me born days.' Recollections jerked stiffly through her mind like an old movie. How many times had she been mounted? After a dozen she had ceased to count. She nodded off and dozed.

Mrs Bellamy, though weary, was on hand clean and neatly dressed to let in Martin's party.

The fishermen unfurled neat coils of rope, turned the

Lutangans on to their bellies, noosed their hands together, and then tied their feet. Some of the Lutangans resisted feebly and grumbled, like children being moved at night, but in ten minutes the whole company was neatly trussed.

Mrs Bellamy and Aidan Stride were sitting round her parlour table calculating the division of fees. In the backyard a bevy of work ladies, clad only in their aprons and looking mauled, were lobbing the Lutangans' clothing on to a bonfire.

Stride was pressing Mrs Bellamy with the case for fees for bystanders. 'Weren't their fault they weren't laid, Mrs B. *And* they handed out the doped drinks.'

Sandford stood out for stud fees only. Stride sulked. Mrs Bellamy bowed. Behind her snored the huge form of Major Ngyoto. The Lutangan's pink tongue lolled. He smiled happily in his dreams, and one of his three slim blonde ladies still sat by his side caressing him lovingly. Her eyes were glazed. She had taken a mouthful of his beer.

Martin walked into the parlour. 'What about their clothes, Mr Stride?'

'Hygiene regs, Stewkly. Can't afford health risks in my factory.'

'But we can't send them home naked.'

'Why not?' asked Stride malevolently. 'They wear no clothes back home.'

'But it's *warm* in Lutanga,' Martin protested.

Sandford said, 'They'll freeze to death.'

'OK,' said Stride, 'they'll wear our aprons and our caps with brand-name. It'll push our product, see?'

So it was that in the morning sun the bos'n and mate of the LCI were hailed from Easterly's harbour-wall to take off a company of drugged Lutangans wearing only Silken Dalliance aprons and little Silken Dalliance hats. The

Africans stumbled into the LCI and immediately dropped off to sleep again. The bos'n recovered himself to ask, 'Their arms and ammunition? Surely – ?'

Martin said authoritatively, 'We've taken charge of them, thank you.'

'Shouldn't I have a chitty for 'em, sir?' asked the bos'n politely.

'Nonsense. You were only told to bring the men, weren't you? They're not on your strength. What's more you've got sixty extra, too, so the First Sea Lord will be delighted.'

The mad service logic appeased the bos'n. Owen cast off and the LCI went astern. 'What was it, sir?' inquired the mate, waving his head over the recumbent Lutangans.

'Sort of fertility rite,' shouted Martin as the LCI pulled away. 'They've had a marvellous time, thank you.'

# 31

At 0400 hours Major Frank Radnage with the remainder of his squadron including six Ferret armoured scout cars was en route for the broken bridge. He had collected from Brackton's outskirts the RE Troop of bridge-laying tanks and special bridging unit. The grinding and clatter of the tank-tracks along the Brackton to Easterly road filled the night, drowning the volley of gun-fire at East Pym.

Radnage had called up Lt Downley two hours earlier as arranged: all was perfectly quiet in East Pym. Radnage had said, 'We make the river crossing at 0700.' He felt at ease. Operation Snuffbox proceeded smoothly. There had been no sound of fighting from Easterly where the Lutangans had been due at midnight. They were not in radio communication for Major Ngyoto had disarmingly confessed, 'Never use the old wireless box below Brigade level, old boy. Better for chaps to bash on regardless.'

When Charles Stewkly heard the convoy of tanks and armoured cars he knew for a certainty that the bridge and not the cutting was to be the Army's main objective. He had only a slight screen of armed men in the woods behind the river. He dispatched Pete to gallop across country to ask Cubbington if he could spare reinforcements. But the Army's feint against the cutting was also in action. Just before 4 A.M. the RE bulldozers and cranes started to clank along the lane from Brackton towards the blocked cutting. Cubbington too had only a few Defenders. Convinced that his ridge was about to be assaulted, he firmly refused Stewkly's request. He said to

Pete, 'But Major Abbot's got three hundred men round East Pym. They'll be free when he springs his trap.'

Pete said, 'But we can't reach him, sir. Otherwise we'd alert the soldiers, see?'

'Can't spare a soul,' said Cubbington testily. 'Listen to that.' Down in the plain the RE vehicles were kicking up a praiseworthy shindy. Pete rode back along Hampden Heights and as he cantered eastwards along the bridle-path through the woods he heard the rumble of the Army convoy beyond the river. He galloped on to report back to Charles Stewkly.

At first light Stewkly saw the armoured Ferrets approach the broken bridge and deploy cautiously either side of it, fearing the marshy ground. They were still painted sand-colour from their Arabian campaign and stood out boldly. They made no attempt to move into hull-down defensive positions. Three halted in line abreast upstream of the bridge; the other three below it. They presented a battery a quarter of a mile wide. As Stewkly was gazing at them, wondering what they would do, they all suddenly fired their mortars. An arc of shells whistled up against the pewter sky.

'Down! Get down!' shouted Stewkly, but the scout-cars fired another salvo. They were firing not high-explosive shells but CS gas. The canisters crashed into the beech branches overhead: the gas burst out. The southerly breeze caught it and swirled it into the wood and up the slope. 'Back!' shouted Charles Stewkly. 'Back up the hill!' His eyes were already burning and his lungs stung. He saw the rising sun's rays touch Major Radnage in his scout-car. The Major was standing up casually in the turret and looking along the wood through field-glasses. He raised the microphone to his lips again and the Ferrets fired their mortars again. This time at shorter range six, then another six shells lobbed over the river

236

and fell in the fringe of the wood. White smoke billowed out. Like a thick sea-fog it rolled into the trees. The river, the bridge and everything beyond it were totally obscured.

Charles Stewkly, cursing his lame leg, dragged himself back up the slope, shouting to the villagers: 'To the ridge! It'll be better behind the ridge.' Above the crackling of their feet in the forest and their coughing and choking, the noise of the bridge-laying tanks could be heard clearly behind the smoke-screen.

The Defenders were still only half-way back to the ridge when the Ferrets fired another round of CS gas, followed by further smoke-shells. The others had run ahead of old Mr Stewkly and disappeared in the swirling biting fog, and it was quieter around him. He stuffed his silk handkerchief with bracken, clapped it over his mouth and nose, shut his eyes and listened. He heard the tanks' tracks on the road below, squeaking and clanking. Their engines raced. Gears whined, then heavy metal banged, swinging down on stone. The breeze which brought in the choking gas and smoke now bore upon it something worse: a small military cheer of victory rose from the bridge.

Charles Stewkly pressed his face to the ground, for the warmth of it made the gas lift. Now the scout-cars will come, he thought, and that will be that. He began to cough. When the bout subsided he heard the Ferrets beyond the river grinding back on to the road to cross their new steel bridge.

'Quick, quick,' he called back up the hill, but his voice was hoarse and thin. He struggled to his feet. The clouds blowing past him made him dizzy. He saw figures, shadowy in the billowing fog. Mr Potter from the village stores, young Dr Quainton and Patricia Fernden materialized and hauled him up.

'Get him out of here,' said Bill Quainton.

'No,' gasped Charles Stewkly desperately. 'To the road, for God's sake!' He started off towards it. Then he heard the Ferrets' wheels clanking over the bridge a quarter of a mile below them. 'There,' he wheezed, 'they've crossed it.' He coughed. 'We must get on to the road.'

The gas and smoke were thinning. They could see the low ridge. Heads of the villagers appeared. 'Come *on*!' cried Charles Stewkly, urgently waving them towards the road. They were shouting against the breeze. The words 'Abbot', 'East Pym', wafted through. He said to Dr Quainton, 'Run back. Get me a flag and six men. We'll stand in the road.'

He could dimly discern the scout-cars crawling slowly up the rise. From behind Stewkly on the ridge the crowd from East Pym continued to approach.

Major Radnage leaned forward from the turret of the leading Ferret. He was holding a megaphone. He shouted firmly, 'Let us through, please. We are coming through.'

Pete appeared racing down the road ahead of the crowd with the flag of St George outstretched. 'They've done it, sir,' he gasped. 'The Major's bloody done it. Got the whole ruddy lot in the village.'

'Everyone?' asked Charles Stewkly, 'And no fighting?'

'Everybody,' said Pete. 'And two helicopters.'

'And no one hurt?' asked Mr Stewkly.

Pete shook his head. 'And all their arms!' Charles Stewkly wanted to kneel down out of relief and gratitude and justified faith in good things. He closed his eyes, then took the flag from Pete and stood firmly in the middle of the road. The mob of villagers on the ridge behind him began to run down towards him babbling of the victory. The scout-cars kept edging on towards him. 'Stop!' shouted Mr Stewkly, but his voice was very faint.

'Stop . . . our land . . . the others . . .' His voice was drowned by the running feet and the shouts behind him.

'Clear the road!' shouted Major Radnage. His scout-car was only a hundred yards from Stewkly and still approaching steadily.

Someone from the wood fired at him. The pellets rattled against the scout-car's armoured flanks. Radnage ducked down inside.

'No!' called Mr Stewkly into the wood. 'Don't fire. Not that way. We must beat 'em without that.' He doubled over coughing, then raised his standard up.

The throng behind his back reached him cheering and clapping. They were thrust forward from behind by the onrush of the victors of East Pym. 'Look out!' someone screamed.

Stewkly turned back from their congratulations. The leading scout-car was upon him. As he turned he slipped. He saw a slice of the driver's face in its armoured porthole, a blur of white numbers, and a great black bullet-proof wheel.

The wheel struck him, bit into his chest and crushed his ribs like twigs. The fractured ends pierced his lungs. Charles Stewkly's legs jerked out frantically like a puppet's. The black front wheel pulverized his pelvis, snapping his spinal column. The scout-car stopped. Major Radnage's appalled face reappeared above the turret. 'My God, you may have – ' he began. He looked down. Old Mr Stewkly's body lay between his wheels. Radnage leapt out, shouting to the scout-cars behind him, 'Quick, all out! Help me here! We've run over a man!' His troopers behind scrambled out of the other five Ferrets and ran towards the crowd round Stewkly.

Major Radnage and Dr Quainton were bending over him. The doctor looked up and said something.

'Dead,' repeated Major Radnage, like a leaden bell. It was the last thing he wanted.

'He's dead.'.The words rustled back through the crowd, like the wind through the top of a wheatfield. 'Old Stewkly's dead.' Heads turned and whispered. The words reached the back of the crowd where the victors of East Pym were still cheering. The cheering ceased. 'Dead . . . dead . . .' muttered the crowd. Its vanguard had flowed on past the six empty scout-cars and engulfed them. The troopers were round Major Radnage's Ferret trying to extricate Charles Stewkly's body by levering up the wheel. But the thing weighed over five tons. All the smoke had vanished. The sun shone brilliantly. The soldiers, suddenly conscious of menace, looked up. Four hundred villagers surrounded them. The crowd inhaled a long moaning sigh like a storm in angry mountains.

A terrible rumble passed through them. They moved towards the soldiers. 'Kill 'em . . .' the crowd murmured. 'We'll kill 'em . . .' the crowd vowed. 'Kill 'em . . . !' the crowd shouted. 'We'll string 'em up!'

At the back of the crowd, enclosed by the villagers were the prisoners from the battle of East Pym. Lt Downley, his sergeants and his men heard the noise of the crowd around them suddenly alter. Hostility stung the air like serpents.

Martin riding back with Sandford from Easterly galloped forward. He had seen the column marching up from East Pym on his right and, as he topped the ridge, a new scene was suddenly projected: a mob in the road; six scout-cars crawling forward; ahead, an approaching crowd; and between the two, a little lame stooping figure with a banner.

He saw the crowd and the scout-cars squeeze together. The banner toppled and went down. His voice called out from the edge of the wood. 'Is it my father? Have they killed him?' He heard the murmur of grief rush backwards through the crowd towards him. He pressed his horse on through them, peering ahead. First the people cursed him for pushing them, then when they turned their heads and saw who he was, sadness sprang to their eyes and they looked away, and he knew from their look that his father was dead. He passed more easily through the heart of the crowd and was engulfed by the shouts of 'Kill them! Hang them!'

'No!' cried Martin, 'No!' He started to fight his way through to his father. He reached the first scout-car's flank and slid from his saddle on to its turret. '*Please*,' he cried in anguish. 'No more. Please leave them. Please.'

He leaned over the side of the scout-car and looked down into the road. There lay his father like a beetle. His stick lay to one side, the broken banner on the other. His glasses, cracked, twinkled on the tarmac. The doctor was there, and young Pete and Patricia Fernden all murmuring to him. Their faces looked suddenly closer to him and blurry as if they were looking out on him through wet winter windows. He squeezed his eyelids tightly down. Something huge, hot and red was swelling between his lungs. It burst. It flowed up through his throat and burst out in a long groan. He found he was kneeling on the road by his father's body. He said, 'They can't move this car.'

Dr Quainton muttered something.

'They can't move it, for Christ's sake,' shouted Martin. 'They can't move it without touching him again.' He jumped up. 'Get them out of here! Back over the bridge!'

The crowd began to rumble again. Martin climbed on to the scout-car. Sandford was there now. And Abbot. Both hauled him up and supported him. Sandford handed him Major Radnage's megaphone. Martin shouted out: 'Put the soldiers through and over the bridge and away

with them. We want nothing to do with them. Nothing.'
He stopped. He put down the megaphone. It bumped
against his knee. He could think of nothing else. He saw
grief and apprehension in the soldiers' faces. He said to
them: 'Go very quickly and take up the bridge behind
you.' He sat down on the turret heavily. His legs and
arms and head felt filled with lead, but his body was like
a numbed light balloon between them.

Major Abbot said to Radnage, 'Get your men out of
here on foot double-quick. I don't answer for what we'll
do to them, otherwise. Get up here and tell them.'

Major Radnage climbed up on to the scout-car. When
the crowd saw his uniform an awful howl ululated through
them: 'Murderer! Murderer!'

Abbot grabbed the megaphone. 'No,' he shouted, 'It
was an accident. We have told the soldiers to go. Just let
them through. They have surrendered. They mustn't be
hurt. Their commanding officer will order them now to
retreat.' He thrust the megaphone at Major Radnage.

The Major looked up towards the ridge and saw the
khaki huddle of his troops from East Pym. He shouted:
'Lieutenant Downley and your two Troops. Retire quickly
and quietly to join me and No. 3 Troop beyond the
bridge. Move now.' He saw the hesitation. He called out.
'You won't be attacked. Major Abbot has assured me.'
The soldiers started to edge forward nervously, but the
crowd made way. When he saw them moving, Major
Radnage put his hand quickly on to Martin's shoulder,
and said, 'I am so sorry. So very sorry. You must know
– '

Martin glanced up and nodded. 'Not your fault. No
one's fault *here*. Just the Government's in the long run, I
suppose.' He added, 'He was awfully lame, you know,'
and suddenly tears spurted.

Major Radnage slid off the back of the scout-car, and joined his two Troops.

Aston Abbot shouted, 'I want a protective escort for the prisoners. Two Dozens up here, please, to marshal them through.'

The crowd writhed as escorts and soldiers extricated themselves. The villagers got on to the verges under the trees. Behind the last scout-car, Lt Downley's party joined Major Radnage's Squadron, fell in, turned righ' and marched away downhill. Dozens of the Defende screened their flanks and rear. The soldiers reached the bridge. Their boots clanked across it. They halted beyon it. Aston Abbot saw Radnage talking to the RE Captain. The bridging tanks lumbered forward. Their cranes came down. The sappers milled around. The bridge sections started to come away.

Wilkinson had come with a sheep hurdle. Martin put his arm under his father's shoulders and started to ease him on to it. But the body felt jointless. The thin broken legs dangled horribly. Martin's face screwed itself up involuntarily as he slid his arm under his father's knees and lifted the body up. Either his father was so light (he had never carried him before) or an excess of nervous strength hoisted Martin's arms, for the small body suddenly shot up head high, as if Martin was presenting it to the people. A low moan ebbed through from the crowd. Martin lowered his father on to the hurdle. Wilkinson, Pete, Abbot took the other corners. His father's body weighed so little, he had to hold one slipping shoulder down. They began to carry him back towards East Pym. The crowd parted to let them through. A few hats came off. Some elderly women crossed themselves. The villagers fell in behind them in a drove.

When the procession reached the ridge they looked back down the slope to the river. The Army's bridge had gone. The Army had vanished. The concourse went slowly on down the road to East Pym. There was quiet talking and a shuffling of 800 feet. Because autumn leaves had fallen on the road and it was dry, a cloud of powdered leaf-dust was stirred up by the feet. It hung in the air behind them. Then it drifted away over the cold ploughed fields and came to rest on the earth.

# Part Three

# 32

The Prime Minister spoke to the nation the evening Charles Stewkly was buried in East Pym graveyard. The day had dawned too bright to last: rainclouds in drifting ridges bowled over Hampden Heights and the River Sedge and the wind set the red crosses flapping on the half-masted flags.

The Vale of Hampden celebrated its first martyr on that boisterous October day. The Stewklys in Meadow Hill had a gap at the head of the dining-room table, a bed which did not need making, hats and coats hanging uselessly in the gun-room, and clothes for the laundry which need not come back. So far Mary Stewkly had surprised her son: she had accepted the death, survived the funeral, coped with arrangements and talked with friends.

No one outside could get into the area to attend the funeral, and there were no letters and no papers. Mrs Stewkly did not know that her husband's death had been on the front pages with the pictures of the Army's surrendered squadron marching out. His name was no longer alive only in the minds of the locals; it was on the lips of editors, politicians, Ministers and of twenty million unknown men and women in the streets of distant cities.

Few widows of countrymen see their dead accorded the praise they merit. Had Mary Stewkly known, the recognition would have astonished her.

Ancilla had helped her and helped Martin. Her own grief had been so enormous that Martin was surprised. He knew how fond she had been of his father – 'like one

247

I wanted, so of course I loved him,' but he had not expected her to be shattered. She said, 'I've lost something more.' He was astonished that she took care of his mother and himself. 'We don't deserve it from you.'

Ancilla changed direction. 'I don't think Mrs Cubbington and Co. are right, darling: your mother's not *taut*. It's more as if she'd been expecting him to die for years.'

'Because he wasn't strong?'

'Well, that *prepared* her. But I think she foresaw that all his preparations for this . . . defiance, this defence would end in his death. She was so calm about it all, about me, about the food.'

'She'd absorbed it all in the strangest way.'

'And him going to die, too.'

'She's very strong,' said Martin, 'in her bumbly way. But you've been a marvellous prop.'

When everyone had gone and there were only the three of them at Meadow Hill, Martin feared the worst. But his mother and Ancilla made scrambled-eggs in the kitchen, and he brought wood into the sitting-room and stacked the fire high. The empty chair in front of the television did mourn at them, but Mary Stewkly went into the gun-room and collected Charles's gardening coat. Things rattled in the pockets: a glossy chestnut, dog-whistle, spare car-key, a ·410 cartridge, a ticket from Brackton Car Park, some Green Shield Stamps from the Easterly garage. 'Oh, here's Jane's collar,' said Mrs Stewkly. There was an old handkerchief too. She popped it in the fire. It fizzled up brightly. She shook out the old tweed coat, folded it, and put it in his chair. Then she patted it, said to her Jack Russell bitch, 'Up then, Jane.' The dog sniffed at the coat, hopped up, circled to make a nest and settled down in a brown and white ball. One amber eye looked warily out: she had only been allowed in that chair before on Charles Stewkly's knee.

'D'you want to listen to the Prime Minister?' asked Ancilla doubtfully. She could not bring herself in that house now to utter his name.

Mrs Stewkly was busy knitting, but she said, 'Oh yes, one should hear what awful *webs* he's weaving.' It was as if she was teasing Charles by mimicking him. Martin grinned at her and she smiled back. He thought, people don't end. They go on in the rest of us. And when I have children . . . He was sitting on the floor between her chair and Ancilla on the sofa. He felt suddenly flushed with happiness, as if truth or something very like it was glowing at the end of a tunnel. He looked up at Ancilla, beaming.

Plain George Robinson's 'Man-to-Man' began with a long-shot of him strolling in tweeds in the garden at Chequers, a Labrador gambolling ahead. He was wearing what he imagined were sensible country shoes, but they were too thin and clean and polished.

His voice, pre-recorded, came over explaining the Hampden situation, as he stooped to sniff at a last rose in a bare bed, and stared sadly out over the golden Chiltern woods.

'Cunning pig!' Martin exploded. 'And God Almighty, he's even borrowed a farmer's stick!'

Ancilla said rather hesitantly, 'I'm afraid he's hired the dog, too.'

Martin looked round and up at her: she was having difficulty in remaining serious. He gave her ankle a loving squeeze, in which there was no sex at all, but a swirl of gratitude, humour and that rare thing, fondness.

Mrs Stewkly said, 'Charles always said one must never trust townees when they ape rustics, because they really despise us.'

'They do think we're stupider,' said Martin. 'It's a legacy from pre-TV peasants.' He was relieved how easily

249

his mother seemed to be thinking of his father in the past tense.

The Prime Minister, free of the hired Labrador but still tweedy, now faced them from the impressive fireplace in the hall at Chequers. He had completed his situation report over his garden stroll. He sat in a winged chair and tapped his pipe sharply out on the hearth. His profile obscured his hearing-aid and his long white locks flopped forward. He had contrived precisely the right mixture of regret and resolution. The tapping staccato pipe marked the start of the second and brisker movement.

'*But in a democracy like ours,*' declared the Prime Minister, '*we can't allow the will of a few rustic and entrenched reactionaries to obstruct the wishes of the rest of us. We have walked delicately in the Vale of Hampden. Probably too delicately. But I'll come to that. We've not threatened these unhappy people with force. We've given 'em incentives and time. That's come out of all our pockets, remember.*' He tapped his trousers, implying a personal contribution to the unaccepted Compensation Fund.

'*How have they reacted? With equal consideration? Let me tell you, my friends –* ' (the Prime Minister with manifest dishonesty stared into the camera's revealing eye) '*They have, under their unscrupulous leaders, replied to our open-handedness with traps, and bandits' snares and mean fascist brutality.*'

Mrs Stewkly exclaimed, 'Oh!' and put down her knitting. She had gone quite pink. Martin said, 'Mother, don't mind what he says. He's a bloody liar. Everyone knows – ' He realized Ancilla was staring at him. He stopped awkwardly.

The Prime Minister was continuing . . .

'*. . . loyal allies from the Commonwealth holding out the hand of friendship, dishonourably drugged.*' Plain George cleared his throat. Ancilla knew he was going to make one of his rehearsed impromptus. '*And from what I hear, my friends, the morals in that agricultural neck of the woods are no better than those of their animals. Worse, in fact. The Commanding Officer of the Lutanga Presidential Bodyguard returned, I may tell you, deeply shocked. The harm that'll do to us in Africa is anybody's guess.*'

Martin could not suppress a hoot of laughter, but his mother still sat very stiffly. He looked round at Ancilla: she was scarlet.

'*But the whole resistance up there,*' continued the Prime Minister smoothly, '*has been conducted, as you might expect, on the squalid level of street gangs. For example, a wretched widow from my staff was lured into the area to be sexually threatened by a gang of motor-cycle thugs.*

'*Happily the youths, seeing the errors of their ways, decided to help the police with their inquiries. They are now outside the Vale of Hampden and in custody. The unhappy widow, who had had of course no access to any confidential matters, is still being held prisoner by*' – he spat out the words – '*by those self-styled gentlemen.*'

'Oh God!' Ancilla burst out. 'That's too bloody much.'

The Prime Minister rose magisterially and took up a manly stance before the fireplace. The cameras followed him up smoothly but did not zoom in too soon for close-up, for Plain George, after movement, needed time to compose his features into sincerity. He continued gruffly, '*A lot of you may have been saying – like good Britons – that we have been too easy with these immoral gangsters. And you are right.*' The camera now moved in. The Prime Minister looked boldly at it. '*Some of the minds which should have quickly snuffed out this nonsense*' (he pinched his fingers as if on a candle's flame) '*have grown negligent and tired.*'

'Someone's for the chop,' said Ancilla quickly.

The Prime Minister continued, '*I have therefore thought it necessary to dismiss the Chief Constable of the County of Brackton, a retired Brigadier whose background did not perhaps inspire the modern . . .*'

'Always envied and hated soldiers and athletes,' said Ancilla.

'*. . . and I must also tell you,*' went on the Prime Minister smoothly, '*that the Home Secretary, feeling responsible for the general situation, has tendered his resignation, and this I have – er – accepted.*'

'He's crazy!' exclaimed Ancilla.

'*I shall for the time being take up the reins at the Home Office myself.*'

'That's his last friend gone,' Ancilla said.

Mrs Stewkly got up. She was walking briskly to the door. Martin went after her. Her eyes were wet. She said, 'Is it surprising that England's so sick, when we have little lying men like that in charge? I'm going to bed, Martin.' She went out.

It was well that she did so, for the Prime Minister was going on, '*and in the mob one of the gangsters' leaders – a landowner called Stewkly – attacked one scout-car and was fatally injured. He has I hear been made something of a hero in his village. But we in Great Britain know how to rate these petty mobsters.*'

Martin was still standing by the door, his face as pale as cheese. But his eyes flamed. Ancilla leapt up and ran to him and put her arms round him. 'Darling! Darling, don't listen to him.' She put her hands over his ears. He took them away calmly. 'We'll hear him out,' he said. 'But if I ever saw him, I would try to kill him.'

The voice now unctuous rolled on . . . '*avoid further fatalities the area will be blockaded. It will receive no light, power, food, clothing or comfort from the rest of Britain. In coarse terms – and coarseness is what these louts*

252

*understand – they will stew in their own juice. Those who have had no part in this uprising and who wish to come in from the cold – and it'll be cold there, I tell you my friends – will, if innocent, be welcomed back. But nothing and nobody will pass in. When the remaining ringleaders have been surrendered, the Vale of Hampden will again come within the law. Till then, they are worse than outcasts. They are literally outlaws. But only, I envisage, for a few weeks. Privation quickly brings foolish little people to their senses.'*

The telephone rang. Martin looked at it. It rang and rang. He said, 'I don't think I can, honestly. It must be someone from outside, who doesn't know, who'll ask questions . . .' His voice drifted off and he shrugged.

'I will,' said Ancilla, taking it up. The Prime Minister had concluded. A trailer for flashing-eyed Rupert Bramble's next 'Vision Now' rolled on the screen. Ancilla said to Martin, 'It's Terry something, a journalist.'

'Oh damn, I forgot. Father used to give him a bulletin every evening.' He moved wearily across. 'He's "Our Man in Hampden", you know.'

'Let me.'

'Can you?' He looked dubious, but leaned heavily against the back of the sofa, as if all his bones ached.

'Give me a try,' said Ancilla, 'I want to help you now.'

Martin raised his eyebrows very high like his father.

'OK,' said Ancilla, 'probably I *need* to help.'

Terry Speen asked for comments on the Prime Minister's 'Man-to-Man'. Ancilla took it apart from head to tail like a cat gutting a fish. Martin sat gazing at her.

She was saying . . . 'No, never owned a dog in his life – never a pet of any sort. You'll find the Labrador was hired for the programme from the Chiltern Kennels, Loosely Row 0717 . . . Suggest Defence Correspondents look up the cuttings about the Lutangans' behaviour in

Aldershot . . . Yes, there were some horrid incidents. It's called Gongo . . .' She spelt it. '*The People* ran a good series about it last year . . . Exactly . . . some local women quite bravely lay down with the African troops to stop them attacking the place . . . Of course, it's very different to the PM's angle. You don't expect him suddenly to tell the truth! Well, he's thrown one Minister to the wolves . . . Naked in a boat with aprons and funny hats?' She started to laugh. 'I don't know. I'll check.' Martin nodded, got up, murmured, 'Darling, our new PRO,' and came across and put his arms round her. She was attractively engrossed.

. . . 'The references to "gangsters" are only his vulgar abuse,' said Ancilla sharply. 'You've got their full backgrounds, haven't you? . . . Good . . . Mr Stewkly, particularly . . . No . . . No, of *course* not. You're absolutely right: he was a really good, gentle man, who'd never attack anyone . . . Me? I'm the widow who's meant to have been kidnapped. Another lie . . . Shergrove, Ancilla Shergrove . . . Yes, that's right . . .' She looked round at Martin, and found ridiculously that she was blushing. 'No, *quite* willingly. I'm an old friend of the Stewklys. I very much admired Mr Stewkly . . . You certainly can.' The line went silent. 'Hello . . . Hello . . .' She clicked the buttons up and down. She said angrily, 'Martin, we've been cut off.'

'Dam' right,' said Martin. And all the lights went out.

'He's started,' said Ancilla and giggled.

Martin felt his way past her into the window and peered out towards East Pym and the Hampdens. All lay in total velvet darkness. He came back into the room. 'Where are you, darling?'

'Here.'

He put his arms round her and squeezed her and hugged her. He leaned forward to kiss her, found her cold nose, brought his mouth down on to hers. Her lips opened, and their tongues quivered and met, playing with each other in her mouth and in his. Their feet entwined still touched the invisible carpet, but did not feel it. They were suspended: the dark air drifted past them.

'I'm done for now,' said Ancilla drowsily.

'Yes, but I love you.'

'Oh, I do hope so,' said Ancilla.

'Yes,' said Martin. 'And?'

'Yes.' She kissed him. 'I do, too. Now.'

She thought, but I was right at Cambridge. And: thank God nothing happened to him in Africa. She said, 'It is all very *un*sensible, as my mother would say.'

'It's extraordinary that you should be here.'

'No, it's marvellous luck that I should be here.'

'You *wanted* to be?' Martin was astonished.

'Yes.'

'Without really knowing why?'

'I don't think we ever realize how we nudge our destinies along.'

Martin's head swam in the darkness, which felt as silent and cool as a pool. He grabbed Ancilla's hand again. He thought: when this happens there is a cocoon around you against pain. He said, 'We must get some nightlights.' He thought: perhaps its more of a placenta than a cocoon. When we burst out, that'll be the end of all things snug. He was in a haze of happiness. They looked out of the window again, standing hand in hand. In the cottages and farms pale candles were quivering. Ancilla squeezed Martin's hand. 'Much prettier,' she said. 'It's like a birth, really.'

'I was thinking exactly of that: me in you.'

'And me in you. That *is* love.'

Martin said, 'Outside things may get rather bloody from now on.'

'Yes, but exciting. And I never came here rest-curing.'

They groped down the passage towards the kitchen, and felt their way through the door where Ronald Cubbington years ago had stood on guard against her. It was lighter outside. They saw the outhouse and found candles and nightlights. Martin stuck them extravagantly about. The kitchen glowed. Flickering golden light flooded the hall. Ancilla was going upstairs with a candle for Mrs Stewkly. Ancilla said, 'Hadn't we better go easy with them?'

Martin said, 'Grace Cubbington here, and Sandford over at Long Hampden have been making rushlights from animal fat for a year, you know. We're quite well prepared.'

Mrs Stewkly was deeply sleeping. Martin and Ancilla peered anxiously at her crinkled face against the pillow. The yellow light drained the pink away. Her skin looked like vellum. Her white hair was awry showing her scalp. Martin thought: how could she conceive these things would happen, when she came from Norfolk to marry a country solicitor forty years ago? Yet she looked peaceful. Martin said quietly, 'Women are amazing accepters.'

Ancilla had been watching him with love as he looked tenderly at his mother. She nodded. 'Accepting *is* the character difference.'

'Between men and women?'

'In every way. On every level.'

'Don't men?'

'Real men don't accept.'

Martin considered. 'Perhaps not.' Then, 'Look at the candles.' He moved between his mother's nightlight and the wall. Grotesque shapes aped him across the wallpaper. He grinned wickedly. 'Look! Hunchback. Hideous, Richard III . . . The English have *always* fought like us.'

'Come on,' said Ancilla. They padded down the corridor making the candles swing and leap.

'Look. On my door. Dog's head.' Ancilla made its jaw bark with her fingers and its ears cock with her thumb.

'I could only do the simple butterfly,' Martin fluttered both hands. 'After you.'

They went inside, laughing, and sat on the edge of her bed. Martin said, 'I've never seen you all over by candlelight. It was usually afternoons . . .'

'Yes.'

'We should save my candle if I stayed.'

Ancilla began to undress. 'The good thing about candles is they do *warm* rooms, don't they?'

'You are beautiful.'

'Candlelight. It's the famous flatterer.'

'No. You are beautiful . . .'

She was naked. Her skin glowed and flickered. She said, 'Beautiful is far too *good* a word.'

He leaned across and stroked her stomach. 'Like a petal,' he whispered. 'Not lustful. Lovable.' He stroked her very lightly again with his finger-tips. She shivered.

'Haven't you seen enough of me?'

'One never has – if you love someone. Staring's like loving.'

'Insatiable?'

'Turn around in the light. There.' Ancilla stopped sideways. 'Now look at your shadow, darling.'

Ancilla slowly turned her head and smiled. She said, 'Well, I do look rather good.' She put her fingers under her breasts so that her elbows stood out like wings and stroked upwards.

'Don't.' Martin stopped undressing.

'Why?'

'It looks like someone else doing it to you.'

Ancilla turned quickly and got into bed. She snuggled

right down so that just her nose showed. 'Aren't you coming in?' she asked in a muffled voice.

Martin slid in.

'You're cold, love,' she said.

Martin said, 'I can't bear the idea of that man.'

'Him particularly?'

'Him. Particularly.'

She did not answer. Martin went on, 'I don't mind others so much. How can I? But he's such a phoney. Such a shit, love. Honestly. Like tonight. Destroying *anyone* to help himself.'

She lay on her back. Martin could see her eye shining. She said, 'Yes, it was awful tonight.'

'But he must always be like that.'

Ancilla said something. 'What?' asked Martin.

'Perhaps he is,' she repeated. 'But if you're a woman living with someone, you do grow to see life through their eyes. If you admire them.'

'Did you?'

'Yes. I saw things almost totally through him.'

'Odd. For you.'

'Hell, I was only twenty-nine when I met him, wasn't I? And then I worked for him, lived there: it was my life both ways – far more than a wife's. Yes, I did admire him. I had to. To *get* to be Prime Minister is admirable, for God's sake! It was thrilling to be at the centre of goings-on which the millions of the world only read about.'

'Of course,' said Martin sourly. 'A seat on the stage.' But he had noticed the word 'was'.

'To hear the problems *first*. And, when decisions were being made, to see the men making them.' She turned full-face to Martin willing him to understand. He nodded. Ancilla went on, 'I can't admire him now. After how he's acted and what he's said. Things are quite altered. Not just you: that was later. But being here – from this angle. Admiring your father. Discovering what you all felt and were doing. Seeing that thing one's always taught and never learns: seeing "The Other Side". Martin, it's the first time for five years I've been a week away from him. It's the first time ever I've been *on* the other side.'

'With his enemies.'

'As you were when I looked at you from Downing Street.'

'Fickle.'

'No.' She rolled away and considered carefully, feeling his knuckles with her fingers. 'I don't think fickle is fair. I was completely constant for five years.'

He said fiercely, 'I loathe the idea of that old deaf phoney clambering about on top of you.'

'He didn't.'

'What?' Martin twisted over to face her. 'What?' he asked, suddenly guessing, but wanting to make her say it.

'He isn't like that.'

'Oh no,' exploded Martin, sitting up. 'Another bloody queer.'

'No, he doesn't like boys. He doesn't like men. He doesn't like women to make love to.'

'Well . . . Well, what? He wanted you. You were there. What did he do?'

'If a man's very powerful and cruel at work – '

'Yes. OK, a sadist.'

' – he's sometimes, in private, the direct opposite.'

'Count Masoch?' asked Martin incredulously. 'Watching you in bed with someone? Acting your servant? I can't believe it.'

She didn't answer immediately.

Martin said, 'He couldn't risk a third person. The blackmail . . . Who was it?'

'No third person. Not watching me making love. Not really being a servant either. Can't we leave it?'

'But you began it.'

'Only to explain to you – because it seemed to mean a lot to you – that he never – in that way – made love to me.'

'"Made love". Ugh!'

'Right,' she flashed out, 'he never bloody laid me, never stuffed me, never put his – '

'Shut up, Ancilla! Please.'

'Well, can't we leave it, as I said? I don't want to say it.'

'Because you're ashamed?' asked Martin surprised.

'I wasn't remotely ashamed then,' she answered. 'He wanted it. I wanted to help him. But I am ashamed now, because I see him differently. And in words it'll sound ludicrous. These things do.'

'Try.'

'I had to shut him in a cupboard,' she said quickly, and hurrying even more went on, 'he had to beat on the door, hammer at it – like a sort of prison, or purgatory, or a sort of womb. He'd plead with me, *beg* me to let him out. He'd scream he was sorry, never do it again – '

'What?' Martin interrupted. 'Never do what again?'

'Nothing in particular,' said Ancilla impatiently. 'It didn't matter what, for goodness' sake! He'd pray to me to let him out. He'd moan out a babbling confession of things done wrong. That he was sorry for. Then I'd open the door. He'd be kneeling on the floor. Begging to be forgiven. When I opened the door, he'd crawl out.'

'Like a bloody dog.'

'Perhaps. No, it seemed more like a penitent.'

'Before a priest? To be scourged? Or perhaps before a goddess?'

'The same. I could pardon him.'

'Was he dressed?'

'Fully.'

'You?'

'No,' said Ancilla.

'Black boots, I suppose,' said Martin as crossly as he could.

'Black stockings,' said Ancilla.

'Honestly? And high heels?'

'Yes.'

'Nothing else? No whips? It *is* ridiculous,' said Martin giving her a squeeze. 'Go on. You didn't wear a maid's uniform or policeman's helmet by any chance?'

'No, nothing else,' Ancilla said more comfortably. 'He'd just crawl out and kiss my feet and beg to be forgiven.'

'The Prime Minister!' Martin began to laugh. 'Is that all? Like a shaggy old dog!' He started shaking with laughter. 'Down Fido! Down! Bad boy!'

'Shut up, Martin.' But Ancilla sounded as if she was about to giggle.

'Shan't. Good old Fido. Our Prime Minister! No, theirs!' Martin let out a guffaw of mirth and began to tickle her. 'Laugh it out, love. Laugh it out.'

'Stop,' she squeaked. 'Stop.' Then she began to giggle, then to laugh, then to howl with laughter. They clung together, shaking with great explosions. 'I can't *breathe*,' gasped Martin. 'My eyes,' said Ancilla. 'I'm blubbing.' Their laughter eased. They lay entwined. Sometimes a little tickle set Martin off again. 'Fido,' he'd say and start to quiver.

'No more,' said Ancilla firmly. 'A joke's a joke.'

'That joke quite over?'

'Yes.'

'Promise? For ever? No more of it ever?'

Ancilla kissed him. 'I promise. I've laughed it out.'

'Good,' said Martin and began very tenderly to make love to her.

When they woke up it was still dark and one candle burned on the dressing-table. Its reflection stared back from the black window. Martin said, 'D'you remember that poem I sent you when you went away?'

Ancilla's brow wrinkled. 'You were always writing me things. Rather good and sad and loving.'

'But when you went to Greece,' Martin persisted.

'Nothing.'

'Well, to Crete or wherever you were with those people.'

'No. Nothing from you . . . You were busy with Ruth.'

Martin agreeably squeezed her arm. 'Before Ruth. I wrote you such a sad piece about going and forgetting. *Your* going. *My* forgetting.'

'No, I never got it. Can you remember it?'

'Yes. It's the candlelight and loving you again. Listen. I called it "Separation".' He began slowly, touching her ear lightly with his finger:

> 'Each night you brush more softly on the pane
> Of my reflection. But your face elusive –
> A flitting bat at dusk – escapes my light,
> My love, and dances to the shadows.
> I who stretched arms towards you, to the sun,
> Turn on my pool again: no eyes, no stars
> Reflected in its stare but my bare thirst.
> Leaves curl, the petals furl beneath
> This anaesthesia of separation.
> Drowsing, I seek your flutter at my window,
> Feel on my eyes only the darkness wash,
> And your distant whisper dies in sleeping sighs.'

Ancilla asked, 'Did it? My whisper die?'

'Yes.'

Ancilla said, 'I wish I'd seen it. It's so sad.'

262

'You'd have come back?'

'Probably. Did you curl up? "Petals furl" . . . I love that "anaesthesia of separation" . . . It's true. You get numbed. Locally and generally.'

'It's all worked out for the best,' said Martin. 'So long as you don't flit off again. I can't be anaesthetized any more. It does kill one bit by bit.'

'I'll not flit, darling. Was it really like turning to the sun, turning to me?'

'I thought so.'

'Now?'

'Yes.'

'How marvellous.' She rolled into his arms.

# 33

It was strange at first in the Vale, waking up without electricity. But hands which used to grope for light switches now scrabbled for matches to light candles, or took tapers to the embers of woodfires. Ashes retaining the night's heat slumbered greyly. You puffed on the ruby glow behind them, dropped on a nest of dry twigs and they burned bright for breakfast.

Had the Vale of Hampden contained towns or modern housing estates, with electric or gas cookers, preparing food and heating homes would have proved very difficult. But the farms and cottages of East Pym and the Hampdens and the little houses and shops of Easterly had open hearths, Agas and Rayburns and old stoves snoozing in unmodernized kitchens. Pots could simmer, kettles were always warm on hobs, back-boilers heated water.

If there had been gas, the Government would have cut it off. There never had been. Though Easterly was on the North Sea it was too far from the direct pipelines to the Midlands to make a few villages worth an expensive detour. It was their own fault for living off the beaten track. The State could only aid the big majorities.

Over the last two years, Richard Sandford had combined with Ronald Cubbington in making charcoal. Their foresters had turned charcoal-burners in the early summer, for the woodmen's fathers recalled getting four times the charcoal from green May wood than from September trees when the sap is sinking. Under a pale-green frilly dome of leaves, the foresters burned great piles of wood under smothered flames and stacked the hard blocks of charcoal. Beech-wood was not, unfortunately, the best yielder, though far better than birch and pine. Best were the chestnuts and the oaks, and the saws bit greedily into the old trees.

Cubbington and the two local merchants had been stockpiling anthracite, coke and coal, over the last nine months, but Sandford was anxious to show the inhabitants immediately that charcoal was not much less efficient than modern fuels and that it was cleaner and sweeter-smelling, and far cheaper. 'Think of charcoal grills,' he told the cottagers, and Stewkly's great horse-drawn wagons came creaking round the villages with sacks of charcoal and peat-blocks, toffee-brown and smelling like smoked honey, cut from the old turf-bogs along the Sedge. Henry VIII had granted the Easterly fishermen peat-cutting rights four centuries ago when he was encouraging the build-up of the Navy. They had not been used since sea-coal started coming down from Newcastle.

The first fuel deliveries were sponsored by the Committee, and a bundle of candles and a clump of nightlights was presented to every home. The candles were a special gift from Mrs Stewkly. She had inscribed on each bundle the last words of Bishop Hugh Latimer burned at the stake in Oxford in 1555, for being a Protestant: '*Be of good comfort Master Ridley, and play the man. We shall this day light such a candle by God's grace in England, as (I trust) shall never be put out.*'

Below this Mrs Stewkly had added: 'Latimer was the son of a Leicestershire yeoman, born not 50 miles from here.' And because Martin had teased her, saying, 'They'll complain, Mother, that their name isn't Master Ridley,' she had scribbled a PS: 'Ridley, another Bishop, also burned for his beliefs. Cranmer quite right: England now free to worship how we like or not at all!'

'She's marvellously mad,' said Martin affectionately, as he and Ancilla were jogging from East Pym to the Hampdens with their cargo of fuel and light. The pair of heavy Cleveland bays in front of them were young, green and still rather fiddle-headed. They needed a few weeks more between the shafts, and the near-wheeler had not yet learned to brace himself against the breeching-straps to brake the great dray down inclines. The more experienced carriage-horses were in the hands of the novice drivers. There were few cars for them to shy at (for petrol was being hoarded) but there was an abundance of horse transport: draught-horses, mighty Shires, hackneys, cobs and ponies checked to stare at every other dray, dogcart, wagonette, barouche or ponytrap trotting smartly towards them with clip-clopping steel shoes and whine of iron rims and squeak of springs and creak of leather.

Their drivers were plunged into a new world of old conveyances. Everybody stopped to examine not only the quality and manners of the horse or pony, but the colours of each equipage, and each other's bits, bridles, traces, brake-blocks, shaft-lengths, travelling-rugs and brass night-lanterns. Experience and advice were freely swapped along the lanes. Children ran to gateways staring and followed the spinning yellow-spoked wheels of dog-carts as they whirred through villages. As with motor-cars outside, the speed of one vehicle was compared with the comfort of another.

Ancilla demanded, 'Pray, let me take the ribbons, my lord Stewkly,' as Nether Hampden's Norman church jolted away behind them, and the lane ran straight past green turnip-fields creamy with hurdled sheep towards Hampden Magna's spire.

''Pon my word, Miss Ancilla,' said Martin, 'you handle

me high-steppin' beauties like a Nonsuch, a veritable Corinthian!'

'Gad!' cried Ancilla, really springing the wagon along so that the bare elms in the hedgerows went rushing past like winter in their faces. ''Tis do-gooding the tenants, we are.'

'That's late nineteenth-century Irish, not Regency. And they'd lynch us if they thought so. We're all free men here – really free now.'

At the edge of Hampden Magna they stopped to watch two horse-teams working in the fields. The brown belts of arable had been tractor-ploughed before the blockade, but here on a sloping bank a pair of shires were easily pulling a seed-drill, dribbling winter wheat. On the opposite slope, yellowy-pink in the sinking sun, two more pairs pulled harrows. The men plodded behind their teams and were glad to stop to catch their breath. Gulls squawked over the tilled land, snatching up grubs.

By the time they were bowling back through East Pym, chimney smoke was rising in ash-blue question-marks. Martin and Ancilla had encountered on their delivery round not quite content, but the sort of excitement the local fair engendered and a surprised relief that things were working at all.

The absence of letters had so far distressed very few, since more bad news and rubbish had come through the post than cheques and good cheer. But the papers were missed. Radios, powered by batteries, continued to relay the world's astonishment at Britain's brutal isolation of the Hampden area. As Mr Potter remarked in his village stores, as he rationed out supplies, 'S'like seein' your photo in the *Mirror*, hearin' Hampden, Hampden all the time from London.'

Rationing in village groups of 400 bellies presented little difficulty. Potter knew exactly who and how many lived in each cottage, and he exercised his discretion fully, seeing that the old and the babies got special allowances. Old Mrs Trimble's hearing being none too good, her radio was on maximum volume, so she went through batteries very fast. 'Stands to reason they never could work rationing fairly from Lunnon,' said Potter reasonably, over his sacks of coarse-milled flour and the cottage cream cheeses made from the surplus milk. 'How'd they know about Mrs Trimble? Or the latest baby? Or me cousin's latest vegey-bloody-tarian fad?'

Cubbington asked Martin and Ancilla in for coffee. He shook Ancilla's hand, haw'd and humm'd, and got out finally, 'I apologize . . . About the manner I treated you . . .'

Ancilla said quickly, 'You were right to doubt me.'

Cubbington's long pale face almost smiled. 'I hear you were grand with the Press. That'll shake the bugger, no mistake. Which reminds me, Martin: about batteries. We're going to be main short and I never thought of them, I confess it. Slim's old man at the garage is charging up accumulators. But he's not got that many, and he's got to use diesel till he can fix the generator to the water-mill.'

Martin said, 'Why can't we smuggle in small things like batteries?'

Cubbington nodded. 'Sandford sent a lad across here on a pony this morning with a message. Owen the fisherman's trying to get north by sea with a shoppin' order. The freddy factory's out o' latex, o' course.' He looked at Ancilla and his face flushed like a raspberry. 'I do beg your pardon, Miss Shergrove.'

Ancilla laughed. 'That won't shock me.'

Martin said dubiously, 'We could try to get through to Brackton – Sandy Potts, Flighty or me.'

'No. Don't. You're known. So are they, and Flighty's

wanted. We're all crooks by their lights – all the Petitioners. They'd nick the lot of you.'

'If I could get in a little way to a telephone, without getting caught . . .'

'Who'd you ring?'

'Terry Speen, the reporter. He wants our news. We've got to get it out. He could supply us with things.'

'He might betray us,' said Cubbington.

'What?' said Ancilla, 'With exclusive access to a big news story. Not him.'

'She's right,' said Martin.

'Give the ruddy lie to Plain George?' asked Cubbington.

'Down Fido,' said Ancilla softly, and Martin started to laugh.

Cubbington stared.

'Joke about the Prime Minister,' explained Martin. He delighted in it: the villain had vanished, leaving a ludicrous, kinky clown. He squeezed Ancilla's hand and added, 'Why don't I take shots of the abandoned helicopters, scout-cars, arms and equipment? Defeated army stuff, and good propaganda.'

While Martin and Ancilla were photographing the area, Richard Sandford was on his way to a business conference with Aidan Stride. The horse-drawn omnibus which had been used as a quayside whelk-stall every summer since the war, was now plying its Edwardian route from one end of the fishing village to the other. It made, at Stride's request, westward loops as far as the Silken Dalliance Factory mornings and evenings to deliver and collect the lady-workers.

Sandford could easily have ridden straight in across the north Downs, but he longed to ride in the bus. It was drawn by four horses and driven by the old son of his father's last coachman. There was a sepia photograph of his father in sailor suit and cap over long blond curls, taken the day the omnibus first ran. So Sandford rode his hunter into the village and popped it into one of Mrs Bellamy's old stables where Major Ngyoto's company had been so pleasantly overcome. He had a sniff round her potheen distillery while he waited.

The creaking omnibus was crammed. From the open top-deck mothers and children waved and shrieked at friends as the dazzlingly painted vehicle crept along. Morale bubbled. The defeat of the Lutangans and the British armoured squadron inflated the people of Easterly with effervescent pride in themselves and faith in their leaders. Except at Silken Dalliance. Here the ladies were fractious after the long night of Gongo and the withdrawal of Stride. There was no work to occupy their nimble fingers and they were muttering. So Aidan Stride had hailed one of the pony couriers which were now plying through the area. For a bob letters and messages were cantered from one edge of the Vale to the other. Stride's note summoned Sandford 'to discuss a project of priority importance, Yours etc. Aidan Stride, Chief Executive.'

'I've had to send three parts of me work-force home,' Stride complained. 'And now I can't rely on that Owen providin' reg'lar latex deliveries ex-Hull.'

Sandford was startled by the new business-supplement jargon. Stride continued, 'You heard he was headed off las' night by the bleedin' Navy? They're pinchin' out me supply route, Sandford. Fired 'cross Owen's bows, they did. Only squeaked back under the cliffs. Buggers!'

'Owen was crazy to think he'd a chance of beating the blockade.'

But Stride was booming on, '. . . so, seein' I'm in sole charge – executive control bein' terminated above me – I must seek reg'lar economic use o' both machinery and woman-power. So . . .' With the casual flourish of a

Hatton Garden merchant revealing a 50-carat rough diamond, Aidan Stride laid an object on his desk. 'Know what that is, Sandford?'

Richard Sandford cautiously picked the thing up. It was 8 inches long, surprisingly light and of a smooth but grainy texture. It was hollow like a giant's finger-stall, tapering from about 3½ inches wide at its open end to about an inch and a half at its closed tip, which was topped with one of Silken Dalliance's famous feathers.

'A dildo!' exclaimed Sandford impressed.

'In slang terms. Medically it is a – ' he glanced at a piece of paper – '*Penile Prosthesis* or *Artificial Phallus*. Dare say our Japanese competitors has a name for it, too. But I prefer to term it The New Elizabethan Cod-piece.' He looked firmly at Sandford, ready to rebut criticism.

Sandford hesitated. 'I rather think – cod-pieces were worn more for show.'

'Exactly,' Stride nodded.

'And that the dildoes were – er – actually used. The French call them *consolateurs*, I believe.'

Stride, looking keenly interested, noted this new term. 'More for the ladies' pleasure, basically? Harems an' such – general female dissatisfaction?'

'You *have* made a study, Mr Stride.'

'I think I've done me ground-work.'

'And your – er – object would please both. *And* serve as a contraceptive. It's a brainwave!'

Stride bowed his head modestly.

Sandford asked, 'What are they made from?' He felt the material.

'Reeds from the River Sedge. Look at this texture.' Stride stroked it lovingly. 'There's nature for you: all softened by natural beeswax in a secret compound.

Smooth, creamy . . . See how they're blended together, Sandford. A little miracle.'

'By hand?'

'This one is, bein' a one-off prototype, as we say, but me machinery can easily be adjusted to press 'em out. The latex solvent tanks will adapt to the rush-beeswax synthesis.'

'Really?'

'I was an engineer first, you know, Sandford. Afore I moved into management.'

Sandford gazed at the object uncertainly, for he had not seen an erect penis since the war except his own and that not recently. 'Isn't it – er – a bit on the large size?'

'Life-size,' said Stride crisply.

'Oh.' Sandford felt himself blush. What a failure he must have been.

'African life-size,' amended Stride, having relished the landowner's discomfiture. 'Major Ngyoto's 's matter o' fact. He permitted me to make a beeswax and resin cast of his organ during his preliminaries in Mrs Bellamy's back parlour.' He recovered the object which Sandford had dropped with some distaste. 'Look,' he said demonstrating the bulges and flanges with a craftsman's pride, 'real life.'

Sandford was silent. He stared at it. 'Comfortable?' he asked.

'Try it.'

'Oh no,' said Sandford quickly. 'No, thank you. I fear my days for those are past.'

'Now that's where you're wrong,' Stride said fervently. 'Which is why I prefer the term cod-piece to dildo. More exactly reflects our purpose. For with these cod-pieces no one's day is ever past. That's half my selling-line: the appeal to the more mature. And the other half o' course is: no lady need feel deprived no more, however insignificant is her feller's penny-whistle. "You too can play a mighty organ", I thought for a caption. "Kiss your whistle good-bye." You get the point?'

'Absolutely,' said Sandford laughing. He controlled himself, for Stride was serious. 'Universal appeal.' He meant it. The things would sell like hot cakes.

'Elizabethans always wore 'em,' said Stride gratuitously.

'Earlier too, Mr Stride. From Richard II, anyway, and the days of tight hose.'

'Hose?' queried Aidan Stride. In the days of his insatiable promiscuity he would have let out a happy snort at Sandford's quip. But the businessman in him forbade time-wasting levity.

'Tight stockings all the way up,' Sandford explained. 'Like tight jeans on pop singers – they liked to boast of what they had. It's coming right back into fashion I gather from my daughter in London. So that cod-pieces would be popular for that reason too.'

'Really,' said Stride, impressed. 'There you are then. In the business, how long?'

'Six centuries.'

'Worn and proved by Kings, we could say. By Appointment, perhaps?'

Sandford said, 'You could use the Plantagenet Royal coat-of-arms, of course. But surely a more modern endorsement – a pop singer, footballer, even a film star . . . ?' With a boldness which surprised himself he inserted his finger into the cod-piece. It felt smooth but gripping.

'The grain o' the rush is cut to hold the piece on,' explained Stride. 'Feels real good, don't it? Sure you won't fit it on?'

Sandford shook his head. 'And for the woman?' he asked.

'The ladies here what have undergone controlled experiments with this model have appeared very well satisfied.'

Sandford with a grunt of disgust tried to remove the cod-piece as quickly as he could from his finger, but the more he tugged, the more closely it gripped. His mind now foamed with leaping images of Major Ngyoto, Stride, this thing and the awful girls. He wrenched frantically at the cod-piece, which gripped his finger like a vice.

Stride guffawed. 'Don' worry, Sandford. 'S fully disinfected. That's the beauty o' it. Readily reusable, but with just enough built-in obsolescence for regular repeat sales, see? Run your finger under the cold tap there . . . See? . . . Easy . . . Sales, they're my problem, Sandford. How do we export 'em? I could be a real earner of foreign currency for the area, seein' I am its one industrialist. And we need currency, too.'

Richard Sandford looked at the former shop-steward with deep admiration. 'Mr Stride,' he said. 'You're a genius. You're Freud, Doctors Spock and Kinsey, Marconi, the telephone and all the communications wrapped up together. Get me a dozen prototypes – some perhaps just a size or two smaller – and I'll see they reach interested buyers.'

Aidan Stride opened the drawer of his desk and brought out a velvet show-case made for Cock Cover Jack's planned export assault on the Indian rajahs. But those had been mere contraceptive sheaths, albeit with Silken Dalliance's special feathers. Now on the purple velvet basked a dozen different cod-pieces. Richard Sandford marvelled.

Stride demonstrated tenderly, 'Note the different angles – very important for relaxed hang, stimulated comfort, and total satisfaction.'

'Have you got that written down?'

'Yes, I have my promotional notes.'

274

'Mr Stride, you deserve to make a fortune. I know exactly the person in London with the right contacts, good taste – '

'Your daughter, Sandford?'

'Yes.'

'I would have suggested her meself, but not knowin' if she'd be accustomed to handlin' these products . . .'

'She'll do it very well,' said Richard Sandford. 'We've someone going across today. D'you think we might take the samples?'

'No time like now to make a profit,' declared Aidan Stride, 'as one of the Rothschilds was sayin'. Here's the sales literature I've run off: prices, delivery dates, trade-discounts. Your daughter could get extra copies on better paper done in London, perhaps?'

'Certainly.'

'And she must register the specifications with the Patent Office.'

'If you think that's necessary, Mr Stride.'

'I do. We have the right rushes here, granted. But it don't follow they don't exist elsewhere. And me special beeswax-bonding solution, stiff, yet supple, stimulating yet not abrasive – even that might be synthesized. Particularly by those bloody Japs – on our backs all the time, they are. *And* the West Germans. For these'll go a bundle in Hamburg, mark my words, Sandford. We sold a hundred gross of the old feathered freddies to one circuit o' clubs in Hamburg, just as membership cards for kinky krauts.'

Richard Sandford broke into his reverie, 'Then of course, Belinda will patent both the process and the product.'

The two men shook hands. 'Fifteen per cent sales commission for Linda,' said Stride. 'On a thousand of the big Ngyotos retailin' at a tenner each that's fifteen hundred quid to her.'

'Good gracious, that's marvellous! You do think big, Mr Stride.'

'Only way, Sandford. Only way.'

# 34

Martin and Ancilla waited till dusk and the official departure of the Rev. Fernden's refugees before they rode cautiously down the slope of Hampden Heights. Three mounted Dozens were still patrolling the ridge in case the Prime Minister's blockade had been a trick to disguise another military assault. But in Major Abbot's opinion Whitehall would need a battalion of paratroopers dropped on the area and determined to kill, to have a chance of subduing the Defenders. And the British Army's only Airborne Division was still involved in the European manoeuvres.

The last exodus from the area consisted of the Reverend Frederick Fernden, his housekeeper, three ginger cats and two parrots at the head of fourteen holidaymakers who had been stranded in Easterly. No one else wanted to leave, least of all the five Yorkshire wives. They handed the Rector coarse cards for him to post to their husbands. 'We've been Entertaining the Troops! And how!' wrote Mrs Ethel Birtwistle to lonely Joe coping for himself in Huddersfield. And, lest he failed to grasp their plans, she added, 'Apple a day's sauce for the Goose too and it's more than one apple most days.'

The Defenders' communiqué issued after the Battle of Easterly referred unambiguously to the courage and dedication of five visiting Yorkshire wives, who, placing themselves selflessly in the path of the invasion, had received the brunt of the African assault and thus saved the fishing-village. Joe and his friends, like many a myopic English husband, were fully contrite, far too late.

The five wives now intended to enact what Mrs Birtwistle termed 'Displays and Erotic Competitions'. They were already rehearsing with Owen and four more hand-picked fishermen. 'What with no telly o' nights,' said Mrs Ethel Birtwistle, 'the boys'll want some entertainment.'

'And live stuff's always better,' said her friend.

The Erotic Competitions would be peculiarly reward-ing, because they could be easily rigged. Mrs Birtwistle had found a little gold-mine when she realized how, in gambling-mad Britain, she could bring the lure of betting into the world of sex. The wives picked five jockeys for their unusual races. Training gallops had gone well: the riders were producing firm, consistent times.

The Reverend Fernden, and his small entourage were blindfolded and escorted past the Heffalump Trap, down the far slope, and along the plain under a white flag of truce until they saw the red lights of the Army's road block on the Brackton lane.

'Good luck,' called Flighty Wing, wheeling his horse. 'You'll need it in the bad old world outside.'

He saw the Reverend Frederick Fernden's dog-collar gleam as the Rector turned at the head of his flock. The cats were mewing and the parrots were squawking. The Rector raised a hand, 'God help you, rebellious people,' he intoned, 'and may He bring you back into the Paths of Righteousness, for His Name's Sake.'

'See you in church one day, Rector,' Flighty Wing shouted cheerfully, 'or in Heaven!' and the escort can-tered away across the misty fields.

Martin and Ancilla could hear the other horses' hooves squelching and saddles squeaking as they rode down the escarpment to reach the bridle-path to Mallard's Farm.

The chatter of the Rector's party, the confusion over counting heads for the Army and police, and a busy

278

press conference should, Martin reckoned, cover his and Ancilla's quiet departure.

The Mallards had farmed in the plain at least since Trafalgar year when their family Bible started. Over the generations some of their family had married into the Potters, Plumridges, Trimbles, Wings and Dintons of the Vale. But the Hampdens and East Pym had always been hard to reach beyond the Heights and the Mallards centred on Brackton. In police eyes they had no obvious connection with the outlawed Defenders, but the cousinry of the countryside ran deep as well as wide.

Martin and Ancilla approached the farm buildings cautiously, looking for signs of the Army or the police. Then they stabled their horses in the cow-byre, and Gyp the sheep-dog and Rascal the terrier set up a clamour of yapping across the yard. The back door opened and a shaft of light spurted across the cobbles. Big Leo Mallard stood in the doorway, with his ginger beard stuck out. 'Who's there? Or I'll loose the dogs.'

'Martin Stewkly and a friend.'

'Come in, Marty, quick.' The two men had ridden as boys together in gymkhanas, mucked out the horse-lines as punishments at Pony Club Camps, and shared trailers to the point-to-points. Then Martin had gone away and Leo had grown too heavy. 'An' too dang busy on this dang farm.' His father drank heavily but still looked an English aristocrat: hawk-nosed, piercing blue-eyed, silver-haired, pink-complexioned. *His* mother had been a house-maid at Hull Castle. The old Duke (father-in-law of the Duchess Abbot had met) exercised *droit-de-seigneur* over his servant-girls. The old devil had looked after his bastards generously, finding husbands with decent farms among his tenantry for their mothers. The Victorian Duke had loved to ride across his fields, glancing down at the men who tugged forelocks and the women who dropped curtsies, and seeing his breeding in their faces.

Traces remained in Leo, who said peering, 'Don't tell me, it's Ancilla. Always mind your strange name. Beat me in the jump-off at Easterly Show, 'member?'

Ancilla did. 'You had a piebald pony.'

'Skewbald, she were.'

'Well,' said Ancilla, 'It's nearly sixteen years ago.'

'C'mon inside,' said Leo, 'and keep hid from the windows. There's a main price on yer heads. For Marty and the other leaders. Thousand quid no less. You're on Wanted posters outside the Brackton nick! Sorry about yer ole man, Marty. *Human* feller for a clever man, I always thought. Now what can I do for you?'

'Well, first could I ring the Press in Brackton?'

'Not say you were here, would you?'

'No. And could you post this parcel for us?'

'Sure.'

'And here's a short shopping-list. Some batteries for our radios. And some things from a chemist – that's the doctor's writing, I'm afraid.' Martin began to get out some money.

'Never mind that,' said Leo. 'We'll run an account like. You settle up when it's all over.' He looked quizzically at Martin. 'How long can you hold out, I mean?'

'Long time,' said Martin, 'if we can get some stuff out and in.'

Leo grinned. 'Which is where I come in.'

'If we could just use you and a few other good friends along here as contact-points,' Martin began. They sat round the kitchen-table discussing details. Half-way through Leo gave Ancilla one of his huge, shaggy smiles. 'Hey, weren't it funny when Plain George broadcast they'd nicked you and then you were in the papers sayin'

280

you were staying with your friends the Stewklys? Gor! We laughed here.'

Martin worked out with Leo a system of safety signals for the cow-byre, then went into the cold hall to telephone Terry Speen. He told him about the photographs. 'They're all captioned. You know – "Farmer Charlie Potter, forty-six, with cousin Jack Plumridge, sixty-eight, examining the captured helicopters." And we've got some smashers of the village kids looking well-fed and woolly playing about on top of the scout-cars.'

'You're an organized outlaw,' said Speen. 'But the story now is: Can you last out? Give me some confident stuff to counter the Government hand-outs. They're still saying a few weeks will bring you to your knees.'

'Balls! We're paying no taxes, no rates, no postage and insurance stamps, no licences for cars, TVs, dogs, shotguns – ' Martin started.

'Sure, I'd not forgotten that side. Your *real* wages will double.'

'Well, what we get now we do keep,' said Martin. 'We're not having to pay Civil Servants' salaries any more either, thank God, nor the Health Service – free for foreigners! And we don't have to dish out any more damned charity to the emergent nations.'

'Aren't you one yourselves now?'

'Well, we wouldn't mind some foreign aid.'

Speen said, 'You know the Americans are particularly interested in your story. They see this break-up happening all over: people versus the State. Oh yes, listen – I've had a girl from Rupert Bramble's "Vision Now!" office on to me twice. They want to film "Life within the Vale".'

'They can't get in,' said Martin.

'No, they're going to provide a camera and a film for you to shoot it – '

'Videotape, Terry? I've no idea how to – '

'You don't have to, brother. Straight sixteen mill film camera. Just press the tit and shoot in the right direction. Then bring the film out. With any taped interviews you make. They'll record your voice and your mates over it later, see?'

'Sounds OK,' said Martin. 'But don't for God's sake let the police follow you to us.'

'I don't want my line tapped, either. So I've got different numbers for the next six nights you can ring.' He reeled them off. 'That brings us to next Thursday. Sunday, no number. I'm courting.'

Martin began, 'It's bloody good of you, Terry – '

'Bloody good *for* me, you mean, chum. I'm making more money out of your stories every week than I used to scrape in a year doing "By-Pass Rumpus" or "The Great Sewage Debate". I'll tell Bramble's girl OK to come. She sent *particular* love to Major Abbot, and said he *must* get out for the interview.'

Martin laughed. 'I'll tell him. How do I collect the camera and films?'

'Couriers' post-box. You name it later.'

'Right. Someone called Leo will ring you.'

When Martin and Ancilla left, Leo had their two large haversacks loaded up. They weighed heavily and clanked. 'Spirits and tobacco,' said Leo grinning, 'strictly duty free! You'll get short.'

'On our bill,' Martin said, 'please.' Leo nodded. Martin said, 'You know Richard Sandford's been growing tobacco these last two years. Under the Downs behind Long Hampden Farmhouse and drying it in his barns.'

Leo wrinkled up his pink Wellington nose.

'Oh, it's not too bad,' said Martin. 'Strong, fruity, with just a suggestion of vintage manure. But in fact some of the old ones, like Plum the policeman, love it in their pipes.'

282

They thanked Leo. 'Put out the lights,' he said, and they crept across the murky yard into the cow-byre. Old dung and acid chicken-droppings hung heavily. The grey mare whinnied when she heard them. 'You'll have to learn to be quiet, love,' said Ancilla putting her hand over the mare's rubbery muzzle. They swung their legs over their saddles. The terrier bobbed along, a white blob in the night, following their horses to the eaves of the Dutch barn. Martin's and Ancilla's eyes adjusted slowly to the gloom. As they trotted briskly across the Home Field a bull-finch hedge loomed up bristling: they followed it to the start of the bridle-path. The track had been an old Roman road across the plain following the ground-line of Hampden Heights, then an even larger forest which the Romans had never penetrated. Strips of the track still lingered on its original stone foundations, with the fosse either side overgrown like an Irish bank with a thicket of blackthorn. It was cold: a winter's mist lurked clammily between the hedgerows. Ancilla shuddered. 'Couldn't we canter?'

'Ghosts of centurions?'

'Perhaps.'

The horses' hooves cantering, their nostrils blowing, and the night air rushing backwards filled the darkness with sound. The bridle-path ran directly forward across the plain.

Martin shouted from behind, 'Steady, love. We've got to fork right soon.' Ancilla's grey mare started propping. She remembered instantly the night she was escaping on to the Downs. This time she pulled up so abruptly that Martin's Jupiter cannoned into her quarters. The mare was braced, quivering and staring.

'Hell!' Martin exclaimed. 'Didn't mean that quick.'

'Get back,' whispered Ancilla, 'Turn round. Something there. This mare's radar . . .' She took Martin's bridle and wheeled him round. As they did so, a voice bellowed from about two hundred yards ahead down the bridle-path. 'Stop! Stop there! Or we'll shoot!' They were aware of, but could not see a movement of bodies. They heard a sudden clink of steel.

'Quick!' grunted Martin, kicking on.

Shouts burst out behind. The white beam of a search-light soared over their heads, came down, touched their backs, sent their shadows racing and bounding ahead of their galloping horses. *Crack! Crack-crack! Crack!* Rifle-shots exploded, far lighter and sharper than the noise on films. Over our heads probably. Something whizzed high up: something cracked far on. A bullet whined, another thudded into the bank. Then into the thicket immediately to their right several bullets crashed, ripping terrifyingly through brush, twigs, branches. One just behind them struck a Roman cobblestone and spun off twanging in a ricochet. The searchlight swung wildly away for an instant. As they galloped on side by side Martin pressed down on Ancilla's back. 'Down!' Their heads lay against their horses' sweating necks. Their cheeks were wet and sticky quite close to each other, as the horses' shoulders punched and pulled their bodies along. 'Our backsides – cocked up!' squeaked Ancilla. Her pale face looked as if she were grinning. The searchlight was flicking a white lash in the sky. Over their horses' breath and pounding feet they heard a sound of engines coming behind.

'Here!' barked Martin. 'Left here!' He remembered a gap somewhere in the blackthorn thicket. Somewhere . . . Here it was. 'Get up! Get *up* it, darling! That damn grey mare, they'll spot her.' Ancilla wheeled the mare left at the hairy bank, took a shorter grip of the reins, sat down in the saddle and drove her forward as hard as she could with her heels. The mare crept forward, then hesitated, peering. 'Bloody thing!' Martin leaned forward.

The searchlight came zooming down on them in a dazzle. Martin slapped the mare's rump so hard his palm stung. She nipped out of the pool of light on to the bank and clambered grunting to the top.

*Crack-crack-crack.* Rifle bullets whistled down the bridle-path. Martin felt the swift dart of one just behind Jupiter's tail. Then the horse let out a squeal, sprang at the bank so powerfully that Martin was nearly flung off backwards, cannoned into the grey mare who was hovering on the top, knocked her downwards into the darkness and leapt after her.

'Oh God!' Martin heard Ancilla swearing. The mare was plunging about, snorting, in a tangle of grey. 'You all right?'

The searchlight probing for them was playing on the tall briers topping the bank behind them. Flickers of white light through the branches raced across the field in front. In the bridle-path behind and to the left of them reverberated the roar of engines. 'Scout-cars,' said Martin.

'Here,' hissed Ancilla, 'keep left in the dark strip.' Martin shouted, 'Like the hammers!' The tall hedge on the left ran towards the distant fringe of Hampden Heights. They cantered in its shadow, not daring to go faster for they were blinded after the searchlight dazzle. Anything could lurk just in front in the impenetrable dark. 'Go *on*, Jupey!' Martin swore at his horse, which felt as slow as a hearse.

The searchlight was jabbing and beating about the tangled countryside like a sharp white rod. It silvered the tree-tops, pinkly illumined a barn, raced along white banks, then swung away, growing paler. 'They're mad,' Martin grunted. 'If they cocked it on that bank behind they'd bloody flood us.' His heels drummed against his horse's flanks. He said to Ancilla, 'This rotten horse . . .'

The searchlights swept across a hedge crossing their front. Ancilla glimpsed a gate. 'Darling, look!' she breathed and galloped towards it.

'Look out!' Martin warned, kicking Jupiter along after her. But he had gone suddenly lame behind. He pulled up to a trot. Jupiter's head bobbed and he wobbled. He grunted as he limped. In front, Ancilla's grey mare scuttled for the gate. Martin turned in the saddle and reached down his horse's quarters. He touched something jagged, wet, hot and sticky and Jupiter let out a squeal. 'The bastards!' Martin shouted ahead to Ancilla. 'They've shot him.'

'What?' Her voice came back from the darkness. He heard her rattling with the gate chain.

Behind him the burble and whine of the scout-cars stopped on the bridle-path. Commands rattled out. He heard troops crashing about. 'Get that blood light left!' shouted an officer's voice. The soldiers were striving to clamber up the steep slippery bank. Martin kicked Jupiter on. 'Sorry, old boy, but they'll have us otherwise.'

Ancilla had got the gate open. They were through it. 'Oh, *poor* Jupiter,' she said.

A crackle of rifle-fire staccato as football-rattles spurted from the distant bank and they heard the double slam-slam of bullets thudding into the gate. 'Go *on*, love! Get on, for Christ's sake!'

Ancilla cantered ahead. 'Here!' he heard her whoop. 'A gap!' Jupiter hobbled on after her. 'Here, darling.' Her voice was much closer. They squeezed through the gap. The firing had ceased. Jupiter was moaning on each breath. It was particularly dark ahead. Then the searchlight over their heads lit up the glorious regiments of beech-trees guarding Hampden Heights. They pushed on desperately across the last field and dived under the cover of the trees like foxes to their earth. Blanketed by the great trunks and mass of russet foliage, the cries of the hunting soldiers died away.

'Let me look at him,' said Ancilla, dropping back.

'No, love, not till we're at the top through the barricade.'

'I'm going to.'

'No,' said Martin fiercely. 'If we stop, he'll stiffen.'

'Don't stop. Keep on,' she called from behind. 'Without him you'd have been done.' She peered over to look at the wound. 'It's nicked through the back of his quarters . . . Flap of skin hanging, it'll need stitching.'

'Not through the muscle?' Martin was leaning over backwards from the saddle. His face touched Ancilla's. It was cool and soft, but her hair smelt warmly of her. She was concentrating on the wound, touching it with her fingers.

'No,' she said. 'Anyway not deeply. Lucky.'

'Yes.'

'Three foot farther forward, and – ' she jabbed Martin's hip. 'Not nice. That's what I meant by lucky.'

Her ear was against Martin's mouth. It was ice-cold. He put his tongue into it and kissed. 'I love you. I love you,' he mumbled. She put her hand behind his head and squeezed his neck. 'I love you, too,' she said.

He said against her cold cheek, 'You sound surprised still.'

'I am a little.'

'But why?'

She wondered about it, then said, 'But love is always surprising, when you think about it.'

They climbed on up the hill. Behind and below them the scout-cars droned away. The searchlight went out. Their horses' hooves shuffled through the beech-leaf floor. Their breathing rasped. The escarpment was very

287

steep. At the top loomed the great stockade of tree-trunks. A voice called softly, 'Martin?'

'Flighty?'

'Yeah. Bit rough, weren't it?'

'Yes.'

'All right, though?'

'Poor Jupiter's hit. Otherwise we're all right.' He was riding at Ancilla's side. He put his arm out and round her shoulders and pulled her to him as they rode. 'We're very all right, darling, aren't we?' he whispered.

'Yes,' said Ancilla softly, and kissing they rode on home.

# 35

Belinda Sandford's London life had been embarrassed by the Defenders' early victories in the Vale of Hampden. At work in Bond Street and at home in Chelsea she had ridiculed the idea of her father's and his friends' opposition. She now found them heroes. Strangers quizzed her for the latest news. All across England new cities and motorways menaced shrinking fields and cringing woods. Villages which had survived the threats of Spanish Kings, French Emperors and German Chancellors went down like ninepins before Whitehall's planners. 'If your father and co. can do it in Hampden . . .' said her hosts with admiration and rising hope.

Tales were seeping out of the Vale about the natural foods the healthy Defenders were enjoying. Eulogies about stone-milled wheat, farm-churned butter, and an abundance of home-grown beef from water-meadows and lamb from sea-fresh downlands, were already coursing through affluent and faddish Belgravia. People began to ask, not quite flippantly, who could wangle them into Hampden for a health visit. 'No pollution up there, no disgustin' diesel fumes or chemical fertilizers. *Natural* pheasants, old boy, Rich, gamey. Bread made from grain, not chemicals. And air the motor-cars haven't farted into. Now if one of these quacks ran a *Hydro* there . . . Not that Plain George would let us in, of course . . .'

When the parcel arrived in Belinda's flat mysteriously posted in Brackton but with a long letter from her father and sheaves of notes from a Mr Aidan Stride, 'Manager and Senior Executive, Silken Dalliance Ltd', Belinda was happy to be in touch again. When she saw the samples she giggled: they touched at least her sense of humour. She talked about the cod-pieces at Sotheby's, in her lunch hours, and at people's parties. Everybody enthused. The idea was splendidly *à la mode*, their workmanship capital, their source dramatic. Belinda, gripped by unusual enthusiasm, asked twenty picked people to her flat to drink champagne and study the cod-pieces and their exploitation.

A young man from Christie's, renowned as an expert in eighteenth-century English furniture, extolled the contemporary craftsmanship: 'I'd be delighted to write a little piece about dildoes in general for *The Connoisseur*, darling, bringing yours in as the New Thing. My name must help a bit, you know.' One of the last of the hand book-binders undertook to fashion presentation holders for them. 'Dark-green Italian leather, gold-tooled with the owner's crest or monogram. What a thing for dreary Xmas, 'Linda. How we'd brighten those tweedy stockings of the peers!'

A gawdy brace of new rich who owned a boutique chain gushed, 'This is what our new tight trousers have been screaming for, darling!' Could they display them on their dummies in their shops? 'Lit from below – fantastic shadows! Think of the stir!' Could they take three dozen right away?

Two homosexuals tu-whitted and tu-whooed over them, stroking them with gleeful pipes. An Austrian psychiatrist, popular with the upper classes but short on English and credentials, promised, 'I vill guarantee prodigest market viz my titled-peoples client-persons.' And the keen young American who ran the London office of Coast-to-Coast Fancy-Goods Inc. said his President, Mr Ezekiel Kornkrack, was visiting London right now and could Miss Sandford see him tomorrow?

'Miss Sandford, believe me, you have a fancy-goods line here which will *really* tickle the American consumer.' Belinda burst out laughing but the American was earnestly polishing his glasses.

Her father and Aidan Stride had both stressed exports – 'because Whitehall's sanctions against home trade are going to be tricky to circumvent' – so Belinda immediately accepted the introduction to Mr Kornkrack of Coast-to-Coast.

She would take her samples round to the President's hotel at 6.45. Belinda bathed and scented herself, slipped on her diaphanous-topped dress with her sexiest black stockings and presented herself a little early at the Westchester. Aidan Stride's sales exhortation had ended, 'Full exercise of your female Allure a vital part in selling our Product. Seeing you, buyers must Think Sex.'

Belinda had never felt more excited in her life. Standing between a table-light and a long mirror in the Westchester's mid-Atlantic foyer she noted with deep pleasure first the distinct lines of her thighs and then the luminous interest of a Spanish waiter, a schoolboy and a fat man wearing a velvet cap. She moved in front of them, feeling their eyes follow. My white skin under this black is marvellously sexy. Surely Mr Kornkrack must buy.

When she tapped on the door to his suite, she thought in a startled breath, But I've never before been to any man's hotel bedroom! She started to cough. Mr Kornkrack called out like a bull-frog, 'Come right in, honey, door ain't locked, is it?' Belinda stepped into his sitting-room, holding the velvet-lined show-case in front of her. 'Early ain't you, doll?' Mr Kornkrack's voice honked from the bedroom.

'I thought – ' began Belinda.

'Well, come on in.' Mr Kornkrack made a braying noise like a jack-donkey. Belinda tip-toed to the door. It was open. Ahead of her floodlit on the middle of the large low bed lay Mr Kornkrack sprawled stark naked on his back. He was huge and old and hairy as a gorilla. He wore pitch-black goggles against the glare of his sun-lamps. Even lying on his back his belly reared up like a monkey-skin cushion before curving away into a tangled black jungle from which Belinda hastily averted her gaze. Something very nasty indeed was stirring.

Nothing could be seen of Mr Kornkrack's eyes behind the steel-lined goggles and he neither moved his head nor altered his tone. 'Seen plenty of those, doll, haven't you?' he honked.

Belinda couldn't speak, started to shake her head, then thinking of the sales, nodded. My God! He wants me to fit the things! she thought. And my God! I won't.

Mr Kornkrack's brow wrinkled. 'You're the girl my office fixed, aren't you?'

Belinda nodded.

'Fine,' said Mr Kornkrack. His thick lips opened and Belinda could see a battery of gold teeth and a very yellow furry tongue. 'Come closer, doll. Let's see these charms I heard about, eh?'

Belinda clutching her show-case walked gingerly towards the bed.

'C'mon, c'mon, doll.' Zekey Kornkrack impatiently jerked his bald and sweating head an inch to the left to study her. He swivelled the sunlamp at her. Belinda was hotly aware of the light shining right through the silk. This bloody dress! She squeezed her thighs so tight together that they felt sticky. She could see her face doubly reflected in Kornkrack's monstrous goggles. She looked scarlet in the two black pools, glanced downwards and glimpsed the awful demonstration in the jungle. She looked up again. On either side of the bed stood two raised ice-buckets filled to the brim with cracked ice and bottles of champagne.

'You wanna drink first?' asked Zekey Kornkrack testily. 'You know 'bout ice-buckets, don't you? Ram my arms in every time I'm near it and wow! I can keep at it an hour. Indian Prince's trick.'

Belinda started to shake her head. She ought to leave. But the thought of the orders she might get made her pause. She said, 'A drink would be lovely.'

'Now you've got a real high-class voice,' said Mr Kornkrack, smiling for the first time. 'I like that.' He moved one hand down over his belly to demonstrate the height of his interest. 'Lookey here, doll.'

Belinda immediately looked away.

'Goddarn it,' shouted Mr Kornkrack, 'what the hell game you playin'? We got to get acquainted, haven't we? Let's see what *you* got.'

With alacrity Belinda stepped forward, put the showcase on the foot of the bed and flicked it open. Mr Ezekiel Kornkrack sat bolt upright, whipped off his goggles, stared, looked at Belinda, stared at the dildoes again, and let out a wheezing ee-aw, ee-aw of laughter. He then leaned across the bed, snatched up a silk dressing-gown, and with sudden modesty draped his salute. He laughed again, braying, 'You're the agent with the cod-pieces! My fool manager didn't lead me to expect a lady.' The telephone rang. 'Yeah. Oh. She's arrived.' He snorted. 'Yeah, send her up too.'

Keeping himself covered, Mr Kornkrack swiftly opened a bottle of champagne with a crisp pop and poured a glass for Belinda. 'I didn't get your name.'

'Sandford.'

He handed her the glass, 'I sure need to apologize, Miss Sandford. You see – '

'Your little manager fixes you a lay each time you're in London?' asked Belinda coldly.

'Sure. Like every big London business with overseas contacts. Part of any deal now. Stenographers, personal secretaries often. High-class girls sometimes.'

'Which you like,' said Belinda, 'for an hour.'

Mr Kornkrack nodded vigorously. 'Most of all I like to get a real English aristocrat down here,' he patted the bed. 'And – '

'Mr Kornkrack, wouldn't you like to look – ?'

'Then I take her out to dinner, dance a bit, then back here for the night.' Mr Kornkrack added proudly, 'Laid a Duke's daughter once. Right here in this hotel. All night.'

'You pay them?'

'No,' said Mr Kornkrack. 'London company pays 'em. That Lady Sarah was 200 bucks and knew nothin'. Just lay around. They're usually on the company staff. Get a bonus, mebbe. But when sales are important – ' He leaned forward to study the cod-pieces closely. 'Gee, Miss Sandford,' he breathed. He was so impressed that his natural cunning slipped. 'Wow!' he murmured, touching. 'These are things of real beauty.' He took several out and ranged them in line. 'Dildoes,' he breathed, 'I've always wanted to run these things. You know somepin': What book of the Bible they mentioned in? *Ezekiel!*' He honked trimphantly, 'Chapter 16.'

'But I'm not getting under you for an hour, Mr Kornkrack,' said Belinda quickly. 'Whatever your first name!'

'Miss Sandford, you are a business woman. Sexy though you are.' There was a knock on the outer door. 'That's for that,' said Ezekiel Kornkrack sufficiently, jerking his head towards the knock. 'Come right in, honey. Door ain't locked. Jest wait awhile out there, eh?' He nipped off the bed to peer through the bedroom door. 'Magsie, isn't it?' he inquired. 'Magsie Brown?'

'Magsie Green, sir,' said a nervous typist's voice.

'Brown or Green – what's the odds?' asked Kornkrack crossly. 'They're all crap common.'

'I was here your last visit, sir, after some dictation, you remember?'

'Sure, doll, sure,' said Mr Kornkrack, but he scowled. He closed the door, and muttered to Belinda. 'She's got a few nice tricks,' he allowed grudgingly, 'But no class at all.' He looked inquiringly at Belinda, and extended his hand towards her bottom. 'No!' she said sharply, whipping her buttocks away.

'OK.' He accepted it regretfully, refilled Belinda's glass and sat down to re-examine the cod-pieces. He honked with delight as he handled them, studied them under a magnifying-glass, slid his index-finger into one. He looked with amazement at the Major Ngyoto model, but Belinda had been advised by her father not to mention its African origin to an American businessman. 'A local,' she said.

'Sure are healthy up there.' Zekey Kornkrack flicked through the brochure. 'All from that break-away province of yours. Like the good old American Colonies over again. Taxes, is it? Not wanting to be buggered about any more?'

'Sort of,' said Belinda.

'As used by Richard II!' exclaimed Mr Kornkrack.

'Other kings and princes, too,' said Belinda quickly.

'Like today?'

'Well, hardly yet. These are only prototypes, after all.'

Belinda could almost hear the American tycoon's mind whirring. He asked, 'Have you sold North American rights yet?'

'Not yet.'

'I'd like a year's option on them.'

'Six months.'

'Nine,' said Mr Kornkrack. 'Nine months option from

295

today – exclusive North American franchise – for 10,000 bucks.'

'Ten thousand . . . ?' repeated Belinda.

'Well, 15,000 dollars, as you've extended the option period. And I'd want a first delivery of 100,000.'

Belinda's knees buckled. She sat down on the edge of the bed by Ezekiel Kornkrack's side. She asked weakly, 'Assorted?'

'Sure, assorted. We've all sizes back home, too, you know. And tastes.'

'A hundred thousand . . . But the cheapest Choir Boy size are £5 each! That's a half million pound order!' Her heart was leaping about inside her like a tit in a bird-cage.

'So it says here. You don't think I can move 'em, Miss Sandford?'

'Belinda.'

'Belinda. That's a nice high-class name. Belinda, call me Zekey. I have 1,750 retail outlets across the States. D'you really think I can't sell sixty dildoes from each C-to-C Fancy Goods Store in just a couple of days? What's buggin' you? Finance?'

'A bit,' said Belinda, 'for an order that size.'

'Don't you worry, little lady,' said Mr Kornkrack patting her knee in an avuncular fashion. 'If you let us have the first order at £450,000 I'd be prepared to advance £50,000 of that as an export guarantee deposit.'

'That's another problem, Mr – Zekey. Getting the dildoes to you. The area's officially blockaded, as you know.'

'Yeah, like sanctions in Rhodesia, no aid to Biafra, no tourists in Vietnam, all that old crap.' Mr Kornkrack's bray was scornful.

'But these had to be smuggled out.'

'Smuggled.' Mr Kornkrack savoured the word. 'I sure

like that. Royal cod-pieces smuggled from the Daughters of the English Revolution – no, that ain't it quite . . .'

'But getting them out?'

'Now, Belinda doll. You know how many billions of dollars England owes the USA? You know England can't get any of your Middle East oil without the US says Yes? You know England can't start a war, or end a war, let alone, goddarn it, win a war, without the US says OK? Since your last war, Belinda doll, the USA owns little Britain right up to your furry ears. So you think any goddam ten-cent limey Government is going to stop an export order like this one? Belinda Sandford, madam, you and your friends are goin' to get mighty rich. And I'm gettin' richer.' His hand was still on her knee, and now he slid it up her thigh, turning to face her so that his short silk dressing-gown split open full of menace. 'Belinda,' wheezed Mr Kornkrack, 'one short dry run – not an hour, I swear it – to seal the bargain. Just to test . . .'

Belinda was so invigorated by the colossal deal she had just brought off that she hesitated. She calculated that her 15 per cent on £450,000 would pay her £67,500. She could shut her eyes. But suppose he used the dreaded Ngyoto. Belinda could imagine that gigantic feather-topped thing spearing up and up. Then she thought of the ice-buckets continually postponing Mr Kornkrack's climax and of his great weight and huge belly and horrible hair. She procrastinated. 'To celebrate the first million sold, I promise.'

He nodded. His brain whirred. 'That'll be 'tween Thanksgiving and Christmas then, doll.'

Belinda gasped.

'You'll see,' said Mr Kornkrack.

'There's Magsie meantime,' Belinda said quickly, 'On ice.'

'And she can work for it,' honked Zekey Kornkrack delightedly. 'Magsie!' he called.

'Yes, Mr Kornkrack.'

'Get your shorthand pad and pencil and some C-to-C paper.'

Magsie sounded surprised, 'Yes, Mr Kornkrack.'

'Bring it all here, Magsie, right away.'

Magsie, blonde, slit-skirted with enormous breasts joggling over the top of her frilly pink frock-top, appeared in the doorway.

'Now, don't stare at Miss Sandford, Magsie. She's London Sales Manager for the Silken Dalliance Company of the Vale of Hampden. You know about that, don't you?'

'Yes, sir. They've revolted.'

'And they have a product, Magsie, which will revolutionize the sex-life of the world. Royal, handmade, historic, satisfying simultaneously erotica and vanity, male and female, hygiene and satisfaction. You got that down, girl?'

'Not yet, Mr Kornkrack, sir.'

Mr Kornkrack brayed angrily, but said, 'Yeah, well that can wait. While Miss Sandford's here I'll dictate a Letter of Intent for our deal and option. Then you, Belinda, can check as we go. Right? Have another glass of champagne.' He refilled Belinda's glass and started to dictate, then broke off. 'Drink for you later, Magsie. After.' He seized the huge Ngyoto model and wagged it under Magsie's nose. She let out a little squeak. 'Oh, Mr Kornkrack, but I don't know whether . . .'

'That's what we'll see, doll. That's what we'll see. For myself I'm lookin' forward most keenly to this first trial, as you can see right here.' The experienced Magsie leaned forward obediently to offer a speedy salutation, then blushing poised her pencil over her pad. Mr Zekey

298

Kornkrack with an occasional glance at Belinda for confirmation, and an occasional fumble at Magsie's melon-sized breasts, continued his brilliantly brisk summary of the great cod-piece deal.

# 36

It was PC Plumridge, recovering nicely from his accident, who suggested the use of Potter's pigeons for communication with outside England. Now that Old Plum was officially cut off from Police HQ in Brackton, grey guilt lifted off him like freezing fog off Hampden Heights. He even reassumed, from his wheel-chair, responsibility for law and order over the blockaded area.

There was so far no threat to order, for the armed locals who had routed armies inspired respect, and English Constitutional Law as applied to the land outside the Vale was assumed to be still in force. Charles Stewkly had insisted on maintaining democratic government through the parish councils. These additionally now became the courts for local disputes, a combination he would not have accepted himself. Doctor Quainton remained chairman of East Pym Parish Council, and the Reverend Mike Thornborough remained chairman of the twin Hampden councils. But the vacancy at Easterly was filled by Aidan Stride, who conducted a vigorous campaign on the platform of 'Vote for Your Own and Only Industrialist'.

Stride heard of the gigantic deal from Belinda, via Terry Speen, Leo Mallard, and Flighty Wing. From his new positions of 'Chief Executive' and 'Chairman, Easterly Parish Council' Stride wrote formally to Cock Cover Jack in Brackton, offering to lease the Silken Dalliance factory as it stood for seven years, with an option – at which Jack cackled with mirth – for another twenty-one years. Stride offered too, to take over all the remaining assets at Mr Pennington the Bank Manager's valuation. The Pakistani who had been wringing his brown scented hands over 'diss millstone round my poor neck in rebel hands', flung it off joyfully, seized Stride's offer and had the contract tightly drawn by Brackton's nimblest lawyer. He then obtained permission for its delivery from Inspector Wilson, now acting Superintendent after the Chief Constable's dismissal.

'I divest myself of all enemy assets, honoured Superintendent. No wish whatsoever to trade with these revolting persons who will all shortly puncture, I hope.'

Shifty Wilson delighted in his exercise of local power and censorship, kept the Pakistani waiting, and let him cringe in front of him before pronouncing his consent.

Until the request for the contract, only Income Tax and Rate Demands, electricity and water accounts and requests for the return of stamped insurance cards had been allowed across the river. They were ferried across in a police rubber boat under flag of truce and, in a gesture of defiance, were then always publicly burned on the rebel bank.

Twenty of Jack Potter's short-range birds were smuggled across to Leo Mallard. The Army were patrolling the bridle-path in renewed strength. Uncertain in the dark, and restricted to the lanes by their transport the soldiery kept up regular and noisy patrols. The keeper and the poacher from the Vale humped their wicker-baskets of birds through to Mallard's Farm.

Leo hid the pigeons in his cow-byre, gave Wing and Potts a tumbler of whisky in his kitchen and then said, 'Speen sent a message from the television girl. She's given him the camera and films. Could you wait and take 'em back?'

Flighty Wing looked dubious. If the Vale of Hampden

had not seceded he would have been in Brackton Magistrate's Court last week facing charges under the Game Laws (Amendment) Act. He muttered to Potts, who would have given evidence against him, 'We dursen't hang about.'

Potts asked Leo, 'How often do they come here – the police? The Army?'

'Every day, patrolling,' said Leo slowly. 'But the dogs'll howl afore they're half-way up the bridle-path. Look, I'll nip into Brackton for the stuff. You wait here.'

'What about road checks?' asked Flighty Wing. 'You'd be better ridin' cross-country like us, wouldn't you?'

'They can't stop *us* driving about,' said Leo.

Sylvie Bucket, dropping the camera with Terry Speen, drove on to spend the few nights waiting for its collection with her mother in the grisly back-to-back house in a Nottingham slum. She had told the old woman straight out last time she'd not stay again till they'd a decent bath in the place. This had now been installed with a gas geezer. Sylv lay in it for hours, as the front parlour was clammy cold and the kitchen stank of drains. Old Mrs Bucket popped in to gaze at her daughter from time to time, changing from ogling admiration to raging disgust as thoughts of Sylv's activities kaleidoscoped in her brain.

'Must say you're smashin', Sylvie,' she said, helping with her harsh scarlet hands to soap Sylv's golden back. The American Senator had taken her to Jamaica for a long weekend. "Ow many you 'ad now?'

Sylv opened her eyes. Her mother's gimlet eyes were staring at her out of the wizened face. 'Don't be disgusting, Ma,' she remarked lazily. 'Your *interest* . . . I dunno, coupla hundred, I dare say.'

'Coupla hundred!' Mrs Bucket sprang back from the bath. 'An' you say *I'm* disgustin'! Coupla hundred fellers in yer. Ugh!' She stood at the door, purple as a turkey and gobbling, too. 'And that one-eyed nigger.'

'He's got Fuzz-trouble,' said Sylv, languidly soaping her breasts and thinking about one-eyed Joshua of The Rancid Cheese.

'Good,' said Mrs Bucket. 'Heroin?'

'No,' Sylv was scornful. 'He's a musician, for Chrissake. Only pot. Ought to be legal. He can't play without it. Like actors and whisky. 'Cept no one gets fighting mad on pot.'

Mrs Bucket's gobblings diminished. Sylv was moving about voluptuously in the bath, opening and shutting her long golden legs. Mrs Bucket came closer to gaze. She imagined the tall American Senator looking like Clark Gable, Jack Kennedy, everybody beautiful, bending over her Sylv in Montego Bay, in a great bedroom with a huge view, violins behind palm trees . . .

Sylv said idly, 'The Fuzz'll let Joshua off, if I lead them to that Major Abbot.'

'Abbot? One of them rebels up here? How d'you know him?'

'Took me out after the programme. Then you know what, Ma? He tried to pay me!'

'He *didn't*, Sylvie!' Mrs Bucket was outraged. '*Disgustin'!*' As if you were a prostitute!'

Sylv nodded.

'There's a thousand quid for turnin' 'em in – these rebels,' said Mrs Bucket.

'I know, Ma. We're doing a film on them.'

'And he paid yer, Sylv. Like a whore.' Mrs Bucket crouched over the bath like a witch over a cauldron.

'I told the Special Branch feller I would if I could.'

'Now, *there's* a girl, Sylvie. Puts you in good with the police, gives you a thousand quid of your own, and pays back that bleedin' Major.'

303

Sylv closed her eyes against her mother's hissing venom. 'I might hook him when they come out with the film,' she said. 'But I can't squeal there, or the unit will cop it, Rupe Bramble an' all. Then I'd be right out.'

'You'd lose yer nice contacts, Sylv.'

'Lose me bloody job, Ma.'

'So . . .'

'So I've got to get the little old runt off somewhere on his tod, then ring the Fuzz.'

'He'll not come, Sylvie. They know they're wanted. Treason. Could hang. He'll not come away with you.'

'Oh, he will, Ma. I can make him. Just think if you was him and burnin' for me, really frantic, and saw me like this . . .' Sylv moved her legs in the water.

'Yes.' Her mother's breath hissed. Yes, she'd get him. 'Meantime,' said Sylv, 'Mum's the word, see . . . Don't you want to wash my hair then?'

Old Mrs Bucket knelt down again by the bath's side and with the special shampoo she saved to buy she washed the long blonde hair as tenderly as if each lock was worth a pound. If Sylv had a thousand quid of her very own, that Senator might marry her . . .

The night fog slunk through Nottingham's back streets, and stray cats yowled on the grimy walls.

# 37

Martin and Ancilla filmed for a month all across the Vale of Hampden. Thelma from 'Vision Now' had given them *carte blanche* and helpful advice. 'This should make a 50-minute documentary: shoot 4 hours of film. If you need more, ask us. It's only the taxpayers' money – and that's not yours any more!'

Their resistance was going to be shown in many countries: 'The Landscape which said No.'

'If they see us surviving happily,' said Richard Sandford, 'world opinion might make the Government drop the Airport.'

Cubbington wondered, 'Will we *want* to go back to Britain . . . ?' and stroked his nose.

So far no one was suffering. On the contrary, after nearly three months Dr Bill Quainton noted such a substantial decrease in colds, influenza and bronchial infections compared with the previous five years that he prepared a statistical report for the BMA, and for the WHO in New York. The BMA had not so far replied, but the World Health Organization had issued a statement saying they were extremely interested and were trying to get the British Government's permission to send in a team of observers. Cubbington complained: 'With your report showing how healthy we are, we won't get those Red Cross supplies.'

Dr Quainton, signing himself 'Health Officer, Vale of Hampden Independent Territory', had sent the International Red Cross in Geneva a list of the medical supplies and equipment which the Vale would need to replace if an epidemic should break out. The request had left the area officially by police hands across the River Sedge and the Defenders heard on their radios that Geneva was discussing delivery problems with Whitehall. One Sikorski helicopter would easily have carried all the Vale's needs, but generous elderly Americans, fired by Hampden's fight for freedom and by recollections of Britain's war-time hardships, were subscribing for thousands of Red Cross food-parcels. There were currently being loaded into an American freighter at Cherbourg. The International Red Cross had asked for a guarantee that the boat would be allowed to unload at Easterly, but the Prime Minister was insisting on Britain's right to detain and search the ship. The argument, which might reach the Security Council's agenda, was complicated by the plethora of relief organizations involved. Some of these were now joined by volunteers who wanted to spend Christmas in Britain's last corner of the olde worlde.

World sympathy, even among the emergent African and Asian nations (excluding Lutanga), supported the Vale of Hampden: Britain's Imperial role was still not forgiven. It seemed that the toothless bulldog, mangey lion or paper tiger, deprived of non-Europeans to bully, had finally turned on its own poor peasants. 'Up 'Amden-vale!' was heard in many a distant, hot and dusty street.

Martin and Ancilla seemed to be filming without artifice scenes of an earlier century. Against a backcloth of golden beeches the fields were worked by silent horses and Hereford oxen. Down the quiet lanes between black hedgerows bowled dogcart and carriage, coach and milk-float. Horse-shoes sparked on roughening roads. Easterly's horse omnibus lumbered past the port.

Here the fishing-boats sprang sails again and men heaved at oars inside the limit of the naval blockade. The guardian mine-sweeper dared not come in too close and it kept the big trawlers off in case of smuggling: fishing had not been so good for fifty years. The old smoking-shed flourished again behind the harbour. Kippers grew brown from the smoke of oak-wood chippings, and not from stain. Herring and sole, halibut and plaice were preserved in natural salt barrels. Round the fires the fishing nets were mended and kind Mrs Bellamy circulated her special potheen: 'Spirits of Hampden', flavoured with the sharp berries of the juniper bushes which still abounded in the woods. She was aided in her distillery by three scientific youths who would otherwise have been doing their practical chemistry at Brackton Tech. Martin filmed her, squeezed into her smart Nanny's uniform, presiding over an important tasting.

Then they covered the arrival, changing of horses and departure of the three great four-in-hand coaches. 'St George', 'Britannia', and 'John Bull', looking as if they had cantered out of Christmas cards, plied every hour on a circuit round the Vale, 'taking less time', as one sheepskinned outside traveller put it, 'than those bleeding buses afore our revolution'.

The pony couriers made busy Thelwell pictures as their child-riders, pigtails bobbing and long hair flying, galloped along the grass-verges with letters between the villages. The mail was carried in leather holsters on the ponies' saddle flaps and in wallets on cross-belts on the childrens' backs proudly marked 'Vale of Hampden Pony Express'. The country children found the task more agreeable than netball practice.

Foreign news from London came in through battery radios and Martin showed an elderly huddle in the Fern-dens' Rectory mocking a Ministerial fulmination. The Vale's own news came in daily bulletins from the Commit-tee nailed to the four church doors and announced by

307

church bells. The bell-ringers expressed themselves freely. A tumble of notes, one deep bell tolling, a clattering peal across the fields, gave the inhabitants a foretaste of news good, sad or urgent. The bells signalled the fishing boats in, the start of school or the opening of a market. A parish counsellor or member of the Defence Committee attended each church to answer questions, give advice and listen to complaints. Grievances no longer festered among the grass roots.

The churches became meeting-places again as they had been before the Protectorate, and if services were not attended purely for religious purposes, at least the pews were filled and some philanthropy resulted. The churches were warmer, too, being lit by massed candles in sconces.

Richard Sandford, in a coat made from his own sheep-fleeces, was moving old Mrs Trimble from her cottage for the winter into the Rectory which Patricia Fernden was running as an Old People's Home. 'Pat's done more good in twelve weeks in the village than her droning father did in twelve years sermonizing,' said Sandford.

The clothes were changing even before Christmas. Crude sheepskins were everywhere with round hats of rabbit fur, some with ear-pads. There were long leather coats of tanned beef hide and many sleeveless jerkins. Grey squirrel-skins made muffs and tippets for the women. Men's gloves and gaiters were of rough cow-hide, and so were breeches, neat and snug and made to measure. Home-made shoes appeared like moccasins, but with willow-wood pattens from the banks of the Sedge.

The breaths of the villagers jetted out across the market-stalls round East Pym Green. Lanterns glowed under the striped awnings in the December afternoon. Horses clopped past behind, bringing purchasers on their backs, or goods in carts behind them: woolly fleeces, bolts of leather, wool on spindles, dried teasel heads for combing wool-cloth, rolls of hemp and flax grown in the Vale. Madder roots, leaves of the common woad, and the flowers of the bastard saffron were all on sale as dyes. There was a fortnightly horse fair where ponies and donkeys changed hands along with 'quiet lady's hacks', 'strong draught horses', and 'pairs of high-stepping hackneys, guaranteed fast and quiet to shoe'.

There were fortnightly cattle- and sheep-markets in Charlie Potter's farmyard at Church Hay, but the Corn Exchange took place in its original building on Easterly's quayside, recently used as the drab depot for the now closed supermarket. Shopping was done either at the door as the carriers came round the villages with their caravans of home-made wares, or at the weekly general markets in East Pym and Easterly. Carts lurched in, creaking with local produce: potatoes, wooden plates, pewter jugs, honeycombs, sea-salt from the marshes, braces of rabbits, hares, pheasants and partridges, pickled beetroots, home-made game-pies, hams, salted bacon, nuts from the hazel-thickets, walnuts from the great trees, preserves of gooseberries and mulberries, honey-sugar, beet-sugar, flagons of elderberry wine, rosehip syrup, dandelion wine, kegs of home-brewed beer, local cider squeezed out in the circular horse-press of Hampden Magna, and bottles of Mrs Bellamy's fiery 'Spirits of Hampden'.

Martin took the BBC's camera into the bank which Mr Pennington opened at any reasonable hour at a ring of the bell. PC Plumridge insisted on appearing in this scene. He sat importantly in his wheel-chair, very still – ''case the snap gets blurred' – clutching a shotgun and wearing his old helmet on top of his now very long hair. He had spent his convalescence reading history-books from Easterly library, and was convinced that he was going to be remembered by posterity as the sole representative of the old order at the birth of the new.

Hair everywhere was grown so long that young and old tied it back in bows behind their heads. Beards and side-whiskers bloomed. Razor-blades were easy to smuggle in, but the eighteenth-century clothes made for eighteenth-century hair-styles. Leather trousers, wool sweaters knitted by the fishermens' wives (rainproof because of their natural oils) and yellow lambswool jackets went naturally with a general hairiness. Dirt was not prevalent. Soap was refined from animal fat, and scented with dried lavender, rosemary, laburnum, or rose-petals. The ladies claimed their skins had never felt so soft with them nasty detergents. And the water helped: soft from the rain off roof-tops into tubs, soft from the Sedge and the Mere, fresh from the wells and delivered by ox-drawn watercarts to distant cottages.

Martin's sequence in the Bank showed some money passing, but batches of cheques were generally exchanged for others. There was talk of a special currency later on. Ancilla recorded Mr Pennington with a silvery beard and flowing white mane discoursing on 'internal liquidity and credit financing in this Independent territory. Bankers made a mystique of money in Britain, as I recall. Here we generally exchange goods and services in kind. Debts are a small problem when everyone knows his neighbour and no one can abscond!'

He explained that since the area paid nothing for imports its budget was securely in balance. With sizeable exports for foreign currency in the pipe-line, the area would be one of the few in credit in the world. 'A minor Switzerland . . .' He pointed out in fairness to Britain that the Vale of Hampden did start with a clean sheet. 'No debts for winning wars,' he said. 'And our armed forces are unpaid!'

Martin and Ancilla then approached the vexed question of Silken Dalliance. Some elderly Defenders feared further publicity for it: the whole of Hampden might seem bawdy, even sex-obsessed. But the firm had landed the biggest fancy-goods order since Britain's last big toy firm went bankrupt. The £50,000 deposit from Coast-to-Coast against their £450,000 order had already arrived, part in cash and part in Letters of Credit from Mr Ezekiel Kornkrack's American bankers.

The funds had been brought via Brackton by Belinda Sandford in the sable coat she had bought out of her commission. She left the money at Mallard's Farm, and Flighty Wing had brought it back across the border with her message: C-to-C would be sending in a helicopter just before Christmas to collect the bulk cod-piece order. She would fly with it to confer with Mr Stride and spend Christmas with her father. Mr Kornkrack saw no difficulty about landing C-to-C's helicopter on East Pym Green. Kornkrack always alerted Washington when trading with backward or awkward small countries. The Secretary of Commerce in Washington had already spoken to the US Ambassador in London on his behalf: Grosvenor Square would smooth the way with the British Government.

To meet the gargantuan American order Aidan Stride's industry, in the manner of expanding enterprises in the world outside, had sprouted ancillaries. The men who had casually reaped the rushes from the river-marshes were now organized into squads within the newly-formed Giant Stride Rush Company. Stride had acquired rights over the unwanted marshlands and in order (as he put it) 'to provide for a further expansion in raw material demand', he now planted a further 200 acres of reed-beds with irrigation-ditches and connecting tracks.

The plucked rushes, bound in sheaves with twisted

reeds, were brought up in an almost continuous donkey-chain, trussed into panniers on the animals' shaggy flanks. This stage was handled by Stride-On-Transports. The track followed the Sedge to the hump-backed bridge on the lane where Martin had rescued Ancilla. Just above the bridge Stride had dammed the river to flood more marshland.

A sluice through the dam ran with renewed and harnessed vigour into the water-mill and this drove the flails which pounded up the rushes in their tanks.

The rush mixture, like wet *papier-maché*, was floated farther downstream on wooden rafts to the edge of the Silken Dalliance Factory. Here horses and carts daily delivered loads of fresh beeswax from the third of Aidan Stride's new enterprises, Beestride Incorporated, which owned rows of trim beehives scattered over warm banks in the Vale west of the Downs. The wax was stored in the vats which had formerly contained the synthetic rubber. When the rush compound was ready for mixing, the beeswax vat was warmed over hot charcoal fires – 'impartin',' as Stride boasted, 'a tender fragrance to the dildoes' – and poured into brewers' pans rotated by donkeys harnessed to spokes. The final mixture was then ready for the moulds along the work-benches: here each variety of ten, No. 10 'Choir Boy' up to No. 1 'Major Ngyoto', was in the hands of groups of girls. 'Gives 'em pride in their work,' said Aidan Stride, 'to specialize in types.' Each week he gave a Golden Phallus and a weekend for two at Sea View to the lady producing the best-made cod-piece.

To handle the C-to-C order Aidan Stride had instituted 3-shift, 24-hour working in Silken Dalliance. The flares, candles, and rush-lights burned seven nights a week in a golden radiance against the darkling Vale behind. Stride was everywhere in his new domains urging his workers forward with tempting bonuses for craftsmanship and minatory suspensions for sloth.

'Carrot and stick! Carrot and stick!' cried Stride, like some parrot Tory of the sixties. 'Can't whack that combo for Prodi-bloody-Tivity!' The system triumphed. Almost all the women in Easterly were employed in Silken Dalliance. Most of the men and boys worked for the Giant Stride Rush Company, Stride-on-Transports, or Beestride Incorporated. A dismissal from one meant no employment in the others. Workers watched their steps, but Stride crammed their pay-packets. Food certainly cost more, but light, fuel, and transport were cheaper. And everybody's pay doubled without tax and National Insurance contributions. As Mabel said, taking home £25, "S'mine to spend now, innit, as I please? Not to bleedin' waste on strikers in Scotland, or grants to backward coons.'

A new rich were emerging in Easterly, and, as they could not spend their money on motor-cars, washing-machines or television-sets, they began like Victorian tradesmen to buy their own houses and horses-and-carriages. They spent each week on local food and drink, wood, charcoal and candles. No distant manufacturer benefited by a penny. They bought local clothes and local furniture, carpets and tapestries. As things were needed, cottage-industries restarted to provide them. Money revolved locally. The whole Vale flourished.

Aidan Stride, richest of all, bought a motor-car. Not one of the three hundred jacked-up on bricks in garages, but the one he had always desired: Mr Granby Browne, MP's Rolls-Royce. For good measure, and under the same contract, he bought Browne's house, and installed three girls from the factory as his servants.

To be so close to the Boss was a great honour, even if

313

Mr Stride did make them wear uniforms of saffron-dyed home-woven linen, with little white aprons and caps from Hampden's cottage lace-makers. The girls had been picked for their looks and were ready to comply with the Boss's most intimate demands. Certainly he rang handbells for them in the night-hours but it was only to order more sheets of the special parchment produced by Sandford from his sheep- and goat-skins. This was an industry Stride craved: he only made mediocre paper as a by-product of his rush-pulp. Sometimes he summoned a decanter of Mrs Bellamy's 'Spirits of Hampden' or Mrs Stewkly's elderberry wine. He worked most of the night in front of the log fire in his bedroom, an expensive fox-fur round his head, and wearing only his ponyskin night coat. The girls, eyeing his bed, were never invited into it. Those sexual junketings were all behind him. 'Sowed enough wild sperm to found a nation,' he would declare, wagging his head. 'Shockin' waste of business energy.'

Thus Aidan Stride, resembling a Victorian merchant in his furry overcoat outside his servant-crammed house, featured at length on Martin and Ancilla's film. They filmed his men reaping the rushes by the flashing water, the boys binding them into russet bundles, the long donkey-trains awinding, the mill-wheels turning, the buzzing bee-hives, the beeswax cargoes and the throbbing factory.

They filmed the horse-teams and the red-brown oxen ploughing glossy furrows through the stubble as the gulls shrieked and pounced behind. They filmed the sheaves of wheat and oats and barley drawn from stacks, spread in a circle on the ground and threshed by trotting horses pulling hurdles round and round. The women, leather-jerkined, with woolly caps like chain-mail helmets at Agincourt, stood in the sea-wind winnowing: casting the husks into the breeze so that the corn fell and the chaff blew away. The older women and the children gleaned in the fields, picking up the grain for their chickens, pigs and rabbits. They had the pickings of wood and hedgerow too: kindling sticks in peeling brittle bundles came in on pony-back, and sacks of white wood chippings were gathered where the axes bit into the forest trees.

# 38

Before Martin and Ancilla could film the cottage lace-makers or Mrs Ethel Birtwistle's Displays and Erotic Competitions (the fishermen were chary of general release) an urgent order arrived by pigeon-post from Rupert Bramble. He wanted the film ready to show on Christmas Day. It would go round the world: Dickensian, Battle-of-Britainish, a Christian Community in action . . . Quaint, rousing, religious: perfect BBC seasonal fare. He must have the films back and record the interviews not later than the day after tomorrow. He wanted to talk to at least five leading lights including Ancilla Shergrove. Sylv, passing the message to Terry Speen, had inserted 'and Major Aston Abbot'. She was staying in Brackton to make all the location arrangements.

Secrecy for the interviews was vital. The BBC believed that Bramble and his camera-crews could be convicted of 'Comforting Her Majesty's Enemies' if they were caught talking to the Defenders. At the least they would be guilty of what their lawyers called: 'Misprision of treason: knowledge and concealment of treason, even without any assent to it.'

Martin rode over alone with his cans of film and met Thelma and Sylv at Mallard's Farm. Thelma said, 'Rupe's coming up tomorrow with the unit. We'll have your stuff processed and rushed for him in our Midlands Studio. When can you get your lot out? And where will Rupe chat?'

'We thought – ' began Martin.

'Natural,' went on Thelma, shaking her grizzled

316

shaving-brush hair, 'backgrounds of wild woods. I see you as hunted animals – stricken deer.' Thelma's hand, dough-heavy as an unbaked loaf, thwacked the talc cover on her map. 'Look here, Stewkly.'

Martin caught the silver-blonde's eye. It winked. A bright tip of pink tongue flickered through her lips. Martin wanted to suck them. He grinned at her. Thelma nudged him. 'Why not there?' he asked Thelma, putting his finger on the barn between Hampden Heights and the Roman bridleway where Ancilla and he had nearly been killed. 'By night?' he asked.

'We'd have to light the barn to film.'

'Impossible,' said Martin. 'So it's a daylight interview. We'll have to create diversions.'

This is what Major Abbot had advocated to the Committee. 'I intend to use *their* scout-cars firing smoke-shells over both the Brackton lane cutting and across the Sedge at the broken bridge. They'll assume – I hope – that we're trying to break out on at least one front. With luck, they'll divert forces north and south, letting us slip out in between.'

'I'm thinkin' you should stay back here, in charge, Aston,' Cubbington had said gravely.

Abbot had darted a look at him and blushed. 'No, no. Plenty of good men among the Leaders. Bit of authority'll do 'em good. I gather Bramble particularly wants my views as the military commander.' He had puffed out his lips and made his small burbling noise. 'After all,' he had added modestly, 'the Battles of East Pym and Easterly were the first defeats British armed forces have suffered in Britain for nearly two hundred and fifty years! There must at least be a note in future military histories about our strategic planning and our tactics.' There had been a murmur of approval: the victorious commander should naturally attend. And the commander, bowing politely, had lusted for Sylv's body.

In Mallard's Farm, as Martin worked out the interviewing schedule with Thelma, Sylv smiled often and opened her eyes boldly and moved around the kitchen-table with that confident presentation of breasts and buttocks based on knowing exactly what men crave.

'Are you now on the Committee?' she asked, leaning very close to Martin. He knew her accent was affected, but she gave off a wonderful warm erotic scent and she was a fabulous golden colour. Through her tight oatmeal sweater her nipples wiggled cheekily and her trousers tightly caressed the twin curves of her little bottom. He could see how old Aston had been crazy for her.

'You've not taken your poor father's place then?'

Martin shook his head.

She said, 'I look forward *very* much to seeing Aston again.'

Thelma scowled at her and jutted out her chin like a stone buttress. She loathed Sylv's little voice when she was doing her social-graces line, and she ridiculed the dependence of all men on Sylv's body. She tapped the mooning Stewkly person. 'How long will your diversions keep the Army from our barn?'

Martin shrugged. 'They may not work at all. An hour at most. If – '

'Not long enough. We've got to set up.'

'Couldn't you get the crews in first?'

'They'd give it all away. Smoking, chattering, lights. Hopeless little wets.'

'Not if you were here with them, surely?'

Thelma shifted her heavy bulk and gave the grunt of a pig with its back scratched. 'I could keep 'em quiet for an hour. With Sylv's help.' She cocked one bushy eyebrow.

'Not that Sylv'd let a bod from the unit even kiss her backside, would you, Sylv?'

Sylv pouted. 'Certainly not!' She looked lingeringly at Martin. 'But they run errands for me all day, y'know. Just hoping.'

The rendezvous was fixed for 11 A.M. next day. Martin warned Thelma, 'We may not be able to get out. You realize that? And if there's danger here, we'll all bolt back.'

'Understood.' Thelma thrust out her hand, caught Martin unawares and gripped his shoulder.

As Martin was going to the back door with Leo, he smelt, then felt Sylv at his side. She took his hand. She put into it a tissue-paper parcel. 'For Aston,' she whispered. 'He's to open it *secretly*, see? *Make* him come, won't you?' She moved her body against him like a cat, suddenly stroked him softly, then glided off. The kitchen light which had seemed at first so harsh after the candles of the Vale, was touching her silver-blonde hair like a halo.

'What a one!' Leo chuckled. 'Gor, Martin! I'd love to mount that and ram her across the bullpen!'

Martin grinned, embarrassed by her effect. 'Aston'll be like a chained bull tomorrow, poor bastard.'

# 39

At 0945 hours one troop of the Defenders' captured scout-cars roared noisily into position on Hampden Heights. Simultaneously and in full view of the army and police detachment blocking the road beyond the broken bridge, the other troop of three scout-cars advanced steadily towards the Sedge and then deployed into the woods downstream.

Their noise and movement whipped up a flurry of interest beyond the river. Men in khaki and blue uniforms trotted busily about, imparting authority's careful blend of urgency without panic. Then on the hidden road from East Pym they heard the rumbling thunder of galloping feet. Orders snapped out, cracked along the Army's defence-line. A cloud of dust rose from the dirty road and a cloud of steam hung over the racing horses like a Jovian mantle on the hill's brow. A hundred horsemen agog for action after three months peace galloped over the ridge four abreast, pitchforks flashing. They swept down the slope and then swung away left-handed into the woods along the Sedge.

Acting-Superintendent Shifty Wilson had been down to the broken bridge for his regular morning inspection, but was on his way back to Brackton when the first reports reached him by radio. 'They'll swim the stream with cavalry,' he deduced confidently. 'Probably starving and desperate.' He called up Major Frank Radnage. 'Can you send me reinforcements from Brackton Lane?'

But it was Saturday: most soldiers had gone home on

forty-eight-hour passes. Regiments which under Wellington, Kitchener and Montgomery had conquered tyrants now worked a five-day week.

'I'll send one Troop round from the cutting,' began Radnage, 'and I'll tell the CO – ' He broke off. 'Hang on, Wilson.' But he kept his microphone button pressed down. Wilson heard him exclaim, 'Smoke, Sgt Muldoon? Three scout-cars?' He came back to Wilson, 'Look, they're probably breaking out here. We'll have 'em all now. Colonel Bradenham will come up with HQ squadron and we'll catch the lot of 'em at last. Just hold the riverline for an hour with all your police.'

Wilson started to protest but Radnage cleared down. Immediately Wilson was called from the bridge-head. 'Heavy smoke-screen now coming down three miles east of the bridge, sir.'

Bugger them, thought Wilson agitatedly. The breakout was coming in his section across the marshes. His men would have to march there on foot. Why hadn't he been allowed the mounted men he'd asked for? The rebels were quids in. He drove rapidly back to the bridge-head. The men would grumble like hell. They'd take a good hour to get across those bogs. Now with cavalry . . . My God! If they got out and encircled him! 'Quick, quick!' he snapped at his driver. 'This is an emergency. Not a ruddy ceremonial!'

Thirty minutes later the party for the TV interviews collected behind the Heffalump Trap on the Heights. Majot Abbot was in a state of triumphant lust. Not only were armoured forces under his command threatening a panicking enemy on two flanks, but he had in his pocket Sylv's little present: a pair of her delicious knickers with the lipsticked message 'Welcome Home'. He felt like Nelson poised for Emma Hamilton, and both his eyes had barely closed all night. Now wet and protruding they swivelled along the ridge as the field-telephone rang from the cutting and couriers galloped up with reports from the bridge. Between orders, he thrust his hand into his pocket and squeezed Sylv's soft, fragrant gift of promise.

Richard Sandford, now the most senior of the Committee, remained in charge behind. But Aidan Stride was arriving. He had sent curt word to Cubbington and Abbot that as the area's only industrialist he would accompany them. He was driven to the rendezvous in his Rolls-Royce and helped up the hill by Mabel his personal assistant, with her fat friend – 'my woman of all-work' – humping a suitcase of clean clothes. Ancilla and Martin, sitting together on their horses, watched his triumphant progress.

'Are we a little democracy, because he's made a fortune?' asked Martin. 'Or not one, because he's suddenly superior?'

'English democracy,' said Ancilla, 'Very complex. And hived off, like we are, it recreates itself.'

'I like the "we",' said Martin.

'You not riding, Stride?' asked Cubbington again. An indifferent horseman himself, it warmed him that Stride, the great entrepreneur, could not ride at all.

'No. I'll walk down.' He looked arrogantly up at Cubbington, 'Spent me youth ridin' other sorts, y'know.'

Ancilla grinned. 'You were *famous*, Mr Stride.'

'Yes, some days and nights, I remember . . . But that's old stuff now.'

Ancilla and Martin were staring into the Vale. About a mile north of Mallard's Farm their eyes had caught movements: quick glints of uncamouflaged metal. The barn was less than a mile away, below them. They saw the cab of Leo Mallard's red tractor parked on guard in the Roman bridleway. Northwards to their right they saw the fringe of the smoke-pall fired by their scout-cars. It was oozing slowly westwards like shaving cream over the flat fields where the police white Jaguars had suffered their accidents.

Major Abbot glanced at his watch and, at that instant, heard a further *crump-crump-crump*. It was the second salvo of his smoke-shells. As they fell, his scout-cars opened brisk bursts of fire with their machine-guns. Obscured on the ridge behind their smoke they might have been firing directly down at the Army instead of horizontally over their heads. Immediately pandemonium broke out along the bridlepath below. One scout-car, then two more emerged like tortoises from behind a huddle of straw-stacks. They were followed by six half-track troop-carriers crammed with helmeted men. The convoy turned north and roared with straining engines and clattering tracks towards the Brackton lane cutting.

'Good!' exclaimed Abbot, grinning at the others, who all started to chatter. 'Shush!' He held up the now military hand which had till then been urgently kneading Sylv's pants in his pocket. Behind them to the south-east, two miles as the rooks were agitatedly flying, lay the broken bridge. Faintly in the cold December air came the pop of other shells, the chatter of distant machine-guns. 'Let's go!' cried Major Abbot, squeezing his horse down the hill. Flighty Wing and Sandy Potts, on their quickest horses, scrambled on ahead and fanned out right and left to act as scouts. Cubbington followed, grunting uncomfortably as his huge hunter slithered and propped down the slippery slope. Then came Ancilla on her grey mare and Martin on Viceroy. Finally on foot, solicitously supported by Mabel and her fat friend, came Mr Aidan Stride grumbling as rich businessmen will about the importunities of press and television.

The camera-crews were already set up in the lee of the black-planked barn. Rupert Bramble's thick glasses flashed impatiently in the lemon-tinted sun. He wore a fur coat to his ankles and a wide-brimmed purple fedora. Thelma, booted against the mud and topped by a tweed cap ministered to him with coffee and armagnac from a thermos. The technicians lounged about on straw-bales, fertilizer sacks and cattle feeding-troughs, with the indolence affected by experts in strong Unions.

As Major Abbot cantered ahead across the last field, he saw a flash of silver-blonde hair and a golden face. A grunt of uncontrollable greed bubbled from his lungs and burst through his lips. His face was flushed and his eyes flashed like dark stones in a stream, as he swept into the barnyard. The cameras panned with him as he swept off his badgeless khaki cap in the general direction of Miss Sylvie Bucket and Mr Rupert Bramble.

The impact was dramatic. His long ginger hair stood out. He wore a home-made sheepskin coat, lengthy as a Household Cavalryman's great-coat. His corduroy trousers were stuffed into rough calfskin boots. Thus far he might have been a Cromwellian yeoman. But his shotgun was slung across his back, and loosely tied under his jaunty beard was his old Rugbeian scarf. His black charger's neck gleamed with sweat, and it pawed the ground.

Sylv's lovely eyes opened with generous abandon and she shimmered forward, gazing up at the horseman. 'Aaarh!' Major Abbot let out a growl of delight and squeezed his horse forward to meet her.

'Keep turning!' Bramble snapped to the cameras.

The Major stooped from the saddle and with a clawing bear-hug gripped Sylv under her armpits, hoisted her up on to the pommel and planted huge hairy kisses either side of her little face. As he did so, Martin and Ancilla cantered together into the yard, with Cubbington pounding just behind, anxious about precedence. Over the sheepskins, fur hats, steaming horses, leather-chaps, glinting gunbarrels, the whirring cameras panned, tracked back and panned again.

'Very good!' A smile exposed Rupert Bramble's gigantic dentures. His glasses sparkled. What a picture! Elan. Confidence. Romance. Drama. And then, across the field with his attendant minions, strolled Aidan Stride like a tycoon in his park. The astonishing ex-shop steward had, if the newspapers were right, just landed a large American order for some fantastic hand-made titillator. What a story for our times, breathed Rupert Bramble: Success, a fortune, perverted sex. And perhaps on top of the revolt the fall of a Government.

For here too, was the Prime Minister's ex-mistress, beautiful to look at, pink face glowing, dark hair as loose over her sheepskin collar as a cavalier's, side by side with young Stewkly whose father had been martyred by the Army.

The rebel party started to dismount. 'No, stay there,' snapped Bramble. 'I like you up there. If the gallant Major could perhaps liberate my assistant.'

Abbot reluctantly rotated Sylv, but his palms ran over her breasts as she slid to the ground. With her face at his knee, she whispered, 'Later? Promise. My car.' Major Abbot nodded and grunted with a wild delight.

Aidan Stride, assisted by Mabel in the barn, was changing into a dark wild-silk suit commandeered from Granby Browne MP's deserted wardrobe. Bramble, seated on a rostrum of golden straw-bales, confronted the Defenders like an orchestral conductor. He'd draw a great theme from them, he swore. Behind their backs lay the russet slopes of Hampden Heights and his large mikes beyond the barn were picking up the thump of shells and rattle of machine-gun-fire. The sounds were rather faint, but more would be dubbed on from stock at Television

Centre, producing the cannon-rolls for his symphonic variations.

Ronald Cubbington, well briefed by Mr Pennington the banker, spoke earnestly about the Vale's booming economy. 'What we're short of, we don't miss, I tell you. And you'll have seen Doctor Quainton's – our Medical Officer's – report to the World Health. Well-nigh unbelievable some of the figures . . . No, so long as Red Cross gets some drugs to us, we can exist for ever, thanks. That bum in Downing Street can't starve us out.'

Ancilla was questioned, as she had expected, about loyalty. Bramble bit into her. 'No,' she answered, 'I don't feel a traitor. I am loyal to this country, but particularly to this land here. To the British people, but particularly to my friends in the Vale. More loyal now perhaps, because before I served a politician.'

Bramble ground his dentures, for she had diverted his next personal question, and her reply was too good to be edited out. Instead he asked, 'You're rich and have excellent connections. Can you possibly call yourself a democrat?'

Ancilla laughed, looking marvellously illuminated and charged with energy. She said, 'Well, no one now has any *connections* with the Vale at all . . .' at which even some of the camera-crews laughed. She added, 'Nor am I wearing Balenciaga or sitting in a Rolls! I've no money here. No authority. I do what I'm told.'

'Unpaid?'

'I feel what we're doing is right. Right for us, selfishly. But just as right for the future of everyone outside. That's why I love it. I've never felt that before.'

Martin interposed. 'We rule ourselves now. We can *touch* our problems, argue them, decide. You can't get that – ever – from a distant government that drags you along like a tin can behind a truck. That's why we won't have it again.'

'Never?' asked Bramble.

'Never!' shouted Abbot, out of camera.

'Never!' boomed Cubbington.

'Not so long as we live here,' Martin said.

Bramble asked him about his father's death. Martin was fair. 'The Army didn't mean to kill him. And he – as perhaps you know – was always unarmed. He swore after the last war he'd never kill anyone else. He wouldn't even shoot pigeons. There was no question of him threatening anyone.'

'But his martyrdom was something round which your resistance crystallized?'

'We were pledged already. It wasn't my father's death that strengthened all our resolves. It was the way that man – your Prime Minister – made use of it.' There was a mumble of agreement. Martin was scarlet. He went on, 'We knew that if Robinson could poison even that, then we could never deal with him.'

Ancilla said quickly, putting her hand on Martin's arm, 'It sickened me.'

'Sickened a lot of us.' Bramble noted that one camera was still recording Martin's grief and fury, and the Prime Minister's former mistress gazing at the rebel with sympathy and love.

Aidan Stride, sleek as a merchant-banker lunching in the Savoy Grill, appeared at the barn door. Bramble, goggling at the transformation, gestured politely towards a straw-bale. 'If you're not too smart, Mr Stride . . .?'

Stride had found cigars, too, in Browne's house. He permitted Mabel to light one for him, kneeling in the mud. 'As the only industrialist in the area . . .' he began. His tones rolled richly on. Bramble sought to snap the flow of references to his activities. The man was as boring as a stockbroker. But your final product, Mr Stride?' he demanded. 'Can't we see this mystery?'

Stride snapped his fingers. Mabel opened a show-case. One camera zoomed in. Stride began enthusiastically, 'Silken Dalliance's cod-pieces, once used by Royalty, hand-made by craftsmen in a dozen sizes. A magic mixture bringing proud content to man and woman.'

'I can't advertise, Mr Stride,' Bramble cut in sharply. 'We have to edit out all plugs.'

'Even a million dollar export order?' asked Stride sarcastically, admiring the ruby end of his cigar.

'A million – ?'

'It is,' said Stride. 'For Coast-to-Coast Fancy Goods Inc. of New York and California. And my London agent reports firm orders for another £100,000 worth here and on the Continent . . .' He was in full voice again. 'Craftsmen . . . the modern role of titillation . . . exclusive patent . . . dildoes, a social asset . . . made by free men to free men . . .'

His bravura magnificently completed, Stride glanced at his watch, changed tone, and said to Bramble, 'I've hundreds of workers in me organizations back inside. I've got to get back to keepin' the Vale's economy buoyant. Right? So good day to yer, Bramble. Come, Mabel and you.' Carefully in his polished shoes, he picked his way past the horses and walked briskly back across the meadows to the woods. Mabel and the fat lady toting the suitcase pattered behind him.

Bramble immediately turned to Aston Abbot. The Major had dismounted so as to get closer to Sylv. He had his hand behind her buttocks and was stroking and squeezing them so feverishly that his eyes were glazed. He snorted with surprise when he heard Bramble call his name and saw the cameras swing towards him. He removed his hand furtively and took a step forward, muttering to Sylv, 'Hold the horse, love.'

'I'm just a soldier,' said Major Abbot, glaring directly into the camera's glittering black eye in which he glimpsed himself inverted. 'But I believe in freedom. And I believe that a few people you know – and who think like you – are more important any time than millions of strangers. I fought for Britain and for UNO, all round the earth. God knows what for! Not for Britain's benefit, that's obvious. Why, we couldn't even protect our property and planes abroad from bandits! I wondered then: what's the point of having armed forces at all?

'What I learned around the world is this: No army, no force however strong, can hold down *people* against their will. We learned in India, Africa, Egypt, Cyprus. The French learned in Algeria. The Americans took bloody years to learn it in Vietnam. *We've* shown it here. Power can't oppress people any more. Because we *matter* more than Whitehall – '

But there swept across the plain the wild shrilling of distant whistles. 'Red warning!' cried the Major. 'Our scouts! Quick. Turn. Gallop for home.' The squeal of the half-tracks turning on flintstones was only a thousand yards away in the bridleway. Cubbington wheeled his huge hunter, smote its backside with his cane and thundered away across the field in a flat gallop. Sods of black earth came ballooning back from his horse's hooves. Martin and Ancilla turned to Bramble, 'We're sorry, but' – grinned and galloped away. Aston Abbot's black charger had somehow got free from Sylv and was careering off, bucking and kicking at its loose reins, towards the woods. Martin tried to grab its bridle as it pelted past him. But, 'Go *on*!' shouted Major Abbot from the yard. 'Leave me. I'll follow.'

The scout-cars and the half-tracks reached Leo Mallard's broken-down tractor jamming the bridle-path. There was a tremendous roaring of engines and shouting. The television-crews were bundling their equipment – cameras, cables, sound-booms, dollies, mikes and lights – into the large green BBC vans. Rupert Bramble dived into his car.

'Quick, Thelma! *Quick!*' he shrieked. 'Drive me away!' Thelma bounded in with her notebooks and seized the wheel. Sylv said to Abbot, 'I've my Mini. Hop in. We'll hide you.' Abbot saw his horse disappearing with the others into Hampden Heights. Sylv seized his hand, took it under her coat, tugged it between her legs.

Bramble was gone, tearing down the track to the Brackton road. The two BBC TV vans lurched off. Abbot looked northwards. The half-tracks had pushed Leo's tractor into the ditch and were creeping slowly past, cocked-up on the bank. They would reach the barn in three minutes. 'OK,' he said. 'I'll drive.' He sprang into Sylv's Mini, skidded on to the track, squeezed past one van, then the next, and reached the Brackton road. Left lay nowhere. Bramble had disappeared from sight to the right. Abbot pursued him. Then after a mile, there was a lane to the left and a finger post: 'Trout Inn and River only. No Through Road.' He swung left.

Sylv squeaked, 'Where?'

'Pub I know,' grunted Abbot. 'Lie low.'

'Why not Brackton?' protested Sylv as her Mini bounced down the ruts. 'Look out for my springs,' she said crossly.

'I will, love, I will.' Abbot immediately slowed down, dived across, grabbed her and began to kiss her like a maniac. 'I'll look out for your springs,' he mumbled. 'Like I did before.' The Mini zigzagged onwards down the slope to the river. He saw in his driving mirror only a

330

hump of empty lane. Ahead beyond the beseeching arms of the line of pollard-willows the River Sedge flashed like steel in the noon sun.

'I've got to stop,' he said. He ripped her sweater upwards and when he saw her breasts thrust one, then the other into his mouth, flicking the nipple between his tongue and his top teeth. His beard tickled her belly. She wriggled. But she relaxed. She could telephone from the pub. His hands had dived downwards under the band of her pants and his fingers tangled through the fringe of his target. But she kept her thighs pressed tight. 'Wait.'

'I can't, Sylv.'

'Wait till the pub.'

'I'm sick for you, Sylv.'

'Greedy, you mean.'

'No, crazed. Hooked. Sunk.' He reached at her breasts again. The smell of her, even had she been hideous, would have driven him mad. He sucked at her nipples, rolled them, nibbled them, mumbled between them, 'Like a moth in a bloody flame.'

'Come up here, then.'

She opened her mouth and let him kiss her while his hands fumbled her breasts. The old brute was sexing her up. She thought of Joshua and the thousand pounds. 'Quick,' she said, 'to the pub. I can't wait either.'

He dashed the Mini round the corner of the grey stone pub, and parked it out of sight. It had been the home of a ferryman in the last century before they built the bridge, now blown up, five miles downstream beyond the end of Hampden Heights.

'You've been here before,' said Sylv, as suspiciously as a virtuous bride.

Abbot grunted, 'Knew a girl once.' But he was out of the car and across to the kitchen-window and tapping on it in a moment. He does move fast, thought Sylv. Fit, he

331

must be. He could really keep at it. A thrill suddenly coursed through her. His beard suited him. Well, mebbe she'd let him have her. Just once before she rang. Abbot had disappeared into the kitchen. It'd be fair, thought Sylv, for a thousand quid. And she wanted it. She crossed her thighs and squeezed them. Yes, she would let him.

The publican peered at Abbot. 'The Major! I wouldn't have known you. You shouldn't be here. There's a reward – '

The urgency in Abbot's face silenced him. Abbot pulled him to him, muttering, glancing round the kitchen.

'OK, OK, we're empty. The room over the front then. You had it before. You've no bags, I suppose.'

Sylv had though. 'Very expensive looking,' Abbot remarked.

'A feller gave them me for the weekend. Said he couldn't take mine with his to Montego Bay.'

'That's why you're so brown.' Abbot was panting up the steep stairs behind her. She was wobbling her little bottom in front of his whiskers.

'All over,' said Sylv in the bedroom under the eaves. 'We'd lie out in his boat. Look.' She stripped off her trousers and her pants in two flowing movements and in a third lay back naked on the bed. She looked round for a telephone. 'It's a pretty little room, I must say,' she said. 'Come on, love.' He had plunged forward like a diver and she caught his head tight between her knees. Now she opened them and put her hands behind his head and pulled him up between her spreadeagled thighs. 'Come on, sex me up there.' She held him by the ears. His beard tickled the inside tops of her thighs and she wriggled. She was still looking for a telephone while his head was buried. Inside that cupboard, other side of the bed, blast it. Then she began to wriggle and heave and pant because of his pleasuring tongue. Her body arched upwards and

332

her hands gripped the back of his head pulling him into her more deeply. She strained upwards like an acrobat. Abbot, goggling upwards, saw her marvellous breasts, her face pink, eyes shut, mouth open, little pink tongue flicking. She jerked once, twice, sucked in a huge gasp, jerked a third time with a scream of ecstasy, and fell back. She was wet. Her hair was tousled. She breathed in and out, long and relaxedly. Her legs were still splayed. She ran her fingers through his hair. 'Fantastic,' she murmured. 'Fantastic . . . A little rest . . .'

Abbot was patient. He had all the afternoon till the December dusk fell for his return. Sylv dozed. He gazed at her, touching her lightly with fingers and tongue. After a little she said, 'I'm hungry. Could we go down?'

'I've ordered it up here. Safer.'

Sylv involuntarily pouted.

Abbot asked, 'D'you mind?'

'No. What is there?'

'Champagne and smoked trout. Sirloin and a bottle of burgundy.'

Sylv bounced up. 'Smashin'! You're a love.' She got off the bed and peered into the little bathroom built under the sloping roof. 'No bidet,' she complained. 'I'll have to have a bath.' She started to run it.

Abbot went downstairs to see about lunch. Leaving the bath running, Sylv nipped across to her bag on the dressing-table, and extracted the piece of paper with the Brackton Police telephone number and the Special Branch extension. She brought it back to the telephone and sat down on the bed. She thought: I'll not hurry, and if I hear him comin', I'll not ring. She was looking at where she had lain, seeing Abbot's head, feeling his tongue and mouth working such joys. She had not let him have her yet. She must let him first to be fair. She felt excited again. She put down the piece of paper. It'd be his last lay before years in jail. Costing the country a thousand quid for the tumble, too! Sylv giggled with delight, and popped happily into her bath.

# 40

When after two hours there was still no sign of Aston Abbot scurrying across the fields into the woods, Martin said, 'I'll have to go and get him out.' There was no argument: only Ronald Cubbington remained on the ridge. Ancilla had ridden back to Meadow Hill to help Mary Stewkly who in the steaming, spicy scullery was half-way through her third distillation of elderberry brandy. Aidan Stride and his staff had left in his Rolls-Royce before the others had galloped back.

Cubbington said, 'Turnin' things over as I was ridin'. Aston told me he'd a row with that girl last time he screwed her.'

'Did he?' Martin was staring down into the plain from Cubbington's observation post. 'Never told me that.'

'Ah. Tried to pay with money,' said Cubbington. 'Dare say he didn't offer enough. They want jewels usually, don't they?'

The smoke-screen had long since blown away. At least two Troops of heavy Saladin armoured cars were blocking the Brackton lane, while the police and the rest of the Army were sweeping southwards all along the plain at the foot of the Heights. Two collections of half-tracks, scout-cars and police Land-Rovers were congregated round the barn where Bramble had interviewed them.

'What I'm sayin',' Ronald Cubbington pursued the point, 'is that it's ruddy odd the bitch is so hot to see him again.'

Martin looked round sharply. 'She'd sell him for the reward, you mean?'

Cubbington nodded, finger against nose, 'Be revenge, wouldn't it?'

Martin scowled and pointed. 'He couldn't take her to poor Leo's, could he? Look at the police there.'

'If he went to Mallard's we've lost him,' said Cubbington coolly. Then he burst out, hammering his saddle flap with his fist, 'Bloody stupid over-sexed stoat. He'll put us all up the creek. Always was like this. Hey!' He broke off. 'He used to take the girls to a pub by the river!'

They peered towards the distant wriggle of the Sedge, but the sun was in their eyes. They glimpsed only flashes of the water where sunlight spangled it, silhouetting the protesting willows like scarecrows on its banks.

'Well, it's possible,' said Martin.

'He'd not be darn fool enough to take her into Brackton.'

'He wouldn't *want* to. But she's so bloody sexy.'

'Ah,' Cubbington agreed. 'She'd be a public convenience though.'

Horse hooves squelched up the bank behind them. A courier appeared through the trees with messages. 'Bad news from Charlie Potter,' he bellowed. 'All the pigeons came back in a flock. Leo Mallard must have loosed 'em from the farm lest they'd be cotched. And here's their last note out.' He held out the tiny roll of paper to Cubbington: '*Police squatting no more safe no Major here.*'

'That Leo's a good man,' said Martin. 'Hope the police can't prove he's been helping us.'

Cubbington turned to the other document. It was a report from Richard Sandford on his home-made parchment. It read:

'*US Embassy Trade Mission plus Int. Red Cross reps arrived by boat Easterly this* A.M. *Interested to buy all local products. Anxious provide additional finance.*

336

*Brought Letters ex-Linda:*

(1) *She arrives plus Head of C-to-C Fancy Goods in helicopter tomorrow to collect Silken Dalliance order;*
(2) *Has had wide inquiries London re tourism here for health (seriously!);*
(3) *(seems most unlikely) Archbishop of Doncaster seeking Government permission to visit us;*
(4) *(even more unlikely) commercial attache Russian Embassy has contacted her, not for order, but to visit! In view of above, imperative Committee meet tonight. Calling session 8 P.M. at R.C.'s.'*

Even Cubbington's monumental mason's face flushed. 'Humming,' he said leaning from his saddle to pass it across to Martin. 'The meeting's fine. I better meet the Yanks.'

'*Trade* Mission!' Martin exploded. 'I can't believe it!'

'Who'll be looking after them now?'

'Mr Aidan Stride whom God preserve.'

'Might be a Government trap, y'know. Plain George sendin' men in disguised as Yanks.' Cubbington wagged his dolorous face. 'Anyway, you get that old bull Aston back. Pluck him off her.'

'I'll have to walk down from the far end,' said Martin, 'I'd never ride down, even on Viceroy.'

Cubbington cantered back into the Vale with the courier, and Martin rode southwards along the ridge till he reached the last outpost on the bluff above the river. He handed his horse over to the sentinel, and set off stealthily down the escarpment. It was almost as steep as a cliff and bristling with thorn bushes. Martin slithered down swearing and gashing his face and hands on the thorns. He thought: I'll never get that sod back up here. He stumbled, pitched, wrenched an ankle, then crashed head-first into a blackthorn-bush with such force that the thorns pierced his scalp and broke off like red-hot needles. He swore as sparks jazzed behind his eyelids. He wouldn't be able to get that sex-crazed old fool out past by Mallard's either. He lay against the blackthorn staring back up the cliff above him. He contemplated going back. But they dare not leave Abbot outside. One more effort. He scrambled onwards down the slope.

The going was immediately easier on the plain. Large water-meadows stretched out towards the river where in summertime bullocks grazed the dark-green grass and crowded under the white-candled chestnuts to dodge the gadflies. Now the fields were sere and empty. The bullocks were fattening in distant farmyards.

Martin loped along the blind side of a huge cattle-proof hedge, crawled under a thicket of blackthorn and emerged like a mole on to an overgrown towing-path. It could not have been used since the bluff at the end of the Heights had caved in. The track was still stony and an avenue of willows made a faded nave of interlacing branches. Stooping double Martin scurried along. The air was dank with brown and bitter river-smells. The water, full of debris and froth, gurgled coldly through the rushes. After a mile he saw a wooden boat-house, its paint flaked off in blistered strips. There was a gap in the boards and he saw a punt moored inside and a notice: 'Private. Trout Inn.'

He walked on more carefully, and the tow-path swung right disclosing above a sloping lawn the grey stone pub. Dusk was filling the wet air, and there was a light in the kitchen and in the room above. It was worth trying. Martin ran past the rusting iron tables on the lawn to the kitchen window and looked in. A man and woman and a boy of about fifteen were sitting in old chintz chairs round the stove. They had their ears cocked towards the ceiling. Their eyes flicked upwards at the beams, then at each other, and they were laughing.

Martin had to tap a finger, then rap his knuckles three times on the window to be noticed. The woman looked round first. Her eyes widened. She clapped her hand over her mouth. The man strode across and flung open the window. 'What yer want?' He stared angrily at Martin. 'Who the hell are you?'

Behind him the woman and boy had risen behind the table. The boy started to slink towards the door.

'I'm a friend of Major Abbot's.'

'What's yer name?'

'Stewkly, Martin Stewkly.'

The man peered at him. 'You're covered all over with blood,' he said plaintively. 'I can't see . . .'

The woman came across and stared at Martin. She asked, 'Have you had an accident?'

Martin shook his head.

'Been shot at by them? Come out from the rebels, haven't you?'

While she was looking at him, Martin heard the noises which had been entertaining them. From the bangs, groans, shudderings and cries through the thin plastered ceiling it seemed that several people were tupping like rams. The woman said, 'Is your father – ?'

'Shush,' said her husband. 'What's your dad's name?'

'It was Charles.'

'Come in,' said the man. 'Your friend's here.' He cocked his head. But there was silence above the ceiling now. Martin whispered, 'Has she telephoned?' The man nodded.

'Where? London? The BBC?'

The man said, 'No, Brackton.'

Martin waited. 'Did you overhear?'

The woman answered. 'I put it through for her – We only have the one line, y'see.'

'But you heard *something*?'

339

'Only saying where she was.'

'Oh, Christ! And what else?' asked Martin desperately.

The woman shrugged. 'Not much I heard. She'd got something – would they collect it. Something like that.'

'That's it. She's betrayed him,' swore Martin, 'to the police.'

'Didn't sound like that.' The woman was dubious.

'But it was,' said Martin fiercely.

'For the money,' said the man.

'The reward,' added the woman, nodding. 'That thousand quid.'

Martin looked carefully at her. Perhaps they were all in it together and were contentedly waiting. The man recognized the thought. He said quietly, 'I'm a cousin of Leo Mallard's. We're with you.' He held out his hand. Martin took it slowly. 'When did she ring?' he whispered.

'About ten minutes back. He was down here, getting another bottle iced. I thought then, that's a bit shifty. But you know girls; thought mebbe she was ringing her husband, her office, or another boy-friend.'

The boy butted in, 'The feller was down here with a bucket, fiddlin' about.'

'Quick,' snapped Martin, 'show me the way to them.'

They darted up the squeaking stairs and paused on the landing. It was low and dark. But there was no need for further directions. Light beamed out: the old door was not even fully closed. From inside rhythmic tumblings, hot panting and thunderous gruntings were again in spate. Satisfaction sounded close at hand.

Martin got to the door in three strides and pushed it open. The girl's upright golden back was towards him, bouncing up and down like a jockey at the trot. She was astride Aston Abbot. Her head was flung so far back that her silver-blonde hair was flopping against the arched small of her back. She was moaning like a dog at a door.

Abbot's hands reached up, gripping her breasts as if they were handle-bars. His legs, feet and toes, braced out towards Martin like a divingboard, were jerking and flicking the golden body up and down. Abbot's left eye suddenly moved from its enraptured gloating gaze. Under his arm, under Sylv's arm, behind her breast and face and flickering hair he saw Martin. He froze. Sylv pumped on, yelping, 'Don't stop. Don' stop. Don' stop. Don' stop!' Her hands shot questioningly downwards. She stopped, looked at Abbot's eyes, flung her head round, saw Martin, cried out like a child, dived forward on to Abbot, realized this extra revelation, scrambled off him, rolled sideways, tugged wildly at the sheet, got it over her buttocks and buried her head in Abbot's side.

'What the bloody hell are you doing?' shouted Abbot, wrenching at the sheet which was curled under Sylv. 'You bloody rotten stinking Peeping Tom!'

'Shut up!'

'What?' Abbot's eyes goggled. His face was purple and wet with sweat. There was a champagne bottle on the bedside-table above the telephone. Abbot grabbed it to hurl at Martin.

Martin said, 'She's sold you. To the police. For the reward.'

Sylv jerked her head round under Abbot's armpit. She was still scarlet. Her huge eyes and moist mouth hung open. 'I've not,' she swore. 'I've bloody not.'

Martin looked wildly round the room. He went to her bag on the dressing-table under the window. He picked up a piece of paper, glanced at it, and said, 'You telephoned ten minutes ago.'

'She didn't,' said Abbot.

The publican and his wife pressed forward in the doorway.

'Get out!' growled Abbot.

The man said firmly, 'She did phone, Major. When you were gettin' the wine.'

'Did you?'

'To the BBC,' said Sylv. 'To Thelma.'

'In Brackton?' asked Martin sceptically. He read off from the piece of paper, "22322". Your writing?'

Sylv paused, then nodded. 'Where the Unit was staying', she muttered. 'Aston said not to say, but I *had* to tell 'em. My job depends – I shouldn't be here,' she babbled on. 'Rupe Bramble's gone . . .'

'Can I ring this number?' asked Martin, politely.

Mrs Mallard said, 'I'll put you through.' She creaked downstairs.

Sylv stared at Martin with her eyes very wide. Martin thought: if she's really bitched him, she'll try to sex me up now. She put out her tongue-tip and wriggled it around between her lips. Martin gazed. Her soft mouth so exactly resembled –

Abbot cut in, 'Oh, come *on*, Martin!' But he looked uneasy. The line clicked and Martin said, '22322, please.' He was still looking across at Sylv. She was raised sideways on her elbow, so that Martin could see both her breasts hanging and quivering as she breathed. Sylv seemed about to say something, but she just watched. The ringing-tone buzz-buzzed in his ear, and stopped. 'Brackton Police Station.' Martin held the receiver across to Abbot. The voice repeated, 'Brackton Police Station. Please give your name.'

Abbot snatched the telephone. 'Mata Bloody Hari,' he shouted into it and plonked it down. There was a long pause. He lay back. Finally he asked Sylv, 'D'you want to say anything?'

She shot up in bed, showing everything. She was so ablaze with anger that her neck and the top of her breasts were flushed. She said, 'I *was* going to ring them, yes.

342

But, when you started to kiss me I couldn't. It was the TV Unit I rang. Brackton 43771. Ring 'em there – '

'Was it?' said Martin. 'I'll ask the woman.'

'Don't worry,' said Abbot. 'If you'll excuse me.' He swung his legs over the side of the bed. He asked Martin calmly, 'No time to bath, I suppose?'

'Don't be crazy. We can't waste one minute more.'

'For Chrissake!' swore Sylv. 'I've not told the bloody Fuzz.'

Martin went out, without looking at her.

'I had their number, because they'd *asked* me to ring,' said Sylv furiously. 'I decided not to, for Chrissake.'

'It'll be a long walk anyway,' said Abbot, dressing rapidly. He called out to Martin. 'They'll not let her telephone again will they?'

Sylv shouted, 'Can't I change me bleedin' mind, because I *fancy* you?'

Martin's voice came mumbling up from the kitchen. He was making arrangements with the publican. 'No,' he shouted up. 'They'll not let her.' Abbot pulled on his corduroys, his leggings, his sheepskin-coat and tied his scarf. He looked into the mirror. He saw Sylv glaring at him. She was panting.

Bloody lucky Martin came, thought Abbot. Good of him. Good to have friends. He was fumbling in his pocket and found her car-key. He held it up. 'This is getting lost, I'm afraid. Otherwise you might get to a box before I can get back and they might hunt me down.'

Sylv crouched on the bed like a tawny lioness about to spring. Abbot looked down at her. 'I've got to get back safely,' he said reasonably. She let out a yowl, but flung herself backwards and lay back with her eyes closed. She let out a long sigh and said wearily, 'I didn't ring them. And I won't.'

Abbot found what he was groping for. He took out

two silver coins, and laid them on her still moist golden belly. 'It's been a smashin' afternoon, Sylv. In every way.' He stumped out as the coins crashed against the wall above the door.

In the kitchen Martin said softly, 'I've borrowed their punt. They say the police-dogs are all out round Leo's.'

They ran down the garden to the boat-house. The mist curled like smoke on the river's mirror surface. The light still beamed from the bedroom. Abbot paused and looked back. 'Oh, for God's sake!' exploded Martin, 'Enough's a bloody 'nough.' He grabbed Abbot's arm and jerked him fiercely into the punt. They pushed it out and floated away.

It was almost silent on the river and they felt snatched out of hot, noisy life into a cool suspended trance. They felt close to one another: allies as men. The skeleton arms of trees wafted slowly backwards. It was still enough to hear each other's breathing. Abbot gnawed his lower lip. Martin quietly related the news of the raid on Leo and the reports from Sandford. Abbot kept nodding. He put his arm round Martin's shoulder and murmured, 'We'll have to hurry.' They were sandwiched between black gliding water and a grey ceiling of mist. The lights of the Trout Inn vanished behind the river's sweep and they heard clearly the baying of the police-dogs on the bank.

It was freezing cold. They huddled together under a dirty tarpaulin which stank of rubber and fish. The current bore them more swiftly forward. A barn owl swept across the mist like a pillow of feathers. The farm dogs were yowling at the Alsatians hunting them. Martin supposed they would hunt his line backwards up the escarpment. He felt suddenly as exhausted as if the lifestream running into him had been cut off. His head lolled on to Abbot's shoulder. Abbot said gruffly, 'Thanks for coming.'

Martin mumbled.

Abbot said, 'I couldn't help it. I was almost certain she'd try to bitch me. But I had to have her.' He stirred under the tarpaulin at Martin's side. The punt had drifted too close to the bank. Filling the gap made by Martin's torpor, Abbot began to paddle energetically. He was trying to command again. He demanded between strokes, 'You think I'm mad?'

'How could I? After all, with Ruth . . .'

'Yes, I'd forgotten that . . . Was that the same crazy – ?'

'Love,' interrupted Martin flatly, aiming to obliterate discussion with the blanket word meaning twenty things to a score of people.

'Love's got dam'all to do with it,' said the Major sharply, thrusting his paddle quickly in and out. Droplets of water illumined by moon-glow through the mist ran down the paddle's edge like pendant diamonds.

'I don't like Sylv. I don't even hate her. I don't know what she thinks or earns or dreams or where she was born or even when. Or if she's any parents. I don't know if she's an agnostic, a communist, a Jewess, a Tory, a Catholic, a paid whore, or a bloody Prog. I don't know whether she likes coffee or cornflakes, or if she can sing a note or boil a bloody egg. As a person she's a stranger! But I know everything about her body. Every fold, crease, lip, hole, wrinkle. Every button that starts that fantastic body, that *motor* going! I could make her body with my hands *now*. Exactly. A replica. Martin, I can *feel* her now, in my finger-tips, in my nose and tongue.'

Martin grunted. Abbot almost shouted, 'I worship that *body*. I would do anything to it and for it. I'll never forget it.' He controlled himself, and asked Martin in a quiet voice, 'D'you know what I mean, at all?'

'Well, with Ruth – '

'Yes, you know then. You were pining sick for her when you came back six months ago.'

'Only six months,' said Martin. 'That *is* crazy . . .' He had to stretch his mind to recapture what he had felt. The feelings returned quite coolly. He said, 'There were other things about her which I loved then, too. So I was sick with jealousy.'

'Well, I'm not,' said Abbot triumphantly. 'I don't mind Sylv's host of men before, after. I wouldn't mind them even at the same time. I don't think her body belongs to me, except when I'm in her – any more than a bottle's *mine* when I drink from it. The *drink* is mine. At the time.'

'Then you can't possibly care.'

'Care? If you mean to care for – Bloody no. But care meaning to *need* – My god, if I hadn't had her for a week and I saw her beyond a firing squad, I'd have to get through to have her and be shot.'

'Yes.' Martin knew more was required of him, but he could only utter, 'It's a madness.'

'Never anyone like her for me,' said Major Abbot, putting down his paddle. 'Not remotely. Like *magic*. A spell . . .' The punt ran smoothly on. The water slapped against the bottom. 'Terrible how the hottest girls are always the greatest bitches.'

'But that's why they are,' said Martin, fractious with fatigue. 'Absolute power corrupts.'

'Power?'

'Is there any greater when one person who is insanely desired holds the other in absolute thrall?'

'Thrall!' Abbot grunted. 'Ridiculous word.'

'Well, that's what it is when you're incurably sexually hooked on a woman. Think of the men Sylv and Ruth have had in their absolute power, screaming to them, begging for them. Look at you. It's the most powerful thing in the world.'

Trees loomed largely on their left. Martin drove his paddle in and the punt swung leftwards. 'We're back,' he said. 'Free again. Free of them, too.'

'Of the bitches?' Abbot fumbled over his head and grabbed a cold branch. A voice called softly, 'Major Abbot?'

'Here. Present and correct.'

'Yes,' said Martin. 'To be free of powerful bitches. Wonderful.' He sprang ashore and yanked Abbot's arm after him. The Major grumbled. Martin said, 'You're not free yet though, you silly old bugger.'

A searchlight leapt across the river bouncing off the flowing water, scything through the trees. 'Quick! Run!' said Martin crossly, lugging Major Abbot after him.

# 41

When the Sikorsky helicopter from Coast-to-Coast Fancy Goods landed with Ezekiel Kornkrack and Belinda Sandford a cheering crowd surrounded the cavalcade of decorated wagons and donkey-trains drawn up on East Pym Green. Drays and panniers bulged with the huge delivery from Silken Dalliance. Aidan Stride, with a Browne cigar and his aides-de-camp, was waiting in his Rolls-Royce by the church.

In honour of the American Trade Mission, the flag of St George and the Resistance flew tautly from the church-tower and farm-chimneys. There was a leaden tinge in the sky: the wind skewered into ears and kidneys. 'Could be a white Christmas,' the old Potter cousins opined, blowing on horny fingers. There had been a restlessness about Christmas in the Vale. The effects of the blockade would be sharply felt: relatives could not visit nor friends correspond. There would be no shopping sprees to Brackton, and no cards, no presents from outside. Young children who did not know, and older children to plague their parents, continually inquired: 'Can Father Christmas get through Plain George's blockade?'

The arrival of Kornkrack, the Red Cross and the American Trade Mission suddenly brightened the outlook. The Mission turned out to be three men under an Assistant Commercial Attaché from the London Embassy, cast forward on to the scent of business exploitation by Kornkrack's Washington inquiry. They missed few commercial tricks which could further political ends. The Vale of Hampden, isolated, but adjoining the North

Sea's gas- and oil-fields had lively power possibilities. This renaissance of craftsmanship, cottage industries and natural foods was also interesting. But the area was not just a commercial proposition. It might provide a tactical bridgehead into Europe. The Progressive Party's unassailable majority had meant that broke John Bull had recently been dancing less willingly to Uncle Sam the creditor's tune. 'A little *local* pressure,' drawled the American Secretary of State, 'always reminds dependent nations how much they depend. Didn't we have Britain *grovelling* to us after Suez? Well now, let's lean on them a little closer home.'

Sandford and Cubbington, aware of the American's axe-grinding amity, used precious gallons of petrol to show the Mission every art and craft in the Vale. Aidan Stride recommended that, as his order book was crammed, the Americans should concentrate on Cottage Growth Industries. 'Plenty of slack there – well behind the area's gross production mean.' So the Mission purred over lace-making in the Hampdens, and tanning and skin-curing in Sandford's barns. Peering over piles of fleeces and skins they watched coat-cutting, glove- and gaiter-making, and the spinning of wool on Easterly's old spindles, and the weaving of tweeds on East Pym's refurbished looms.

They knew the passion for hand-made goods back home, as the revulsion against the mass-produced mounted in the States. They had seen some cottage industries on the remote rocky shores of Scotland and Ireland, but had recognized that these were mainly for the tourists' benefit. 'Here in Hampden, it's a way of life. It's *vital* to them,' they declared. 'Such *dedication* is fantastic!' The spirit of these self-help colonists, threatened by an imperial government, summoned up like a battle-trumpet in disillusioned American hearts proud echoes of 1776.

'Goddammit,' the Attaché remarked, 'we might be back under Washington!' Horsemen rode by and carriages dashed along the crumbling roads. Herds of beef cattle and flocks of sheep wandering biblically to common grazing, held up their wide-eyed progress on the lanes. The visitors touched the traces of the lost American dream. 'Here, maybe,' murmured the Commercial Attaché, fumbling for words to encase emotion, 'is the Ethos of our way back to Truth.' His sentiments were reflected in damp American eyes.

The International Red Cross Party escorted by Dr Quainton assumed the St George's Cross of the Resistance flew particularly in their honour. So they happily exclaimed at the good complexions, white teeth and bright eyes among the young. 'Experiment almost unique!' The Swiss Professor burst out. 'Here we are having Benefits of twentieth-century Experience, with Capital enough, on good Land. Yet we are having no Disadvantages. Nowhere else is such thing possible. Fresh Food, not Tins. No Synthetics, not one. Fresh Air and Exercise – plenty. All early nights. No Pollution. No Exhaust Gases. No Cannabis and Heroin and only natural Alcohol. Here Persons perhaps live to Centuries!'

Patricia Fernden's old people at East Pym Rectory came in for special commendation. They were all busily engaged on group projects, which were actually needed by people they knew. These ranged from knitting mittens or fresh-wool blankets for each other to making woolly teddy-bears and Plain George goblins for their own or friends' grandchildren. 'They 'ave their *personal* "Oxfam",' said the cynical French doctor. 'So they *see* the good being done. And they get warm on close-by gratitude.'

Mr Ezekiel Kornkrack, borne along in Aidan Stride's Rolls-Royce, was not too interested in the very elderly; they did not constitute a major market for his goods. But he quizzed Stride keenly about the children. 'How much earlier does your back-to-nature existence here bring on the libido?'

Stride said, 'The school-kids are a bit busy for that sort of lark so far. And they've no films nor telly nor girdle ads in Tubes to sex 'em up. But they're comin' to it earlier, Kornkrack. I've seen 'em lookin' at my girls. And in the first warm evenings of summer . . .'

'Hayfields,' sighed Mr Kornkrack romantically. 'Young love in the new-mown hay.'

'Using our products,' said Stride, 'by the gross.'

Mr Kornkrack was startled. 'Yes, sure, sure.' He had for a moment been almost shocked by Stride's commercial attitude. Something of the ambience of the area had infiltrated even his armadillo skin.

While they motored on to the factory hundreds of hand-woven panniers containing the beautiful cod-pieces were being stacked inside the helicopter.

'*Made with love for love in the blockaded Vale of Hampden*', ran the announcement in vellum on each reed basket. Kornkrack's advertising agency was already warming up the American market with its series of half-pages bearing the simple query, 'WHAT'S COMING IN FOR NEW YEAR, DOLL?'

Belinda, who had expected to see her father at East Pym when they landed, sat between Stride and Mr Kornkrack. The latter gave her thigh his avuncular squeezes as he repeatedly declared, 'Now this Belinda doll, Mr Stride, has worked for you like no woman's business.'

Stride was engrossed in planning future orders: 'We must rationalize, Kornkrack, to bring down costs. I reckon a range of five sizes – Choir Boy to Buck African – would be ample.'

He had not given Belinda a serious look until he heard Mr Kornkrack murmur like a bullfrog into her farther ear, 'Doll, if this guy don't appreciate your value, you've a top position with "C-to-C" any time you give me the nod.'

Stride immediately studied Belinda. She was still pale, but her cheeks had aristocratic roses in them. Her eyes, which he remembered likening to cow pats – 'dull as all snobs', now sparkled and darted like sunlight through a beck. Inside her new sable coat she looked, he thought, like some Russian princess. He sniffed: she even smelt expensive. He looked at her hands: they were small and white but with long slim fingers.

'Hey, hey!' he murmured, steadying himself. But sex had not yet stirred; he was appreciating her. She's sharp and ambitious like me. But she's got *taste*.

She was whispering to Kornkrack, 'Nods don't mean an hour under you between your awful ice-buckets, Zekey!' Mr Kornkrack honked. Belinda laughed. Stride twisted round farther. He could see her small ear glowing. Nice colour that. His mind shot off on new dildo shades, but was hastily hoisted back.

'For one hour with a high-class doll like you, Linda,' grunted Mr Kornkrack, 'I'd pay two hundred fifty bucks.' The thought of it drove his hairy hand amorously up the creamy inside of her thigh.

'That's four dollars a minute,' said Belinda cheekily, nipping his fingers tight before they could advance farther.

'Just a bit over, doll,' said Mr Kornkrack.

Stride glowered. High-class, that's what she was. Bar young Stewkly's Ancilla there wasn't a snob dish in the area. Belinda looked real good in the Rolls. There would be a lot of sales entertaining in the future. He said toughly, 'I hope, Kornkrack, you're not seekin' to obtain me Sales Manager's services.' Kornkrack's eyes popped. 'Officially,' added Stride. 'And I mean it.'

Belinda looked at him. He was flushed with anger and those wonderful eyes which had by legend kept his lady-workers panting, glared furiously across at the American. Now he beamed them down on her and said, 'Just because we'd no occasion to meet before, Miss Sandford – ' He paused, then added firmly, 'I hope you realize I want to spend time with you this visit.'

'But of course,' said Belinda, rather breathlessly, as the Rolls, richly crunching the gravel, drew up at the front of Silken Dalliance. A guard-of-honour of work-ladies was drawn up, the week's holder of the Golden Phallus standing a little apart and holding it correctly in front of her. The American pressed his enormous nose against the window, steaming it up. 'Gee,' breathed Mr Kornkrack, 'our publicity boys could really go to town on that one.' But he was studying the other ladies too. Flimsily dressed to display their charms they were goosefleshed with cold and hopping from one blue leg to the other. But their breasts were bouncing prettily.

Aidan Stride announced, 'I shall show Mr Kornkrack round the works, my new mills and rush-beds, and then you and I will have a sales conference for future planning, Miss Sandford.'

'Certainly, Mr Stride,' said Belinda meekly.

'I've a few ideas to put to you.'

Belinda bowed her head. Hadn't this man's enterprise made her rich on her own, by her own energy and thought? She was an independent person at last. She had something to hold on to, other than Long Hampden and the need to marry money to keep it in the family.

Mabel twitched open the door of the Rolls and Mr Kornkrack levered his way out, sniffing the air as if to test the profit in it. He waddled towards the line of young ladies who at a sharp bark from Mabel dropped him a bobbing line of nippled curtsies. Kornkrack beamed. 'Fine British welcome!' he honked, wrapping his fur coat round him. Mable started to introduce him to the shivering contingent. Belinda was about to follow him out of the car, but Stride gripped her arm. 'You've nothin' goin' with that hairy fat old buzzard, have you?'

Belinda was surprised enough to hesitate. Stride impatiently squeezed her. 'Have you? I asked.'

'Nothing but business,' said Belinda primly, turning to look at him. She began to chuckle.

'What's funny?' Stride's voice was rough. He jutted his chin out.

'You had such a reputation!'

'You mind?'

'No.'

He stared at her and grinned. He really was marvellous to look at, thought Belinda. She heard herself murmur, 'I suppose someone like me rather wants a lot of experience.'

Mr Kornkrack, inspection over and the girls thankfully dismissed in a whirl of purple thighs, was flapping his arms like an impatient gorilla round his enormous belly. 'You comin', Linda doll? You comin', Mr Stride?'

Stride snatched Belinda's hand. 'Dine with me tonight.'

'I'm meant to be staying with my father.'

'I said "Dine", Miss Sandford.'

'All right,' she smiled, 'I'd love to.'

He gripped her hand and they got out and began to walk around the factory. Stride was a tycoon again, crisp and knowledgeable, impressing Kornkrack, inspiring attention. Belinda walked behind him admiringly. It was crazy, she thought, they had grown up within five miles of each other but they would never have met without this

354

revolution . . . He saw her gaze reflected in the glass door and smiled at the reflection. She grinned back. As she passed him, he said in a low voice, 'All that experience. I've had no more of it since I started to run this business.'

She raised her eyebrows. Mr Kornkrack was stirring the latest beeswax-and-rush amalgam in a vat, while gazing covetously at the young blonde work-lady who overhung the turgid brew.

Belinda said quietly, 'I hope you've not given up . . . entirely. Experience ought to be passed on.' Before Stride could reply, she said, nodding at Mr Kornkrack who was now moving a hairy hand under the girl's apron, 'Our client will need the usual entertainment after lunch.'

'You're right. I'd forgotten,' said Aidan Stride. 'Big Business Gongo!' He began to bubble with laughter. 'That's what I like about you – efficiency.'

'But that's not all, Mr Stride.'

'No. But let's *all* have our dinners – lunches – first.'

Preliminary drinks were taken at Mrs Bellamy's, whose genteel references to the aristocracy and best 'Spirits of Hampden' warmed Mr Kornkrack's heart and loins. His eyes rolled restlessly round the bar and he muttered something to Belinda. She whispered into Aidan Stride's ear.

'The girl on the beeswax amalgam? He'll mean Babs,' he said. He crossed over. 'I can't guarantee her performance, Kornkrack, y'know. She's new.'

The American waved this aside. 'She's got a high-class look.' His eyes settled and started to protrude.

'I'll have her down straight away,' said Aidan Stride. 'Dare say you'd fancy a tickle over dinner. I used to, mind.' They were all repairing to fresh lobsters and Sandford's Hereford sirloins in Mrs Bellamy's dining-room. Mr Kornkrack gurgled and stroked his belly. 'Shell-fish and a doll,' he breathed. 'Pow!'

Stride clicked his fingers for Mabel. 'Get that Babs down here sharp for Mr Kornkrack. And tell her no knicks, lips shut and legs open, OK?'

As Mabel opened the pub door to scurry back to the factory a babble blew in on the sea-breeze. The steamed-up windows had obscured the gathering of a woolly-coated and fur-hatted crowd on the quay. They were gesticulating out to sea. Ancilla hustled in with a message from Martin: 'The Red Cross boat from Cherbourg's half a mile out there. Owen and his lot are bringing the stuff back in their boats.'

Then a surge of astonishment swept through the crowd and broke among the party in the pub. Landward of the freighter, watched by the suspicious Navy minesweeper, the fishing-boats were sailing back filled not only with crates and cartons, but with people.

Owen's boat crossed the harbour-bar with Christmas parcels, ridiculously gift-wrapped, in its sloshy footing. But even stranger were ten smartly-dressed men and women in the jaunty hats, check-suits and overcoats which Americans affect for British visiting.

As Owen's boat ran in alongside the jetty, he shouted up to Martin, 'The Navy's ravin' out there! Their orders is to let through only Red Cross personnel.'

'But are these?'

'No. Tourists. But they've all got Red Cross papers, somehow! And there's scores more comin', wantin' to spend Christmas here. What do we do?'

But the first visitors were already leaping on to the slippery stone steps at Martin's feet. Grunting as they landed, they pounded up with the eager bellows of a hungry beef-herd sighting new pastures.

An argument broke out, fragmented by the breeze, the slapping of slackened sails, the avalanche of food-parcels, cries of inquiry from the crowd's ignorant fringe and the arrival of further fishing-boats laden to the gunwales with shouting tourists sensing an impasse. At this juncture the Easterly horse-drawn omnibus hove into sight. It had been commandeered by Sandford and Cubbington for the American Trade Mission's luncheon. Exclamations of delight and greeting darted between the omnibus party and the newly-arrived tourists. Cubbington and Sandford scrambled down the outside stair and thrust through the crowd to join Martin and Owen. They urgently considered the problem, encircled by confused advice from the locals.

'Friends,' Cubbington called out, 'we're not yet ready to put up as many guests – '

A frustrated howl burst from the assembled Americans, as latecomers squeezed into their backs, querulously asking what the hold-up was.

The inhabitants of Easterly raised a counter-chant:

'We've rooms enough.'

'We'll take a couple.'

'Christmas is coming.'

'But,' Cubbington shouted, 'we're glad to have you with us. If you would put up in our cottages, and farmhouses – '

A roar of approval rose from the crowd like steam. 'But that's what we want.'

'In old English cottages.'

'Farmhouse fare . . .'

'Roast beef of old England.'

'Well said, Cubby,' shouted a local woman. Cubbington's nose traversed stuffily round.

Sandford called out, 'If you'll follow us to Mrs Bellamy's we'll try to arrange accommodation for you all.' He murmured to Cubbington, 'Better send Pony Expresses out to the Council Chairmen and the pubs. Tell 'em to report back with possible *pensions*.'

Cubbington, elbowed by the crowd, looked baffled.

'Put-ups,' grunted Sandford. 'I'll take half a dozen myself at Long Hampden. Belinda might help, if I can prise her away from Mr Stride.'

'I can do three couples in the Manor,' said Cubbington quickly. 'More perhaps, if Grace has help. Our dailies are all weavin' and lace-makin', y'know.'

Martin said, 'My mother can take four at least. We'll get all the coaches and carriages in.' Ancilla and he squeezed out of the throng.

The tourists jostling towards Mrs Bellamy's bourn, saw Martin and Ancilla cantering out of her stableyard, as the first pony couriers galloped along the quayside. The children, playing up to the fresh audience, let off Western shrieks, and ostentatiously slapped their ponies' necks and rumps as they rattled across the cobbles and turned clattering up the hill. Cries of delight and croons of pleasure burbled through the crowd. 'This is genuine,' explained one warm American voice entering the pub. 'No play actin' about it. This is how these people actually *live*, for God's sake!' In a diapason of approbation the new arrivals swept into Mrs Bellamy's bar. 'Do your quaint licensing regulations permit a drink?'

'No silly Government regulations here,' Mrs Bellamy corrected them. 'Only the little rules I make myself. You're not in the rest of England now, I'm glad to say.'

The Americans cooed over the bottles. 'Dandy Lion Liquor! Elder Berries . . . "Spirits of Hampden" 150 proof, my God! . . . Razberry Cordial . . . Parznip Wine?'

The local wines and cottage-ales and home-distilled spirits poured down their eager, salty throats. Then staid carriages and dashing curricles and bobbing governess-carts bore them euphorically away to hearths where huge logs snoozed and candles lit low beams, and there would be fat pheasants for supper with rough-milled bread and salty butter walloped from the churn.

The Silken Dalliance luncheon, swollen by the Red Cross delegates, the US Trade Mission, and the food parcels superintendents, lingered on. The Defenders were flushed with triumphant pride. There was even no need for the gratitude that often grates between donor and recipient. The outside world *wanted* to help the Vale of Hampden. '*Need* to help us,' whispered Ancilla, giving Martin's hand a squeeze under the table. 'Isn't it rather nice for you, love, to be on the receiving end at last?' As the pewter mugs of mead circled the tables, slurred toasts were drunk to the Vale of Hampden and damnation to Whitehall.

Babs had endured a testing lunch from Mr Kornkrack's busy fingers, but she had obeyed orders almost to the lip, opening her mouth only to gasp at a particularly searching probe. Belinda observed the American tycoon's rising colour and murmured to Mrs Bellamy. Two ice-buckets were ceremoniously carried upstairs and Mr Kornkrack and Babs rose to follow these instruments of bliss or torture. Belinda murmured, 'Not more than your hour, Zekey.'

'Listen, doll,' said Kornkrack huffily, as if interrupted on business, 'I'm trying the Buck African this afternoon.'

'Poor Babs,' sighed Belinda, turning her eyes up.

The party dispersed towards tipsy observation of their duties, but Aidan Stride sat on with Belinda, drinking black coffee brought in by the friendly Americans and dicussing the future of Silken Dalliance in sensibly optimistic terms. 'Your man's had his hour,' said Stride at last. Belinda, allowing the redoubtable Mr Kornkrack five minutes grace, finally roused him for his flight back to London.

She said to Stride, 'Babs looks the worse for wear, Aidan. I'd let her off tomorrow.'

Stride's mind was pattering like a jig-saw with his

rationalization scheme. He stared at her, surprised and delighted by her use of his first name and by her solicitous attention to detail. What a help she could be. 'Thanks, Linda,' he said, adding quite kindly to the uncomfortable Babs (the ice-buckets had proved peculiarly efficacious) 'Buzz off home and miss tomorrer's shift.'

'Than you, Mr Stride.'

'And there'll be fifty quid extra for amusin' Mr Kornkrack.'

'It was a pleasure, Mr Stride.'

'Was it?' inquired Stride keenly. 'A 'ticular pleasure?'

'Oh yes, Mr Stride. I've never felt anything like it in all my life.'

Stride grunted. ''Course, you haven't. It's a new model. Weren't it a shock at first?'

'Well, sir, Mr Kornkrack is on the heavy side and does, well, *continue*, doesn't he? But parts of it was fantastic, Mr Stride.'

'Right. Let's have your report on *which* parts on my desk Monday mornin'.'

'Report, sir?'

'Good God, girl, you're participatin' in a titillatin' technogical revolution. I might even upgrade you to Regular Tester.' Babs pouted dubiously. Another five minutes, let alone another hour with such as Mr Kornkrack was more than she could bear. Aidan Stride brushed off her hesitation. 'Ask Miss Mabel to put you on Special Test Trainin'. That way lies promotion.'

Choral Evensong soared from the church behind East Pym Green. 'Till we have *built* Jerusalem,' roared the village basses behind the choir. The Trade Mission and the tourists were like awed travellers to an antique land. Then the sudden roar of Kornkrack's helicopter yanked them back into the present of the world outside. The flutter of the Sikorsky's rotors dwindled and its navigation light vanished over the broken bridge on the River Sedge.

There was still a large fleece-coated, furry-hatted, plaid-cloaked gathering round the braziers and the leaping bonfires outside the pub. They had been drinking spiced ale and mulled sack of much higher alcoholic content than the beer formerly supplied by Brackton Brewery. PC Plumridge, wheeled by his wife Tibby, perambulated from group to group accepting the occasional nip or tankard, while officially keeping his ear to the ground and a check on drunken riding. Celebrators from outlying farms were pecked by wives, then hoisted sozzled on to their horses' backs or into their traps and carriages. Unlike the motor-car, the hungry horses took their owners safely home. Old Plum looked blandly on until he too, was wheeled away by Tibby in the moleskin coat her brother-in-law had sewn for her, from moles her niece had trapped.

The braziers glowed softly through their ashes like setting suns through mist. Firelight rippled on beams through windows. The flares round the Green were doused, smoking, in the clean frosty night. And the sweet floury smell of another bonfire's embers, crackling with chestnuts, wafted across from Church Hay with the high shouts of the children.

Aston Abbot had retired early to bed. His special kindliness to his wife, Davina, had left the General's daughter in no doubt of his afternoon's activities. He was yawning too and his eyes wore sporrans as they always did after one of those awful amatory bouts which meant so much to him and yet never raised in her more than a wish to giggle. Davina felt neither regret nor bitterness. She enjoyed her golf and bridge; Aston played neither. Love, too, was just a question of taste and ability. He returned from his sexual blow-outs rigorously exercised, mentally chastened, with a good appetite and no hang-over. As Davina Abbot remarked to Mary Stewkly, 'It's not as though he ever does it with friends of mine. *That* I couldn't bear.'

This time he had so narrowly missed betrayal, capture, and long imprisonment that the poor lamb must have learned his lesson. She brought him up a cup of warm creamy milk, a bowl of her partridge and hare casserole and a decanter of rose-hip brandy. She left him sleeping as soundly as a ginger-whiskered schoolboy after a needle match.

Ronald and Grace Cubbington had Mr Pennington the Banker to dinner to meet their six house-guests. Now over pheasants, chestnuts from Hanger Wood and elderberry-wine they were creating the Vale of Hampden's Tourist Board. 'Keep it just like this,' urged the Americans. 'Exclusive. Homely. The brave old world. We have a thousand friends back home who'd give their right hands to be right here by your beautiful fireside.'

The Reverend Mike Thornborough was playing host to Patricia Fernden's hostess in the Rectory at a cheese-and-ale reception for the Red Cross delegates. Carols were being bawled out under Dr Quainton's baton as the mummers came bowling up by coach. Old Nurse Dinton sat up on top, cocooned in the rough wool scarf she never finished knitting. She had so little to do at her First Aid Post that she loved to brew herb-tea for the other elderly in the Rectory of an evening. 'The old girl's mixture keeps 'em very spry,' said Thornborough with a grin at Patricia, for the mummers were as coarse and personal as Shakespearian clowns and the audience was loving it. Dr Quainton mopped his brow under the radiant candelabra. 'Better stuff in those herbs than in the pills outside the Vale.'

In Easterly Owen and his fishermen had stacked away

the Red Cross parcels and were slaking their thirst in Mrs Bellamy's when Mrs Ethel Birtwistle stumped in officiously. She was wearing a bright saffron cloak (woven in Nether Hampden) over her see-through crochet dress, and was seeking out volunteers for the five wives' Erotic Spectacle. 'Mumming and carols is fair enough for some of t'visitors,' Mrs Birtwistle announced, 'but these Yanks must have an eye for summat sexy and original.'

'Honest, Mrs Birtwistle,' said Owen, 'they'll not be wantin' that.' In spite of the remarkable intimacy of their relations on stage, Owen never called her Ethel off it.

'What? Yer out of yer mind, yer great slob! A smashin' new audience to send word back home. Now look at our new "Rural Rides" race-game. I mean that's got t'full flavour of country love-makin', hasn't it, Owen?'

Owen and his four friends wearily agreed: applause after those performances was always generous. 'But no competitions tonight, *please*, Mrs Birtwistle.'

Before they adjourned to Sea View where the tourists awaited the Spectacle in the Residents' Lounge, Mrs Birtwistle came to an important arrangement with Mrs Bellamy who still disapproved of these vulgar displays. Mrs Bellamy was firmly booked that night by the head of the American Trade Mission, who felt the need of her comfort. 'I do think all performing ladies in the area really must give up their amateur status,' she announced firmly, extending her little finger genteelly past her beaker of mead. Mrs Birtwistle agreed. Mrs Bellamy continued, 'If we are united we can charge sensible fees, you know. After all, we are doing special kindnesses, for which there are no substitutes inside or out.'

At Meadow Hill old Mrs Stewkly slept snug in bed with her terrier on her woolly shoulder and her bantam on her white head. She was convinced that dear Charles knew exactly what was happening in his beloved Vale, and because she could feel his happiness filtering through to her like the sun's rays through cloud-haze she unfurled and was content. She knew that down the corridor Martin and that lovely Ancilla were curled up together, 'snug as two pet dormice'. It was really so nice – and clever – of God, she considered, to put people together again in the most accidentally-*seeming* way, when one feared them irreparably broken.

In Long Hampden farmhouse, Richard Sandford was waiting for Belinda to return. He regretted she had not been with him for dinner, for he had enjoyed his six American tourists. He had put himself out in the way of food. 'You mean, Mr Sandford, sir, that every mortal thing we've eaten and drunk is off your very own property?' They had also relished his historical anecdotes about the place. He found himself as tickled to be asked as a cat having its chin stroked: nobody roundabout ever thought about Long Hampden's history at all. Now the Americans, after an exclamatory tour and a chilly instant when the dog-ghost scratched on the stairs, were returning with nightlights to their fire-warmed bedrooms. He realized that from their recommendations he could fill Long Hampden with Americans in love with England's past.

Sandford sat on with his toes towards the great log, as big as a man's frame, ticking and crumbling into ash. Then a car scrunched the gravel. His hall was still bright and hot with the glow of sixty sconced candles. Their light radiated over the frost-rimed beds full of bare rose-bushes and illuminated the Rolls-Royce. Aidan Stride and his daughter were kissing each other less with passion than with the affection of equality. Richard Sandford scraped his feet on the gravel. 'You'd care for a night cap, Mr Stride?'

'No thanks, Sandford. Not tonight. I've had a long day

with Kornkrack. And I'll be down at the factory at 6 A.M. y'know. We're doublin' production of the Buck African.'

'Sorry you can't stay,' began Sandford.

'There'll be plenty more times. I fancy your daughter. Seriously. Workwise too.' He hopped into the back of his Rolls. 'Workwise particularly,' added Stride. Sandford saw that he had dressed up Slim's father as a coachman with a cape and low-crowned beaver. The whole set-up was so ludicrous, he started to smile. Stride caught his look, and interpreting it as one of pleasure called through the window, 'Night Linda, love. Tell your Dad about it, eh.' The car swept away.

Belinda came glowing into the hall and put her arms round her father and hugged him. '*Extraordinary* kaleidoscope life is,' she murmured into his ear. 'All the pieces are there. Somebody, something rattles it: shake-shake. Quite different patterns. Why? If *we* don't do it, we're someone's toys really, aren't we?'

# 42

Between Christmas and New Year's Day events tumbled on the Vale of Hampden like a snowstorm. Great logs burned on the village greens and on Easterly quayside. Oxen were roasted, and fat piglets turned on spits. The three churches had overflowed on Christmas Day as the Reverend Thornborough galloped from service to service on his skewbald cob, for the Defenders gathered together in their hundreds to wish each other happiness, exchange news and thank God for their deliverance so far '*from Whitehall's blighting hands*'. The phrase was one of many militant lines from Patricia Fernden's and Mike Thornborough's New Hampden Hymnal.

Light snow lay on Boxing Day when there was a circus in Easterly, a fair on East Pym Green, and parties for the children. The Mere had frozen, suggesting to Major Abbot the possibility of another military attack. But the soldiers, morale low, were away in droves for Christmas with their families. Skaters skimmed hissing across the black stippled ice. Horse-drawn sledges, grandly called troikas, whirled down the lanes in a whine of iron-runners and the rumble of hooves on snow. Snowballs flew back from galloping hooves and out of children's hands and word rushed around the area about Rupert Bramble's Christmas film. The BBC talked of little else. In the world outside the people of England were turning to each other, as they are apt to do every other century, and deciding that Whitehall's blighting hands should bloody well lay off. It was no longer a matter of Chesterton's 'Secret People': '*And a few men talked of freedom, while*

*England talked of ale.*' It seemed the '*the people of England, that never have spoken yet*', were at last rising against the State's oppression. There were marches and demonstrations in other areas threatened by central planning.

'But have they planned as we did, Aston?' Cubbington inquired. 'That's the point.'

'That's how we did it. Two years good organization.' Abbot was crisp.

'More than two years,' said Richard Sandford. 'Ever since the last war people like old Charles were secretly thinking, "We do not *quite* forget."'

Abbot said awkwardly, 'You know, Charles Stewkly wasn't the innocent martyr really, was he?'

'He wasn't fighting when they killed him,' Cubbington was angry. He glared at Abbot.

Sandford said, 'Charles thought of it all. Without him nothing would have happened.'

'Richard is right,' said Abbot. 'We wouldn't have acted.'

'The quiet revolutionary,' murmured Sandford. 'That's the way it always happens in England: quiet men, decent men, *thinking* under the surface. That's why the politicians never notice us. Until, every few hundred years, it's too late.'

The Archbishop of Doncaster, escorted by the Bishop of Brackton, crossed the Sedge by pontoon with police permission. The crammed churches had made the Church move. The archdiocesan party toured the area in a cavalcade of carriages, after which the Archbishop preached to his newly discovered flock from an open landau on East Pym Green. He saw in the Defenders' return to simple things, and to the helping of one another, that renaissance of Christianity which Britain had sought so vainly since the war. 'Opposition from our *material* rulers has bonded you together. You have recreated a Christian community as it was under St Peter in Rome, surrounded by the black threats of the pagan Romans.' (He did not support any merger of the Christian churches.) 'In the grass roots you have found faith,' the Archbishop proclaimed. 'You have found one another and so are finding God.'

The Archbishop, maced and splendidly mitred, then sped about the four parishes in a dashing yellow-wheeled dogcart at the head of his episcopal posse. He blessed from crossroads and straw-stacks and from the tail-boards of hay-wains. He blessed the ploughs and harrows and their team of horses and oxen. He whirled round the tannery and the fish-salters, the looms and the tailors, the smithy and the lace-makers. He even paused briefly outside Silken Dalliance and, without blessing the products, at least shook Aidan Stride's hand with a murmured congratulation on his productivity. 'You are, I feel, the temporal power here, Mr Stride.' The dildo tycoon did not deny it.

As the Archbishop rode slowly down to the Sedge he recognized that a strong emotive force did rise from the area. He could not exactly define the source, nor swear it had a divine inspiration, but it certainly gave off a religious fervour.

Martin and Ancilla were escorting him on their horses. They passed the place where Charles Stewkly had been killed and Ancilla leaned from her saddle and put her arm round Martin's shoulders. The Archbishop saw them glowing at one another and he smiled. They said goodbye to him and rode back to Easterly.

'Something's in the air,' said Martin, trotting along sharply to keep warm and slapping one arm across his chest.

'George has been very silent,' said Ancilla.

'Plotting?'

'He's got a lot on his plate,' said Ancilla mischievously, mimicking his voice.

'But he's doing *nothing*,' said Martin. 'It's bloody odd.'

'He'll never recognize us. That's certain.'

As they rode past the burning braziers outside Silken Dalliance, a Pony Express lad waving a flaring torch galloped past them, shouting something about Russians.

Martin and Ancilla cantered on to the port. The road was cracking up in the frost where the tarmac had worn through. Pebbles and grit spurted from their horses' hooves.

By the time the Committee thundered back to Easterly, elbows waving and heels drumming like Hollywood cowboys, Martin and Ancilla were already ensconced in Mrs Bellamy's bar. They were entertaining four shining-faced Russians in astrakhan hats who were comparing 'Spirits of Hampden' favourably with vodka and treating it with the same tasteless directness. The atmosphere was cordial when Abbot, Sandford and Cubbington strode into the pub.

'Our Committee of the October Revolution,' Martin introduced them.

The Russians chortled and bowed jerkily like clockwork toys.

'Praesidium, yes?' asked one, grinning.

'How the hell did they get through the blockade?' Abbot whispered to Martin.

'They had Board of Trade permission.'

'Impossible!' said Cubbington.

'Yesso,' said the senior Russian, harking to the magic of a governmental phrase. 'New President of Board of Trade after Home Secretary disciplinization. He give us green signal. My name Smirnikov. This person Bolsenski, my assistant.'

Bolsenski comfirmed, 'Gave us definitely OK, Board of Trade President, with most full documentation.'

Cubbington glowered suspiciously. 'Have they got identity-cards?'

Ancilla said, 'Yes, and passes. And there's a genuine introductory letter. I used to know the Minister.'

Smirnikov produced a pack of passes and identity-cards and official letters and dealt them round the table. 'Look!' he cried with a gloat of gold-filled teeth, 'Board of Trade President's especial stampington!'

'But why?' asked Sandford.

The 'Spirits of Hampden' was working sweetly on the Russians and they were under orders to charm the Defenders. Smirnikov murmured confidentially, 'You have full US Trade Mission here.'

Cubbington touched his white beak. 'Well, the Assistant Commercial Attaché and a small team . . .'

'But one has returned with US capitalist Kornkrack and big Western Imperialists' erotical export.'

Martin nodded.

'With order books filled, they are giving out all round London,' cried Smirnikov.

'That's true.'

'They make other exports? And say they pay with good loans, no interest?'

'They've certainly offered us very interesting terms,' said Cubbington carefully.

'And will now grip you, American-wise, by the short balls! For ever crunching – ' Smirnikov ground one huge fist inside the other – 'Like they make with Britain ever since wartime and their rusty destroyer-ships.'

'I don't think – ' interrupted Sandford.

'Exactly, yesso,' said Smirnikov triumphantly, slapping

his palm heartily on the table to prove his point and swat out American dependence like a bluebottle. The Defenders waited, glanced uncertainly at one another and saw with relief that each was equally puzzled.

Ancilla said, 'They mean that if the Americans can trade with us here, so must they.'

'So,' exclaimed the Russians, in unison, 'So, so, so.' Their heads nodded vigorously around the table like tympanists over drums.

'So they pressurized the Government, I suppose,' said Ancilla laughing. 'They want to lend us money too!'

'No great pressure. Small reminder of Middle East oil situation. But powerful reminder of equal opportunity, here yesso. For we are most especially equal here. You know why?' The inflection was that of a statement, and there was further hesitation among the Defenders. Smirnikov inverted his question. 'You are *not* knowing why? Not why we have especially equal opportunity here?'

'Revolution?' asked Martin.

'Military coup?' suggested Abbot.

'No,' said Sandford, 'The balance of power.'

'Trade,' said Cubbington firmly.

'More likely extend the Cominform!' said Aston Abbot.

'Toe-hold anyway,' said Ancilla. The Russians' heads had been swinging around between them. She added ingratiatingly, 'And to help your small neighbourhood oppressed minority.' As she said it, she could not suppress a smile. She added, 'Against imperialist hyenas.'

Smirnikov looked suspicious. Martin started to laugh. Ancilla lowered her eyebrows at him and he said quickly, 'Certainly we're an oppressed minority. Always interested in aid.' He lowered his head as the absurdity of world politics began to tickle him unbearably.

'All of a bit things,' said Smirnikov firmly, nodding

away like a Cossack puppet. 'But one big thing more. We see your film on TV. Right. What does it show? True Communism!' He banged his hand down so hard on Mrs Bellamy's table that the glasses leaped like Bolshoi dancers.

'First proper Communism *ever* in Britain. Serious Communism. Not your wartime joke people or present-time Trades Union lunatic clerks! But big, proper Communism with a heart! Yesso!'

Mrs Bellamy was tired, for she had been engaged by different Americans every night to listen to the woeful tales of their exploiting wives. Continued sympathy towards these rather common people from unspeakable home-towns with their snaps of ugly children, had drained even Mrs Bellamy's great heart and frame. She now stumped across to the Russian party. 'That's not at all a nice way to behave,' she snapped, snatching up the glasses.

'No, no! Please Madam Publican Lady!' boomed the Russians. 'We make great business for you.'

'Please, Mrs Bellamy,' pleaded Martin. He said quietly, 'They were never at a decent school you know. Nothing like Eton near Moscow.'

Mrs Bellamy thawed; she had nannied almost as many Etonians in her nurseries as the Tories had cared for in their Cabinets.

'Very well then. Just one more chance.' She replaced the glasses. 'Not that we want any of your nasty pogroms here,' she said sharply to the Russians. 'You had a nice Czar of your own once, remember. Bolshies – poor Lord Bruncham always called you. Always thought you were waiting for him in his Walled Garden, poor old gentleman. Most of us here are C. of E., I'm glad to say.'

'See of ee?' The Russians repeated and then mumbled among each other.

372

'Christian,' declared Mrs Bellamy flatly.

'Christian! Just so!' said Smirnikov cheerfully. 'Good Communist religion. Share all. Down with the rich and camels. Very anti-imperialist religion.' He added as a small joke, 'And everything always better tomorrow, yesso? Just like ours!'

'We believe in *God*.' Mrs Bellamy, with a wag of her weary buttocks, plodded back behind her bar.

'We also,' said the thin-faced Bolsenski. 'Your God called Jehovah, ours called Working-peoples.'

'No, no!' cried Smirnikov impatiently. He called across to Mrs Bellamy. 'Please. Here you are especially most Communist. That is what I try to say. You have Peasant Collective Industries. You have workers stand together united. You have one party of the people. You have Workers' Councils. These leaders are your Politburo, good lady. You have overthrown yoke of imperialists!'

His rising voice reached a shout and his companions lurched to their feet, swaying with heavy concentration like sea-lions in a circus. 'Long live first soviet socialist republic of Vale of Hampden! Huzzaa!' They screamed, drained their 'Spirits', banged their feet on the seats of their chairs, and flung the empty glasses in a shattering salvo against the bar.

'No,' snapped Mrs Bellamy very crossly. 'That's quite enough – I knew it would all end in tears. You must go back to Sea View like good gentlemen and have a rest.'

The Russians looked gloomily at one another. Smirnikov seized Martin's arm. 'But we wish to make tours of industries. Place firm order books. Offer loans of money. Help equip Peasant Collectives. Make aid for Import-Exports: shipping, airfreighting, all together.' He grabbed Martin's hand and started shaking it.

Martin began to laugh and caught Ancilla's eye. She started spluttering. Richard Sandford began to giggle.

Aston Abbot let out barks of laughter. His face flushed and his eyes popped damply. Cubbington permitted a slow smile to leak across his countenance.

The Russians, suspecting an insult in the laughter, looked curiously at one another and then balefully at the people of Hampden. But the laughter swelled. It infected the corners of the bar. Giggles started snorts and snorts triggered whoops till laughter bellowed. Suddenly the Russians too collapsed into streaming-eyed merriment. Backs were slapped, shoulders punched, biceps gripped. Then the sound ebbed, save for a few last explosions.

Smirnikov said, 'Good to laugh together. Communist peoples are at one. But what is so funny?'

The Defenders on the brink of more mad laughter looked at one another. Sandford said quickly, 'Just happy.'

'Ah, happy,' breathed Smirnikov with another flash of gold. 'Happy, yesso. Thrown off Whitehall yoke. Now we make negotiations.'

'Tomorrow,' wheezed Cubbington. 'All trade negotiations.'

'And tonight,' said Martin, 'a great Soviet solidarity banquet.' He began to laugh again, tottering across to the bar for a private word with Mrs Bellamy. 'Look,' he mumbled trying to keep his face serious, 'those Yorkshire wives.' He jerked his head at the Russians. 'After all, Mrs Bellamy, you have been looking after the Americans quite beautifully. As they both want to help us, I think it ought to be fair do's for both, don't you?'

'They're more entertainers, of course, those wives,' Mrs Bellamy grunted scornfully. 'Their *Spectacles*! Nothing very comforting about *them*.'

'But our Russian friends might be partial to them before bedtime?'

'Very well,' said Mrs Bellamy, 'I'll send up word; I'll

be thankful to have them out of my nice clean bar, at all events.'

But the Yankee dollar, judiciously distributed in the Vale, had already spawned an intelligence network. The Russian delegation had not moved from Mrs Bellamy's bar before the American Commercial Attaché supported by one member of his Mission stamped in. With a frosty nod snapped off like an icicle in their rivals' direction, the attaché bluntly asked Martin, 'What's this about some Soviet Solidarity Banquet?'

As Martin hesitated, the Russian leader quickly agreed, 'Yesso. Tonight. To welcome real Communism.'

'What the hell is this?' demanded the American Commercial Attaché, with a surprisingly angry gimlet look. 'Some kinda joke, Stewkly?' His expression was quite at odds with his previous bonhomie. Martin motioned towards his three seniors. 'Our Committee . . .' he began.

'Local Soviet Apparat,' interrupted the Russian.

'You said you were a democracy here,' said the American querulously. 'By our observation you *are* a democracy here.'

'We are.' Martin, Sandford and Ancilla spoke together. Martin added quickly, 'Our Archbishop says we're a very Christian democracy, too.'

'Vèr' much democrats,' the Russian agreed warmly. 'Like Warsaw Pact peoples.'

'To hell with the Warsaw Pact!' started the second American, who had been particularly lachrymose in Mrs Bellamy's deep confessional bed.

'To hell also with NATO Pact peoples,' said the thin Bolsenski courteously.

'Please,' said Richard Sandford. 'We're independent here. Not members of NATO *or* the Warsaw Pact, thank God!'

'Perhaps of the Commonwealth, though,' said Aston

Abbot, taking up a new point with apparent interest. 'What d'you think, Martin?'

'I don't think it matters,' said Martin.

Sandford said teasingly to the American, 'I suppose we *are* still in the Commonwealth. After all, *we're* loyal to the Crown.'

'Imperial Preference,' said Cubbington drily.

'Jeez!' exploded the Americans. They both swung on to Cubbington like taunted bulls. 'Just listen here,' snapped the Commercial Attaché, 'We have in principle agreed aid to improve your port and cottage industries. We have discussed a Lease-Lend food, hospital and road-improvement programme.'

'All things *we* will do also but better,' announced Smirnikov calmly. 'We have together, Soviet and Hampden peoples, our special political alignmenting.'

The Attaché choked. '*We* have this Special Relationship.'

Martin said quickly, 'I'm sure the Americans would be more than welcome at the Banquet.'

'Not if it's for the benefit of Soviet Solidarity, we won't.'

'Surely,' asked Ancilla, 'it will be for the benefit of the Vale of Hampden?' Laughter started to spring up.

'Trade Banquet,' said the Russians.

'Aid Dinner,' said the American.

'Trade *and* Aid,' suggested Martin.

'A celebration,' said Sandford, 'but on us.'

The Americans and Russians regarded each other warily, like runners settling to their starting blocks.

'Well . . .' said the American, 'if you're hosts.'

'Yesso,' agreed Smirnikov. 'That way we both have more equal opportunity.'

'Now Mrs Bellamy,' Aston Abbot called across, 'Some of your "Spirits of Hampden" for *all* our friendly visitors.'

Mrs Bellamy, clucking like a turkey, tottered forward with a tray. The 'Spirits' whistled down, instilling after several steaming rounds a hazy camaraderie.

'Dreadful thing about your Prime Minister,' remarked the older American, gazing interestedly at Ancilla, as if he were considering her naked and enjoying the thought.

'What!' She flushed crimson, supposing that they had unearthed her relationship with George, and utterly confused that a stranger should mention it.

'You've not heard the news?'

'News? No. When?'

'This afternoon.'

'No, what's happened?'

Conversation around snapped off. Questing faces pointed inwards.

'Found dead,' said the American with the laconic delight of someone bearing dramatic tidings.

'Dead?' Ancilla had gone quite white. Martin slid across to her and held her arm. She asked, 'Suicide?'

'Oh, no,' said the American. 'Why d'you say that? Just an awful accident on New Year's Eve.'

'But we've heard nothing,' said Martin.

'Well, he was only discovered last night in his flat in Downing Street. Shut in a cupboard in his bedroom apparently. Couldn't get out and they suppose he started to panic and had a heart attack.'

Ancilla got up, walked across to the bar, then slumped down suddenly. Her head drooped. Martin went to her quickly. Everyone stared. Her shoulders quivered. Martin sat at her side, put his arm round her waist and felt the warmth of her shaking. He stooped down under her hair and peered into her face. She was smiling. She murmured, 'Oh God, love, it's bloody to laugh. I know it is. But it's such a relief.' She began to shake again. 'And I feel so stupid this evening. The way it ended. Can you see the relief?'

'That he hadn't killed himself?'

She nodded. 'And that he'd found someone else to play his game with.'

'But who? And where is she?'

Ancilla shrugged. 'One of the Garden Girls. There was one he quite *fancied*. Probably terrified by his screams and bolted, thinking he could get out. No handle inside, of course – part of his womb thing, poor George.'

'How bloody,' said Martin. But he could not prevent himself smiling when he added, 'Still, I suppose he went the way he wanted – as they say of other sportsmen who snuff in action.'

Ancilla grinned. 'None of those sports ever with you and me.'

'Never.' He squeezed the back of her neck.

Cubbington came across to them importantly. 'They say Chester's the new PM – Sir Frederick Chester. Home Secretary till Plain George sacked him.'

'Over us,' said Sandford. 'Your father saw him, Martin.'

The American moved in, 'Your radio said Chester takes a far more reasonable view about you. We guess – and I'm darn sure our Russian friends guess – that he'll recognize your autonomy. We think you see, that you've probably won the day.'

The Defenders gazed at one another in a glorious surmise. Then Sandford said, 'We didn't think all your attentions were entirely disinterested.'

The American said quickly, 'If you were officially independent, then with our enlarged port – '

The other chimed in – 'In your tax-free and duty-free enclave – '

'The goods would flow in.'

'And the exports could jet out. We have been considerably pressurized on this point by your Mr Stride of Silken Dalliance and our Mr Kornkrack, two men of much importance.'

The Russians moved happily into the group. 'Yesso,' declared Smirnikov eagerly. 'Jet in. Jet out. Our particular reason for visiting you. We want to talk about our especial plans to give you airport.' Martin and Ancilla stared at him, then looked at each other and back at him. They could not possibly have heard what they thought. Their eyes moved round the three earnest faces of the Committee, attending to the Russians. No one looked startled. Cubbington was simply nodding, 'Silken Dalliance *is* an important exporter. We must move goods quickly to meet demand.'

'Odd,' whispered Martin to Ancilla. 'Thought he said airport.' They stared back at Smirnikov who was waiting to continue.

'Yesso,' he said. 'Export demand most good already. With official freedom you make more trade. You must communicate with outside friends. So we have powers from Moscow, Aeroflot Division, to build you airport.'

Martin looked at Ronald Cubbington and at Aston Abbot and at Richard Sandford. They did not utter. They hung on the Russian's words.

The American Ataché began, 'Now we didn't raise this point earlier because we had somehow thought – ' he broke off hopelessly and looked at his colleague for aid. None was forthcoming. The man was equally stupefied. The American collected himself and continued, 'But we are, of course, in an ideal position to help you with an airport ourselves. We have bases and USAF construction crews already in the Midlands. And we can lease you cargo-planes most competitively.'

Before anyone could reply, the second American

cleared his throat. 'Look,' he said, 'let's put it on the line, friends. Have you read about our latest development for quick airfields: portable flexible runways? We put 'em down – up to Jumbo level – in weeks.'

Ancilla pinched Martin. But the three members of the Committee were still looking seriously at one another.

Abbot asked, 'Flexible?' He inquired with genuine interest. The American Attaché smiled broadly. 'Sure. Lay it down easily across most sorts of terrain.'

His friend expanded, 'Given the required reasonably level length.'

The Attaché resumed the running. 'Now in East Pym, say, if you used the Green and removed only a *few* of the older cottages – '

Smirnikov had been attending carefully. 'Or if the church-tower was lowered,' he suggested. Martin stared at Ancilla.

Then Aston Abbot said, 'Of course we must be able to communicate with our external allies. We're not immune to threats.'

'And we've got to trade,' said Cubbington. 'We're makin' so much here now that the world wants.'

'I suppose Belinda would say,' said Sandford sardonically, raising an eyebrow at Martin, 'that we've got to move with the times!'

'Right,' said Abbot. 'And we're ready to advance now.'

But it was Cubbington who put the understanding into words. 'Frankly,' he said, 'we should talk about an airport.'

Sandford's look had launched Martin and Ancilla. Now they let out wild explosions, shrieks of hysterical laughter. They rose to their feet tottering and, galvanized by mirth, stumbled into each others' arms and reeled down the passage and out into the fresh bite of the night air.

The Americans on one side of the table, and the

Russians on the other looked up, and stared at each other, and shrugged. 'Strain, I guess,' said the American Commercial Attaché.

'Yesso,' said Smirnikov. 'Cut off, as they have been.' He shrugged, then leaned across towards the Americans and said softly, 'If you are doing the runway building, we would build hangars and terminal. That would be correct division of control.'

Ronald Cubbington placed his white finger against his pale beaky nose and scowled down at his glass of Mrs Bellamy's 'Spirits of Hampden'. Major Aston Abbot's large wet eyes rolled to and fro above his pink cheeks and ginger whiskers. Richard Sandford could not meet Abbot's gaze. Like Cubbington he eyed the table. His fingers tapped its wet top. 'And did those *feet*,' he tapped, tum-tum – ' *Walk* upon *Eng*land's mountains green . . .? Tum-tum-ti-tum . . .'

Outside, January's stars sparkled over the Vale of Hampden. Candlelight and fireglow quivered out of Easterly's windows. The place snoozed. The laughter of Ancilla and Martin rattled across the empty cobbled quayside. They looked at one another, fleece-coated, furry-hatted, with streaming eyes and aching jaws.

'Darling,' Ancilla asked, pinching Martin's arm, 'are they all mad now? Or are we?'

'*They* are, of course.' He added, grinning, 'I think. Aren't they?' He pinched her nose.

'Well, an *airport*!' murmured Ancilla into Martin's ear to start them off laughing again.

'It's got to be the old cry, love: Over our dead bodies!'

# The world's greatest novelists now available in paperback from Grafton Books

### Jack Kerouac

| | | |
|---|---|---|
| Big Sur | £2.50 | ☐ |
| Visions of Cody | £2.50 | ☐ |
| Doctor Sax | £1.95 | ☐ |
| Lonesome Traveller | £2.50 | ☐ |
| Desolation Angels | £1.95 | ☐ |
| The Dharma Bums | £2.50 | ☐ |
| The Subterraneans and Pic | £1.50 | ☐ |
| Maggie Cassidy | £1.50 | ☐ |
| Vanity of Duluoz | £1.95 | ☐ |

### Norman Mailer

| | | |
|---|---|---|
| Cannibals and Christians (non-fiction) | £1.50 | ☐ |
| The Presidential Papers | £1.50 | ☐ |
| Advertisements for Myself | £2.95 | ☐ |
| The Naked and The Dead | £2.95 | ☐ |
| The Deer Park | £2.95 | ☐ |

### Henry Miller

| | | |
|---|---|---|
| Black Spring | £1.95 | ☐ |
| Tropic of Cancer | £2.95 | ☐ |
| Tropic of Capricorn | £2.95 | ☐ |
| Nexus | £3.50 | ☐ |
| Sexus | £2.50 | ☐ |
| Plexus | £2.95 | ☐ |
| The Air-Conditioned Nightmare | £2.50 | ☐ |

### Luke Rhinehart

| | | |
|---|---|---|
| The Dice Man | £2.95 | ☐ |
| The Long Voyage Back | £1.95 | ☐ |

To order direct from the publisher just tick the titles you want
and fill in the order form.

All these books are available at your local bookshop or newsagent, or can be ordered direct from the publisher.

To order direct from the publishers just tick the titles you want and fill in the form below.

Name _____

Address _____

_____

Send to:
**Grafton Cash Sales**
**PO Box 11, Falmouth, Cornwall TR10 9EN.**

Please enclose remittance to the value of the cover price plus:

**UK** 55p for the first book, 22p for the second book plus 14p per copy for each additional book ordered to a maximum charge of £1.75.

**BFPO and Eire** 55p for the first book, 22p for the second book plus 14p per copy for the next 7 books, thereafter 8p per book.

**Overseas** £1.25 for the first book and 31p for each additional book.

Grafton Books reserve the right to show new retail prices on covers, which may differ from those previously advertised in the text or elsewhere.